Love Has Many Faces

I dare you to put this book down!

"Love Has Many Faces is a novel that places true friendship under a revealing social microscope and examines all the elements that move it to its triumphant conclusion. Through Robin and Leslie, we see how our own relationships need constant examination as they bump up against wave after wave of social turbulence. Love Has Many Faces will signal the beginning of that examination. Denise Turney is an excellent teacher."

Lee Meadows, Author of
Silent Conspiracy: A Lincoln Keller Mystery

LOVE HAS MANY FACES

Friendship has no limit. It does not court perfection. Find a true friend and you find a circle of love.

by denise turı

Love Has Many Faces

Copyright 2000
Chistell Publishing
First Prining, May 2000

Scriptures are taken from the
New International Version of the Bible.
Copyright 1985, Zondervan Corporation

Published by: Chistell Publishing
2500 Knights Road, Suite 19-01
Bensalem, PA 19020

Cover: Morris Publishing

ISBN: 0-9663539-1-9
Library of Congress Catalog Card Number: 00-131037

Cover Photography
Copyright © 2000 by
Morris Press

Printed in the United States by
Morris Publishing
3212 East Highway 30
Kearney, NE 68847
1-800-650-7888

Dedication

**For my son.
I love you, Gregory.**

Acknowledgements

Thank you to my family. My father, Richard Turney. My mother, Doris Jean. My son, Gregory. My paternal grandparents, Clyde and Emma Turney. My great-grandmother Rebecca Skinner. My brothers, Richard, Clark and Eric. My best friend, my sister – Adrianne. My brother-in-law, Ricky. My nephew and nieces, Richard, Assyria and Samaria. My aunts, Christine and Pat. My uncle Donald. My great-aunt Ruby. My cousins Donna, Monica, Michael and Langston. Thank you for the foundation you placed beneath me, a foundation I stand on today. It has not failed me. To my friends and supporters. To those who read, supported and enjoyed my first book, Portia. To my church family, Norton Avenue First Baptist Church in Bristol, Pennsylvania where the Rev. James G. Evans III and his beautiful wife Sheila pastor and lead. To my Sigma Gamma Rho sorors. To Tim and Essie Stackhouse, a woman who God used to allow the story of Ruth and Naomi to work itself into my own life. To Helen Crawford (I'll never forget you walking around the corner those many times just to see how I was doing). To Cormy L. Williams, one of the sweetest women I know. To Willie J. Murray. To Kizzy Murray – you have an awesome talent; please work yourself to a large platform and sing. To Mary Lambert, thank you for sound Sunday School lessons. To my web site designer, Anna Stevens of ALG Designs – it's been a pleasant journey and we are just beginning! To everyone who has touched my life in a special way, thank you for your love and support. Enjoy Love Has Many Faces!

<u>More Praise for Love Has Many Faces</u>

"A suspenseful tale of the twists and turns which happen when two New York roommates, one black and one white, encounter fame. This is a contemporary story that deals with the subterranean territory of the friendships between women; that is, the fragility, the fissures, and finally the loyalty of agape love."

Maxine E. Thompson, author of The Ebony Tree and No Pockets in a Shroud
http://www.maxinethompson.com

****

"The hit book of the '00. It took me one sitting to read this robust novel. Ms. Turney does an exquisite job of telling each individual tale and pulling you into each character's life and how his or her life is ultimately affected by choices they make and the friends they keep. I guarantee that everyone who reads this book will find at least one character they will see a part of themselves in. You don't want to miss this one!"
Shonell Bacon, The Nubian Chronicles

****

"This book is a page turner!"
Mozella, Herstory Chairwoman

Chapter 1

"Wanted. Artist between the ages of 20-35 to share living expenses with local actress. Must be a woman with a steady job, no kids, and her own car. Race unimportant." Robin tightened her grip on the shopping bag handle. She grit her teeth and thought about Leslie. She hoped she wasn't home. The words to the ad she answered one year ago kept playing in her head. They were the words she believed Leslie used to trap an unsuspecting New Yorker – her. Confusion poisoned her life now. Loud, drug addicted men. Alcoholic rages. Angry bill collectors ringing the bell and calling on the telephone. And now death threats. So much changed in her life since she moved in with Leslie.

Pulling her raincoat tighter around her stomach, she skip-walked until she reached the high rise apartment building. She smiled when she heard children singing choruses of "Rain, rain, go away" while they played across the street in the park.

While she traipsed beneath the building's blue canopy, she nodded at the doorman. A second later, she pushed her wet shoes across the entrance mat. When she looked up, the doorman, his face the color of charcoal, his hands rough and splintered like worn slabs of wood, tilted his cap at her. She grinned and hurried toward the row of elevators.

She was late. She told Leslie she would be home an hour ago.

A tall, shapely woman sporting a short Afro stepped alongside her. She carried a laundry basket stacked high with folded clothes. She nudged her elbow. "What's up, Girl?"

Robin frowned before she said, "Diane's got you doing her laundry now?"

Paulette laughed. "No. I'm just helping her out. She's not feeling well."

Pursing her lips, she worked to keep her thoughts to herself, *"Probably sick from the blood on her hands from all that back stabbing she does."* A second later, she glanced up and saw Paulette's pouting brown eyes looking in her direction. She smiled and said, "Nice of you to help Diane out. You two are so close." Then she twisted her mouth. "Wish these elevators weren't so slow. Think with all the money we pay for rent, management could keep these slow moving boxes better maintained."

The elevator doors opened, and Paulette chuckled. "You're the sweetest, most simple person I know, Carlile, but if you ain't one impatient woman."

She waved and called out, "Bye," to Paulette while they stepped on separate elevators. When the silver doors closed, she unbuttoned her raincoat, moved to the back of the elevator wall, and closed her eyes. The

1

tight jeans she wore made it clear that she was a woman who seldom missed a day at the gym. As usual, she wore a pair of high priced cross trainers. One of the city's top distance runners, she didn't go far without her cross trainers. During her free time in the evenings, just before the sun tucked itself behind the trees, she logged a brisk six to ten mile run.

The elevator ascended. Sighing, she braced herself for the long ride to Apartment 1201.

A wave of silence greeted her when she exited the elevator. She stood in front of the only apartment on the twelfth level and cast her gaze to the floor. A folded note was pushed beneath the door. She kicked it all the way inside the apartment.

Her heart quickened the second she opened the door. Her gaze darted around the room. She looked down the hallway and called out, "Leslie." No answer. Walking down the hall, she went into her bedroom and sat on the edge of the bed. She sighed and thanked God that she was alone. A moment later, she pulled a book out of her bookcase. Crossing her legs, she turned a page in Charles Fuller's latest play. She didn't look up until she heard the security chain rattle the wood of the front door.

Without a "hi", "I'm home" or a nod, Leslie pushed her bedroom door open. Her tall, thin frame loomed in the doorway. The pink cashmere sweater she wore brought out the blue in her eyes. A wad of gum was in her mouth. She chewed and popped the gum loudly. Dropping her bottom lip and sighing, she stood in the doorway with her hand resting on the knob. Across from her, Robin pursed her lips and turned another page in the play.

"Stop acting like you don't see me!"

She sat up with a jolt. She watched Leslie swagger to the center of the bedroom.

"Where were you?"

"I went shopping. Since when did you become my mother?"

"You are so selfish! You don't even care that I got robbed!"

"I'm supposed to know you got robbed as soon as you walk through the door?"

"You said you'd be here!"

"Oh. So, I'm supposed to stay locked up in the apartment while you go out all day just in case something happens? Think I want to be here in case that . . . that . . . that guy calls and starts telling somebody's after you? That somebody's going to kill you? Think I want to be here all by myself for that?"

"I was expecting a very important call and you knew it!"

"Les—"

"I called you!"

"Did you hear what I just said?"

"I can't count on you anymore!"

"Somebody's stalking you and all you're worried about is missing a director's call?"

"I can't count on anybody." Her bottom lip quivered.

"Forget the stalker? Just forget it. Comes with the territory, right? On to other things." She sighed. "I told you I went shopping. Are you okay?"

"Do I look okay?"

"You're always ranting and raving. Let me put it another way. Did you get hurt?"

"No." She crossed the floor and sat on the edge of the bed. "Piece of trash took my diamond necklace. Just snatched it off of me. You'd of thought he was trying to pull a lease off a dog the way he yanked and pulled on me."

"Did you call the police?"

"There you go. You are always trying to follow the rules. You're never going to get ahead until you learn how to break the rules." She shook her head. "No. I didn't call the police. I'll handle that scum myself. If I ever see him again I'm gonna beat him like there's no tomorrow."

Taking her gaze to the ceiling, Robin rolled her eyes. While Leslie cast out threats against the man who stole her necklace, she reminded herself why she came to New York. Despite the fact that she couldn't afford to live on her own, despite the fact that she was still attending New York University as an undergraduate majoring in English, she grit her teeth and promised herself that she would be a success. *"One day I won't have to sit up under you and your mean, nasty ways. I won't have to run home to my daddy. I won't be here when death threats turn to death, when the stalker shows up at the front door. I'm gonna make it as a writer. I'm gonna make it big."*

Leslie pushed her hands against her hips. "Something bothering you?"

She stared at the play. "Nothing."

Leslie sighed and stretched out on the side of the bed. Less than a minute later, she walked inside the kitchen and poured herself a glass of orange juice.

Robin lowered the play beneath her nose when she heard glass crash against the kitchen floor.

Inside the kitchen, Leslie clenched her teeth.

Charles Fuller's play pressed against Robin's chin.

Leslie stood from picking chunks of glass off the floor and counted, "one-two-three-four-five," before she shouted, "Come in here and help me."

"You sure you don't want me to call the police?"

3

"No, Rob. They won't come out to help me pick broken glass off the floor."

"I was talking about your getting robbed earlier."

"I told you I'll handle it, and I will. Now will you help me in the kitchen?"

"I'm coming," she answered while she scooted off her bed. She stared at Leslie's arched back. She watched her push the mop back and forth across the floor.

After she leaned the mop handle against the refrigerator door, she crossed her arms. She peered at the newly cleaned floor before she looked up and said, "Finished."

"And I came in here . . . "

"To help, but I'm finished. Didn't you hear me? I just said 'finished.'" Shaking her wrist, she pushed her way passed Robin and stormed into her bedroom where she loosed the green ribbon tied to the end of her hair. Her blonde ponytail fell limp against her shoulders. When it did, she walked to the front of her dresser and brushed her hair until it was tangle free. Two years ago she rarely styled her own hair. The studio hired a hairdresser to take care of that for her while she was on set, whenever she had a photo shoot, an interview, an autograph signing or an awards banquet to attend. She paid someone to drive to the store and buy her clothes. Grocery shopping was out of the question. Too many avid television watchers and too many moviegoers were familiar with her round, pretty face. Two years ago she was a star.

Robin carried a glass of cola into Leslie's bedroom.

She muttered, "I tell you, Girl," while she placed the brush on her vanity tray.

"Bad day?" Robin asked before she sipped her cola.

A scowl deepened her brow. "Stop trying to mother me!" She snarled. The brush was in her hand again. She drug it through her shoulder length hair so hard, her scalp throbbed.

Robin waved her hand at the back of her head. "Stop making an emergency out of everything. And you probably didn't get robbed. Somebody probably just bumped into you. Everything's an emergency with you. Everything except what's really important. You give no thought to your personal safety. Bringing strange men in and out of here like the front door spins on its hinge."

"Shut up."

"That's the reason you wanted me home all day. In case some director for some small time movie calls. So you'll feel like a hit. What's a standing ovation when it's coming from a crowded room of people who wouldn't know a horrible, pathetic movie if they saw one? Sit by the phone

4

while you go out just in case some director calls. You and your half finished career because you refuse to share the limelight with another actress. I tell you, it took me the longest. It took me the longest to figure out why you put that ad in the paper."

"Do we have to go over that again?"

"You need the money. You actually need the money. You can't afford to live here by yourself. How was the fall, Leslie? You used to be on top of the world, but you and your narcissism took you all the way down. How does it feel to fall so far, to fall so hard?"

"Shut up."

"Not that you don't need to be in this high rise all by yourself, as hard as you are to live with."

"Yea. You don't mind that much," she snapped. "You and your religious beliefs."

Giving a long sigh to the room, she lowered and shook her head. "You know I actually had a good day until you walked through the front door. Even with the rain it turned out to be a beautiful day. Kids singing at the park. It wasn't too crowded at the store. I even caught a few good sales." She stopped and glared at her hands. "None of your ex-boyfriends followed me home." She nodded. "Yea. It actually was a pretty good day. Then here you come."

"So," she said while she plopped, back first, onto her bed. "I had a horrible day."

She thought about the play. In a second, she was gone out of Leslie's room. If it weren't cloudy, she'd go out for a run. With each step she took, she'd ponder the reasons she wouldn't break away from Leslie. True. NYU cut her grant and there went the money she used to pay for her dorm. She had to live somewhere. This was the end of her junior year. Quitting school wasn't an option. The timing seemed so perfect, and yet it seemed so wrong. Leslie and her – desperate for a roommate at the same time. Both of them needing someone to help them meet their living expenses . . . at the same time. They were so different. God, community, education and the spiritual laws of the universe were important to her. Not so Leslie. To her, Leslie seemed bent on causing her pain. Outside of acting, getting laid, sending blood curdling screams through the apartment while she engaged in fits of rage and drinking herself into deeper depression, she doubted that Leslie wanted anything out of life.

Leslie rolled her eyes when she looked up and saw Robin gone. Pushing off her bed, she entered her room. She gawked at her. "Well."

Robin stared at the blank wall before she asked, "So? How was your day? What happened?"

5

"You know I've been trying to get the lead in Roger Morris' Repentance?"

Familiar with the conversation, she took the words to be gibberish, "Yeah."

"After I telephone his secretary, I leave the apartment and take off to look for his new office. You know his old office was on 34th Street, close to Herald Square. Shannon, his secretary, said he moved to 48th Street two days ago so he could be in the heart of the Theatre District." She chuckled. "You know my girlfriend, Teresa. You know how she keeps me abreast of such things. Even she didn't know about this Morris relocation. I felt like I was deliberately left out of the loop while I listened to Shannon run down the details of Morris' move. I hope he's not having financial problems. Traffic was mad. I got tired of hailing cabs, so I just took off walking."

"Your car's in the shop?"

"No. You know I don't drive in the theatre district unless I absolutely have to. I'm not about to risk having one of those culture-less New Yorkers run into my Porsche."

"You stopped hailing cabs and walked? You? Nobody mobbed you for an autograph?"

"Anyhow, by the time I got to 48th Street, my feet were throbbing! I walked over a mile! Did I ever get tired of walking. You know the only time I go to the heart of Midtown is when I want to shop at Macy's." She paused and searched Robin's face. She bit her bottom lip when she saw her doodling on a blank page at the back of the play.

"Screw you and your book!" she shouted before she walked inside the kitchen.

Alone in the bedroom, Robin stopped doodling and arched her pencil lined eyebrows. Emotion filled her eyes.

A moment later ice clinked against the sides of the tall glass that cooled Leslie's hand. Away from the kitchen and lowering her arm to her side, she stopped spinning the glass and stood somberly at the edge of the living room. She watched Robin's back move. She didn't ask, "Who was that?" until Robin pulled her head inside the apartment door.

She closed the door before she said, "Did I tell you about the note that was under the door when I came home?" She walked across the room taking long strides. She handed Leslie the note. "Here." She tapped her foot to the beat of Minnie Ripleton's, *Memory Lane*, while she waited for Leslie to read the note.

"Armstrong having another party?" Leslie asked, sipping white wine. "I wonder what's the occasion this time."

Before she answered, Robin turned partway toward the door. "That was Diane."

"Why didn't she come in?"

"How should I know?" She excused herself by turning her back to Leslie. "You know how she runs around."

"I just asked. You don't have to be snotty about it."

She hedged her off with silence.

"I bet Diane found a job."

Edging passed Leslie, she walked into her bedroom. "She was looking for work?"

She followed her. "Sure. For over six months." All at once, the volume in her voice dropped.

Robin met her glance. "Close your mouth. You don't have room to talk, and you know it. You had the lead in *Michael Come Home*, but Amanda was in it, so you turned it down. Grapevine has it, if you had accepted the lead role Keith offered you personally, Amanda's role would have been substantially smaller than it turned out to be. You'd of been the star." She smiled like a fox before she turned away from her. "But you had to have it all."

Feeling the all too familiar pangs hung over from the decision she made over a year ago, she employed her wit and changed the subject. "Are you going to the party?"

"Nope."

"Why not?"

"Because I don't use drugs."

She tossed her head back and let out a thunderous laugh. "Everyone there's not going to get stoned."

"One person getting blitzed is enough for me."

"I might go."

"Do what you want. I'm not going to try and talk you out of going."

"I didn't ask you to."

"I know you."

She shrieked. "You are so artificial. You are so predictable and phony. You're so afraid to be yourself, always worried about what people think about you. You're paranoid. You don't have a clue what it is to be you." Her brow narrowed and pointed. "I see right through you. You and your bible quoting. You and all that bible reading you do." She nodded. "Yea. I see right through you. I see right through you. You're made of glass. See through and artificial."

"Leave me alone." She pushed closer to the edge of her bed and her alarm clock. "And if I'm see through, then you're blind, because you've got me all wrong. I pay my share of the rent. I keep my end of the deal. I need a place to lay my head and so do you, so don't start in on me. And leave my relationship with God to me and God. I love the Lord, and yes, I'm a Christian. I told you that the first day we met. Don't try to change me, because I don't try to change you. Just leave me alone."

She took a swig of her wine. "I've had a bad day. I have to take it out on somebody."

"So, it's got to be me again? I don't know why I stay holed up in this apartment with you. Every time I start to move you start treating me like I'm somebody, like I'm a human being. I change my mind and stay and I'm stuck with you for another six months. I tell you sometimes, if it wasn't for that lease I signed, I'd..."

She leaned forward and talked so loudly, spit flew out of her mouth. "Say it. Go ahead. Say it. It won't hurt me. All my life if it wasn't for a contract or money, nobody'd give me anything. What were you doing when you were a little girl, Miss Righteous, Holy Rolling, Robin? Well, me. I was busting my hump on a television set. I still haven't seen half of that money. Hmph. But I bet you my father has. So go ahead. Say it. You'd what?"

"Nothing."

Wine in hand, she turned and stomped across the hall. She went to her dresser, and, after rummaging through the second drawer, she pulled out her favorite pair of designer jeans. She hobbled while she took off her skirt and pulled on the jeans. When she looked in the mirror, the woman staring back at her met her favor. The silk, sky blue blouse she wore matched the jeans. "After an hour, I found Roger Morris' new office." She twisted her mouth and buttoned the jeans. She chuckled before she added, "The highlight was speaking with his secretary face to face." She paused and brought the woman into view. "She's attractive. A little short, but attractive. A little talkative, but attractive. A little plump, but attractive. She promised to give Roger my message and telephone number." She chuckled at the thought of Roger Morris needing her telephone number. "On the way home, I bumped into this wino." She pinched her nose and grimaced, the smell of week old liquor on the man's clothing again familiar to her. "I gave that poor excuse for a human being a piece of my mind. He was so dirty, and did he stink! He was rank!" She fanned her nose with the side of her hand. "He had the nerve to act like he wanted to hit me. Good for him he didn't." She lifted the wine off her dresser and took a sip, "I was in a vicious mood. I would have given him some work."

Robin narrowed her eyes and pointed her brow.

"I went to Vander & Mahn to check on my diamond, see if the jeweler fit it into the gold band. My mom's had that order in for me for at least a day. My father paid good money for that diamond to be fitted. It should be fitted. That pissed me off. One whole day and it's not fitted yet."

8

She looked across the hall into Robin's bedroom. "Can you believe that? I guess it's a good thing though. I probably would have only had it stolen if it was ready." When Robin was mute, she piped, "Let's get a bite to eat." Lowering her head into her hands, Robin moaned, "Why me?" When she raised her head, she asked, "Why don't we cook for a change?"

Leslie climbed atop her bed and lay on her side; her knees were pulled close to her stomach. Above her head was her radio on/off knob. She pushed the knob up and breathed evenly while Aretha Franklin sang her 1960s hit "Respect" and drowned out the low hum of Robin's radio. "No." She said, changing her mind, "I'm going to take a nap and go out for a salad or a boiled turkey sandwich later." Her voice raced behind her thoughts. "You know, there's a new salad bar two blocks from here. It's nice . . . cozy. I've been there twice. You ought to go sometime."

Robin was silent.

"You know, the other day I almost locked my keys in my car again. I'd lose my head if it weren't screwed on. Nobody forgets their keys are in the car when they lock the door as often as I do." She sat on her bed. "What are you cooking?"

"A fish sandwich," Robin called back from the kitchen.

While the fish thawed in the sink, she walked into the living room, and, standing next to the picture window, she entertained thoughts of walking onto the terrace and sitting on one of the two cushioned lawn chairs. Leaves swung full circle under the wind gusts. Watching the leaves spin, she turned away from the window and walked to the sofa. Snapping her finger, she remembered, "The mail!"

"Where are you going?" Leslie asked when she heard the front door open.

"To check the mail."

"I thought you said—"

"Diane put that envelope outside our door. I told you that. I didn't get that out of the mailbox."

"Well—"

Robin sighed. "What is it, Leslie?"

Leslie lowered her voice. "I already checked the mail."

"So? Did I get anything?"

"N-N-No." She waited. When she heard Robin return to the living room, she reached for her purse. She might have been robbed earlier in the day, but one thing she'd held onto – the letter. It was typed on an old typewriter. Some of the letters were jagged and raised. Opening her purse, she took out the letter and held it in her hand. Her heart raced. Her hands shook while she opened the envelope.

Hi Leslie,

"You don't know me, but I know you. I know exactly who you are. I know where you live. I know where and when you were born. I know you've got a fine looking roommate now. No longer carrying your burdens alone. Watched you come up on TV. Been to all your movies. You're all right when it comes to being pretty. But one things sure; you've got something I want. If it wasn't for me you never would have made it this far. I'd of cut you and all your people off a long time ago. I still hold that power. You just don't know all about it. I'm gonna get you, Leslie. You and your pretty new roommate. Better tell her to look over her shoulder when she walks down the street. I'm close."

She turned the envelope over and cursed to the empty room. "I didn't expect a return address, but I can't even make out the postmark!"

Down the hall and sitting cross-legged, Robin relived the most important things she picked up about Leslie and her parents at their first meeting. She gazed across the room for five minutes before she called out, "Les?"

Silence.

"Les?"

Silence

"Les?"

"Yea?"

"Be careful."

"What?"

"At the party tonight."

"What are you talking about?"

"Just be careful."

Chapter Two

Crisis. That's what Leslie was. A crisis. If she wasn't in the middle of an emergency, she was just coming out of one. It was as if she existed simply to try the depth of Robin's faith. Because she was in between steady, decent work and had been since she met her, Robin refused to desert her, leaving her alone with her own insecurities. She'd seen her curled on the floor crying to a band of unseen demons, pleading with them to turn her loose, to set her free from the fits of jealousy, the deep self doubt, the heart wrenching loneliness that tormented her. She always prayed for her. Picked her off the floor and helped get her into her bedroom. She'd rub her back and tell her, "Everything's going to be all right. God's going to work it out. Trust God. I know God will work it out." She'd seen her too stoned to make her way to the toilet. The pee would smell up the apartment. Those long days, days that spilled into the night and stretched out until she couldn't tell which was day – which was night - everywhere Leslie went she left a trail of stale urine. After she came home from work and before she went to bed, she always washed her off. Changed her clothes and put her back in bed. She stood by and listened while she wept to bill collectors, "I'll pay you as soon as I get a gig. Don't take my car. Don't take my jewelry. You already took two of my houses. Don't take it all. Don't take everything from me. Leave me something. Something of my own." She hugged her after her quiet sobs turned into loud, heart breaking wails. She hugged her and told her, "I'll help you pay some of your bills. You'll get back on your feet again. God's going to fix it. Watch and see."

"Don't leave me. Don't leave me. Don't ever leave me," she would scream while Robin hugged her.

"I won't," she always promised afraid of the sound of her own words. She used the words like they were magic. She only spoke them because she wanted Leslie to pull herself together. Stop wailing. Stop clinging to her. Be strong. Be strong so she could walk off and leave her without feeling guilty.

"Christianity is about being there when someone needs you. It's about being a friend. A lot of people don't know what it is to truly, really love another person. Most people don't have a clue. When you love someone, you'll stay even when the chips are down. Don't be a fair weather friend. Be a good Christian. Be a true friend." Reverend Keith Julian, Robin's pastor, gave her those words when she came to him complaining about how impossible her roommate was. He never met Leslie. "But I never said she was my friend," she wanted to call back. Although she nodded and said, "Uh-huh," she walked away from him feeling like a cracked egg. She'd exposed herself, shared her true feelings, and he left her unfixed. She knew Leslie's misery was becoming on open channel. Its venom was seeping into her own life. It was reminding her too much of her own heartache, her own disappointments. One thing was certain. She knew she would not answer a newspaper ad and move in to live with another woman again – ever. She felt stuck, shackled to Leslie and betrayed, tricked. *"Wanted. Artist between the ages of 20-35 to share living expenses with local actress. Must be a woman with a steady job, no kids, and her own car. Race unimportant."* She would never forget the ad Leslie placed in *The Daily New Yorker*. She dressed like she was going to a job interview the day she went to meet her. Her knees shook, and her throat kept turning dry. "All that for this," she told herself when life with Leslie became so taxing she thought about returning home down South. But then she thought the better of it, usually after Leslie employed one of her sympathy tricks. Life with Leslie was hard, very hard, but time got by. One year to be exact.

She was the only person who managed to live with Leslie when she was out of work. It was noon before she crawled out of bed. Once out of bed, she paced the apartment like a caged animal. Within days, her nervousness worked its way onto her flesh and became skin rash. Hard, red bumps clustered at the edges of her mouth, the sides of her face, and went up her neck and arms. All her time was spent waiting for the telephone to ring. In all her conversations, she was quick; sarcasm coated all her words. Because she didn't want to miss important calls and claimed she needed to rest, she ordered Robin to answer the telephone on the first ring. Fully settled into her diatribe, she instructed Robin not to laugh or talk loudly, perchance her laughter or conversation would flood the apartment and silence a knock at the door or the ring of the telephone.

Months later and overcome with relief, she found herself hugging Leslie. While she embraced her, she reminded her that, "You landed the lead because you're a great talent. You have an enviable skill." She was careful not to mention the fact that the B movie would likely never make it to mainstream theatres.

Leslie, a product of Hollywood from her youth, once was a dominant figure in the movie and television industries. She began her acting career at the same age Robin's father, Theo boasted Robin started reading -- three years old. As it was with most child actresses, Leslie's first job was a commercial. During those early days, she advertised toothpaste, tights and two popular lines of children's clothing. She signed her last commercial contract when she was fifteen. Between her first and last commercial shoot, she worked as the lead character in Christine Simpson and Jerry Stone's series, *Gardenia's Life*. To increase her exposure, she posed for magazine layouts and made several appearances on the nationally syndicated, hit television weekly, *Friday Night's Hot Spot*. *Gardenia's Life* ran 250 episodes and secured a top-ten slot on the Nielson Ratings the first 196 episodes. After *Gardenia's Life*, she received more than a hundred motion picture offers. One she gave a great deal of consideration. After months of legal wrangling, she turned the offer down. Her confidante, Teresa, a Beverly Hills hairstylist and confirmed Hollywood gossip, telephoned her and suggested, "Let's have lunch." While they enjoyed an entree of soft shell crabs and a basket of buttered sweet bread at the Fisherman's Dock, Teresa made a point of telling her, "You know that movie you told me you were thinking about taking on? Well. I don't think you're going to want to hear this, but Amanda Gaynor's in it. Supporting actress."

Her agent, Donald Riggs, visited the apartment and made several desperate attempts to persuade her to accept the role. "Yes, you're an established actress," he nodded after she cited past achievements. Three hours later, frustration moistening his armpits and his brow, he stood and closed their conversation by reaching to the back of the living room sofa. He grabbed his leather jacket and assured her that she couldn't afford to bypass the opportunity to work with an Oscar bound screenplay. "Besides," he added with his jacket on, "If you reject this offer simply because Amanda's the supporting actress, you risk being labeled a spoiled, maladjusted child star. And," he called over his shoulder, his briefcase in his hand and the unsigned motion picture contract inside the briefcase, "You know what that means."

Winter 1986 New York City's evening skies took on a darkened hue. Leslie's refusal to work with Amanda Gaynor turned to jealousy-- turned to nausea after Robin and she opened the door to their wide screen television and sat on the living room sofa. They stared at the television bug-eyed while they watched Amanda, dressed in a calf length, gold, silk gown hurry onstage to receive her Oscar. The movie Leslie was given first opt to play the lead, female role in but refused to work on won a total of five Oscars: costume, special effects, supporting actor, supporting actress and leading actress.

Three thousand miles from where Robin and Leslie sat gawking at the television screen Donald voiced his disapproval of Leslie's decision to three distinguished gentlemen, men who wielded enormous power in the entertainment business. That evening Hollywood's elite began to talk. Night of the 1986 Oscar awards presentation Leslie's refusal to accept the leading role opposite Amanda Gaynor in *Michael Come Home* proved detrimental.

Robin scratched her scalp and yawned. So many times while she worked to soothe Leslie's fears and pad her insecurities with the fluff of empty compliments, she pondered the cradle of her mania, her deepest hurts, her broken strength. The answer came to her one spring day a year ago. It was the day she met Leslie's parents, Arnold and Joyce Fletcher.

Arnold wore a pair of designer jeans and a blue blazer the day Leslie drove her to their home in Mellton, Connecticut. Joyce wore a flowered sundress. She smiled throughout the entire visit. Robin found her to be docile. She thought Arnold, with his piercing sea-blue eyes and his deep, raspy voice, was striking. Yet, the way he barked orders at Joyce then followed the orders up with a wink to her sabotaged the bulk of his appearance. She tagged her mental image of him with a harsh label -- ugly. They didn't reveal much of their shared lives to her during the two-hour visit. Not until she bid them farewell and climbed again inside Leslie's Porsche did the facts become known. Leslie talked non-stop the entire drive from Mellton to New York City.

She told her, "My parents were high school sweethearts. They married in their late teens. Two years after they wed I was born. I don't know how many times Mama's told me that she endured a long, sixteen-hour labor giving birth to me. She never says it, but I think, on many days, I'm nothing more than a child who reminds her too much of the man she regrets marrying -- my father." Placing her head against the driver seat headrest, she turned on the Porche's cruise control and licked her lips. "Like my dad told you, he works at Mellton's leading law firm. He's a senior attorney." She chuckled. "Even with all the secrets Mom and he try to keep, I knew he'd tell you that. He's always bragging about himself." She laughed outright. "As you can see, his being an attorney has brought a fair share of financial comfort to my mom and him. That's how they got that big house in that quiet suburb." She laughed. "Well. That and the money they stole from me while I was a kid acting fourteen to sixteen hours a day, a kid who didn't know any better. You know. Thought my parents cared enough about me not to rip me off for millions and millions of dollars. You know? " Turning on her left blinker, she moved into the fast lane and sped passed a man who was driving the 55 mph speed limit. "Then again, if I hadn't been a child star and Dad didn't work as an attorney, he and Mom would probably steal their way into an upper class neighborhood." She shook her head and twisted her mouth. "Such show offs. Goodness! Do they ever care what other people think about them." She sighed. "I don't know if you could tell, but my parents' marriage is more for show than it's for real. I know it sounds awful, but I don't think they really love each other. But divorce and have people start talking about them -- never." She laughed again. "Dad doesn't think I know, but he has a lover. Now, her -- I think he loves her. In fact, he's had a few of them. One woman, a dumb red head, almost cost him his life. Turns out she was some psychotic crook's girlfriend. I mean, this psycho guy was into some of everything. Drugs. Prostitution. I even heard he made a few hits on people who got in his way. Anyhow, when he found out about his girlfriend and Dad . . . talk about a triangle. We got death threats, prank calls, the whole nine yards. Don't think my mother turned her back on Dad. Never. She stuck by him through the whole ordeal. Said it was all the red head's fault. To this day my mother cannot stand to see a red headed woman. But the red head's out of the picture now. Ten years ago she turned up missing."

Robin glanced at her out of the corners of her eyes. She nibbled her bottom lip and hoped she wouldn't stumble onto a passageway leading into her past that would cause her pain, deep emotional haunts.

"I think Dad's had his current mistress for about twenty years now. He always kept more than one, but I think she's the only one now." She smiled. "Like I told you, I think he loves her." She shook her head. "I really think he loves her. He used to take me with him when he drove to the florist and bought her flowers. I was real young then. I don't guess he thought I was old enough to figure it out. He'd order a dozen of roses and ask to have them delivered on the same day, but when we went home, I never saw any flowers for Mom." She laughed then she turned and looked Robin squarely in the eye. "Mom got him back though. She still does. Know what she does?"

Shaking her head, she answered, "Un-un." She prayed for her to stop revealing her family's problems.

"You don't know?"

Her brow pointed and shaped into a V. "No. I don't."

"Wonderful shopping sprees! Mom spends nearly every dollar Dad sweats to earn."

She stared at Leslie while she watched her toss her head back and laugh -- laugh loud, laugh long and hard.

"Loehmann's, Macy's, Bolton's, Anne Taylor's, designer suits, dresses, designer jeans, silver, crystal, gold, diamonds, you name it; my Mom buys it. When I was growing up, I loved shopping with her. She never said 'no'. Nothing was outside her limit. She shopped like we had money that would never end. Every week she did."

When she felt Leslie's gaze at the side of her head, she turned and asked, "Your dad never said anything?"

She arched her shoulders. "I don't know. I never heard them argue about money. Besides, with the way Mom answers to his every whim, any way you look at it, Dad wins out. The only thing I ever heard Mom complain openly to me about were the parties the law firm hosted. She said Dad always made her stand in the background. She couldn't talk too much or assert herself in anyway. Dad was always drinking then, Mom said."

Shaking her head, she added, "That man sure loves his scotch. And Mom said he would spend the evening telling joke after joke. Everyone would laugh and guffaw. Mom said most of the jokes were directed at her. And you see how handsome my dad is. He keeps himself in shape. I have to admit he's an attractive man even if he is my father. He doesn't miss his days at the gym. No, Ma'am. The women in the neighborhood love everything about him. They're always giving him compliments. I think he's slept with a few of them. I think Mom knows."

She stared at the road while Leslie pulled onto the turnpike.

"And do you know what my mom did once?"

"No. What?"

"She broke down and told her troubles to the town gossip, the one and only, Lisa Butcher. Lisa lives five houses down from my parents. She lives in that pretty, red brick house I pointed to when we drove down the street. Mom said Lisa kept pouring her more and more tea that day while she, my gullible mother, opened up and told her too many secrets. Mom said she even broke down and cried in front of Lisa. What a mistake." She shook her head. "I'm not sure about Mom crying because I wasn't there, but I do know this. People gawked at, talked about and made fun of my mother so bad after that, she spent six months talking to a therapist." Releasing a thick breath, she continued with, "I suppose people didn't want her to make it clear to them how imperfect Dad and her marriage really was."

"Looks like the whole town's perfect to me. Everybody's yard is so evenly cut and edged. I've never seen so many pretty houses and lawns one after another. Those folk look more proper than my mother, as hard as that is to pull off."

"Mellton's the kind of place where sports standouts are the high school heroes. High school tournament games sell out months in advance in Mellton. The thing I like the most about the city is how it looks in the winter. After a hard snow, Mellton is absolutely beautiful. Looks like a scene out of a movie. Mom always made the best buttermilk pancakes in the winter. She likes to cook, but she never cooked that much in the summer. Said the kitchen got too hot with the stove and oven on. I have to admit, Mom and Dad looked good together, especially when Mom was really happy, and she loved winter. If I remember correctly, Dad never hit her in the winter. You know. Thanksgiving. Festivities. Office get-togethers. Company coming over. Christmas and all. Beat the fool out of her after she pissed him off any other time of the year." She turned and looked at Robin. "Of course, they didn't think I knew, but you can only hide so much with make-up." She gazed out the windshield. "My parents have been married for twenty-five years." She chuckled. "In a way, I guess they are the perfect couple.   Mom's perfected the illusion that Dad has her eating out of his hand, when, in fact, she's the one who's pecking the top of his head."

Robin swallowed hard.   She wondered what she had gotten herself into.

Chapter Three

Robin sat up with a jolt. She wiped her eyes and wondered how long she had been asleep. Pushing off the sofa, she went into the kitchen. The smell of fish rushed up her nose. After she cleaned the fish, she tugged on a baking pan until it was free of a mixing bowl, skillet and blender.

The fish in the oven, she crossed the floor and walked inside the dining room. She opened a bureau drawer and grabbed a small, decorated box. Sitting in one of the dining room chairs, she took the lid off the box and smiled. Pictures. Pictures. Pictures. Memories and the faces of good friends beckoned her. The first photo she took out of the box was of her girlfriend Dinah. She laughed when she recalled pranks they played on each other while they were dorm mates at NYU. Soon she held pictures of Betsy and Loretta.

Growing up with the trio in Johnson City, Tennessee brought joy and a sense of security to her. Attending to the pomp of high school dances, football and basketball games and track and field meets left the quartet no time for boredom.

She shuffled a handful of pictures. Then she stared at a young boy's smiling face. She remembered the boy. He was one of the kids she met when her sorority, Sigma Gamma Rho, visited The Saint Vincent Children's Ward a year ago. He was the little Jamaican who giggled every time one of her sorority sisters or she, dressed in clown suits, blew up a balloon or pulled the tips of their ears and made a funny face or winked at him. Staring at the picture of him resting in the bed, his head bald, his face pale, created a lump in her throat. She had to turn away from looking at him. He reminded her too much of her little sister, Sonia, a girl who died of leukemia when she was only four years old. An only child -- that's what she became after her sister died. An only child and the person who reminded her mother too much of death. Although she was oldest, her mother made it clear to her that if she had to choose just one child, she'd always pick Sonia.

She dropped the picture in the box and buried it.

Grabbing a handful of older photos, she pressed her elbows against the edge of the table and spread the pictures. In one of the pictures, her sorority sister Loretta and she wore big, floppy hats. Looking at the hats reminded her of how she used to dress up in her mama's clothes when she was a girl, and she laughed.

She stared at four pictures. They were of her high school graduation. In the first picture her mama, dressed in a silk dress, and, she, in her cap and gown, stood with their arms draped over one another's shoulder. Neither woman smiled. In the second picture, her four grandparents, all in suits and old fashioned hats, and she hugged one another's waist. In the third picture, her father, dressed in a three-piece suit, held her around the waist with his thick, strong arms. He was leaning to the side and planting a kiss on her cheek. In the fourth picture, her mama, dad and she stood shoulder to shoulder with their hands gently cupping each other's waist. None of them smiled.

She sighed. High school graduation for her started on a bleak note. An hour before the commencement ceremony, her mother, Marcia, demanded that she wear her hair down, show off her long, black curls. "The one good thing about you, your hair, and you keep it up. Girl, when are you going to learn? You are not Sonia. Sonia had a face suited for any hairstyle. Sonia had a pretty, round face. Your face is long, and you know you have a pointed chin. You can't wear your hair any kind of way. So many styles just don't look good on you."

"She was a baby, Mama." Her bottom lip quivering and as if deaf to her mother's requests, she stood in front of her bedroom mirror and gathered her hair into one hand and prepared to pin it into a bun.

At the end of the short, heated confrontation, Marcia turned and told her, "Yea. You're graduating, but where are you going?" The remainder of the evening, she pouted and criticized her hairstyle, the way she slouched when she walked and how she forgot to buy "Thank you" cards for family and friends who gave her gifts and money for graduating from high school.

For seventeen years, she watched Robin grow up, yet, for her attention to detail, her constant concern, her hand that guided, disciplined and betrayed, she found it impossible to vision her daughter as a grown woman. She found it impossible to release the person who was ten years old when her little sister died. While Robin was in New York City, she pressed her for personal information and demanded that she telephone no less than twice a week. Robin greeted her demands with insolence and anger. Her freshman year at NYU, she didn't telephone home for eleven months, and, when her mother telephoned her, she complained that she was busy with Rush, finals and dating.

Graduation loomed fresh again. In three semesters she would graduate from NYU. For the second time, she made Marcia the center of attention and Theo proud. Her recent conversations proved to them that her writing career was progressing well. Until she sold her first play, she earned a living working at Mills Clothing, a large factory twelve blocks from the high rise.

Pushing loose strands of hair off her face, she put the lid back on the box and walked into the kitchen. She made a fish sandwich and rounded the corner.

As soon as she entered her bedroom she started turning the 96-channel television knob in fast circles. Two minutes later, rather than spin the knob a third time, she punched the power button and watched the screen blacken. Instinctively, she sat on her bed and turned on the radio. A disco song buzzing in her ear, she sipped cola. "Leslie, do you want some--" She stopped talking, bit into the fish sandwich, stood and looked across the hall. "Sleep. Here I am trying to make conversation, and she's asleep."

One song later, her bedroom was quiet. She walked inside the living room, and, parting the drapes, she looked out the picture window. She watched the wind blow through the trees. The weather was cool and cloudy just like this on the day Sonia died. It was a late night telephone call that changed her family tree. "Come to the hospital now." That's what her mother kept telling her the doctor said. By the time they got there Sonia was dead.

Wind rattled the picture window. Crossing her arms, she whispered, "Sonia, why did you die and leave me? You were supposed to grow up. We were supposed to be roommates. Not me and some maniac of a woman. You and me, Sonia. We were supposed to be best friends." Nibbling her bottom lip and swallowing hard, she released the past and returned to her bedroom. After she slipped into a pair of wooden clogs, she grabbed her purse and checked to make sure she had twenty dollars. Door keys in hand and her purse strapped over the crest of her shoulder, she closed and locked the front door and entered the hall.

While she walked to the parting elevator doors she wondered if Diane's party started. When she turned her wrist, she glanced at the diamond watch Leslie bought her for her birthday last year from Tiffany's. The delicate hands on the watch told her it was 7:30. She hurried inside the elevator.

She declined Diane's invitation to attend her party because she refused to be subject to another night of ridicule. When she moved to Apartment 1201, Diane threw two parties, both on a Saturday night, both within the first month she lived in the high rise.

Diane laughed when she turned down her offer of drugs. She wanted her to "loosen up" and let her show her how to do blow. That night while she backed away from the white, powdery substance, she made references to God and scripture.

The daughter of a movie director in the twilight of his career, Diane knew more Hollywood secrets than *The Daily Fact*. Well dressed and witty, she announced celebrity secrets while she made her rounds tapping shoulders at the parties she hosted. She and her girlfriend Paulette, a leggy Broadway dancer, kept their noses in other people's business. They instigated marriage breakups and took decent single men from their steady girlfriends. Robin's best revenge against Diane was Diane's pale, pimply face. She stepped off the elevator and reminded herself how unattractive Diane was. She wouldn't miss not showing up at the party, even if she was the only absent, single resident.

The wind picked up and battered her face when she pushed the apartment entrance doors apart and stepped beneath the canopy. She lowered her head, crossed her arms and braced herself for the evening chill before she left the cover of the canopy. The first thing she did was to hunt a newspaper stand. Her search led her to Rascals, an East 22nd Street American cuisine restaurant.

A single *New York Times* remained in the box. She dropped two quarters in the newspaper machine and pulled out the thick newspaper.

Dinah and Trish told her about Rascals. It was one of their favorite weekend eateries; she had not once been inside before. She ordered herbal tea when the waitress approached her window table.

Steam curling off the top of the tea and the waitress gone, she settled into her search for a good movie. Her finger went down the pages in the "Weekend Movie Clock" section until she saw *Into The Night*. She stared at the title of the newly released movie directed by Gavin Paris. Then she stood, and, as quickly as she entered Rascals, she exited it.

Wind sucked at the door, and rain attacked her face like a gun full of pellets. The sky had gone black. She labored to catch her breath while she ducked around the nearest corner and ran inside Loew's Department Store to purchase a raincoat and an umbrella. All in one minute, she told the cashier not to bag her purchase, grabbed the receipt and left. It was 7:50. In ten minutes, Loew's would close for the day. She thought the rain quickened when she stepped on the sidewalk. With a flip of her thumb, the brand new black umbrella popped open. Beneath the umbrella, she took quick steps getting down the sidewalk. Moments later, when she turned and looked over her shoulder, Loew's was a small blur.

Through a throng of businessmen, women managers and CEOs, police officers, housewives and retired, elderly men, most scurrying to automobiles, taxis or buses, home from work and the start of the weekend, through a huddle of umbrellas, she pressed her way. Amid the throng, was a tall, stocky woman. Her head was covered with a copy of *The New York Times*. One block ahead was the Chelsea Cinema.

Stopping at the crosswalk and turning her head from side to side like a tin soldier, Robin lowered her foot into the street. A Volkswagon sped past her. In its wake was a rush of mud and water. Both landed on Robin and the stocky woman.

Satire filled the woman's voice, "Bum!"

The noisy wind stung Robin's face. Cars screeched and honked. Robin felt center of a symphony of confusion. Though she darted her gaze while she walked, she didn't see a man, two suits fresh from the cleaners flat against his back, approaching. Inches apart, the man and she turned and checked for oncoming traffic.

Their elbows touched. Robin, her footing loose on the wet pavement, tripped on the heel of the man's shoe. She fell hands first and palms down to the street. When she peered up, a flood of headlights greeted her. Horns screeched. She mounted to her knees, but remained tangled. Her pant cuff was caught beneath the heel of the man's shoe. The man lost his balance and fell partway on her back. Her face smashed against the pavement. She broke her fingernails so close to the skin, they bloodied her raincoat and blue jeans when she stood and pushed her hands down the lap of the raincoat and the legs of her blue jeans. Impatient automobile drivers cursed her while she hobbled to the other side of the street. "I'm sorry. I'm sorry," she called out while she crossed the street.

"Senorita." The husky, alto voice startled her. When she turned, she looked the stocky woman squarely in the eye. The woman wiped her jeans with a pink handkerchief. "Como le va?" The woman gave her no time to answer. "Creo que ya nos hemos conocido."

She looked at the woman softly. She wondered how she could tell her she didn't understand Spanish.

The woman continued. "Acabo de terminar mi trabajo."

She scratched her temple and tried to recall the last time a stranger mistook her for a Puerto Rican.

"Como se llama usted?"

Mrs. Brown's fifth grade Spanish instructions in Johnson City returned to her and she answered, "Robin."

"Que bonito. Que sucedio?" The woman paused and looked quizzically at her, "Que pasa?" The woman waited briefly for her to answer then she continued with, "Asi es como es. Como llueve! Usted no tiene mucho de estar aqui, verdad?" The woman never stopped wiping her jeans. "No importa. No me importa nada. Me voy. Vostros as lavis." The woman opened her purse and handed her a wad of clean tissues. "Tengo que ir. Tengo que irme. Tengo mucho que hacer Acso sea esta el que usted quiere?" The woman turned to leave.

She took the wad of tissues inside her hand, smiled and nodded at the woman.

"Al anachecer," was the last thing the woman said to her while she stood outside Chelsea Cinema holding her black umbrella and the wad of tissues in one hand. Without a word, she watched the woman walk away from her down the sidewalk.

Then she climbed the cinema steps.

"Four dollars and fifty cents," the clerk told her.

She reached into her purse for ten dollars.

"Four dollars and fifty cents," the clerk repeated while she popped a wad of gum.

She started to stutter, "I-I-I don't know what happened to my money. I had close to twenty dollars."

"No money. No ticket."

"But I had—"

The clerk smirked. "Looks like your friend did more than clean you off. Looks like she cleaned you out too. And," the clerk stood from her seat. "Looks like she and her friend with the suits across his back are gonna have a good time at your expense." When the clerk returned to her seat she was laughing.

Running down the stairs, Robin called out to the husky woman and the man she'd bumped into earlier. "Hey! Stop! Stop! Stop!"

The couple raced around a corner then down a dark alley.

Robin stood at the edge of the alley watching their feet move. A moment later she returned to the cinema box office. Straining to smile, she looked at the clerk and said, "As long as they needed the money. They didn't take my purse. They must be poor. I just hope they make good use out of the money they took from me. Buy something decent to eat. Who knows? They might have kids. I know it's a scam they're running. I also know it's better to give than to receive. God'll make it all right. God will work everything out just fine. I just hope something good comes of what they just did. Somehow I hope God blesses it."

Arching her brow, the clerk laughed and asked, "Girl, where are you from?"

With a heavy sigh, Robin turned and bound down the steps and walked into the night. Her pace was brisk. Her head erect. She walked in the center of the sidewalk, away from buildings and the street. She gripped the umbrella and readied to turn it into a weapon should someone jump out at her. Fluorescent lights from office buildings, shopping marts and all night diners lighted her path. On her way home, she passed the Hudson River, dark and still at this hour. Further into the city, she saw the General Theological Seminary and Saint Peter's Church. Three more blocks and she would be home. Chinese, Italian, French, Spanish and English words clashed inside her head. In effort to tune her passersby out, while she walked, she examined the architecture of old buildings.

Thomas Clarke bought the Chelsea estate over two hundred years ago. History told her the place where she lived wasn't always desirable. Though its groans had turned into low murmurs, Chelsea's buildings and other bits of its landscape seemed to bare some of the old pains. She wondered what living in Chelsea was like then, delinquent boys, teenage gangs and promiscuous young girls decorating the night, carousing for trouble. Suddenly a very sharp social thought stabbed her and returned her to reality. In 1750 she would have been a tortured slave, at best, a docile maid. Of Leslie and she, only Leslie could walk Chelsea's streets free of ridicule and accusation two hundred years ago.

The start of the century, the city's film industry found its root in Chelsea. The 1950s brought the district's housewives into the workforce. The 1960s brought Civil Rights to the district's country which supposed itself to be founded upon those same truths two hundred years before, and Chelsea, keeping stride with the nation, changed and became one of New York City's most desirable places to live.

She rounded the corner and looked up at the building she called home. On the opposite side of the street was Mavis' Homestyle Restaurant, her favorite place to eat. While she pulled her door key from her purse, for tomorrow's breakfast she decided on a serving of country ham and eggs. Key in hand, she looked up and greeted the doorman. "Hi."

"Good evening, Ms. Carlile." He watched her walk to the elevator. Dirt only showed on her pant cuffs. Her fastened raincoat concealed much of her mired jeans, allowing her to maintain appearance. He shook his head after she stepped on the elevator and the silver doors closed behind her. "Ump! That girl sure is pretty."

Bertha, Kathleen and Aretha, the first people Leslie introduced Robin to when she moved into the high rise, were on the elevator. Bertha wore a pair of tight black pants and a loose fitting blouse that exposed most of her small breasts. Kathleen wore a pair of tight designer jeans and a green, cotton blouse. Aretha, leader of the trio, wore a fedora hat, purple shirt and purple silk pants. A bazooka parted her lips. She raised her arms and clapped her hands. Bertha and Kathleen mimicked her. "Ssaayy, Rob."

"What's up, Aretha?" She chuckled.

"Let's get this party started."

"You're too much, Aretha." She shook her head and grinned.

"That's right. That's right."

"You don't see us?" Kathleen broke in.

"Hi, Kathleen and Bertha."

Bertha tapped the top of her head. "Hey, ba-be."

"Hey, hey, Rob." Kathleen said with a chuckle.

"You three are headed back to the party, huh?"

"You know it," Aretha answered.

The bazooka pierced her ears. "Aretha, why don't you quit?"

"Sorry." Aretha teased as she lowered the bazooka to her side.

She scraped her foot on the elevator floor. "Who's at Diane's?" She turned and looked at Aretha.

"You mean, who ain't there."

"Is the party jumping?" She asked, folding her arms across her chest.

Kathleen bumped her shoulder. "Aren't you coming?"

They looked at her.

"Naw. I'm not going. You know that's not me."

Aretha draped an arm around her shoulder and tapped her elbow. "Yes. We know." Then she pecked her cheek. "We love you anyway."

It was Bertha's turn to hug Robin's shoulder. "We all do."

"Sure, Girl. We love you even if you don't like to party."

"Thanks." She turned and looked at the last one who spoke to her, Kathleen.

"So, what are you going to do tonight?"

"And don't tell me you're going to sit in that apartment reading and writing."

She turned from Bertha to Kathleen.

"You do spend too much time in that apartment. You need to come out more."

"Aretha, all of you, I was just out."

"Where'd you go?"

"To the movie. An--"

"What did you see?"

"Dag, Bertha." Aretha turned up her nose.

"Yea, Girl. You're digging, aren't you? If she said she went to the movie, she went to the movie."

"Shut up, Aretha and Kathleen. Rob, what movie did you go see?"

"Gavin Paris' new movie."

"Ggiirrll, I've been wanting to see that. Was it good?" Aretha asked.

"I don't know."

Her brow went up. "I thought you just said—"

"Some woman picked my purse."

She stepped back. "What?"

"Um-hmm. You heard me right. She was working with this man who knocked me clean into the middle of the street."

"Get out of here."

"Yea. But they must have needed the money or they wouldn't have stole from me. The woman was very nice to me. After I ran into the guy and fell in the street she helped me. You know how hard it was raining outside. She wouldn't stop helping me until she made sure I was okay."

She arched her brow. "Rob?"

"No. No, Aretha. Everybody's not bad. Everybody's not out to run a game on someone else just to be running a game. I really think the woman was in need. She might have kids to feed. I mean. You never know."

Aretha shook her head. "Girl, you need Leslie as much as she needs you." Then she tossed her head back and laughed. "That's why you two are together. You need each other. You take care of her when she falls off the wagon and she protects you."

Robin narrowed her brow. "I don't need anyone to protect me."

"Rob, you're naive. You're very naive. Les protects you in ways you know nothing about. Every time somebody says something bad about you or teases you, she just about loses her mind. That woman has cursed more folk out for teasing you. Now you two fight differently. You fight with faith and prayer. Les, she'll just flat out curse somebody out if they hurt you.'" She shook her head. "But you don't know. Les, she doesn't tell you those things." She laughed. "Oh, but what am I saying. I almost forgot. You don't need anybody for anything. For a split second, I forgot. Most people I know can't do everything by themselves. I have to remind myself that you can do everything alone. You don't need anybody. Your faith is enough."

"It is."

"Rob, you use religion as a crutch." Kathleen looked Robin squarely in the eye. "You're emotionally and psychologically as crippled as Les, me, Bert and big head Re."

Aretha popped Kathleen in the back of her head.

Kathleen grinned and winked at Robin. "Don't pay her any mind. She doesn't know better." Her grin returned to a narrow brow. "Aretha's right. You and Les do need each other. Les protects your rainbow. She knows what you do each time you look at her. She knows you take out your ruler and measure her then measure yourself next to her. She knows when it comes to keeping religious traditions you'll always stand taller than she does. But she knows you need her. If it wasn't for Les, you wouldn't have that religious rainbow you walk around gazing up at."

Robin turned up her nose. "Rainbow? Les? The two have nothing in common."

Kathleen chuckled. "Don't tell me you haven't noticed how good you feel about yourself now that you have Leslie to practice being a good Christian on."

Aretha frowned when she turned and looked at Kathleen. "Stop. You're being mean."

Robin's gaze darted from Aretha to Kathleen to Bertha. She swallowed a lump in her throat.

"Religion makes you feel like you measure up—"

"All Christia—"

"I didn't say all Christians, I said you. I'm talking about you, Rob, not a roomful of people. Just you. You. That's the reason you go over board with religion. It makes you feel like you're somebody, and you are. I'll be first to tell you that. But deep down inside you don't believe it. That's the reason you're so religious. Like Kathleen said, you're emotionally and psychologically crippled like the rest of us." She laughed. "Why do you think we're such good friends? But you'll be the one the world will call good. You don't get drunk. You don't even drink. You don't get high. You don't get laid. You're not gay like me, Bert and Re. Girl, you're just keeping your corners square on all sides. But we're a circle of friends." She nodded. "You better believe we are. One of us gets hurt, we all go down. We stay busy taking care of each other. Now that you know. We beez friends down to da bone."

Robin shook her head and smiled. "Kathleen, you are one crazy woman. Child."

Bertha craned her neck. "Kathleen, you and Aretha shut up and leave Rob alone." Then she asked, "Rob, you okay? Getting robbed and all. Girl, you all right?"

"Yea. I'm okay. I didn't get hurt, and I only had nearly twenty dollars on me." Then she turned and faced Aretha, "Anyhow, I heard the movie's good. I heard it's about a South African journalist. He falls in love with an American businesswoman. Basically, it's a love story, but it also deals with some serious social and political issues. You now Gavin." She smiled as if she knew the director personally.

The elevator doors parted and Kathleen, Aretha and Bertha stepped into the hallway. Robin talked to them through the space in the doors. "Go see it. All three of you. I plan to try to see it again. I know it's good."

"I'll go see it." Bertha assured her with a farewell wave.

"We can go see it Monday." Kathleen suggested to Bertha and Aretha.

"Well, Kathleen, I can't hold this elevator forever."

Aretha was quick. "Yes, you can."

"Maybe I can." She took her finger away from the elevator control panel's 'open' button. "But isn't it a shame I'm not going to?"

The elevator doors closed, but not sooner than Aretha, Kathleen and Bertha pressed their heads together and screamed, "Bye, Rob!"

With her back pressed against the elevator wall she lowered her head and grinned sheepishly. Running into them lifted her spirits. She

27

promised herself to finish reading the last pages of Charles Fuller's play. Afterwards, she planned to write the outline of her sixth play. She brainstormed on her way to the 12th floor. If she got five pages of script on paper before retiring to bed, she'd call the evening a success. Talking about Gavin Paris' *Into The Night* fueled her desire to become a published playwright.

Even before she opened the apartment door, she expected Leslie to be at Diane's. Admittedly, she threw Middletown's ritziest socials. It was the glass tables lined with cocaine and liquor that posted "keep out" signs for her. Besides the narcotics at Diane's all-nighters, she especially avoided watching Leslie get blitzed. Dealing with the after effects of her 'highs' alone in their apartment was hard enough.

When Aretha, Bertha and Kathleen walked through the door to Diane's apartment, Jeremy Weaver's *Gracious Woman* sent a loud chorus' of "I've got to have her" into the hallway. Tucking in her butt and stomach, Aretha edged passed a dancing couple.

Diane spotted Bertha and waved the hand she held a joint in, "Bert!"

She turned, "Yea?"

"Over here!" She drew her with the swing of her arm.

Bertha pressed her way through the crowd with a string of "excuse mes."

"It's jammed in here." She pushed loose strands of hair off her forehead. Behind her stood a television producer snorting a line of cocaine. "Excuse me," she said when she bumped his hip with her elbow.

"Ain't no party like an Armstrong party, because an Armstrong party don't stop." Diane's voice raised and sailed across the room.

"You've got this party jumping, Girl."

"Diane Armstrong knows how to throw a party." Diane teased, brushing the top of Bertha's shoulder.

"I'm glad I came. I almost didn't catch this one."

"I'm glad you came too."

"Where's your girl Paulette? Out stealing some man?"

"Stop laughing, Bert. Paulette's not that bad. And. Hey. Can she help it that she's beautiful and men fall all over her?"

"I guess not." Shaking her head, she looked down into a sofa. "Hi, Leslie."

Leslie's head bobbed when she turned and looked over her shoulder. Her pupils were dilated. "He-he-hey, Bert."

Diane chuckled. "I see you had a good time, Ms. Fletcher."

Bertha cornered Diane with a stare while she addressed Leslie. "Let me take you home. You're bombed."

Leslie uncrossed her legs and shifted on the sofa. "No. Naw. No. I'm okay."

"Are you sure?" Bertha asked, leaning close to her shoulder.

"She's okay."

"Be quiet, Diane!"

"Bert, this is my party and Leslie's a grown woman."

Bertha searched Leslie's face for a plea. Seeing none, she grew silent and stepped away from the sofa.

Robin sat on the living room sofa with a pen in her hand and a composition notebook resting on her lap. For two hours she bent over the notebook; her neck ached while fresh ideas filled her head. Her hand dashed across the paper. She wrote feverishly. She promised herself no rest until she completed the first act of a play.

Midnight turned into early morning. Robin sat with a second pen between her fingers. Trying to work the knot out of her neck, she turned her head in one big circle and let the ballpoint pen slide from her fingers onto her thigh. Except to shift her hips and cross and uncross her legs, she hadn't moved since she sat at 10:00. The bottoms of her thighs were sore and numb. Her buttocks ached, and her vision was blurred. Slowly she pushed herself off the sofa, stretched her arms over head and yawned until her throat whistled. A second later, she bent and rubbed her buttocks and the backs of her thighs. She walked, stretched and yawned in unison until she reached the edge of the picture window where she pulled the string on the side of the window. She watched the floor length creme colored curtains close.

Tending to her writer's ailments, she massaged the center of her spine. She kept a hand on her spine while she walked to the sofa and almost sat. The notebook impeded her. She yawned before she bent to see on what page she ended. The top of page twenty. On her way to the bathroom, she dropped the dry ink pens inside the wastebasket at the edge of the living room. Her T-shirt drooped over her belt. Her jeans were unfastened. Her plait was unraveled, and the cuffs of her jeans dragged the floor.

Warm air filled the apartment. Her mind void of Leslie, she checked to see that the apartment door's deadbolt was locked then she slid the door's safety chain into place.

She set her alarm clock for 9:30, took a light, green chiffon dress from her closet, placed a pair of shiny, black pumps in front of the dress which she hung from her closet door knob and walked to the mirror and looked in. Her shoulders lowered. She was too tired to roll her hair.

Gospel music filled her bedroom. Reaching into the bookcase along the back wall, she pulled down the Bible. Her reading was mechanical. Psalms 119:13-16: "'With my lips have I declared all the judgments of thy mouth. I have rejoiced in the way of thy testimonies, as much as in all riches.'"

"Oh, God, help me get my desires in order." She sighed. "'I will meditate on thy precepts and have respect until thy ways. I will delight myself in thy statutes: I will not forget thy word. Blessed art thou, O Lord: teach me thy statutes.'" She read until the words warmed her spirit, "Blessed art thou, O Lord: teach me thy statutes."

Zipping the Bible closed and undressing she switched her bed lamp off, sunk beneath the warm covers, and, turning to her side, she fell into a restful sleep.

A band of crickets filled the night with noise. Central Park was quiet, even the homeless abiding there slept. Candy wrappers and sticky bubble gum littered the park's walkways and bicycle paths. One block from Central Park, an old woman slept in the corner of a parking garage. Drug controlled pedestrians mulled about Madison Square Garden dull and listless. At the back of the sports facility, a garbage can was pushed to its side by the wind, and bits of trash spewed over the parking lot. All night shopping marts, donut shops, 24-hour grocery stores, hospitals, bars, nightclubs, all night diners and 24-hour dry cleaning stores remained open.

Trucks lined Mills Clothing Factory's parking lot. Union Square, with its coffee shops, discos and old bookstores, dwarfed a teenage girl who walked up and down the sidewalk wearing a short, tight mini-skirt and a pair of six-inch pumps. On Edgewater Avenue a nineteen-year old slept on his back in the corner of a stranger's garage. A heavy, soiled rug, two torn blankets, a rusting bicycle, and a bag stuffed with little girl dresses cluttered the garage. The boy slept beneath the green rug. The musty odor emitting from the rug failed to bother him. He slept soundly. Hitchhiking, running, walking beaten paths and drinking from muddy waters he made his way from Maryland to New Jersey three nights ago. Though his aim was home in the Bronx, he hadn't left the garage since he found it.

Edgewater Avenue in Ridgefield, New Jersey was less than a quarter mile from Interstate 95 which, even at this hour, was noisy with cars, trucks, Rvs and motorcycles speeding North to Niagara Falls and Canada and South to Philadelphia and Delaware. The passing automobile headlights cast a flittering glow over Edgewater Avenue. Below Interstate 95, children slept with their legs and arms stretched across their beds. Smiles lighted their faces while dreams made fantasy come true in their heads.

The day was May 25, 1988. Temperatures escalated. Winos and late night party-goers danced a wobbly step with boarded building fronts, street light poles and ghosts of drunkenness that always haunted them at this hour. The smell of vomit coated the air and burned in sober pedestrians' noises. Out of open view, a wino worked to settle his nausea by gripping his stomach with his left hand and vowing to God with his right hand that he would never drink again.

It was Sunday.

Robin rolled to her side and wiped slobber from the corners of her mouth. On the opposite side of the apartment door, Leslie coiled with indignation. She pounded her fists on the door. She yanked the knob, but the safety chain refused to break. Her head throbbed. She slid to the floor and hung her head. Urine pulsed in her bladder. She looked up when she heard the elevator car ascending. Alcohol bubbled in her stomach and turned to vomit in the time it took her to push to her feet again. She couldn't get a man she met at Diane's party out of her head. He stared at her most of the night and wouldn't stop making advances at her despite how rude she was to him.

The moving elevator car grew louder. She took in a deep breath and jerked the door so viciously the safety chain banged the wall.

Robin raised her head and squinted. She crawled on all fours off her bed. Her feet dragged across the shag carpet. Her toes wiggled and cracked. Her arms hugging her shoulders, she braced herself against the cool air conditioned room. She stumbled to the door. While she listened to Leslie bang the door, she fumbled with the chain.

The elevator chimed and 12 lit up. Leslie jerked on the door again. When the elevator stilled, she jerked on the door and shouted, "Get up, Rob! Wake up! Wake up! Get up! Let me in! Open the door!"

Robin pulled back on the safety chain.

"Rob, please! Please! Someone is coming! Rob! Oh, Robin, please! Open the door! Open the stupid door! Robin! Rob!"

Wrapped inside her maroon, silk robe, she unlatched the safety chain and cracked the door.

Leslie stuck her nose through the crack. "Let me in, Rob. Somebody is coming. Somebody must have followed me. Let me in. Now."

She yawned and sent her sour breath brushing against Leslie's nose.

The elevator doors parted, and Leslie pushed against the door. "Let me in."

She ran the back of her hand across her face, and brushed her teeth with her tongue. "Come in." She said stepping away from the door. Then she turned and walked toward her bedroom.

Leslie slammed the door closed, but not before she turned and watched a shadow get back on the elevator.

At the edge of the living room, Robin shook her arms and let her robe slide down her shoulders and onto the floor.

Following her footsteps, Leslie stumbled over the robe. "Will you pick this thing up? I could have been killed tonight, thanks to you. If that won't work, now you're gonna try and break my neck?"

She waved her hand. "I'll get it in the morning."

Leslie bent and snatched the robe from the floor. She threw it across the foot of Robin's bed before she hurried into the bathroom.

The bathroom door slammed to a close.

Moments later, her stomach having emptied itself in the commode, she entered the kitchen and gulped down a glass of ice water. It wasn't long before she ran into the bathroom again.

Not until she sat on her bed did it occur to her that she could have lost consciousness had she drank another glass of white wine. She knew she was stoned and was grateful that the high would stay with her most of the day. She lay on her back then, a second later she sat up on her elbows. A sharp pain knifed her temples; she lay down again. She climbed beneath the covers. While she rested under the haze of drugs, she forgot about the man at Diane's party. His name was Jack. Though she was lonely and searching for a sexual escapade, he turned her off with his hard advances. "Keep your hands to yourself," she snapped at him after he coddled her breasts. She found his language, dotted with gender related slang, offensive. All night, his breath was hot like fire and funky. Had she not spent the evening dodging his balding head, Diane's party, Bertha, Aretha and Kathleen cutting a mean step until they left at four, would have been the highlight of her week.

Diane's apartment, with its large entrance hall, was the most eloquent apartment in the building. The living room, the first room guests saw after they walked through the entrance hall, gave the apartment a sophisticated look with its cathedral ceiling, light green drapes and oak floor. The room's sofa, two studio chairs and one lounge chair were made of forest green leather. Two floor lamps kept sentry on opposite ends of the sofa. Framed pictures of Diane and her parents lined the walls. Entertainment magazines and a vase of gray, silk flowers covered the room's only coffee table that was carved from dark oak.

The reading room was Diane's favorite. In it was a sofa, two high back chairs, a stone fireplace, two end tables, a ceramic bowl filled with gray, silk flowers and a wall length bookcase.

The dining room seated fifty. Tall candles rested in Roman candlesticks midway across a long stonewall table. Burgundy, upholstered chairs lined the table's two longest sides. A large, wood framed mirror shadowed the dining room table. A mural made from Indian design covered the room's second largest wall.

The kitchen seated thirty. The tops of its two tables were made of glass. All its chairs were made of brown leather. Crystal chandeliers lighted the room. Stove, oven and refrigerator were non-conventional in size. To the right of the kitchen and next to the master bedroom, was a small dining area. It was from here that Diane prepared and ate most of her meals.

The master bedroom was decorated in yellow. A thin patchwork quilt covered the room's king size, contemporary waterbed. Tan and yellow curtains hung from the ceiling to the floor and covered the room's two windows. Six copper and bronze "ladies in hats" hung from the walls.

The bathroom, black and yellow, boasted a large, round, sunken tub and a black marble sink and vanity case. Square mirrors covered all the walls in the bathroom. Two black, cotton towels were neatly folded over a gold towel rack.

The guest bedroom was the last room in the apartment. Its walls were off-white and its furniture, each piece bought from Ethan Allen, was European in appearance. White drapes enclosed the high bed and one dresser. A thick, shag carpet covered all but the outer edges of the polished wood floor.

Resting beneath the covers, Leslie took in a deep breath and rolled her eyes. She turned to her side and tried not to vomit.

The alarm screamed "Amazing Grace." Robin balanced herself on her palms then dabbed at the edges of her mouth where cotton formed over night. Her hair was loose and tangled. The corners of her eyes were caked with sleep. Her jaws were sunken, and her eyes were tiny beads. She pursed her lips, raised her arm and scratched her armpit. Though cool air pierced the stubble on her shins, must and sweat clung to her pajamas and body. She crawled off the bed and punched in the button on her alarm clock bringing "Amazing Grace" to an abrupt end and welcoming the ghost of silence into her bedroom.

Her toes cracked while she walked toward the living room. She stretched her arms over head and yawned.

In the living room, she pulled on the string at the side of the picture window and opened the drapes. "Ugh!" She turned away from the window. Sunshine beat warmly into her back. She figured she'd have to stand in the shower for ten minutes before she woke. With a light breath, she covered the sides of her face in her hands. After morning worship, she planned to run seven easy miles through Central Park.

Before she left for church, she told herself to open all the windows so birds could fill the apartment with noise. Turning, she stared out the window and marveled at God's creation. "The greatest artist," she whispered when she turned away from the window and walked into the bathroom.

She lowered her head beneath the spigot and splashed cold water on her face. After she splashed and washed her face, she slurped the water until her stomach jiggled.

With a beach towel wrapped around her torso, she departed the bathroom and trotted down the hall. She passed Leslie's room and found her snoring lightly. Although she hoped to eat breakfast with her at Mavis', listening to a low buzz rise and fall with the rhythm of her chest, she arched her shoulders and decided to let her sleep.

Adjusting her half-slip, she pondered the many places Leslie could have set the keys to her Porsche. She stepped in front of her mirror and straightened her slip for the last time. Her image met her approval. The chiffon dress snuggled her hips and showed off her small waistline. After pinching cologne behind her ears and on her wrists, she pulled down on the dress and picked lint away from its hem.

Before she departed the bedroom, she checked her purse. She frowned. Leslie's snoring had risen a volume. Not only did she need the keys to the Porsche; she also needed money. She crossed the hall. "Leslie. Leslie. Leslie." She whispered while she gently rocked her shoulder. Stepping back, she took in a deep breath and screamed, "Les-lee!"

Leslie sat up like a jack-in-the-box. Her head clanged like smashing cymbals.

Robin raced after her and stopped outside the closed bathroom door, "Leslie?"

"Wwwwhhhhaaaatttt?" She moaned, her head resting against the commode.

"May I--"

"The keys to the Porsche are in my purse. Have a nice time at church."

"Leslie?"

"Now what?"

"You okay?"

"Yes, but I don't think that's what you really want to ask me."

"Want me to get some medicine?"

"Thanks. No."

"I'll bring it back before I go to church."

"Rob--"

"Okay."

"Bye."

"Bye."

She turned away from the commode and stared blankly at the door. "You're not leaving." Her voice rose and fell like a roller coaster.

"I know." She was hopeful.

"Why not?"

"Want some breakfast?"

She raised her hands to the rim of the toilet seat. She almost chuckled. "Breakfast?"

"Yes. Breakfast." On the opposite side of the door, Robin smiled.

"Rob, I can barely hold down what I ate last night."

She chuckled before she said, "Maybe if you hadn't blown a gram of coke and drank a bottle of white wine . . . I know it's your favorite . . . you wouldn't be kissing the toilet right now, you sad puppy."

She crawled to the bathroom door and turned the handle until her head stuck out. The first things she saw were Robin's feet. "Help me." She called, extending a hand.

Wrapping her arms around Leslie's waist, she scooped her off the floor and onto her feet. "You need all the help you can get, Girl."

"What were you saying?" She asked, vomit coating her breath.

"I invited you to go to breakfast with me."

"Thanks."

"So, go?"

"I can't, Rob. I'm sick. I'm never going to drink like that again."

"Let me see," she said, tilting her head toward the ceiling, "When was the last time I heard that?"

"About a week ago."

"Right."

"You think I'm nuts, don't you?"

"You're a stone mess. So? No breakfast?"

"I can't."

"Then, can I have ten dollars?"

She stepped back and laughed. "I knew it. I knew it. I knew it all along."

Standing in front of her, Robin laughed equally as hard. "I only need ten."

"Rob. Get out of my face. You know I'm broke."

"I know that dear old Mom and Dad keep you happily supplied. As a Fletcher only child and with parents who'd do anything to see you on top of the world again, we both know you'll never be truly broke."

"Pplleeaassee."

She patted her foot and extended her hand. "Whatever. The ten please or maybe you'll need me to be quiet when I come home, so, let's make it twenty."

Walking to her bedroom, she granted her request when she picked up her purse. "Here."

"Thanks. I still wish you'd go to breakfast with me."

She walked to her bed and sat, "I wish I could."

"What are you going to do? Lay in bed all day?"

"No. Later, much later, I'm going to get up and take a shower. It looks like a nice day outside. When I get up, I think I'll take a walk."

"Yea? When I get home from church, I'm going running."

"Sounds good. Well, you better get out of here."

"Yea. Take it easy. Say. I'll be back around two."

"All right."

"Easy."

"Easy. Have a good time."

"I wish you'd come to church with me."

"I will one day."

"Promises. Promises. Bye."

"Later."

When the door closed, Leslie lowered her back to the bed. She wasn't asleep twenty minutes before she bolted upright. She was screaming. Shaking her head, she cried, "No. Don't kill me. Please don't kill me." A second later, she raised her hands and rubbed the spot on her neck where the masked man in her dreams had his hands around her throat.

Chapter Four

Reverend Keith Julian stood in the doorway of New Salem Baptist Church with his right hand raised. Across from him, the congregation held their hands midair. Their heads were bowed and their eyes were closed. "Now may the Lord rest, rule and abide between you and me until we meet again. And all the people of God said--"

The church sang in unison, "Amen."

Nearer the choir chamber, a voice called out, "Rob."

She turned and smiled. "Hey, Jennifer. What 'chu been up to?"

Jennifer O'Neil, a tall, dark skinned woman with a model like figure, pushed loose strands of hair off her forehead. "Same ol', same ol', Girl. You know how it is."

"I know, Girl. What are you doing later?"

She pressed her shoulder into Robin's. "If you think of something, I'm game."

"Wanna go to the rink? You can skate, can't you?"

"Girl, please. Is that a joke?"

She shrugged. "No?"

"Robin Carlile, you know I'm mean on a pair of skates."

"Skating? Skating? Did I hear somebody say skating?"

Jennifer recognized the voice immediately. "Hi, Willie. You look nice today." She smiled while she eyed his tall, dark frame.

Willie gawked at Robin. "I don't look nice, Ms. Carlile?"

She grinned into, "Well."

"Un-un, not always."

With a quick glance over the top of his shoulder, he teased, "Be quiet, Thelma. I was talking to Robin."

"You always look sharp, Willie," Jennifer enthused. "You look extra sharp today, that's all."

He patted his chest and chuckled.

Jennifer, Robin and Thelma's voices rose when they turned and faced a newcomer, "Roger!"

"Hi, girls." The collegiate sprinter clasped his hand over his mouth and took a step backwards. "Forgive me. I meant, hi, ladies."

Thelma chuckled and popped the crown of Roger's head with the corner of her purse, "Listen."

Behind them, Tim and Johnny clapped their hands over their heads. "Hey, what up?"

Jennifer turned, "Hi, Johnny . . . Tim."

"Church was good today, wasn't it?"

Jennifer turned. "It sure was, Tim. I almost slept in. I'm glad I didn't."

"I was tired this morning too, Jennifer." Thelma added, planting a hand on her hip and joining her friends on their walk outside of church. "Sometimes I get tired of coming to church too, and on Wednesdays I really have to press my way."

The friends rocked and leaned into one another's shoulders while they laughed. "Know what I'm talking about, huh?" Thelma asked, catching her breath. "But, I come to praise God, and, in that, I always receive a blessing."

Robin nodded emphatically. "There you go."

"And you know what?"

Thelma and Robin's voices chorused, "What, Girl?"

"God is good. I come to church to thank and praise Him. I come expecting a blessing."

"Amen," Johnny agreed.

As usual, Jennifer was loudest, "Praise the Lord!"

Willie pushed his shoe across the sidewalk, "Tim, are we singing at three?"

"Oh, yea. Willie, we are-ah-going to sing at Mount Calvary."

"You don't sound too sure of yourself, Bud-de." Robin said shaking her head and laughing.

"We are."

"At three?"

"Yes, Roger."

"Because last time--" Roger's laughter peaked. "You didn't show up, Bud-de."

"Well, I extended apologies. I must have said 'I'm sorry' a thousand times."

Johnny snaked through Robin and Jennifer until he neared Tim. "And you still aren't sorry."

Robin and her friends laughed until Reverend Julian looked up and called out, "Johnny?"

He clapped his hands and took the volume out of his laughter.

Further down the sidewalk, First Lady Theresa shook her head and smiled. Reverend Julian glanced at his wife. Then he smiled too.

Johnny sprang off the church steps onto the sidewalk with the agility that made him one of the nation's top collegiate basketball players. "Reverend and First Lady." He said seconds before his feet touched the sidewalk.

Reverend Julian's smile stretched across his entire face. "What's going on, Johnny? How's school coming? Still majoring in Chemistry?"

Theresa's dimples deepened. Her dark, brown eyes sparkled. Reverend Julian and her three-year old daughter, Lana, shadowed her calling, "Mama. Mama. Mama." Their four-year old son, Jama, who resembled his tall, slender, bearded father, stood next to Johnny's calf peering up at him.

"Nothing much," Johnny said, answering Reverend Julian's first question. "School's coming along fine. I should finish the year with a 3.30 gpa or a little higher. And, yes. I'm still majoring in Chemistry."

"Excellent."

"I plan to work as a disease control researcher after I graduate."

"That's good. It's always good to prepare for the future. I'm glad to hear you're doing so well. Remember to always give something back to our younger brothers and sisters. Be an example and spend time with the younger folk. God can use you to make a difference."

For an early Sunday afternoon, the parking lot of Mavis' Homestyle Restaurant, on the corner of 21st Street and 10th Avenue, was atypically crowded. Robin circled the lot twice before she put the Porsche in reverse and waited for a Toyota Celica to back out and leave an empty space.

She pulled an Aretha Franklin gospel recording out of the cassette player, turned off the ignition and stepped outside the car. Though Leslie never spared the keys to the Porsche, she wanted to drive her own car. Her mechanic promised it would be ready for pick up in two days. Last year, every four to five months, she found herself driving the nine-year old sports car to Robbie's Auto Center to have either a diagnostic test run on the engine or the transmission repaired.

With summer approaching, she told herself she'd use car repairs as a good excuse not to visit home. When she called home two days ago Theo answered the phone. "I'm going to be working lots of overtime this summer, Baby Girl. Old Man Jackson's got us busting our humps. He's trying to move the shop into a new building. Don't ask me why. You know how long we've been in this building on Monroe Drive. Got to be fifteen years. Jackson's just trying to make changes. Just trying to make things look new. But it's the same ol' same ol'."

She smiled when she heard her father laugh. She smiled until he cleared his throat and asked her, "Wanna talk to your mama?"

"Ah-Dad, I've got to go. I really shouldn't have called. I'm in a crazy hurry. You wouldn't believe how I'm always rushing around. I'm telling you. There's always something to do. But—" It was her turn to clear her throat. "Tell Mama I said hi."

Summer.

When Sonia was a baby, if Theo worked a lot of overtime and the weather was hot, Marcia would take Robin and Sonia into the hills of Middle Tennessee. They always carried a lunch basket with them. Robin would help Marcia spread a blanket on the ground. Sonia's legs would kick. She'd squeal, laugh and blow bubbles. Marcia would hug Robin and sing to Sonia. She'd tell happy stories, read from books like <u>Charlotte's Web</u>, <u>Pippie Longstocking</u> and <u>Curious George</u>, and tell corny jokes. Robin would laugh and smile up into her mother's face. They'd spend hours like that, just the three of them, soaking up the cool mountain air.

   A hostess escorted Robin to a window table. "Nice day outside, isn't it?"

   "Yes," she nodded. "It is."

   "Here's your menu an--"

   She raised her hand. "I don't need one. Thank you."

   The hostess pulled the menu close to her chest. "You've been here before?"

   "Many times."

   "Good." She smiled and stepped away from the table. "Your waitress will be with you soon."

   "Thank you."

   While she waited for a waitress to approach her table and take her order, she looked out the window. An elderly man hobbled down the sidewalk wearing a pair of running shorts, a T-shirt and sneakers. Pumping his arms fiercely and gulping air, he moved slowly passed Mavis'. Robin covered her mouth and tried not to laugh. A police cruiser pulled into the parking lot. Seeing the cruiser, all Robin's thoughts went to coffee and donuts. Two teenage girls walked in front of Mavis'. They talked non-stop. Across from them, an aging couple strolled hand in hand. When the couple neared the top of the street, a boy and a girl sped around the corner pedaling bicycles. They laughed while they raced each other down 21st Street.

   Robin turned away from the window when she heard a voice at the side of her head.

   "Ma'am?"

   She gazed at the waitress. "Hi."

   "Hi. How are you gettin' along today?"

   "I'm doing all right."

   "Good. Ready to order?"

   "Yes."

   She raised the order pad and waited.

   Robin talked fast. "A slice of country ham, two scrambled eggs and a large orange juice."

"Okay. I'll be back with your order in a bit. May I bring you a glass of ice water?"

"Please?"

"Comin' right up."

She took the rhythm out of the waitress' step. "May I ask you something?"

The waitress turned and faced her.

"Where are you from?"

"The South."

"I thought so. You have a Southern accent. I'm from Johnson City, Tennessee."

The waitress grinned. "Really?"

"Really?"

"Well, how about that? I'm from Louisville, Kentucky. I sure am."

Robin teased, "Really?"

The waitress leaned close to her and chuckled. "Really."

"How long have you lived in New York City?"

"Two years."

"Oh, yea?"

"Yea. I've seen you in here before. You always get ham and eggs."

"Yes. That's my favorite."

"Well, hope I see you soon, and, who knows, maybe I'll see you down South one day."

"Maybe."

"Let me hush so I can put your order in."

"Good, but, first, what's your name?"

"Michelle." She extended her hand, and Robin took it inside hers and shook it.

"Good to meet you Michelle. My name's Robin."

"Do you like New York?" She lowered her voice and twisted her mouth.

"Doesn't sound like you're crazy about it."

"It's all right. I miss the South."

"What brought you here?"

"Thought I was gonna be an actress. It's kind of funny. I came all this way to be an actress, and I ended up busting tables and being a waitress. I could have done that in Louisville."

"Don't laugh. You never know what'll happen."

"Yea. I suppose."

"Trust God."

"Thanks."

41

"I better let you go."

"If you want to eat."

Alone at the table, Robin dug through her purse. After she pulled out six quarters, she walked to the newspaper machine at the entrance of Mavis'. Dropping the coins inside, she retrieved a Sunday edition of *The New York Times*.

Right away she turned to the sports section. While she read yesterday's college football scores, she reminisced. She was glad she stopped by Mavis'. Its atmosphere reminded her of a restaurant in Johnson City that her father used to take her to. It was smaller than Mavis', but the food was just as good. Theo took her to the restaurant on the Saturdays after she brought home a straight A report card. She always ordered ham and eggs. She giggled and asked, "Really, Dad," while he told her about the large mouth bass he caught when he was a little boy, just about her age. He winked at her when she told him how much she liked some new cute boy in school. The first few times he took her to the restaurant she looked at him and asked, "Why didn't Mama come?" He always hung his head and mumbled, "She wasn't feeling well. But you know if your mama was up to it, she'd be here. She's real proud of you and all those good grades you keep making." He was her father. She forced herself to believe him. When she got older, to keep him from feeling shame and herself from being hurt, she stopped asking, "Why didn't Mama come?"

Turning away from the newspaper, she gazed out the window. A couple and their two children were coming into Mavis'. From the way they were dressed, she could tell they were coming from church. She nodded when she saw them. She was glad she went to church this morning. Reverend Julian's sermon weakened her fears and her deepest heartaches. It strengthened her resolve to be a great writer. Pushing her spine against the chair, she called up the sermon he preached less than an hour ago.

"The story of Job proves that each of us has a purpose," he preached to a congregation of nodding heads, a chorus of 'amens' and a flurry of waving handkerchiefs. "Despite humble beginnings, great loss, sickness or death, we can overcome. Sometimes life challenges us what seems like too much. It seems like there's one storm after another raging in our life. One setback after another. Storms come, and storms go. But, I tell you my brothers and my sisters we can make it through the storm. Look at Job. He lost all his earthly wealth. He lost his children. His wife told him to curse God and die. His friends proved themselves to be unfriendly. He couldn't count on them when he needed them most. But Job trusted God. In season and out of season he did. Job lived with purpose, my brothers and my sisters. Even in life's great storms he did. Job knew there was a bright side somewhere. He knew there was a lily in the valley. He knew God loved him and didn't just put him here for any ol' reason. Job knew his life had a purpose. And I tell you church, I do believe one of Job's purposes was to encourage people. He never gave up. He refused to quit. Job's story has encouraged millions around the globe. Job had a purpose, brothers and sisters, and guess what? So do you. Live like you matter. Live like you're somebody. God has a great purpose for each of us. That's why he gave everybody a special gift. Each of us has a gift from God that's tied into God's purpose for us being here. And I tell you, my brothers and my sisters we've got to use our gift. God is no respecter of persons. If we don't use our gift, it'll lose its power in our life. Hear me now, Church. We all have a purpose. Each of us has a gift from God. Use yours. Use yours," he concluded his sermon while he pounded the podium. Around him churchgoers shouted "Yes, Lord" and "Tell the truth".

Robin stared at the theatre section in the newspaper. Pushing her fears aside, she promised God that she would tell the stories he spoke to her heart.

Monday mornings were hard for Leslie. The last two weeks, they had been especially hard. Watching Robin shower and dress for work then peering out the living room window and gazing down on the street to see New Yorkers hustle to offices depressed her. She spent the day sulking in her robe. She lay on her bed or on the living room sofa staring at the ceiling. She dreamed incessantly. Her hopes for renewed film success never ended. Her heart ached when scenes from the past surfaced. She kept seeing herself on a set concentrating on her lines, rehearsing close ups, performing relaxation exercises and reporting to make-up and wardrobe even before the sun yawned in the sky. While working on the set of *Gardenia's Life* she climbed out of bed at four in the morning Monday through Saturday. Anxious to step into her character and glad to have a job that paid her $20,000 a week, she lived to work. The series consumed her. Her identity became lost in her character. By the time she worked on the set five years, an unrelenting boredom settled around her life. The set's appearance rarely changing, being constantly at odds with the sitcom editor, lighting technician and her stand in, she performed more for the cast and crew than she performed for the television audience. She worked hard to convince the crew on *Gardenia's Life* that she was happy.

Despite her efforts, she became increasingly difficult to work with. The senior hairdresser complained about her mood swings and threatened not to work with her again. Gossip columnists circulated rumors about her erratic behavior. Her drying episodes increased. She held up the set by switching hands in close-ups, master and medium shots. The director complained to the producer that she was purposely ruining the camera shots.

A senior writer pulled her to the side and told her, "On the set is not the place to air your personal problems. You better get it together."

"Money makes people anxious," Arnold told her over the telephone.

"Yea. Yea," she responded flatly.

"Being in the business as long as you have, you know how much money is involved in bringing a television series before a national audience. Stop acting like a spoiled brat. Everything's not going to go your way, not on the set, not in life. You know your mother and I raised you right. Start behaving like it." He would continue while he hoped for her to be more like her mother, submissive and tolerant. "The producers and directors have an awful lot of faith in you, Leslie. You can't quit just because you don't feel up to it."

"I know, Dad. And don't worry. I won't quit and make you look bad. I would never do that. Of course, you've always been there for me. Always supported me. How could I ever even think about quitting and making a man like you look bad?"

Days she spoke to her father she lost sleep at night. His criticisms and his snide remarks choked her attempts to rest, to relax. The next day on the set, muscled by emotion, she called on skills she learned in college Fine Arts courses. She drew strength from the fact that, though her spirit contrite, she was able to rise from bed at a time in the morning when most people were still turning over. Her lines were always well rehearsed. Her make-up was rarely smudged. Her wardrobe was never stained. She was familiar with the day's set (she made it a point to know where every prop and set marker was the night before the next day of shooting). At the close of each day, she took pride in the fact that she mounted the courage to complete a full day's work.

Four years. It had been four years since she worked on a decent set, starred in a major role. To deal with the stress of being unemployed, times Robin was out of the apartment and she was alone in her robe, she wept until her shoulders heaved. Robin in the apartment, she was mean and unforgiving. "These last four years have added ten years to my life," she moaned to Robin at least three times a day.

Without make-up, a mask she no longer wore while in the apartment which was most of the time she looked haggard, years older than she was -- twenty-three. Robin, busy with part-time work at Mills', charity work and her writing career, not once revealed to the media or the public the details of Leslie's distressing life. "Too many bad mixes in my system," Leslie whispered to the empty apartment whenever she felt herself on the brink of a nervous breakdown.

Even during her deepest depressions, she couldn't stop her thoughts from going to Amanda Gaynor. Amanda was a polished actress. She studied her portfolio. At forty years old, Amanda had eighty movies to her credit. Her work in each movie was outstanding, unforgettable. Though it pained her to admit it, she knew the real reason she didn't accept the lead in *Michael Come Home* was because, opposite Amanda, the flaws in her craft would reveal themselves. Working with a seasoned actress like Amanda, she knew the camera would catch the times she relied on technique instead of emotion, let the audience see the few times she, nervous and unsure of her talent, forced realism into her lines or seemed detached from the pulse of her character. Twenty years in the business and it continued to be her shortcoming that she turned applause and awards into weapons, weapons she turned upon herself. Applause gone and the awards not forthcoming, she turned to alcohol and cocaine to help her face the world.
****

For the first time in over a year, she woke before Robin. While she made her way across her bedroom floor and into the bathroom, she vowed to find work. She pushed the bathroom door open, turned the cold water on, and, listening to the water gurgle, she watched it go down the drain. She laughed at the water and wondered how she would look washing a row of tables in a smoky restaurant. She was tired and it was only 7 a.m. Hollywood's most powerful producers and directors knew who she was. They had Donald's address and telephone number. She wasn't a giggling, naive dreamer fresh from Connecticut. Assistant directors stopped calling to schedule her for screen tests eight years ago. Outside the cinema, she had not the slightest inclination on how to survive. With each passing day, she grew more afraid to telephone friends, talk to business associates or contact Donald.

"Good Morning, New York!"

Reaching for the radio at the edge of the bathroom sink, she turned the volume down.

"Today is gonna be a hot one! Temperatures are expected to soar into the mid-nineties. That's right, folks. Today's gonna be a cooker!"

Twenty minutes later, showered and dressed, she stared at a frying pan. Two eggs and two pieces of wheat bread lay on the kitchen counter next to the frying pan. She knew the sound of eggs and grease popping would coax Robin out of bed. Taking her hands off the counter, she walked to the refrigerator and pulled out a pack of margarine. After she laid the pan on the stove, she sliced off a chunk of margarine and watched it fall into the pan.

Margarine melting in the pan, she walked to the refrigerator and took out a gallon of milk. Just as she stabbed the eggs with a fork, she turned toward the kitchen doorway and listened to a familiar noise.

Robin stood on her bed and stretched until her fingers neared the ceiling. She yawned while she climbed off her bed and walked to her dresser. When she walked around the corner of her bed, she bumped her knee on the bed's sharpest point. Using one hand to massage the sore spot on her knee, she hobbled into the bathroom. She pulled off her nightgown and panties and stepped into the tub. Cool shower water splashed her face and body. When the cool water touched her lips, she pushed her head back, and, catching water in her mouth, she spit a gush of water into the air. Next, she combed her fingers through her hair and shook her head from side to side. Water splashed onto the shower floor and inside the marble shower wall. She shook her head until her scalp began to tingle. Then she switched the shower off.

She hugged herself while she shivered and ran out of the bathroom then across her bedroom floor to her dresser. Cool air bit the backs of her thighs until she pulled her dresser drawer open, and, her cotton panties on, jumped into a pair of corduroy pants. When the towel fell from her body to the floor, she fastened her bra and pulled a 5K road race, T-shirt over her head. In the afternoon she planned to run her regular, brisk, five-mile route through the Chelsea District. Monday through Friday, she conditioned herself for her weekend road races. Saturdays she went to a local track and field and clocked herself in quarter mile to three-mile runs. The quiet, forsaken track and field was safe. It was her haven. Sometimes she went there just to walk and enjoy the evening air. Weeds and tall grass filled the inside edges and all the cracks in the oval asphalt track. Her Saturday runs were her shortest and hardest runs of the week. Twice she ran until she fainted. Both times she came home and told Leslie, "I don't feel too good. I'm so tired and there's this tightness in my chest. To top it all off, while I was timing myself today, I passed out."

Her eyes wide, Leslie screamed, "Go to the doctor. You pass out and drag yourself in here and tell me. What can I do?"

"It's nothing. I was running. I must have run too hard. Next thing I knew my heart was racing. My chest got tight and bam! I was on the ground. Just-like-that. I passed out."

"Fainting isn't something you should take lightly, Rob. You should go see a doctor. Don't try to be a hero. Just go get checked out. That's all I'm saying."

Shaking her head, she said, "I shouldn't have told you. I should just have kept it to myself. I'll be all right. I'm strong as a racehorse. Look at me." She faced Leslie and raised her arms. "I'm a picture of health."

"All right," Leslie conceded, "But the next time you pass out you go to the doctor."

Leslie pressed her elbows against the kitchen counter and stared at the face of the past. Once she was the envy of Hollywood. Now she feared losing the Porsche if she fell back two months in her loan payments. A salty tear inched down the side of her face and pounced onto the bread of her egg sandwich. The telephone rang with few intermissions four years ago she mused while she stared at the egg sandwich. Though a pretty woman, she conducted her sexual affairs with great emergency. Fans followed her down the street and begged her for an autograph. Four years ago it was hard being Leslie Fletcher. Gazing at the egg sandwich, she let out a deep breath and moaned, "That hasn't changed."

A second later, memory brought her father's voice to the front of her thoughts. "People only like her so much the way they do, because she's young, cute and spunky. She has a cherub face. She won't always be young and cute though. And once she loses her youth, something we all must forsake either by living longer or dying young, she won't be cute anymore. No longer young and cute, fans, producers, writers and directors will reclassify her spunk as meanness. Our young, cute, cherub faced daughter won't be spunky anymore; she'll be an imp."

She recalled the conversation she overheard her father having with her mother more than fifteen years ago as if it happened yesterday. She was pressing her ear against the dining room wall listening to her parents while they sat in their favorite lounge chairs in the living room. She hated her father for unleashing his harshness to create such conversation about her, his daughter and only child. She hated her mother for allowing him total freedom to engage in the conversation. She despised her mother's submissiveness and complacency. A viciously mean man, at a young age, she knew her father's anger needed curbing. Now a woman herself, she realized her father didn't love her mother. By the time she was seven, she saw him parade three adulterous relationships before her mother, a woman who took it in, seemingly untouched by it all. One of the services she saw her mother able to provide the family was the courage to curb her father's anger, and not once did she even do that.

She spun on her heels and turned back toward the egg sandwich. Her father's words stung in her ears.

It was her mother who started the scrapbook filled with magazine and newspaper clippings on her. Her father kept abreast of her financial achievements. Her mother knew which editors and reporters chronicled her successes; she sent them holiday greeting cards and birthday presents. Her father knew the details of each of the contracts she worked under. He knew how much each performance she worked on paid. He knew the approximate start and finish time of each commercial, magazine or newspaper layout she was assigned to complete. He pushed her to do more commercials, television series and specials. His persistence both annoyed and encouraged her. She was determined to prove to him that she didn't need him waiting in the wings to perform, to bring the audience to its feet, to succeed.

She turned and faced the egg sandwich. She would never forget the words her mother spoke to her the day after her sixteenth birthday party. They were the kindest words she ever spoke to her, since she couldn't remember her pulling her close and saying, "I love you."

"Leslie, you can't remain a child forever," she advised. "You must grow into a woman. And, honey, I want you to be a strong, healthy woman. I want you to have a lot of inner strength. Most of all, I want you to be happy. You can't live for anyone other than yourself. For, darling, please never forget, on Judgement Day, you will give an account for all your thoughts and deeds. No one will be represented in your stead, and you will represent no one but yourself. So, you see what a tremendously great waste it would be to spend your life living for someone, anyone else."

When she started acting on the set of *Gardenia's Life*, her parents telephoned every day. Arnold inquired as to her hourly itinerary. He wanted to be able to assess whether she was over working or not working enough. Before he returned the receiver to its cradle, he handed the telephone to Joyce. While he glared at her and mouthed the words, "Long distance prices are going up, even while you speak," she fumbled with her necklace or earrings. "How're you doing, darling?" and "Behave. Do what the producers and directors tell you to do. Be good. Bye. Take care," was the most she felt she ever had time to say to Leslie.

Three years into *Gardenia's Life*, Joyce feared Leslie was growing up too fast. Hollywood's vices, the wild parties where tables were lined with alcohol, speed, Quaaludes and cocaine, weren't unfamiliar to her. She heard the ladies' room conversations when Arnold and she attended award banquets in support of Leslie. She went against the living arrangements the production company secured for her. She heard rumors that the middle-aged actress Leslie lived with paraded men about her house. She considered such behavior poor mothering. The only thing that kept her from moving to California was Arnold. He said he needed her home, and, since she was his wife, he told her with him was where she belonged.

At fifteen, Leslie saw musical groups hurry to the top of record charts only to plummet a short one to two years later. She found it strange that children who kept themselves awake at night dreaming of becoming famous were often products of dysfunctional homes. More often than not, she witnessed Hollywood destroy those same children after they became adults with their nighttime dreams fulfilled. She came to understand that Hollywood didn't create giants or stars of people. It couldn't. It had not the ascendancy for that, and, after more than fifteen years in the business, sensing that the greatest achievements in life were never the product of magic, she began to caution herself not to count on the mirage called Hollywood to make her dreams come true.

She came to believe that Hollywood created vapors, people who lost their true identity in their recent performance, people who vanished with their first commercial failure, people no one saw or heard from again. If she hadn't heard television and movie executives openly joke about an actor or actress' box office failure, she would have emphasized with them, heard their pleas. Met with their laughter and ridicule, she came to detest their hankering her to be on time for shootings, motion picture premieres and publicity photo sessions. The fact that they spent millions of dollars on a movie she was cast in scored few points with her. Her patience with their alter egos and cruel games was famished.

She turned away from the kitchen counter and arched her shoulders. Perhaps producers and directors recently were fair. After all, it appeared she too was but a vapor. She lowered her hands and crossed her arms. There was no universal law that stated she was guaranteed lasting fortune and fame. There was no universal law that tucked her dreams safe with God and said they had to come true.

The last three movies she starred in were huge box office failures. Director, David Whootson fought Phillip Radcliffe, a filming industry president and financial tycoon, to have her in *A Long Way Home*, the last major picture she starred in -- a comedy flop. A month after *A Long Way Home* premiered in New York City, she was embarrassed to look David in the eye. He was the only director she ever considered a friend. It was an awful time in her life. She took to drinking.

She kept her arms crossed while she walked out of the kitchen, through the dining room and into the living room. She plopped down on the loveseat. For the first time since she moved into Apartment 1201, it occurred to her that not once did Robin collect a paycheck from the entertainment industry. Robin's dream of fortune and fame was merely fantasy, an embryo. She regretted being famous only now because she felt fame betrayed her. She was convinced it turned on her as it turned on many of her predecessors.

She stood. "At least I peaked," she comforted herself. "I triumphed." To consume time, she entertained the thought of enrolling at New York University and taking a few graduate courses. Robin and her sorority sisters were happy. They didn't spend days in the prime of their lives groping with clinical depression.

She walked to the picture window and stared out at the open sky. She could drive to NYU and pick up graduate school enrollment forms later in the week. Robin, Dinah, or Betsy could advise her on which professors to take. They knew who all the better instructors were. Because acting was an unstable profession, she told herself to build as many bridges going from Hollywood to the rest of the world as she could.

To pay for her tuition at NYU, she considered doing local theatre. She missed performing on stage before a live audience. She told herself theatre would sharpen her acting skills. "I should have listened to Mama." She found herself saying. "I should have gone after my master's degree." Robin and her sorority sisters' conversations came to her and filled her mind with noise. "To be happy and not combating long bouts of depression," she wished out loud.

　　　　She stood at the edge of Robin's bedroom. "You ready?"

　　　　Robin turned and stared at her. "Ready?"

　　　　She lowered her head and cast her gaze to the floor. Annoyance crept into her voice. "Yes, ready? Are you ready to go?"

　　　　"Go where? "What's wrong with you?"

　　　　All at once, she buried her head in her hands and wept.

　　　　Robin watched her back heave and listened to her voice choke. Sympathy was not something she offered her. Her patience was expired with her rash decisions and outrageous jealousies. She tired of hearing her complain that her fans no longer appreciated or cared about her since her fan mail dropped off drastically two years ago. She didn't think Leslie respected her fans. Watching her deal with celebrity, she vowed to always respect her fans, to the point of willingly signing autographs, even while dining at a restaurant with family or friends.

　　　　Nightly she went to her knees and prayed earnestly to God that Leslie would find work. Until then, she wanted to grab her by her shoulders and shake her. She wanted to scream at the top of her voice at her that the world was no longer watching her, that it was okay for her to fail, to stop performing. The past month she frequently over heard her talking to Joyce on the telephone. She always cried bitterly into the receiver before she hung up. Visits by train or car home to Connecticut were becoming weekend retreats. Her constant complaint was that no one cared about her and that all of her once devoted fans proved to be thankless.

　　　　Twice, after combing the streets and want ads, she found her work, but Leslie was firm. She would never accept work outside of the live stage or motion picture industries. Any other job was beneath her. When she told her she looked for hours to find her the two secretarial jobs, she shrugged, swore under her breath and told her, "I don't need your help to get a job."

Raising her head and wiping her eyes dry with the back of her hand, she sniffed hard. After she pulled the keys to her Porsche out of her purse, she sniffed hard again. Then she walked into her own bedroom and grabbed her leather jacket. "Wrong with me?" She asked while she looked over her shoulder.

Robin was silent.

"Nothing's wrong with me." She shoved her arms into the jacket sleeves.

Robin pursed her lips.

She walked to her bed where there was a stack of typewritten papers. "Don't let me forget these." She piled the stack of television and motion picture screenplays into the crease of her arm. Not in eight years had she been willing to screen test for a role. Last month she decided not to renew Donald's contract. She was pleased with his work. She couldn't afford to pay him.

She turned and looked over her shoulder at Robin. 'No. I can't leave without these. And guess what?"

Staring blankly at her, Robin asked, "What?"

"I'm going to NYU later today. I'm gonna see what kind of graduate level theatre classes they have."

"Mmmm."

She blinked fast. "But first I have to get to some screen tests." She looked down at the papers in her arms. "Can't forget these."

"No. We wouldn't want you to do that. Would we?"

She clenched her teeth. "Not we." She said stabbing herself with a finger in the chest.

"I should have known that. Nothing you ever do includes me. It's always only about you. I'm glad I already knew your supposed kindness wouldn't last longer than two seconds."

"Shut up." A second later, she raised her hand and shook her head. "Let's not fight this morning. Come on." She waved Robin toward her. "Let's have breakfast at Mavis'. My treat." She was in the hallway, but Robin still hadn't moved. "Lord knows I need to start doing things for other people and stop being so selfish." She looked back at Robin before she walked toward the apartment's front door. "Well, come on. Get your purse and jacket, and let's go." Silence. She neared the elevator doors, then she turned back. At the edge of Robin's bedroom, she grinned like a fox. "Don't you want to go?"

She was quiet.

Moments later with tears in her eyes, Leslie boarded the elevator and rode to the main floor alone.

In the afternoon Leslie was supposed to stop at Robbie's Auto Center and pay Robin's repair bill with money Robin gave her. With fall semester starting in two months, Robin needed her car. Betsy telephoned from Johnson City at 6:30 in the morning and reminded her to register for classes in two weeks. She concluded the conversation by encouraging her to brainstorm for ideas for the fall sorority rush. They also had to vote for officers, as usual, making certain each of them held an office. They discussed voting Trish, Dean of Pledgees, and Robin, President. They talked about writing and performing a play that detailed the sorority's history. Last year they planned four dances, two in the fall and two in the spring. Anna, most likely to be the sorority secretary, sold them on the idea of a skating party. Loretta and Sharon planned a fashion show, and Dinah sold them the idea to schedule two renowned African American historians to speak at the campus in February. This was their final year. They wanted to leave New York University their legacy. Sharon, a talented seamstress, sewed a dress and jumpsuit for each of them. It was her goal to make them the sharpest sorority on campus, even sharper than the Deltas, their toughest Greek Show competition. Last year they lost twice to the Deltas, both times in the spring. Before the start of the academic year, they choreographed new steps. There was also a possibility that Trish could run for a regional office.
****

The Porsche pulled alongside the curb. Leslie sat against the back of the car seat. She sighed, and, looking at the car ceiling she said, "I'm already tired, but, I'll get a job even if it kills me. I'm not going back to the apartment unemployed. I have to get a job." She sighed again and rested her chin atop her fist. "I can't give up. It's hard, but I won't give up." She rubbed her forehead and shook her head. "I have to get a job."

She stared through the car window before she opened the door and walked inside Robbie's Auto Center. Fifteen minutes later when she left Robbie's and entered the warm, late morning sun, she looked up and called out in disbelief, "Rob!"

She turned and faced the Porsche. Before her was the woman she hoped to avoid until late in the evening when she returned to the apartment. To the side of her were two teenage boys engaged in a game of crap. Behind her walked a pair of elderly men engaging in long, slow conversation.

The wind blew through her braids while she walked down the sidewalk closer to the big steel entrance doors of Mills Clothing Factory. "Thanks for paying the mechanic for me. I didn't have time to stop in there before I went to work. They're always so busy. I just didn't feel like standing in a long line. Did you tell them I'll make a final payment tomorrow when I pick up my car?"

"Yea. I told them."

After she thanked Leslie again for paying her mechanic with the money she gave her last night then bid her God-speed during her job search, she turned on her heels and resumed her walk to work.

Leslie watched her through the Porsche's rearview mirror. The nearer she went to the factory, the more mired her hopes became.

It took both hands for Robin to open the factory's steel, entrance doors. Once inside, the doors clanged to a close behind her, shutting out Leslie. In an instant, she entered a world of loud sewing machines and row after row of women sitting in front of piles of expensive fabric.

She smiled as she passed her co-workers on her way to her assigned station. "Hi, Liz." She called out, flipping her hand in the air.

Elizabeth Chung, a seventeen year old, Chinese woman, stopped her. Two tall boxes of wire hangers were pushed beneath the wooden table she was stationed at. She reached and grabbed an armful of leather dresses and laid them on the table.

Not unlike many of the factory's employees, Elizabeth dreamed of making it big in the motion picture industry. Beth Ashie, a forty-year old woman born and raised in Ghana, Africa, was the factory's oldest employee. Married at fourteen, she was the mother of eleven children. Monday through Saturday, she completed her back breaking assignments at the factory. She worked hard so that her husband and their children could move into their own house in the finer parts of Harlem leaving the dirt, cold and poverty of the ghetto as a distant memory. Elizabeth, Robin, Beth and Juanita Andrews, a nineteen year old Puerto Rican who dreamed of making it big as a pop singer, were a passionate quartet of friends.

There are four Mill's Clothing Factories in the United States, making Mill's one of the nation's largest clothing factories. The New York City branch alone employs over one thousand people. Two New York City day shift managers, Patricia Brown and Robert Jones, often joke with the seamstresses and packers that they would gladly switch jobs with them to avoid facing the messy piles of paper work always cluttering their desks. They manage from a distance and encourage a strong passion for the arts. It is because of them that Robin finds juggling work, school and writing doable. Outside the steel, factory doors, no one guessed laughter had a place inside the concrete building that housed the latest fashions designed directly from Paris, Africa, India, the United States and France.

Robin pulled a stool away from the table and sat beside Elizabeth. She rested her elbows on her shoulder.

"Hi, Rob. Guess what?"

"Yea, Girl?" She asked, turning and looking into Elizabeth's dark, brown eyes.

She looked over the crown of her shoulder at Robin. "Girl." Narrowing her eyes, she looked at her and grinned. "Girl."

"What?" Her brow was arched.

"Girl!"

"Oh, come on."

"Girl."

"Elizabeth"

"Girl." She pressed the point of her head against the top of Robin's head and laughed.

"What is it?"

"There's a new guy."

"And?" Robin stood.

"And . . There's a new guy here." She pumped her eyebrows and giggled.

"Okay, Chung, forget you." With a wave of her hand, she turned and headed in the opposite direction, away from Elizabeth.

She lifted an inch off the stool and raised her voice. "And he's black and good looking!" She returned to the stool.

Robin threw her hands against the swinging doors and walked into the next room. She was smiling.

Chapter Five

Push. Push. Push. The skateboard landed on the ground before it bounced across the street and scrapped the edge of the opposite sidewalk. Sunrays beat down on Robin's back and neck. She left her umbrella at work. It didn't rain all day. A runner brushed her shoulder and looked down 22nd Street. Lifting his legs and pumping his arms, he ran against gravity until he reached the end of the street.

Robin smiled when she glanced over her shoulders. New York City's faithful distance runners were out in great numbers. It was mid-evening, the time most walkers and runners took off on their daily training course.

Push. Push. Push. After pushing the skateboard three blocks down 22nd Street she stopped and wiped her brow. Her chests heaved. She struggled to catch her breath. A block later, she picked up the skateboard. Drawing in a deep breath and placing one hand over her heart, she decided to carry the skateboard home. She nodded at a woman walking her dog. The woman returned her nod, and she put the skateboard on the ground. She crouched and rocked from side to side until she reached the end of the street.

Her stomach growled. She passed the El Grande, Mama's Best, The International House of Pancakes, the 21st Street Diner and Mavis' Homestyle Restaurant. Each restaurant, distinctive aroma emitting from its chimney, sent a message of hunger to her mind and stomach. By the time she reached the apartment building's entrance doors, she was famished and her heart was racing.

Five weeks separated the last time she and Leslie saw one another. Telephone conversations between them were long and detailed. Leslie wanted to know if she talked to the Porsche dealer, told him she was going to pay the loan off next month. Robin wanted to know how hot it was in California. Leslie wanted to know if she talked to the apartment manager, told him she'd catch up on her share of the rent in a couple of weeks. Robin wanted to know if she had been in any earthquakes. Leslie wanted to know if her mother sent her the money she asked for a week ago. Robin wanted to know if she had stopped drinking now that she was riding the crest of another career wave. Leslie wanted to know if New Yorker's were raving about her new movie.

Six months prior to this latest separation, Leslie was busy working with Gavin Paris on a new movie. In her work, Robin found cause to be happy. Since she started working with Gavin, Leslie changed. She no longer screamed and cursed at her. She smiled with sincerity. She even laughed hard and without envy or indignation. Robin told her friends at church that God answered her prayer for Leslie to secure employment and with one of the industry's leading directors.

Working on the latest set kept Leslie away from New York for weeks at a time. The apartment seemed to carry a death silence while she was away. At night loneliness settled around Robin until she felt choked with solitude. She'd never been all by herself before. The apartment seemed to grow larger with each passing day. At the edge of midnight when stray cats cried into the blackness, she thought about Sonia. Every loud meow sounded like Sonia calling out to her. To silence the cries, she whispered long, panic stricken prayers. "God, keep me safe. Keep me from all hurt, harm and danger. You know I'm all alone. I'm here all by myself. God, don't let anybody come in here and hurt me. Keep me safe, Lord. Keep my mind and my spirit, Lord. Don't let anything bad happen to me. Don't let me be scared, God. Don't let me be scared. Don't let me be scared about Sonia. Lord, don't let anything hurt me. Don't let anything come at me. . . ." She prayed until her eyelids grew heavy and she started to yawn and nod. She slept with the television on. During the day when she skimmed weekly and monthly news and entertainment magazines, she smiled when she saw Leslie's face. Moviegoers admired her talent. She had regained her angelic presence. During one of their telephone conversations, Leslie chuckled and said, "I'm big time again."

The crew on the set of the Gavin Paris' *When All The Flowers Bloom*, Leslie's last movie, shared a professional and a personal camaraderie. Gavin would have it no other way.

He was a simple, energetic, man who set high standards for his staff, higher standards for himself. He had thirty years and over one hundred films of working as a director to his credit. He refused to feed alter egos. No one on his set was pampered. He worked on a low budget. He left no room for tantrums or fits of jealousy. He only worked with actors and actresses who agreed to a contract clause that stated: "I understand that during the course of the making of this movie, if I, without good cause, do not show up on set for work, I could lose one day's pay. If I refuse to arrive on set on time, I may lose one day to one week's pay, depending on how many hours and days I detain production due to my lateness or absence."

Leslie didn't know anyone except Gavin the first day on the set. Between takes, she spent the first week in her trailer. A week later, she struck up a friendship with a make-up artist and one of the stuntwomen. It wasn't long before she struck up friendships with the entire crew. For the first time in ten years, she looked forward to going to work.

Filming on *When All The Flowers Bloom* ended five weeks ago. Donald wasted no time finding her work. The movie she worked on now put her in the center of a stellar cast, but she was not happy.

Robin sighed when she walked inside the apartment building. Since October, she sold two plays to college drama departments. She hoped to finish the play she was under contract to former Broadway director, Richard Steinberg for, this week. At Leslie's advice, she signed Derrick Hall as her agent, her publishing house and stage show go between. Twice she met with Patricia and Robert at the factory and requested they cut back her hours.

She nodded at the doorman before she made her way to the elevators. She spoke to a pair of women she knew, pressed the 'up' button and waited. A male friend stepped around the corner, and she lifted her head. She smiled and waved at him. They walked close to each other and entered into a conversation the opening elevator doors cut short. "Stop by later. Are you still singing and networking in the business? I miss talking with you." She said ending the conversation and stepping on the elevator.

"Yea. I'm still singing, and I'm good. Hey!"

Pressing the 'open' button, she stuck her head between the elevator doors. "Yea?"

"Some guy was around here looking for your roommate."

"Oh, yea?"

"Yea. Said his name was Jack. Said something about a party months ago. I guess Leslie gave him her number. I don't know. He was around here asking about her."

"Never heard Leslie mention a Jack. Sure he wasn't just a fan?"

"I don't know. He didn't act like it. Acted like he knew her. He knows where you two live."

She waved to him while the doors closed. On the elevator, her head bowed, as if controlled by a string and not will. She shifted the skateboard in her hand and thought about Leslie. She whispered, "Thank you, Lord," when she thought about how the stalking calls stopped a few months ago. She wondered what Leslie was doing and wished the director would release the crew for the weekend, so Leslie could fly in from California. It scared her that their careers would flourish and send them thousands of miles, months . . . years apart. It scared her that success would cause her to be alone, especially at night.

Unlocking the door to Apartment 1201, she went into her bedroom and pushed her skateboard under the bed. Then she went into the dining room and checked for notes from Annette. Leslie and she hired Annette Combs to be their secretary six months ago. Annette was another tool they used as proof that their careers weren't growing them apart.

She grabbed a pile of phone messages and a thick stack of fan mail addressed to Leslie c/o Donald Riggs Acting Agency. She walked into the kitchen and pushed a frozen dinner inside the microwave. When she stepped back and opened the refrigerator, a sinking feeling came over her. She took the pitcher of orange juice off the shelf and poured herself a glass. The last six months Leslie and she visited one another on major holidays. They ate together on Thanksgiving and exchanged presents on Christmas. They hollered, "Hey, girl!" when they passed each other on busy thoroughfares in Manhattan while Leslie completed a round of community service commercials as a penalty for the stack of overdue traffic tickets she accumulated over the last year.

A potholder padded the aluminum dinner tray. Robin carried the frozen dinner, now hot, into her bedroom. After she laid the tray on her dresser, she fell, face down on her bed, reached overhead and turned on the stereo. The radio was turned to WPMZ, an AM gospel station. She sighed before she mounted to her elbows. She lifted her arms overhead and pulled off her T-shirt. Next she stood and pulled down her blue jeans. Last weekend, after tithing, donating to the United Negro College Fund, the American Heart Association, the United Way, the Center for Better Mental Health and the National Writer's Union she treated herself to a shopping spree. She bought shoes, dresses, nightgowns, and a designer purse. A new leather coat hung in her closet. Its hem brushed the top of a new set of tan luggage pushed to the back of the closet. A $5000 oil painting of four bright-eyed African American children running down a steep hill covered with dandelions sat on the dining room floor next to the bureau. She told herself to ask Annette to help her hang the painting.

To tighten her schedule and "make a difference," as she told her dad, she worked with Derrick to arrange college campus speaking engagements. She was also busy laying the groundwork for a television documentary on religion and its effects on African American society. Enlisting the aid of fifteen prominent African American historians and ten widely respected African American theologians, she hoped to complete the documentary in three years and sell rights to PBS. For Thanksgiving and Christmas magazine editions, she was scheduled to interview with two leading African American literary journals.

Outside entertainment endeavors, Sigma Gamma Rho consumed much of her time. Eight rushees pledged the sorority the first week in September. The 60's dance the sorority sponsored was a huge success. Over five hundred students attended. After paying the food and soda bill, Sigma netted over one thousand dollars on the dance. Dinah moved through the dancers dressed in a tight, white sweater and a purple mini skirt. Heavy mascara and eyeliner and artificial fingernails accentuated her outfit. The knee length boots she wore only served to make her look increasingly outlandish. Betsy and Loretta wore short, tight green dresses. Sharon looked like a motorcycle rider flanked in her brown leather pantsuit. Pictures of the Temptations, Stevie Wonder, the Supremes, Vandelles and Smokey Robinson and the Miracles were blown up and taped on every wall of Room 202W in the Student Center. Betsy and Loretta styled their hair in a pageboy. They wore big, looped earrings. Their faces were hot with make-up. Trish and three Kappas posed as Gladys Knight and the Pips. When time for the talent contest came, Trish and the Kappas took the honors. Anna, wearing knee length, black, leather boots and a snug, mini skirt, won the apple-bobbing contest. She and an Alpha entered the talent contest and sang an Ike and Tina Turner hit. They took third place. Robin, an avid Aretha Franklin fan, lip singed "Respect" and finished second in the talent contest. After the dance, rather than return to their dorms, most attendees milled into the streets in search of more fun and loud music.

"*President Ronald Reagan discusses sending troops to Lebanon.*" Robin uncrossed her ankles and said, "Oops!" when she ripped a page of the newspaper. Flipping the pages, she stopped when she read, "*Carl Lewis breaks his own long jump record. Can he break Bob Beamon's monumental leap?*" Turning the sports page, she saw no distance race coverage. She twisted her mouth until she came across a letter to Ann Landers. She sat forward and stared at the newspaper. Halfway through the letter, she shook her head. She said, "Heaven, help us." when she read the plea from a twelve-year old daughter to her mother. In the letter, the girl begged her mother to stop belittling her, to accept her as she was.

She folded the thick *New York Times*, returning it to its former state, before she pushed off her bed. Turning off the stereo, she walked into the bathroom.

Water splashed across her face while she smiled and turned her head from side to side. Her two plaits slapped the sides of her face when she turned her head in the shower. She ran her hands over the top and sides of her head and helped the water get down onto her shoulders. The cool, prickly water loosened the ends of her plaits. The soap plucked salty sweat and dirt gently off her skin. Soon, she decided to wash her hair. Gold colored shampoo cooled her palm and filled her hand and ran through the cracks between her fingers. Half an hour later, her body was wrapped in her favorite beach towel -- the one Theo ironed a skateboard to the front of.

In front of her bedroom mirror, for the first time it occurred to her that all her hair accessories came from Miss Lillie's Flea Market. Miss Lillie's Flea Market was in Queens. It used to be a barbershop. It sat across from the old high school track and field she held her Saturday timed runs at. The school, Young High School, was closed five years ago. It spent three years as a school for adults seeking their GED. It stood alone in the surrounding woods, one block away from its track and field.

The curling iron cost a mere $1.50. Each morning when she plugged it into the outlet at the side of her bed, within minutes it was piping hot. Miss Lillie told her she used it only five times, and she knew Miss Lillie didn't lie. From the hair accessories to blue jeans to tea kettles dating back to 1910, worthy collectibles to her, Miss Lillie's presence shadowed her bedroom.

Dental floss, a yellow toothbrush, jars of hair grease, pink, sponge hair rollers covered her dresser tray. Two wrist watches, one hadn't run in over a year, balled pairs of sport socks, bottles of shampoo, one extra large bottle of strawberry hair conditioner, a tub of facial cream, talcum powder, Ben Gay and a bag of half eaten jelly beans cluttered the oak of her dresser.

When the dresser drawers were closed, revealing more of the room, a tall navy, blue filing cabinet came into view. The first drawer of the filing cabinet was crammed with plays and short stories mailed to theatres and slicks that were not returned. The second drawer was crammed with plays and short stories mailed to publishing houses, rejected and returned. The third drawer was half full with scribbled on ruled notebook paper detailing plots for plays and novellas. The fourth drawer was half full of plays and short stories mailed and accepted for publication. Because the second drawer was crammed to the top, sometimes the papers spilled to the back and fell into the third drawer, she wrote feverishly. Tomorrow another file cabinet, also navy blue, was to be delivered from Office Requisitions. She planned to use it to file letters of correspondence between Derrick and her.

Presently, her interest aimed at college drama programs. Through major schools like the University of Southern California at Berkeley, the University of California at Los Angeles, New York University, SUNY campuses, the University of Tennessee at Knoxville and the University of Tennessee at Chattanooga, she hoped to gain national exposure. In between cranking out five and six act plays, she ate frozen dinners, worked at the factory fifteen hours each week, and caught four to five hours of sleep at night.

At nine o'clock tomorrow morning, she was meeting with Derrick. He wanted to discuss two stage play contracts with her. His voice rolled with excitement when he called earlier, briefing her on the projects before she walked to work.

Tomorrow's meeting with Derrick on her mind, she let out a deep breath and placed her comb, brush and a jar of grease on her dresser. Her hands empty, she walked to her wastebasket and dropped a ball of hair inside. She wiped her hands on her butt before she saw a note scribbled on a piece of purple stationery. Peering down at the note laying on the edge of her dresser, she wiped her hands on her butt once more.

"The only thing I didn't get to was Les' fan mail. Rob, I did get to your fan mail. That girl from USC wrote again. You might want to write her back. Some guy stopped by and asked for Les. Said his name was Jack. Said he met Les at one of those Armstrong parties. Talked about Les' father too though. Said something about a red head. Don't know. You know that Leslie. Have a good day. Rob, tell Les (I know you'll pass this message to her), that guy she's seeing. What's his name. Jimmy? Well. He called and he came by once. And Rob, your sweetie Michael called. Said to call him as soon as you got in. Said it was urgent. Sounded like he was in some kind of trouble. Let me know if you need my help. Talk to you later. Annette."

Chapter Six

Michael Henderson introduced himself to Robin the same day he started working at Mill's Clothing Factory. That weekend he asked her if she wanted to go to the movies. She answered yes, and, later that evening, while they were eating garden cheeseburgers at a sidewalk cafe, he revealed to her the truth of his past. She coiled in disgust when he told her about the summer he spent with his uncle and aunt in Maryland. She found it hard to believe that for a month he crept into the garage of a young couple's suburban home on Edgewater Avenue and slept through the night.

She gawked at him while he talked. "My parents told me they called my aunt and uncle for days. When they kept getting busy signals, they contacted the New York City and Maryland police departments. When my parents found me, I was dirty, scared and hungry."

"What did your aunt and uncle do to you? Why did you run?"

"I was supposed to spend the summer helping them at their hardware store." He hung his head. When he looked up his eyes were pink with emotion. "They beat me and used me as their lookout man while they trafficked drugs." He lowered his head and swallowed hard. "I wasn't there a full day before it started to happen."

Robin softened her gaze. She leaned toward him and laid her hand gently atop his. Heat from his hand went into hers. When it did the pace of her heart quickened. She smiled longingly into his eyes and swallowed a lump of emotion.

"I'll never forget the day my parents found me. My mom couldn't stop hugging and kissing me. My dad kept patting my back and asking me if I was all right."

She squeezed his hand then she sat back. "I admire your strength. I really do. Just don't know why you didn't just go home to start with."

"I was scared. I don't know. I had this fear, this hard feeling in my gut that my aunt and uncle were chasing me. Everywhere I went, I felt like a shadow was following me."

She leaned forward. "But certainly they would expect you to go home. Certainly, if they wanted to find you, they'd look for you there."

He shook his head. "No. They knew I hadn't called my parents. They kept very close tabs on me."

"But you'd be safe at your parent's. They wouldn't let anything bad happen to you. They'd protect you."

"It's not that simple. My aunt and uncle aren't people who live on the right side of the law."

"Well. Why did your parents send you to—"

"Do you think they knew? Knew my aunt and uncle's hardware store was a front? Knew how violent and dangerous my aunt and uncle are?"

Her eyes swelled. She lowered her voice. "They threatened you."

He spoke matter-of-factly, "Every day. Every single day they did. Getting busted for drugs ain't no easy rap for a black man. You know that."

"I know. It's just so wrong. Selling drugs. It's murder. I don't care how you look at it. I really don't. Selling drugs is murder."

"I didn't want to do it."

She raised her hand. "Oh, no. I'm not talking about you. I'm talking about all the other people that d—"

He bowed his head.

"Bu-bu-but, I admire your strength. I mean. To break away from that and come here. All the way here by yourself. Thumbing rides and all. It's obvious you didn't want to sell drugs. You wouldn't have left if you wanted to do it."

He was silent.

"Life doesn't always go the way we want it to."

He peered up at her.

"It's how it ends up that counts. You're on the right track now."

He gave her a half nod.

"Don't discredit yourself. It took a lot of guts for you to leave, to come all this way by yourself. To run. To just take off. That takes a lot of guts, a lot of inner strength."

He lowered his head and worked at a smile. "Yeah. Strength. It's gonna work for me one day."

She smiled softly. "Oh, yeah?"

He nodded. "Yea. It's gonna help me become one of the world's greatest dancers. My best friend, he's from Venezuela. We dance together. You ought to see us." His eyes swelled. "J. T., my friend from Venezuela, Joe Joe and this guy named George and me put together a singing group called Rival. Every Saturday we sing and dance somewhere. We win all the contests we enter." He looked deep into her eyes. "I want to dance on Broadway. I want to dance all over the world." Then he leaned forward and told her, "I'm glad I met you. I'd like to keep seeing you. I can tell you're a good woman. I can trust you."

The telephone rang four times. "Hello. You have reached 555-2244. This is Mike. I'm not available right now. Leave your name, number and the time that you called and I'll get right back with you. Peace."

"Hi, Baby. It's me. Annette gave me your message. Call me as soon as you get in. You know I'm here if you need me."

She paced her bedroom. Thirty seconds later, she picked the receiver up again. She watched the console light up.

The telephone rang four times. "Hello. You have reached 555-2244. This is Mike. I'm not available right now. Leave your name, number and the time that you called and I'll get right back with you. Peace."

She read Annette's note again. Then she picked up the receiver.

The telephone rang four times. "Hello. You have reached 555-2244. This is Mi—"

Bowing her head, she ran her fingers over the top of her hair. She released three deep breaths. Turning on her heels, she hurried into the living room. She walked from the loveseat to the picture window back to the loveseat back to the picture window. At the side of the picture window, she pursed her lips and walked into the kitchen. "Just have to wait until he calls me. Just have to trust God and wait," she said while she scanned the countertops.

Michael. If he needed her and things were good between them, she ate when she thought about him. If he created emotional distance between them, she starved herself.

A loaf of wheat bread. That's all that lined the counter. She opened the refrigerator, then the freezer. She didn't stop hunting food until she pulled a frozen dinner out of the freezer. Forty minutes later, after she tossed the aluminum dinner tray, messy with gravy and bits of turkey, inside the kitchen wastebasket, she turned on the stove and prepared to grill a cheese sandwich. While the sandwich browned, she poured herself a tall glass of iced tea. Her glass filled; the pitcher emptied. She lay the pitcher in the sink, flipped the sandwich and wiped her hands on her skirt. When she finished grilling the cheese sandwich, she laid the skillet in the sink and told herself to wash dishes later.

She nibbled her bottom lip while she hurried into the living room. Her fingers pressed the buttons quickly, hard. 555-2244. "Honey, it's me. I'm going out. Need to relax. Had a busy day at work today. Missed you while you were away from the factory taking a personal day. I won't be out long. About half an hour. Leave me a message as soon as you get in. I'll call the second I get back. I love you."

The receiver again in its cradle, she returned to the kitchen. Tucking the grilled cheese sandwich inside a plastic bag, she walked into her bedroom, pulled her door keys off the dresser and left the apartment.

It was a clear day outside. She wanted to go to the park and watch the children play. Heat massaged her neck the second her feet met the sidewalk. Soon after she left the confines of the apartment's canopy, she began to sweat.

Nearer the park, laughter, riddles and children's nursery rhymes rushed to greet her. The closer she got to the park, the tighter her stomach became. She reached down and cradled her abdomen with her free hand. Warmth from her hand incubated her stomach, and the spasms subsided. When they returned, she felt a familiar twinge. She feared the worse and thought about running back down the street to Loew's Department Store to purchase a box of sanitary napkins, but thought better of it. Her body always gave her a generous warning before her menstrual cycle started. Sandwich in hand, she made her way to the swing set and wiggled herself into a free swing. Her feet hit the ground in slow rhythm when she pushed off the ground.

A pair of high heel pumps crashed against the back of the wall before Leslie turned and pushed the closet door. A small crack remained in the door. When she turned and saw it, she walked back to her closet and slammed the door. Amanda Gaynor ate away at her like a raw nerve. "I don't like her. I just don't like her." She shouted to the empty apartment. "Amanda, that's good. That's it. That's exactly how it should be done." She continued, doing a poor imitation of director, Alex Whittell. "Leslie, a little more emotion. You're supposed to be mad. The audience won't be convinced with that take. Come on. I know you better than that." She rocked her head from side to side and paced the bedroom floor. "Amanda, I can see you've really been brushing up on your character. Leslie, maybe you've been working too hard. You're work looks forced, and you look tired. Leslie? Are you tired?" She scowled and tried to shut Alex's voice out of her head. The harder she tried, the louder his voice boomed. "Amanda! Amanda! Amanda! Leslie! Leslie! Leslie!" All at once, she lifted her arms to the crown of her head then thrust them to her sides. "It's too much! I can't take anymore!"

For her, life on the set of her latest movie was like running a steeplechase. In order to maintain a moderate level of influence, she had to compete with Amanda. They jockeyed and vied for Alex and two senior screenwriters' attention. It made her wish she hadn't read the script. Halfway through reading the script, she fell in love with Melinda Brown, a single mother who worked two jobs while she tried to raise her three children and keep her ex-husband, a drunk and a womanizer, at a safe distance. Her liking for the script over shadowed the fact that Amanda was among her supporting cast.

She walked into the dining room and shook her shoulders. She shivered every time her mind's eye cast a picture of Amanda being coy with Alex. Likely the two were lovers. It would end next week at the finish of shooting, she knew, but she was jealous. She didn't like Alex; she thought he was narcissistic. He was one of Hollywood's prominent directors though. She refused to sit back and allow Amanda to wrest a career stepping stool from beneath her.

Alex was cordial with her. She believed he never purposely took sides where Amanda and she were concerned. Besides, she heard through the grapevine that Amanda wasn't a skilled lover.

She shook her head when she rounded the corner and walked inside the kitchen.

The movie's only major player tolerable to her was Beth Tolson, one of the industry's leading female screenplay writers.

The refrigerator door closed, and she pounded the counter with her fist. Her throat was parched. She stared at the empty pitcher in the sink until she felt her blood rise. Satisfied to drink ice water, she pressed the glass she held in her hand against the ice dispenser on the side of the refrigerator door then reached for the sink's spigot.

Ice clinked against the sides of her glass and her hand grew cold while she walked into Robin's bedroom. She walked to the dresser and checked her messages. She frowned when she saw the stack of unopened fan mail. "Annette probably didn't type the letters I asked her to or send the check to the Society for the Homeless." She fumed under her breath, certain that her fans would accuse her of being hard now that she hadn't responded to their letters or given to charity. "But she writes Robin all these notes." Grabbing the stack of messages from Annette, she balled them into her hand without reading them and threw them in the wastebasket. "And where's Rob?" She turned and asked the empty room. Then she thought about Michael and figured Robin and he were at his one story flat, kissing, cuddling and holding hands which, she assumed, was as far as their physical intimacy stretched. That was at Robin's discretion, she knew. For, though she would never reveal it to Robin, being the woman she was, she saw clearly that Michael was experienced sexually. It was also clear to her that he didn't believe it necessary for a woman to maintain her virginity until she wed. If Robin wasn't careful, she knew, Michael would loosen the fears that girded her religious thoughts. She knew Michael would tempt her with his honey, thick voice and tight muscled body – tempt her and seduce her.

She entered the bathroom. She stared into the tub. A crooked grin crossed her face when she saw hair and scum circling the tub. She jammed her hands onto her hips and stood akimbo. "She didn't even rinse the tub out," she growled a second before she turned and headed toward the dining room.

In the dining room, she scanned the tabletops. When she didn't see a note from Robin informing her of her whereabouts, she narrowed her brow. A second later, she walked to the dining room table, pulled out one of the chairs and sat.

She was the leading actress in Beth Tolson's movie. Amanda's lines weren't as significant or as long as hers. Beth, a grandmother-writer and a confidante of hers since the days she worked on the set of *Gardenia's Life* made certain of that. A good friend of one of the senior writers on *Gardenia's Life*, Beth visited the set of *Gardenia's Life* several times. Those times, despite her temper and long bouts with depression, she charmed Beth with her grown-up manner, robust laughter and quick wit.

In the movie she currently worked on, *Betrayal*, Teresa Michels, played by Amanda, frauds Melinda Brown, played by Leslie, in a two million dollar insurance scam. Teresa has an affair with Melinda's estranged husband, Mark, a retired Army Lieutenant. Following an automobile accident where Melinda is hit head on by an intoxicated driver, Jonnie White, played by Shirley Hollidae, and left partially paralyzed, Mark takes out a two million dollar insurance policy. When Melinda questions the policy increase, Mark tells her he wants to assure that she will always be able to afford medical check-ups and lengthy physical therapy sessions.

At the time of the accident, Melinda's two sons are away from home attending college at a nearby university. The boys and her one daughter are spoiled. Rather than love his children, Mark chooses to pamper them with toys, clothes and money. Melinda and her daughter, Jennifer, played by Kay Schlitz, engage in bitter conversations throughout the film.

Melinda doesn't have solid friendships. She doesn't get along with her grandmother. During her weekly visits home she grows angry with her father when he gives into her mother's whimpers. Since she was a little girl her mother and she haven't seen eye to eye. To compensate for the disastrous relationships, near the end of the movie, she checks herself into a private psychiatric hospital. There she learns to open up, confess her recent sins of aggression and malice. Her group consists of nine people, mostly women. It is through the group interaction that Melinda learns that crying is okay and that failed relationships do not take happiness forever from a person's life.

Teresa is a forty year old, childless woman who married six times. In between and during her marriages, she comforts lonely husbands and teaches insecure men the art of sexual intercourse. Besides the men who spin in and out of her life like they are attached to a revolving door, her only company is her black, show poodle. Her poodle, Tiffany, makes her a moderately wealthy woman, winning at least forty dog shows a year. Her lavish Westwood California condominium is crowded with plants. The pastel colors in the rooms of her condo are unlike her personality. Honoring her wishes, her men only visit at night.

Though it is by accident that Teresa and Mark meet and become lovers, it is no accident that Teresa maintains Mark and her relationship as long as she does. One day early into their affair, Mark blurts, "I almost forgot about that insurance policy I took out on Melinda after she had the accident. It was for two million dollars. Since our divorce isn't final I can get some of the money. I plan to do just that."

After Teresa convinces Mark that he is entitled to all of the money since he is the one who took out the policy, they concoct a scheme to fraud Melinda out of the entire two million dollars. The last scene shows Teresa, Mark and Melinda in a courtroom visiting the past, and, through the request of a judge, secretly unraveling the keys to the movie's plot.

For Leslie, depicting the scenes from Melinda's life is mentally and physically draining. At night she collapses into bed.

Hoping to quiet the jealous demons wrestling with her soul, Leslie walked to the china cabinet. Bending her knees, she tugged on the cabinet handle until a long, skinny bottle of white wine fell between a stack of plates and a wooden salad, bowl set.

A dry chuckle slithered from her lips after the first ounce of wine dribbled down her throat. She chuckled because she knew Robin hid the wine. She gulped the wine and poured herself another glass. Moments later, with the bottle in hand, she walked into the living room and sat on the edge of the sofa. When she turned and looked out the picture window, the weather invited her to sit on the terrace.

She turned her glass upside down and emptied the wine into her stomach. Turning and looking out the picture window again, she told herself to remain on the sofa. She didn't feel steady enough to brace the terrace rail without her stomach turning in big, nauseous circles.

Wine ran down the insides of the glass until it reached the rim. Lines etched deep into her face. Loose strands of hair moved atop her head when she combed her fingers across her scalp. It didn't seem fair that Amanda had fewer lines to memorize and rehearse than she did, and, yet, in the last seventeen minutes of the movie, she was given the most lively and memorable dialogue. "Amanda always wins." She said, pushing the living room coffee table with the soles of her feet.

The apartment door opened and closed. She failed to hear Robin's feet thump across the kitchen floor.

Robin cut into her misery when she switched the power to her stereo on and turned up the volume. Tramaine Hawkins sang a pretty gospel song. Her rich, alto voice filled the entire apartment.

Robin stared at her answering machine. No blinking light. Picking up the receiver, she dialed fast. 555-2244. "Mike. Honey. Baby. Are you there? Are you there? Are you okay? Please call me back. I'm getting worried. Are you okay? Call me as soon as you get in. Okay? All right? Okay? I love you."

When her voice silenced, Shirley Cesaer was singing one of her top-selling tunes.

Standing over the kitchen sink, she watched cold water slide over ice cubes in the glass she held in her hand until the cubes cracked. "'This is the day the Lord made. We will rejoice and be glad in it.'" She chimed sipping on the ice water and reciting Psalm 118:24. She repeated the verse of scripture until she entered the living room.

Glass in hand, she stopped at the edge of the living room and stared at the sofa. "Les!"

Leslie sat her glass and the bottle of wine on the coffee table. She raised one arm and pushed it at Robin who walked toward her and the bottle of wine gape-eyed.

"Les." She opened her arms and prepared to embrace Leslie, rescuing her from the drunkenness.

"The sofa's too close to the window. I always told you that." When Robin reached her side, she fanned her face with her hands and slapped Robin's arms with imperfect aim. "I'm okay."

Robin's voice was soft, near a plea. "Les."

"No." She waved her hands. "I'm okay. I don't need your help." Then she sat up and blubbered recklessly, careening Robin's mood and spirit as she went. "You're so perfect. You're always right. You never make mistakes. You don't get drunk. You don't smoke. You don't get high. You don't cry. You're never jealous. You don't even screw your boyfriend. You're an angel! You're so good. You should live a little. You sit around here doing nothing besides write. You're unbelievable. Did you write a story about graduating from high school? Did you write a story about the first time Michael kissed you?"

To support her rocking emotions, Robin stood stoically.

"This is a joke! You and me . . . roommates . . . it's a joke!" While she tossed her head back and laughed, Robin stared at the empty wine bottle. "Michael and you . . . Michael's not in love with you, Robin. You're his ticket to the top. He's going to be a much bigger dancer than you'll ever be a writer. First he's got to get virgin Robin in bed, though. Then you won't be so good anymore." A naked honesty glared at her when she stopped and peered at Robin. She shook her head while she lowered it. "Oh, Rob. I'm sorry." Emotion choked her words. "Amanda always has the last word. I worked my butt off in the movie, and who gets the last word? That slut! She sucks up to the directors and producers', and she gets the last word. I try to make it off skill alone, and I don't get anything. Yesterday I over heard Alex telling a friend on the telephone, 'If it wasn't for Amanda, the movie wouldn't have a final scene.' I work my butt off and he says something like that. When he tells someone I'm doing a good job, he sounds condescending." She stopped and shook her head in her hands. "All my life it's been something. All my life. If something goes right for me, it never goes right for long. Sometimes I wonder why I stay in this blood sucking business. This has to be the hardest business in the world. People turn against you quicker than you can say 'I give' in this business. Everyone's watching their own back." She paused and took a deep breath. "Mama and I fight all the time. We don't get along at all anymore." She shook her head. "I work my butt off and someone else steals the last seventeen minutes of the movie. Story of my life. Why I expected more, I don't know."

When Robin looked into her eyes, she thought they looked like two dark, brown marbles. Shooing her further down the sofa, she pulled her skirt around her legs and sat down beside her. She lowered her head and covered her face with her hands. "Something's wrong with Michael."

Chapter Seven

It was Friday, October 23, 1988 and the last day of shooting on *Betrayal*.

"Les! Les!" A white scarf tied around Amanda's neck was the perfect accessory to compliment the short wool skirt and the stripped blue and red cotton blouse she wore. A small hole set off the back of the blouse.

In *Betrayal*'s final scene, Mark rushes to Teresa's Westwood condo before Melinda stomps inside the insurance company. After Teresa sprints to his car, he accidentally sticks the cigarette he is holding against her back and creates the hole in the blouse.

Days earlier, after she curses and screams for half an hour, an insurance company executive shows Melinda the insurance policy Mark forced her to sign while she was prescribed heavy medication and under going therapy. Rage takes her blood pressure to its peak when she reads sections of the policy that give Mark full claimant authority as her primary beneficiary. She fights back tears when she scans the policy and sees that Mark used her voluntary stay at a private psychiatric hospital to prove she is mentally incompetent. The fact that Mark and her daughter meet at the insurance company and confess to the company president that she is chemically unbalanced, something they claim impairs her decision making abilities, brings her to a breaking point.

In *Betrayal*'s final scene, she wears a large T-shirt with a cluster of balloons printed on its front. The T-shirt reaches below her thighs and covers most of her blue jeans. She wears a dirty pair of tennis shoes. She is sitting on bleachers watching her sons play in a university baseball game when it all comes together for her. Watching bats swing and feet race, it isn't long before she slides off the bleachers and dashes across the field to the parking lot and her ten year old, orange Pinto.

"Les." At forty-one, Amanda was an incredibly beautiful woman. She had the figure of a twenty-year old. Her hair was a natural gray, something that embarrassed her until she reached thirty. Magazine editors and radio and television talk show hosts telephoned her publicist no less than twice a day to request that she be in their periodical or on one of their hit programs. Movie offers were mailed to her agent until they stacked high on the corner of his desk. Since college, she ran six miles a day five days a week. To add muscle tone to her trim, shapely physique, she drove to the local health spa three days a week and lifted weights.

She tapped Leslie's trailer door once before she turned the knob and waited.

Leslie rocked in her make-up chair, then, pushing her feet off the floor, she turned the chair in one full circle. She leaned close to the mirror and brushed her hair.

"Les?" She called again, folding her arms.

Leslie tightened her grip on the arm of the brush. She narrowed her brow and stared into the mirror.

Amanda tapped the door one last time before she leaned her shoulder into the door and stepped inside the trailer. "What are you doing, Girl?"

"What are you doing, Girl?" Leslie mimicked, turning the question in her head. Amanda's stroke of kindness left her bewildered. She pushed her feet off the floor and turned the chair partway toward the door. From where she sat, she could see Amanda's dark shadow looming in the doorway; it stretched out across the trailer floor and beckoned her.

"Yea?" Her voice was dry and coarse.

"Ready?"

She placed the brush on the dresser. "Yea."

"Les?"

She turned the chair toward the mirror.

"Leslie." Amanda said, straightening her shoulders and pulling down on the hem of her blouse.

Leslie tossed her hand in the air and rolled her gaze toward the ceiling, "Go ahead."

Amanda's hands knifed her hips. She frowned down at the top of Leslie's head. "I didn't come here to fight with you." Her breath thickened. "I didn't mean to ask you this either," she took in a deep breath and let it out before she continued, "But can you please tell me why you're so evil, so enraged with jealousy? I try-try-try to be friends with you. I have offered to help you with your scenes time and again. When I speak to you on set, you pretend not to hear me although we both know better than that. You're a woman who lives with her ear to the ground. Why? I don't know. Really don't know why you even bother. You're a thing of the past. A has-been who was given a lucky break. Don't blow it. This picture is about more than you and your failing career. There are hundreds of people who need this movie to be a hit. I'm trying to help you by offering to work with you after shooting. Your lines still need obvious work. But do you listen?" She turned up her nose and growled, "You're a mindless devil, a miserable woman, a lunatic of an imp."

Leslie glared at her.

She placed her hand on the flat of Leslie's shoulder. "Why are you an angry, washed up, has been?"

Leslie sprang from her chair and stomped across the trailer floor. She snatched the door open.

Amanda followed her. She propped her foot against the arch of the door, turned and faced her. "Tiss. Tiss. Tiss. Little jealous imp."

Leslie's gaze went to the ceiling. She rolled her eyes before she faced her.

Amanda turned to leave.

Leslie closed the door and returned her gaze to the ceiling. Certain everyone on the lot figured she was spoiled, she kicked at the floor and cringed. Her mind hurried to the past where she always found excuses for her behavior. The thoughts grew loud in her head until she pushed her shoulder against the door and sent it crashing against the side of the trailer.

"Why am I angry?" She hollered at Amanda's moving back.

Amanda grinned like a fox before she turned. "She does listen."

She pressed her shoulder against the door arch. "I'm not a has been."

Amanda turned and faced her. "How old are you, you precious-precious child star? How many years have you been at this?"

The gathering crowd of supporting actresses, actors, and prop technicians prevented Leslie from turning and racing to the safety of her trailer. "Twenty-six."

"All grown up now, right?" Her grin grew. She saw the crowd beginning to circle Leslie's trailer.

Leslie was mute. She studied Amanda's demeanor.

"Too old not to know how to handle being second best on a movie set, if you ask me. Too old to throw fits and tantrums every time you don't get your way. But, what am I saying. I'm talking to a woman who is narcissistic, an egomaniac."

"And how old are you, Ms. Trying to sleep her way to the top?"

"Too old for it to be good manners for you to ask. And I'm not sleeping my way anywhere. If you could only find the decency to be more discreet about your many quickie affairs."

"Amanda?"

She nodded curtly. "Go ahead."

Leslie took in a deep breath and stood on the trailer's second step. She met Amanda's stony gaze with a brave stare. "Just wanted to make certain I had all of your attention. Wonders never cease. Amazing – absolutely amazing that you manage to work at all the way your mind reverts to sex. The way you scheme. Spend all your day thinking of the right men to give a blow job so you'll land another acting job." She shook her head. "It's truly amazing. Really. It is."

"Oh," She turned partly on her heels. She faced the crowd more than Leslie's trailer now.

Leslie grinned tautly. "That said, what do you have against me? Why would you feel it necessary to call me a washed up, has been?" She searched for Alex. Once she found him, she stared at the bald spot at the top of his head. She knew he thought she was looking directly at him. "And the movie's almost over. This is the last day of shooting."

Her grin taut and her face flush, Amanda turned away from the crowd. In an effort to regain her composure, she twiddled the hem of the blouse. "I don't--" Her gaze went to Alex.

"You called me a has been less than a minute ago! You came in my trailer and called me a has been! Totally unprovoked, you walked in my trailer and called me a washed up, has been less than a minute ago! So what do you mean, you don't hate me?"

"I don't hate you, Les. Sweetheart. You misinterpret things. You're paranoid."

"Paranoid?"

"That's right. Paranoid. Sensitive. Unsure of yourself." She looked squarely at Alex. "I don't hate you, Les. Honey, I have no reason to hate you. I'm pulling for you. I keep trying to help you in the shots we do together, but you just don't seem to want to follow through."

It was Leslie's turn to be coy. She stood akimbo and smiled into, "Why. Of course, Dear."

When she returned to her trailer to grab her costume, her smile widened. Alex may have fixed the script so Amanda had the last line, Amanda may have orchestrated the gathering crowd, but on this set, she, Leslie Fletcher, had the final word.

Alex moved through the crowd and stood outside Leslie's trailer door.

When she grabbed her costume and re-opened the door, his presence caught her unawares. He grabbed her forearm and squeezed it until she flinched.

"What do you think you're doing?" He took one hard look at her, then all at once, his tone and demeanor changed, "Look. I've . . . we've . . . " He stabbed the center of his chest with his finger. "We've all been working non-stop on this movie. For the past few months I've been getting by on three to four hours of sleep a night, many nights not even that. I'm a married man with five kids. My oldest is only ten. It's not easy." The volume in his voice increased. "All of us, the writers, costume designers, special effects people, make-up artists, everybody on the entire set has been going at it night and day rehearsing lines, editing and cutting and making sure props are right to insure this movie comes off right. I appreciate your hard work, Leslie, but you're not the only one who's been busting their tail! I don't appreciate you causing a scene on the last day of shooting." Lowering his head, he paused and ran his fingers through his hair. When he looked up, he was shaking his head. "Everybody told me not to work with you. People told me not to sign a contract with you. Writers from *Gardenia's Life* told me not to work with you. And they should know . . . all the years they tried to work with you. But I didn't listen. I will next time, though. I can tell you, this'll be the last project we ever work on together. I promise you that." He turned to leave. "I promise you that!" A thought prevented his footsteps, and he faced her again. "Don't think I need you either. A less skilled actress is better than an uncooperative actress any day." He shooed her with the side of his hand. "Don't you ever forget that. It may very well be the most valuable thing you learn from having worked on this set." He called out to her over the arch of his shoulder when he turned and started walking away from her. "You'll never make it in this business with your attitude. You're finished!"

Alex gone from her sight, color returned to her face. It took the last ounce of her will to stop herself from stomping to the back of the trailer, where her two travel bags were, and, her arms flailing, grab then stuff her shirts, jeans, socks and sandals inside the bags. It took all of her will to stop herself from swearing her way off the set. Inside her trailer, she decided the sooner she finished shooting and cleared the lot, the simpler her life would be. Dressed for the next to last scene, her feet thundered the ground while she walked. All she could think about was the way Alex turned Amanda's slander around until it appeared to be her fault. Newspaper and magazine writers, pushy directors and producers were trying to ruin her career. She felt certain of that. It seemed they lived to see her suffer. Yet, she refused to satisfy them. She refused to give up. She stomped across the lot and told herself to never quit.

Every eye turned watchful and fell upon her when she approached set. Alex ducked his head and turned away from her glance. Amanda went immediately to her spot on the floor and stood cross-legged on the scotch tape that formed an X on the ground.

"Everybody take your places," Alex boomed. He unfastened the first two buttons on his shirt before he continued. A looser collar didn't rid him of the guilt that choked his conscience each time he glanced at Leslie. "Shoot!"

She quickened her stride and walked next to Amanda. Before she passed her and took her place on the set, she mumbled, "Alex's wife'll take care of you. She won't be too happy to find out her husband has been screwing a forty something piece of easy. So, don't concern yourself with me, Honey. Alex's wife is your biggest worry right now. You have to get passed her first, Dear."

Aware Leslie wasn't discussing business with Amanda, Alex shoved his head into the camera and stared through the lens, careful not to make eye contact with anyone on the set. Part of him wanted to call out, "Cut. Second take," and start the entire day over, but he knew better than to trust these types of confrontations to fantasy.

Mark took his place next to a rusting, silver Honda Accord. He held a set of car keys in his hand. After Alex called out, "Shoot!" Mark started mumbling to himself and fumbling with the lock in the door. "Come on, now," he said, talking to the car, after he climbed inside and stuck the key in the ignition. "Start on the first try. I really have to get out of here. Melinda's got to be on to us by now. I have to hurry. Come on, Baby. Go." He said, patting the dashboard and turning the key.

The engine revved, and he pressed the gas. When he sped passed Teresa's apartment, he waved. She returned his wave from where she stood peering out of her living room drapes. Grabbing her purse, she hurried down the steps taking them two at a time.

"Cut."

Everyone turned and looked at Alex.

"That's perfect. That's exactly how I want to portray Teresa in this scene. The audience has to know how crucial it is that Mark and Teresa reach the insurance company before Melinda. I want the audience to pull and root for Teresa and Mark. I want the audience to take sides. Some of them will cheer for Melinda, and some for Mark and Teresa. None of the characters is a saint. I feel good about this movie. You all are doing a wonderful job. I want you to know that." He almost turned and looked at Leslie. "I really want you to know that. All of you, and I thank you. Okay." Glancing over his shoulder, he cued a cameraman into position. "Let's start where we left off. Take two. And shoot!"

A line formed around the insurance company service desk. Janet Douglas, the company president, stood and walked toward Mark and Teresa. Inches away from them, she extended her arm and shook both their hands. "I was expecting you." Turning her back to them, she escorted them inside her plush office. "Come in and have a seat."

"Thank you." Mark said, before he turned toward Teresa and glared at the top of her shoulder.

"Thank you." Teresa smiled and said, following Mark's unspoken order.

Janet walked behind her desk and gazed at a thick pile of manila folders. She handed them to Mark. "Does this clear everything up? You've already seen these, right?" Trusting that he had, she went on. "All policy changes have been made. We have been careful to meet your request." She leaned back in her swivel chair and eyed them suspiciously. "This does take care of everything, doesn't it?"

"Yes. This takes care of everything. Thank you so much. I appreciate you and your staff's patience, attention to detail and promptness in this matter. I know it's sudden. It's just that my wife--"

Janet's glass, office door slammed to a close. A scowl tore into Melinda's face. She thrust her shoulders forward with each step she took.

Pulling up the hem of his pants, Alex squatted and examined Leslie's expression, her behavior, her walk. Though he tried not to, his face broke into a smile. He'd seen Leslie perform more than a hundred times and he still hadn't figured how she was able to perform with such focus. He beamed with pride. He knew hers was a rare skill.

"Is here!" Melinda screamed, breaking up Mark's words.

Janet sprung to her feet. She spread her hands across the top of her desk and leaned forward. Though she couldn't place when and where, Melinda's face was familiar to her. "Come in." She said cautiously. "I suspect you're the wife." That said, she nearly turned to see who spoke the words. It alarmed her that everything was coming to her so easily. Words rushed out of her mouth. "Pull up a chair."

"I'm not sitting!" Melinda tossed her purse on top of Janet's mahogany desk. Two balled pieces of tissue, three tampons and a dirty brush fell out of her purse when it touched the desk. Across from her, Mark and Teresa sat mute.

"Is there a problem?" Janet tried to soften her mood.

"You're a part of a big insurance fraud. It's all a scheme, a grand scheme."

Janet braced the edge of her desk and took in a deep breath. She said, "Excuse me," then released the breath.

Melinda raised her voice. "Fraud, Lady. F-R-A-U-D, fraud. Fraud, Lady. Fraud!" She pounded Janet's desk with her fist.

"Ma'am, please do sit down." The hair on the nape of her neck began to rise.

"I'm not crazy! I'm not crazy!" Melinda screamed with a narrow brow.

Mark turned away from his ex-wife and stared at the wall.

"Mark, give me a cigarette," Melinda demanded. When he dug through his jacket pocket and pulled out a slim cigarette, she waved it aside and snorted. "Do you really think I need anything from you?" She chuckled before he got the cigarette back in his jacket pocket.

"N--"

"Shut up!" She snapped before she reached for her purse and pulled out a long, low tar cigarette. "Hello, Teresa. How are you doing today?" She didn't give her time to answer. "Not going to speak?"

"Hello." Teresa whispered dryly.

"Can't face me, can you?"

Teresa looked up, "Hello."

She waved her hand across the point of Teresa's nose. "Don't look at me. I don't want to speak with you."

"Cut!" Alex screamed. When he stood, he applauded. Several cameramen, prop artists and special effects people joined him. The applause subsided, and Alex continued, "Let's take a break and finish with the court scene in twenty minutes. Beautiful! Beautiful! Beautiful! Leslie, you're excellent! You're absolutely excellent! Bravo!" He blew everyone kisses. "Susan," he called to his secretary who left her trailer to watch the final two scenes, "Order everyone a dozen red roses! Excellent work! Very good! Especially you, Leslie. Yo—you—you were good. You were very good."

Chapter Eight

The door closed gently behind Leslie.

"Les, is that you?"

"Yea!" She called out, reaching down and pulling off her shiny, black pumps.

"Come in the kitchen! I'm making us a snack!"

"Is that what I smell that stinks so bad!" She walked across the carpet barefoot after she pushed her luggage against her bedroom wall. She carried her pumps in her hand.

"Shut up, and come in here. Tell me how your day went."

"You sound excited to hear about it." She stuck her head through her shirt collar and pulled her shirt off.

"I am." Robin stuck her finger in her mouth and licked it free of ketchup. "So, come in here and tell me all about it. Tell me! Tell me!" She opened the oven door and stuck her head inside.

"What's the matter?" Leslie asked, her chest growing cold with only a bra on. "Something burning? Smells like something's burning."

Robin pulled her head out of the oven and turned up her nose. "Look." She pushed the scalded pan under Leslie's nose. "I was trying to baste chicken, and look what I did. It's burnt to a crisp. I don't know how I let this happen. I kept coming in here checking on it." She lowered her shoulders and laughed. "Let's go out to eat."

"Sure. Tell you what."

"What?" Robin asked walking to the sink and laying the pan inside.

"I'll cook dinner next time."

She laughed. "Sure."

"No. I will." A smile went across Leslie's face.

"Yea, right."

"Can't you believe I'll cook dinner tomorrow night?"

"I believe you."

"Where'd you get that?" She asked, looking at the green apple in Robin's hand.

"Michael got it for me on his way home from dance rehearsal."

"Oh, yeah? How's he doing?"

"Okay."

"Really?"

"Les. He had a setback. And it's just a rumor anyway." She grinned.

The volume in her voice went up. "It is. Michael's not involved with drugs." Her brow grew tight. "I'm tired of this haunting him. Michael doesn't take drugs and he doesn't deal in drugs. I don't care what people say. He's a good man. He's a very good man."

"Just say you love him and leave it at that."

"I do love him. I'm in love with him. I love him. I don't want to live without him."

"There you said it."

"And?"

"And. And. And. And love is—"

"The greatest force around."

Leslie nodded. "Yeah." She turned and faced the refrigerator. "And I still haven't eaten anything today. I'm—" She stared at the apple in Robin's hand. A second later she opened the refrigerator and looked inside. "We need to get some groceries in here, Girl."

"If we stopped wasting so much food, we'd have some groceries."

"That's true," she said, shutting the refrigerator door.

"What were you looking for, anyway. Something in particular?"

"If you stop munching on that juicy apple, I won't be hungry." She turned away from the refrigerator and faced her. "I wasn't looking for anything in particular."

Making jest of her hunger, she chewed the apple slowly. "Ummm. It's so cold and refreshing and satisfying and juicy! Girl, this apple is juicy!"

"And all we have in the refrigerator is half a loaf of rye bread." She opened the refrigerator and stuck her head inside. "Not even half a loaf." Then she closed the door again.

"We do need groceries."

"Robin, stop eating that apple and give me a slice."

"Nope." She jerked free of Leslie's grasp.

"All right, then." She nearly lost her footing when Leslie grabbed her arm, and, pulling the apple to her mouth, took a bite. She stepped back flabbergasted, "Excuse me!"

She rubbed her stomach in small circles. "That hit the spot. I was so hungry. Now all I need is a glass of water to wash it down with."

"Pig." She turned the apple until she found a spot without teeth marks, then she took a bite. "You never told me how the last day of shooting went. How did it all go?"

She followed Leslie into her bedroom. "You don't want to know."

"Yes, I do." She said, taking another bite out of the apple.

"Not as well as your writing."

"Thanks."

"You deserve it. You've been writing for so long. It's time you got a big break. And besides, you're good."

She quoted scripture while she walked to her closet to grab a jacket. "'The fear of the Lord is the beginning of wisdom: a good understanding have all they that do his commandments: his praise endureth for ever.' That's why I write well. I really believe that." She said, slipping her arm into her jacket sleeve. "If you obey God, God will bless you."

Leslie smiled and stretched an arm across her shoulder. "Come on. We've got a lot to talk about. After I jump into a pair of jeans and a sweater, let's grab a bite while we talk."

A thousand stars twinkled in the sky of the world's most famous city. The falling rain gave the night sky a bright glow. Rain danced off the moon and sent a majestic orchestra of heavenly music across the city's streets, sidewalks and housetops. Six days it rained in New York City without intervention. Mud puddles circled the corners of inner city and suburban homes. Worms and snails inched through back yards. The cool, night air was loud with singing insects that would chorus the city's many distinct boroughs and neighborhoods the entire night. Motorists scurried narrow passageways in search of food or entertainment. They sprayed muddy water on the fronts of pedestrian raincoats, dresses, pants and autumn jackets. Rain fell so feverishly the first two days of the storm, cars stalled over the city. Twice, from the picture window of the apartment, Robin watched a group of thieves press their way around a stalled car and strip it of its tires, steering wheel, front seats and stereo. Before the rain, the air was hot and humid. Shirts and dresses clung to the backs of chief executive officers and branch managers walking in the World Trade Center during the day. Because there was acid in the rain, the Statute of Liberty stood tall and green, her torch eroding in her hand. Environmentalists across the nation talked about cleaning the nation's symbol of hope and freedom, but nothing except the acid rain washed the statute free of dirt and debris.

Since the start of the rainstorm, ticket sales dropped at theatre and movie box offices. Not even famous Wilson, Gershwin, Hansberry, Ziegfield or Hammerstein plays were well received in this weather. Law offices, loan firms, even banks and small restaurants closed one to two hours early beginning the second day of the week long storm that dashed across the city in shots of lightning and loud bursts of thunder, flooding residential homes. Macy's, Alexander's, Lord & Taylor's, Saks Fifth Avenue and Loew's managers pressed their noses against their store glass, office windows and wished God would change his mind and resort to something other than torrential rain to cool New York City. Grateful for cooler temperatures, which they were certain would help mend the sun cracked East Coast farm land and city sky line, the same managers turned and walked back to their desks. Money woes prevented them from sitting long. The steady rain was eating away at their profits.

At midnight, thunder drummed housetops and woke irritable babies. Lightning pierced curtains and lit up entire bedrooms. Frightened by the display, toddlers crawled beneath their bed covers and buried their heads.

From New York to Florida, weather reports echoed national sentiment that, if not for the falling rain, the country would have borne the tribulations of a long, hot summer.

When Robin pressed the button on the arm to her umbrella, a New York Giants emblem burst into view. She watched Leslie's shoulders weave and bob while she walked beneath the high rise's canopy. When she caught up to her, she bumped her elbow and called out, "Let's go," over her shoulder.

Leslie hurried and walked in step with her.

Robin stopped halfway into another step. "Where're we going?"

"How about Mavis'? You like going there."

Her eyes brightened. "I wonder if Michelle's working tonight?"

"Well," Leslie said waving her forward, "Come on."

Her brow narrowed. "I wonder if Loew's is still open. I should buy a raincoat."

Leslie stopped walking and rested one hand on her hip. A vagabond stumbled passed her and asked for five dollars while she rebuked Robin with, "All those raincoats you've got in the apartment, and you're talking about buying another one?"

"Yea." Before the vagabond stepped beyond her, Robin handed him five dollars. A second later, she bounced on her toes and dashed across the street.

Leslie watched her reach the other side of the street before she raised the hem of her blue jeans and ran across the street after her. They bumped shoulders and laughed when they rejoined. Neither thought about how eight months stood between this and the last time they spent a night on the town sharing one another's company.

In front of Leslie, Robin pulled on a set of heavy, glass doors and walked inside Loew's Department Store. Once inside, she closed her umbrella and shook her head. "Whew!"

Leslie combed her hair with her fingers, "Really."

"It's getting cold outside too."

"I know," Leslie lowered her hands to her sides. "Maybe I should buy a raincoat too."

Robin pursed her lips and shot her a glance, "Ump!"

"Oh, Rob. I don't have half as many raincoats as you do. Besides, I'm getting cold. Look at me. I'm shaking."

"I see." She said, throwing her gaze to the arch of her shoulders.

"Look, Rob." She pointed to a long rack. "There's a pretty yellow one."

"Where?" She turned her head.

"Over here. Come on." She walked toward the rack. "I'll show you."

"Goodness." Robin said, standing firmly on the shiny floor and catching her footing.

"Be careful. Don't fall." Leslie called out without breaking her stride or turning around.

"This raincoat is cute." Robin pulled the yellow raincoat off the rack. "I wonder if they have anymore." She pushed the tip of her finger inside the corner of her mouth while she stood on her toes and looked down the rack.

Leslie arched her brow. "Why?"

She answered matter-of-factly. "You wanted that one, didn't you?"

"No. I was showing it to you."

"You wanted it." She walked down the aisle and pushed raincoats apart so she could examine them.

"I think it's cute. I don't want or need it. You don't need it."

"I know." Robin stopped midway down the rack. "Do you see one you want?"

"Well--" She twisted her mouth. "Do you like this white one?"

She shrugged. "It's all right."

Leslie hung the white raincoat on the rack. "You don't like it."

"Not really."

"How about this blue one?"

"Look!" Robin turned and faced the cashier. She called out, "Excuse me."

"Sure." The cashier said, looking up with a smile.

"May I ask you a question?"

"Sure. Go ahead." The cashier's smile was contagious.

"Whose yellow raincoat is that you're holding?"

"Yours, if you want it."

Turning away from the cashier, she looked at Leslie. "Les."

"Wait a minute. Let me tear off the tag. I got it from the storeroom couldn't have been five minutes ago. It's the last one like it we've got. We got a shipment in this morning. We sold out already. We're getting another shipment in tomorrow, and I bet you they'll be gone by the time I come on at three." She chuckled, "Raincoats are the only thing we're selling fast right now."

"You sold out that quickly. Really?" Robin asked.

"Really."

"Wait!" All at once a tall Jamaican woman shouted. She leaned passed the checkout counter and stared into Robin's eyes. "I've seen you somewhere before."

Backing into Leslie's shoulder, Robin tightened her grip on the raincoat and filled her chest with a slow, deep breath.

"You're a writer, aren't you?" The cashier didn't give her time to answer. Her eyes darted from the Jamaican woman's smiling face to Robin. "One of the day shift cashiers told me you were a writer and that you shopped here, but, I didn't believe her. You're Robin Carlile, aren't you?" Again, she didn't give her time to answer. "One of your plays just opened on Broadway, didn't it?" Her smile wide, she left the cash register and walked to Robin's side.

Leslie pinched Robin's rib and whispered, "Forget the raincoat. Let's get out of here."

"Let me get a camera, so I can take a picture of you." The cashier stated plainly. "I'll get some cards for you to sign. Will you wait? Will you wait?"

While the cashier searched for a camera and a box of cards, Leslie ducked behind a row of dresses, scanned the aisles and advised, "Rob, let's get out of here. People are starting to come into the store. If we don't get out of here now, a crowd could form. As quiet as you are, you won't like that." She pulled on the raincoat and recalled the worst experiences she had with autograph seekers. "Fans aren't always nice, Rob."

The cashier returned, her hand bracing her pounding chest while she worked to catch her breath. "Okay. Get over there by those raincoats you were looking at. Scoot to the left a little bit. Okay. That's perfect. I wish someone were here to take a picture of you and me together. Okay. Smile!"

The flash exploded in Robin's face. "Give me the cards, so I can sign them. I've got to be going. I really have to get out of here."

"Okay. As soon as you sign these cards for my girl friends, Mom, Dad, brothers and sisters."

She swallowed hard when she counted the thirty cards. "How about just for you and your family?"

The cashier turned her head and softened her gaze. "Please?"

Robin raised her hand. "I really must go."

The cashier consented. "Okay. Sign ten."

"Fine. You certainly are welcomed."

"Sorry. Thanks."

"You're welcomed."

With a chuckle, the cashier added, "Sorry. I've been so bossy."

Robin waved the entire scene from her memory with a turn of her hand. "Forget it."

"Will you sign thirty?" The cashier asked with another chuckle.

Robin tossed her head back and laughed. "I have to go. I'll sign ten."

Leslie stood behind her clinching her teeth.

The cashier leaned over Robin's shoulder and guided her while she signed the cards. "That one's for Donna. That one's for Kim. Sign that one for Triss. And that one goes to Bobbie. No. B-o-b-b-i-e. She's a woman."

Robin looked up before she answered curtly, "Thanks."

"How's your actress roommate?"

She almost turned and looked over her shoulder. "She's fine." She raced the pen across the bottom of the cards.

"Her name's Leslie Fletcher, isn't it?"

"Didn't she just finish making a movie?"

"I heard it was supposed to be good."

"How old are you? The same age as Leslie?"

"How is it being her roommate? Do you like each other?"

As if her head was a revolving door, she turned and faced each questioner recently gathered around the cash register. Her heartbeat quickened when she saw she had two more cards to sign. Fear cleaved her tongue to the roof of her mouth. She didn't answer any of the questions.

"When's your next play coming out?"

"Are you ever going to write a book?"

The crowd of ten pushed the cashier's back against the cold, steel of the cash register drawer.

"Bye." She climbed to her toes and handed the cashier the signed cards. "What's your name?"

The cashier smiled passionately. She promised herself not to forget her display of kindness. As a show of gratitude, she vowed to go see each of her plays. "Tracey." The crowd turned and looked at Tracey who continued to wave at Robin. "Bye, Robin!"

"Bye, Tracey!" Robin called out. A second later, Leslie crouched close to her side and they sped through the exit door.

"I'm glad we got out of there." Was the first thing she said when Leslie and she planted their feet on the sidewalk.

Leslie stared at her blankly. "What were you trying to do in there?"

"She was nice."

"Your first round of signing autographs." She smiled in recollection of the first time someone approached her and requested that she sign an autograph. "How does it feel?"

She shrugged.

"When the cashier looked hard at you, I knew something like that was going to happen."

"I got that feeling too. I wanted us to pay for our raincoats and book, but we didn't make it in time." She softened her gaze and lowered her voice. "You know I hate attention. Plus, I'm not for autograph signing anyway. God put all the stars in the sky."

"I'm glad nobody recognized me."

Glancing at Leslie's make-up-less face and the hole in her faded jeans, she snickered. "Your mother wouldn't recognize you in that get up."

Leslie looked at the hole above the knee in her jeans. She chuckled when she met her stare. "She probably wouldn't."

Robin swung her arm in one wide circle and called Leslie to her side. "Come on. We still didn't get any raincoats. But, never mind raincoats. Let's get something to eat."

With a skip hop, Leslie sped down the sidewalk. "Let's go!"

Outside the door to Mavis', they stopped to catch their breath. While Robin sucked in thick gusts of air, she thought about Michael and the hours they spent lifting weights at NYU's gym.

Michael also jumped rope a lot. Because he was a dancer, he wanted spring in his step. He was taking ballet at night school. Street dancing and bee bop were natural art forms to him. He told Robin that he started dancing when he was four years old. He was known as "jam" in the borough he lived in. While outdoors and not working, he kept a blaster strapped over his shoulder. Living in a stranger's garage polished his street knowledge. Without turning and looking over his shoulder, he knew when someone was behind him. From across the street, he could tell when someone was watching him, staring at him. He could spot fear in a stranger's eyes. Even if they weren't carrying a camera or gazing excitedly at buildings and plastered ads, he knew who tourists were. Just from their walk. He could tell. It wasn't unusual for him to make the night streets his stage. In the spirit of a spin, sometimes he bumped a metal garbage can and sent it clanging to the ground. Barking from a few neighborhood dogs was the only response he got. The months he lived with his parents after his return home, he shut the door to his bedroom and danced for hours in front of his bedroom mirror. He mowed lawns to earn cash. Soon he had six floor length mirrors nailed side by side to the longest wall in his bedroom. Behind his closed bedroom door, he danced until his body became a frenzy of motion and sweat pumped out of his pores and soaked his shirt and pants. On the streets, he challenged radical hip hop dancers. He mastered the pop, spin, moonwalk, shake, and break. Besides stuffing shirts in cardboard boxes at Mills', he worked as choreographer for two local singing groups.

Balancing his appetite for dance, was Robin, a woman whose intelligence, independence, determination and perseverance worked like aphrodisiacs; they pulled him in different directions. Because Robin was a born again Christian, Michael assumed her virtues and biblical morals brought goodness to his life. When he placed his thoughts on her, which was every day and night, sometimes he cried. Yet, he rarely laughed hard, guffawed until his knees quacked and his shoulders rocked, unless he shared her company. To touch her was to send his body into spasms of nervousness. The endless 'nos' she brushed against the tip of his ear when they caressed, their hands climbing over one another's arms, thighs and bellies emptied him of passion and courage. When she showed herself to the door of his apartment, he held himself by the shoulders and rocked until sleep found its way through the songs played during radio station WPTZ's Quiet Storm into his tired, lonely body. Robin answered that she had no sexual hang ups the dozen times he asked. One of those times, she read I Corinthians 6:13, "Meats for the belly, and the belly for meats: but God shall destroy both it and them. Now the body is not for fornication, but for the Lord; and the Lord for the body." While he listened to her read from the Bible, ire burned beneath his skin, and, turned his sexual energy off. "Sexual intercourse within the bonds of marriage is beautiful," she was careful to inform him each time he raised the subject of sexual intimacy, "but outside marriage sexual intercourse is only sin."

However frustrating, the way she quoted scripture proved to him that she was sincere in her quest for righteousness. Although he didn't agree with her sexual principals, there was an unspoken quality about her that kept him coming back to her -- that made him telephone her late into the night.

Late at night over the telephone, his deep voice kept her from sleep. The upward turn of his thick lips, quickened her heart. She answered him candidly when he asked her, "How does it feel when I kiss and stroke your body's secret parts?" She told him, "Maintaining celibacy isn't always easy. To overcome temptation, I pray, read the Bible and fast."

Leslie smiled while she walked inside Mavis'. "Don't tell me you're getting out of shape, Rob."

She placed her hand over her heart and pressed down. She breathed fast, deep – hard. "I don't know. I can run a marathon and catch my breath in five minutes. Then sometimes I walk halfway up a hill or down one block, like we just did, and I find myself panting for the longest. I don't understand." She stopped and chuckled. "Maybe I'm supposed to be running instead of walking."

They stood next to Mavis' cash register, close to the "Wait To Be Seated" sign. "No. You're supposed to be a writer." She rocked her finger from side to side. "And don't you forget that. Don't you ever forget that."

"I can't. I think I spend more time thinking about writing than anything else. Sometimes I think I think about writing too much. Les, you know, I see movies working themselves out in my head. After watching a news flash or reading a good article in *Essence* or *Ebony*, I can pump out a story or a play in a matter of hours. It takes so little to get me started. I'll probably die with my head laying on top of my typewriter keys."

Leslie smiled warmly. "I think this is the hostess."

"I hope so."

"Me too." She circled her stomach with her hand. "I'm hungry."

"Yea. This is her. She just grabbed two menus."

"If she ask where we want to sit, what should I say?"

"Say, next to a window facing the street."

"You can't get enough of watching people get along, can you?"

She arched her shoulders. "Guess not."

"Hi, Ladies." The hostess stepped in front of them and smiled before she turned and walked into the main dining area. They followed her to their seats.

"I'm getting hungrier by the minute." Robin said, kicking her heels together beneath the table the hostess guided them to. Turning her head and looking out the window, she wrapped the end of her thick braid around her finger. "I wonder if Michelle's working tonight. We've been hanging out together on the weekends for the longest. Michelle's good people. She really is."

"She is. I like her." Leslie said, resting her chin in her palm and pushing her chair closer to the table. She looked hard at Robin. "You said she's from Kentucky, didn't you?"

She continued to look out the window. "Louisville."

"Have you been to Louisville before?"

She turned away from the window and faced her. "I pass through Louisville every time I go home, but I've never spent much time there."

"What's the South like?" Leslie asked, sipping her ice water.

"You know we've been living together for three years, and you never asked me that before."

"You never asked me much about Connecticut either."

"Leslie, we live in New York City."

"New York City isn't Connecticut."

"I know that, but as close as they are, it could be."

Her gaze softened. "Connecticut's a quiet . . . well, the city I was born and raised in is quiet, a quaint, little town. You saw the street I grew up on the first time I took you home with me. Anyhow, it was a good city to grow up in. It's one of those cities where everybody knows everybody. In the neighborhood I grew up in, Mama said people were too nosey. She said they always tried to get in Dad and her business. Winters there were heavenly when I was growing up. When I was growing up, once or twice a year it snowed at least a foot of snow. Our front yard looked like a winter wonderland in the early morning then. My friends and I would put on our boots and tromp around in the snow. We'd pull our sleds from our parents' garages and slide down this steep hill close to my parents' home. This girl named Darlene was my best friend. I wonder what she's doing now. She was so tall for her age when we were growing up, and that was eighteen years ago. She's probably six feet tall now. I'd like to see her. She had this funny laugh and a high pitched, squeaky voice. I loved to listen to her talk and laugh. You'd like her if you met her. She was a cut up, and I know how you like to laugh."

A waitress stepped next to them.

"Does Michelle work tonight." Robin asked, looking up at the waitress.

"No. She's on day shift this week."

"When you see her, tell her Robin said hi, please."

"Oh, you're Robin?"

"And I'm Leslie." Leslie offered with a smile.

"Nice to meet you." Then she faced Robin and said, "Sure. I'll tell Michelle you said 'hi'. I'm sure she'll be happy to hear from you. She talks about you a lot. She came here to be an actress, you know? Like you." She turned and faced Leslie. "I heard about your new movie."

Leslie sat against the back of her chair and arched her brow.

"It's getting great reviews. Michelle talks about you a lot too, although I don't think the two of you have ever met." She turned to Robin again. "Robin, we've all heard about you. When am I going to be able to go to the bookstore and buy a juicy novel you wrote?"

She sat up. "One of my plays is open on the West Coast. A play I just co-wrote recently opened at NYU. Thank God they're both doing well. You won't see a book written by me in the bookstore for a least another several years. I plan to concentrate on plays for at least a few more years. My dream is to sell a screenplay to a medium sized production company. I'm a little scared, but I know I can do it."

"You will."

"Thanks."

"So now you're going to get Leslie hooked on Mavis' home cooking." She turned and smiled at Leslie.

89

"I'm glad she is. The food and the service is great here. I really like the atmosphere."

Robin crossed her arms and leaned her elbows on the edge of the table.

The waitress raised her order pad close to her chest. "So, what will you two be having tonight?"

Robin ordered first. "I'll take four pancakes--"

Leslie was disbelieving. "Four!"

"Four."

"I know you said you were hungry, but, my goodness!"

"Four pancakes, a side order of sausage, two scrambled eggs and a tall orange juice."

"You are hungry," Leslie exclaimed.

"Leslie? Your order."

"Four pancakes--"

"Four!" Robin chuckled.

"Four!" The waitress chimed jokingly.

"Four pancakes. Oh, the same as Robin, except I want grapefruit instead of orange juice."

"All right," the waitress said, taking their menus. "I'll be right back."

"Hurry. We're hungry."

The waitress called, "Be quiet, Robin," over her shoulder.

"Yea. You be quiet, Rob." Leslie pursed her lips and teased.

Alone with Leslie and her own thoughts, Robin turned and looked out the window. "Remember when we first met?"

The rain picked up. It drummed Mavis' roof and splashed the side of the window Robin sat next to. Looking out the clear, glass window, she felt embraced by the darkness. It made her feel anonymous, a fleeting feeling she treasured.

"Goodness." Leslie's eyelids fluttered.

"You were desperate for a roommate."

"And you were desperate to leave the dorm, you and your broke self. And before you say it, yes, I was broke too. More than that, I was tired of being alone." She said, sipping her water.

"I had to find a roommate and fast. I think I had ten dollars in the bank the day I moved in with you."

"I remember you saying how much you just had to find a roommate the first time we met. That's exactly what you said. I can't take one more day of being this broke is what you said. You were wearing a sweater and a pleated skirt. I thought you were coming for a job interview or something.

And you just loved the idea that I lived on the top floor." She smiled in retrospect.

"I did. I don't know why. I just did."

"You put up with me and my zillion moods right from the start. God bless you. I don't see how you do it." She shook her head and sipped her ice water. "I don't see how you do it."

Robin turned away from the window. "Sometimes I don't see how I do it myself." She wiped her nose with her napkin.

"Catching a cold, Girl?"

She cocked her head, sniffed and turned her gaze against the window. "Hope not."

"So, you're putting your novel writing on hold?"

"I need to. I have too much going on right now. It's very important to me that I get involved in the community. I want to schedule a few college and high school speaking engagements. If I don't make a difference, if I don't contribute something to the community, then all my writing's in vain, because I will have done nothing."

"You're so hard on yourself."

"I don't think so. I just want to accomplish my goals, fulfill some of my dreams. I want to live a satisfied life. I have to be busy sometimes to do that."

She nodded. "That's true. I know when . . . well, you know too. When I don't have anything to do, I literally go crazy. But being a writer is easier than being an actress. You can organize your time better than I can. The studio monopolizes my time. I wish I could work with the same level of freedom you can. You're your own boss."

"You're your own boss too. Neither of us has to clock in or be to work at a certain time." She paused before she added, "Well, except for me at Mills."

Leslie leaned back in her chair and arched her brow. "What?"

Robin shook her head. "I forgot. You do have to be to work at a certain time. But, you love it. Like you said, when you're not working, you become temporarily insane."

She sighed. "Yes. But, I suppose it comes with the territory."

Robin turned away from the window and faced her. "You know I always wanted to be famous, since I was a little girl. I always thought I would be a great Olympian. I used to watch sprinters race in high school. I admired their speed and form. But I'm no sprinter. I never could run fast enough. Then I wanted to be a singer, but you know I can't sing. I can't hold a note to save my life." She chuckled. "I was ten years old when I started writing. I remember, I used to write this play about these girls who lived in the projects, and I forced my cousin, who's one year younger than I am, to listen. She cringed when I bossed her into my bedroom where I read the play. But soon she started asking me to read to her. I only read new material. Sometimes I had to tell her I didn't write anything new yet, so she'd have to wait. That made me feel good, her wanting to hear the play I was writing. I lost that play. I wish I still had it. I'd like to laugh at my early writing." She looked out the window a moment before she returned her attention to Leslie. "When I was twelve, I started on my first novel. It turned out to be four hundred pages. I finished it when I was eighteen. I cried when I finished it. One of the main characters died of cancer. He was a star athlete. It's strange. I felt like the characters were real. I missed him when he died, and my heart went out to his wife. And I wrote the story." She chuckled again. "I'm glad I'm a writer. I wouldn't want to be an actress. I don't like getting attention. You know how I love anonymity. I like to walk through crowds totally unnoticed. I even get like that in church sometimes. I wouldn't want people asking me for an autograph or to take a picture with them or their children. I hope that never happens to me." She stopped. "Well, it already did, but that was an accident."

It was Leslie's turn to chuckle. "It always is."

"I guess you can't avoid it."

"Not unless you become a hermit, and neither of us likes our privacy that much."

"Goodness, no." Her eyes swelled. "Oh. I forgot to tell you. Some guy named Jack has been looking for you."

Leslie sat back. "Jack? Who is Jack?"

"I don't know. Said he knew you. Annette said he came by a few times and mentioned your father. Maybe he knows your dad."

Shaking her head, she said, "No. I don't think so. Dad never mentioned a Jack. Doesn't mean they don't know each other, but even if they did, why would he be looking for me?"

"I don't know, Les. Maybe he's an old boyfriend."

"Goodness, no!"

"Goodness, no, what?" Michelle cast a shadow over Leslie's right shoulder.

Robin turned away from the window and smiled. "Michelle!"

"Hi, Rob. Guess what, you two."

"What?" They chorused.

"I ran into Dinah, Betsy, Loretta and the gang. They're out in the parking lot." She pointed her thumb toward the window.

Robin followed her thumb to the edge of Mavis' parking lot. "Really?" She stood and looked out the window.

"Yes."

Before Robin could scoot from behind the table, Janet, the waitress, laid two large plates covered with pancakes, eggs and sausage, on the table. "Here are your orders." She turned and looked over the top of her shoulder. A smile widened her face. "Hi, Michelle, Girl." She enthused while she pushed her hands down the front of her apron.

"Hi, Janet. How's it going tonight? Is it busy?"

"It's not that bad. Larry's being a pain, but you know how he is."

"Yea. What else is new?"

"I'm telling you. Enjoying your night off?"

"Enjoy isn't the word. Girl, I needed this. I was getting tired of this place. But, I can't quit. I need a job. I need to eat." She looked at Robin and smiled.

When Robin met her glance, she went to her toes and waved over the crown of her shoulder. "Hi, Dinah, Betsy, Loretta, Sharon, Trish and Anna."

"You all eating here?" Janet asked, stepping back with a raised brow. "I just told Michelle tonight's not been that busy." Her long face stretched into an infectious smile.

"We all are hungry, and Mavis' is the place to go when you're hungry. You know how it is," Trish piped.

"Let me see," Janet said, turning and hunting for empty tables. "Let me try to sit all of you together. I know you want to talk. I already took Robin and Leslie's orders. As soon as I find some empty tables, I'll take your orders. Michelle, are you eating here tonight too?"

Pushing Robin closer to the window with the wave of her hand, she sat. "Might as well." She grinned like a fox. A second later, she propped her elbows against the edge of the table and smiled at the thought of being a customer.

Sharon, Trish, and Janet pushed and pulled until they fit four long tables together. That done, Janet let out a deep breath. "Now I can start taking your orders." She brought the thinning order pad inches beneath her nose. "I'll start with you, Sharon. Since you helped move those heavy tables. I know you're hungry. You're next, Trish."

Sharon pushed out her chest and said, "I'll take a cheeseburger, small fries and a medium coke."

Janet's hand sped across the pad. "All right, Sharon."

Five minutes passed before she had everyone's order. When she did, she excused herself and went quickly into the kitchen area.

"Trish, did you all go to the regional convention?" Robin asked as soon as Janet excused herself from their table.

"That's where we just came from." It was Loretta.

"Who went?" Robin wanted to know.

"Me," Dinah said, sticking a finger against the center of her chest, "Trish, Loretta, Betsy, Sharon and Anna."

Robin's voice was flat. "Everybody except me."

Loretta threw her hand down. "Oh, Rob. We know you're busy with your career. We know once your career's off the ground, you'll have more time to hang out."

"I hope so." Guilt went like a chill up her spine, and she balled her hands until they became two tight fists. "I don't see you all nearly as much as I used to, not nearly as much as I'd like to. You probably think I forgot you."

Anna pursed her lips. "Ggiirrll."

Pulling herself forward until her stomach brushed the edge of the table, she combed her fingers through her hair and asked, "How did the convention go?"

Each soror gave her their version of the week-long convention. They didn't tell her how much they sacrificed to make the trip.

Since graduating from New York University in June with Bachelor of Arts degrees each of the sorority sisters secured employment. Sharon and Trish gathered their courage and took out a joint business loan and opened their own day care center -- Ma Bee's Love & Care. Loretta taught Algebra three days a week as an Associate Professor at the University of Tennessee. Dinah worked as an executive secretary at Tilson Construction, a leading East Coast construction firm. Betsy, a great lover of the outdoors since she was a toddler hovering around her mama's knees, trained horses in Gatlinburg, Tennessee's Smokey Mountains. Anna, a physical therapist, brought the lame back to health with the balls of her hands and the kneading of her palms at Trenton, New Jersey's Helene Fuld Hospital. National unemployment figures nearing double digits, even Dinah, who usually complained, "I didn't go to college to be a secretary. I majored in Business Administration, so I could be an office manager," was grateful for her job.

Betsy crossed her arms and legs after she gave Robin her version of the going ons at the convention. Then she pushed her back into the seat cushion. "So, Rob, what's been going on with you?"

She was quick. "Right now I'm working on a play with two masters, Michael Hammer and Roger Jones." The crown of her head pointed toward the table. "My work load is starting to get to me." A lot of air came from between her lips. "I think I'm doing too much." She raised the crown of her head and the volume in her voice. "Michael and Roger are great to work with. The only down side to working with them is that Michael is a perfectionist. I don't like the way he pushes Roger and me. They're both in their forties. I'm a kid to them." A smile tugged at the corners of her mouth. "Every time they look at me, I think they imagine their daughters." She smiled. "I'm grateful for the exposure. I'm young. By the time I'm as old as Michael and Roger, my career should be further along than their careers are. At least I hope so. Not that they haven't done well with their careers. They have. They're two extremely talented men. They're sharp as razors. They're shrewd. They're gifted. Roger's a genius. I tell him that all the time. Working with him and Michael is a good career move for me. I'm working with two of the most well established playwrights in the business. I know I'm blessed to be able to work with them. I'm learning so much from them. They're unselfish with their talent. They want to show me all their tricks. I'm glad."

"When do you think you will finish the play?" After asking the question, Anna stuck the last slice of her grilled ham and cheese sandwich inside her mouth and started chewing.

"We should be finished in a few months. We have two more scenes to crank out."

Loretta enthused, "That's not bad."

"No. It's not." Her voice went flat. "I'm starting to run out of energy, that's all."

Pushing her empty plate to the center of the table, Loretta uncrossed her legs and looked her squarely in the eye. "You need to rest. Sounds to me like you're pushing yourself too hard. You don't want to wear yourself too thin, Girl. Take a break after you finish this play. You can always start on another project later. We all need a hiatus every now and then. Don't overdue it."

Sharon examined the faces circling her. "Yea. Be careful, Rob. Be careful that you don't overdue it. Remember. Atlantis wasn't built in one day. I keep telling you that, because I know how you are. You get these ideas, and you think you can fulfill your biggest dreams all at once. It takes time. All good things take time, Girl. I know you know that." Her gaze went down to the crown of Robin's nose. "You just need someone to remind you from time to time, because you forget."

"I know." She stopped herself from turning away from her friends and looking out the window. Out of the corner of her eye, she saw a throng of teen-agers strut down the sidewalk. They laughed, opened their mouths and wagged their long, pink tongues when they passed Mavis' window. She worked hard to ignore them. "I'm a perfectionist. I got it from my dad. I don't know. I feel my best when I push myself hard."

"Well, how are Michael and you doing?" Trish asked.

Before she could answer, Loretta stood and looked out the window. She squinted and stared into the night. "Rob, aren't those the three girls Les and you hang with sometimes?" She arched her shoulders and pushed her nose close to the window. Robin and Leslie looked over the tops of her shoulders.

Leslie's eyes ballooned. "Aretha!" She extended her arm and tapped the window. "Aretha!" Diners on the other side of Mavis' turned and gawked at her, but Aretha, staggering away from the window, failed to hear her. Drawing in a deep breath, she went to the ends of her toes and screamed, "Aretha!"

Robin veiled the next words she spoke with motherly concern. "It's going to storm again. They're drunk. We have to get them home. We have to get them out of the impending rain. It's going to pour. It's started lightning like crazy again, and that thunder's really booming." Before another word went outside her mouth, she pushed her way to the end of the table and ran out of Mavis' entrance doors. "Aretha!" She called while she ran.

Two businesses down from Mavis', Bertha and Kathleen pressed their backs against the brick of a twelve-story Bank of Manhattan building. Despite their present immobility, they managed to keep alcohol and narcotics from interfering with their greatest plans, with their lives, with their jobs. Not so Aretha. She called out sick from her job at the post office twice a week. She had for the past month. Bertha and Kathleen spent hours encouraging her to sign herself into a detox center. "I'm okay," was the only response she gave them.

"Aretha?" Leslie spoke softly while Robin and she stood on opposite sides of her.

Aretha mumbled while she staggered. Her shoulders brushed the side of the bank building. Leslie's knees buckled. "Help me get her up, Rob."

"Sure. You get her around her right shoulder and I'll get her around her left."

She leaned her head back and glanced at Robin. "You're stronger than I am. She keeps leaning to the right. You come over here."

"All right," she said, walking around Leslie.

"Wait."

She looked over the top of Aretha's shoulder at Leslie. "What?"

"Where're we taking her?"

"Not a bad question. I hadn't thought of that."

"We have to get Bertha and Kathleen home too. But we have to take care of Aretha first. She's five sheets to the wind. She's cranked."

"I know." Robin almost twisted her mouth. The potent scent of liquor attacked her nose and burned.

"Tell you what."

"What?"

"Let's take them to our place." A second later, Leslie turned and looked over the arch of Aretha's shoulder. "Trish, did you drive your car?" Trish's nod was slow coming. "Yes." Leslie's gaze crossed the sorors' faces. "Who else drove?" Sharon almost whispered, "Me."

Leslie nodded then she gave out orders like she was an Army drill sergeant. "Let's put them in Trish's car and drive to our place. They can spend the night there and dry up." She grabbed Aretha's shoulder. "Come on, Rob. Let's get her to Trish's car first."

Breathing deeply and taking short, choppy steps, Sharon, Anna and Trish walked Bertha and Kathleen to Trish's black convertible. Aretha drunk and sleepy, Robin and Leslie were forced to try to carry her, the soles of her shoes getting hot while her feet dragged across the sidewalk, to Trish's convertible.

The walk from Mavis' to Trish's car proved short in comparison to the walk from the parking lot of the high rise to Apartment 1201. Bertha leaned all of her weight into Anna's shoulder while they stood in the elevator. Beside her and pressing her shoulder into Trish's back, was Kathleen.

All the shots of Snotz they gulped at Pete's Tavern made them giggle and talk from the first to the twelfth floor. Aretha moaned when the elevator reached the twelfth floor. Ridding its veins of alcohol and cocaine, her body convulsed and sent a stench of vomit spewing across the elevator floor. Pulling white napkins they took from Mavis' out of their purses, Anna and Trish pinched their noses, bent to their knees and cleaned the vomit off the elevator floor.

When the elevator reached the twelfth floor, Robin ran down the hall. She stuck her key in the door. Before she turned the knob, Leslie and Loretta dragged Aretha to the side of the door.

Moments later, Betsy helped her walk Kathleen and Bertha inside the apartment. Her mother-like duties complete, Betsy gulped in thick chunks of air. When she left Robin's bedroom, she went into the living room and plopped down on the sofa.

Bertha and Kathleen lay on Robin's bed. Aretha was sprawled across the bathroom floor. Her arms hung limply around the top of the commode. She was semi-conscious. If Dinah hadn't walked into the kitchen to pour herself a glass of ice water, Aretha's head bumping the bathroom wall would have gone unnoticed. The women gossiping and laughing in the living room while the television flashed different pictures across its screen would have wiped her from their memory for the remainder of the night.

Leslie heard Dinah scream, "Help!" first. Ire and disgust pumped into her thoughts when she followed Dinah's voice and ran into the bathroom and saw Aretha on the floor. In Aretha's hollow, open eyes, she saw familiar demons. Unlike Robin, she knew Aretha was an addict, more than a recreational drug user. Yet, she wanted to kick her and pound her head against the commode. "Come on, Dinah. Let's get her up." She said, peering up at Dinah.

Before they could raise Aretha to her feet, Robin called out, "Les? Dinah?"

Leslie pulled up on Aretha's shoulders and grunted before she answered, "What?"

"What are you two doing?"

Dinah turned and shouted down the hall. "It's Aretha again!"

"What?" Robin asked walking away from the living room.

"It's Aretha!" Leslie answered at the top of her voice while she pulled up on Aretha's shoulders.

Robin stomped the rest of her way inside the bathroom. "Not again!"

Leslie rolled her eyes and stood erect. Aretha fell against the commode. Leslie sighed and went like a slinkee to the floor. "Yes, again." Aretha's head fell into her lap.

"I can't tell you! I can't tell you! I don't know where she is! Stop hitting me! Stop! You're hurting me!"

They looked down at Aretha. They watched her arms flail and her legs kick. "Who is she talking to?" Dinah asked.

"She's drunk," Leslie snapped.

"No! No! Stop, Jack. You're hurting me. Stop! I don't know! I don't know! I don't know where she is! Stop!"

Dinah took a step back. "Who is Jack?"

Robin turned from Dinah to Leslie. "That's what I want to know."

As if silence were her only friend, Leslie crossed her arms and said nothing.

After she glared at the side of Leslie's head, Robin released a thick breath and reached for Aretha's feet. "Well?" Her eyes ballooned when she peered at Leslie and Dinah.

Leslie climbed to her feet. "Come on, Dinah. Let's get this helpless girl off the floor."

Dinah's voice went like a torn paper airplane through the air. "All right."

They grunted, sighed, pulled and pushed Aretha away from the bathroom floor into Robin's bedroom and onto the bed.

Robin faced Leslie and Dinah after they finished laying Aretha on her bed. "What do you say to a glass of 7Up?"

Dinah dabbed at drops of sweat on her forehead. "I say, all right."

Leslie inhaled deeply. "Me too."

Sipping 7Up, Dinah leaned against the kitchen counter and said, "Aretha's got to get herself together."

Robin swallowed her soda then she ran her tongue across her teeth. "She does. If she doesn't, she's going to regret it. She might not have a serious drug problem. She might not be an addict, but she does need help to get it together. She needs God. She needs God in her life. Whether she admits it or not. She can't do it alone. Everyone needs God. We all need our creator to survive, to endure, to make it."

Leslie twirled her glass and clucked her tongue against her jaw while Robin and Dinah discussed Aretha's fate. Then she rolled her eyes and cut into Robin's summation of Aretha's plight with, "So, Rob? You're not spending the weekend with Michael? You two mad at each other or something?"

Dinah sipped her soda. "Yea. How are Michael and you doing?"

She answered quickly. "We're doing good."

Leslie moved the next words out of her mouth like they were rocks going in and out of a sling. "Sure. Michael and you are doing good. Why not? Everything about you is good. Just one thing. Rob, you are so private, so quiet. You do good interviews. You're good copy. But, in person, especially around strangers, you hardly say a word. I don't know why you're so quiet." She closed her mouth and leaned toward the end of Robin's nose. "People won't hurt you." Then she moved away from her and stood erect. "You should trust people more. You don't confide in anyone. Me." She let her head go back, then she shook it. Her soft, blonde hair bounced against her shoulders. "I'm dating Drew Moore. He's half black, half Indian. He's gorgeous." Her eyes swelled. "We've been dating for about two months. I'm crazy about Drew." A smile took the corners of her mouth up. "I don't know. I might let myself get serious with him. And a love maker." She turned away from Robin and tapped Dinah's forearm. "Drew's an excellent lover. Making love with him is out of this world. He's so attentive and caring. It's like I'm the only woman in the world when he's around. That man sure knows how to handle his business." Taking the brightness out of her eyes, she changed the subject and invited Robin back into the conversation. "You need a good friend in this business. If you go too long without a good friend in this business, you could wind up a lonely hermit. Everybody needs somebody." She looked hard at Robin. "Nobody needs to be all alone. It's not good to be all alone, and I don't think it's human either. It's just not natural. We all need somebody, and we shouldn't be too proud to admit it."

Robin spoke evenly. "Thanks for the lecture, Leslie, but, I do trust people. And I'm not afraid of anyone. Nor am I too proud to admit I need other people. Michael and I get along fine. Because I'm a young play writer, people make a big deal out of me. The talent is from God. He gave it to me. He can take it away from me. I know where all my blessings come from. Artists make it to the top and forget God. They forget where their blessings come from. Oh, they say, 'I'd like to thank God' when they receive an award, but they don't live for God. You have to thank God with the way you live your life. God's not impressed with lip service. If a person tries to live right in this business, folks label them as homosexual or freak. If you get stoned or drunk every night, lie, cheat and lay every attractive newcomer, you'll fit right in."

"Now, Michael. I could see why he would have trouble trusting someone."

She glared at Leslie.

"After what you told me he went through in Maryland." She lowered then shook her head. "I'm surprised you two are together."

"What happened in Maryland?"

"Nothing, Dinah. Leslie's just spouting off again as usual."

Leslie sipped her cola. "Sure about that, Rob?"

"What do you say we change the subject?"

"I just thought since we were talking," she shrugged, "Might as well talk."

"Nothing's sacred with you, is it?"

"If you call peddling drugs sacred."

Dinah arched her brow. "What?"

"Never mind, Dinah. Leslie's off the hook right now. Ignore her. I do it all the time."

After she turned from Robin to Leslie then slowly back to Robin, Dinah asked, "So, how's Michael's career coming?"

"He's working in a musical right now. There are forty dancers on the set. They put in fourteen-hour days. Michael said this is the hardest he's ever worked. He comes home sore and stiff every night. I've been giving him massages, and he soaks in Epsom salt in the tub."

"How does he find time to do it all? I know how you do. You're a workaholic. You deny it, but you are. But, how does Michael manage? Don't tell me he's a workaholic too."

"Dinah, Michael's not a workaholic and neither am I . . . I don't think. I just like being busy. I need to be busy. I get bored fast. Anyway, Michael wanted to stop dancing for awhile, but I encouraged and pushed him to keep dancing. He was born to dance. Dancing is his talent from God. He should glorify God with his God given talent." She smiled into the next words she spoke. "I love to watch him dance. This weekend he's dancing in a show in Atlanta. That's why I'm not with him." She gave Leslie a quick glance. "He's going to be in Atlanta for two weeks." She looked at Leslie again. "Sometimes he thinks our careers are pulling us apart, but I don't agree. I think two people can grow and work to reach their goals and remain in love. Don't you?" Turning on her heels, she faced Dinah and waited for her answer.

Dinah nodded emphatically. "Yes. I think two people can have separate goals and work toward them and remain in love. I think both partners in a relationship having a realistic goal in life is a major key to the relationship's staying power, so long as those goals aren't so different they tear at rather than strengthen the relationship."

Robin's brow arched. "How do you mean?"

Dinah rested her hand against her hip. "I mean, if a man wants a wife who's home most of the time or if a man wants a wife who only works nine to five, and the wife wants to be a top manager or vice president at a large corporation, that marriage is going to have problems."

Robin's brow lowered, and she smiled. "That's true."

"That's what I mean."

"And Michael thinks I have more freedom with my career. Leslie said that just tonight." Smiling at Leslie, she continued, "I guess it's true. I can take a break from writing whenever I feel like it. In some small ways, I suppose writing is one of the less stressful jobs a person could choose, but definitely not where money is concerned. Many writers have to supplement their income with another job." She paused. "But writers are born. I don't think they are made. You can't make a writer. I don't care how much schooling you give a person. It takes God to make a great storyteller. A person's either born to be a writer or they're not." She lowered her head and shook it. "You can't make a writer. There are too many heartaches, disappointments and rejections in writing. If God doesn't call you to this profession, you won't last."

Dinah crossed her ankles and grinned like a fox. "Back to couples. I bet Michael didn't want to go to Atlanta without his boo. I bet he wanted his number one girl to be there with him."

Blood rushed to her face and she lowered her head. "He did want me to go to Atlanta with him. I wanted to go too. It's hard for us being away from each other like this. I'm counting the days until he returns. He calls me three to four times a day." She chuckled. "He calls me before I get out of bed each morning, and he calls me at night when he knows I'm getting ready to go to bed. His voice is the first thing I hear in the morning and the last thing I hear at night." She smiled hard. Then she lowered her head and added, "But, I feel it's best I stay here and finish my obligations to the plays. If the show in Atlanta lasted just this weekend, I would be there. But the show's scheduled to run two weeks. Michael's dance group is performing at a row of theatre/dinner houses. I can't be away from New York for two weeks. I'm under contract right now."

"I understand." To reassure her, Dinah repeated herself. "I understand."

"I know you do. It's just that I know I'm not the most outgoing person in the world, and everybody knows I need my space. Except where Michael's concerned, of course." She smiled again. "I love him like nobody's business. He's a very special man in my life. I need him right now. We have a wonderful relationship. He gives me my space, and I need that. He's not controlling. He is simply a wonderful, affectionate and giving man. I have never met a man like him before. He understands me without my having to explain how I feel. We know each other. It's like we were meant to be together. I've never told anyone this before, but I really believe that we are soul mates. I trust Michael explicitly. I'm never so happy as I am when I'm with him. He cracks me up. You know Michael. He has a marvelous sense of humor. He's all I've ever wanted in a man. He's an answer to my prayers." When she grinned, her jaws went out like two fat, ripened plums. "He does have a jealous streak, though. Once this guy came up to me when we were at a restaurant that had an open floor and asked me to dance. Michael was using the bathroom. When he came back to our table and saw me dancing with that guy, you should have seen his face. I danced one song with that guy then I told him I had to go."

Dinah smiled at her upturned mouth. "Most women like that. Do you like when a man gets jealous over you?"

She chuckled into her answer. "Yes. I guess I do. I do like to feel like a man's protecting me. For some reason it gives me the impression that the man loves me. Although, I have to admit, I know for a fact that Michael loves me. Deep down in my soul I know that. He doesn't have to say or do anything. We love each other. I thank God for what Michael and I have. It's rare."

Dinah nodded. "I think any woman who had a man who cared about her the way Michael cares about you would feel that way. Michael's a good Brother."

A second later, they turned and looked at Leslie when they heard her voice break up their conversation.

"I wish I had someone to make me feel that way."

"I just thought you said--"

"Oh, Dinah, he's mostly a bed partner."

"Well, why don't you stop looking for decent men in indecent places?"

"Rob."

"No. It's true. You expect to find a good man in a bar. That's crazy."

"Well, Rob, sorry to burst your bubble, but everybody's not like you. Everybody doesn't have your life style, your protective life style."

She waved her hand. "Oh, shut up, Les."

Moments later, they moved their conversation into the living room. . Scenes of make believe flashed across the wide screen, color television set. Apartment 1201 hummed with laughter and gossip until four o'clock in the morning. Sleepy from sitting in the living room for more than six hours, the women stood from their places in the living room.

Robin flipped the remote control and the television screen blackened. The living room came under a potent silence. Darkness filled the entire apartment. Robin ran her hands along the living room's longest wall until her fingers bumped into the light switch. With a flip of her finger, she brought light blaring into the room. Ten minutes didn't pass before her sorority sisters pulled on their raincoats and bid her and Leslie good-night. Out in the hall, their brows pointed when they saw a bald man standing outside the apartment door.

"Are you looking for someone?" Trish asked.

"No. No." The man answered, turning and going down the stairs.

Chapter Nine

Snow and icicles clung to the tops of houses, apartment buildings, department stores and office complexes. Because it was seven o'clock in the morning, few dog paw marks created tracks across the snowy lawns. It was January 2, 1989. In a few hours, department stores would be loud with bargain hunters combing through clothes racks and stacks of toys looking for after Christmas clearance items. Temperatures dipped well below the freezing mark. Except for merchants and bargain seekers, New York City's sidewalks would be bare.

Dogs yelped, barked and pushed their tails between their legs when their owners snapped their leashes around their leather collars and led them outside. Twice J. F. K. International closed its runways due to low visibility, it snowed and the wind blew so hard. Visitors to the city were trapped inside Greyhound and Trailway's terminals waiting for the next bus home. Four lane highways were plowed into two lane freeways, while two lane streets were salted into one lane roads. Snow piled four and five feet high against curbs and tall buildings. Grocery store counters lay bare, because residents panicked when newscasts of the first real winter storm aired.

While Leslie struggled through another New York City winter, Robin went horseback riding, fishing at Rudder's Creek, skiing in Gatlinburg and hiking in the lower altitude of the Smokey Mountains. As usual, winter in Tennessee was mild. Robin filled her days shopping, cleaning out the attic and garage with her dad, going out to eat and to the movies with former high school classmates and attending East Tennessee State's theatre department's local performances with Dinah, Betsy and Loretta.

For the first time since they graduated from high school and took off for the East Coast, Johnson City wasn't boring. This Christmas, home in Johnson City, the quartet was inseparable. Though no one uttered a word, each woman believed this would be the last winter they would spend together. It was Thursday. Since they planned to end their winter vacation on Saturday, nostalgia clouded all their activities and conversations. The two weeks they shared in Johnson City refreshed their souls and sent a renewed sense of hope into all their thoughts. They visited their favorite high school hangouts twice. Shoney's Big Boy. Elroy's Drive-Thru. The Putt-Putt Course. Nelson's Drive-In. The South Side Mall. Pigeon Forge. Silver Dollar City. They were the women who knew more about each other than anyone else did.

Monday nights at home in Johnson City, they piled inside Loretta's gray sedan and visited high school running partners. They searched Johnson City's department store aisles grabbing leather jackets, sweaters, blue jeans, dusters, pumps, skirt suits and dresses. There wasn't an East Tennessee State University or Kingsport High School basketball game they missed. Friday afternoons, they played putt-putt golf, indoor tennis or racquetball. Early that first Saturday morning, Betsy, Dinah and Loretta went ice-skating. Robin, ever the writer, walked to McCory's Five and Dime store half a mile from her parents' home, and bought a stack of ruled notebooks and two reams of bond, typewriter paper. When her friends allowed her, or, in the wee hours of the morning, she put the idea for a new play to ink.

Knee-hi stockings hung over the rim of the tub and around the edges of the sink. Hand, facial, body towels and wash rags hung neatly over a towel holder nailed to the back of the bathroom door.

Robin stuck her head out the bathroom door and called, "Mama?"

Before she answered, Marcia rolled her eyes and took in a deep breath. "Yes?"

"Are you busy?"

"Robin, you know I am always busy. Why would you ask me a question like that?"

She arched her brow, and took her ear further outside the bathroom door. "What, Mama?"

"Yes. I'm busy!"

Widening the crack in the door and pulling a towel around her waist, she talked at the top of her voice. "What 'chu doing?"

"Child, what do you want?" Marcia asked, tilting her head and placing one foot on the bottom stair.

"A clean towel, please?"

"There are towels up there!"

"I know, but," she brought the corner of the towel wrapped around her lower torso to her nose. When she raised her head, her brow tightened. "They're dirty! Mama, this is the same towel I used yesterday!"

"Girl!"

"Mama, please!"

"I'm busy!" She turned sharply on her heels and walked through the living room and the kitchen into the basement.

Scowling, Robin turned her back to the hallway. She wanted to slam the door closed, but, fearing her mother's certain wrath, she pressed her hands against the door and brought it to a close quietly. In front of her, on the shelf below the medicine cabinet was a radio. She turned it on. When she did, her hand bumped into a small picture frame. Lifting the frame off the shelf, she gazed at its back. She made the frame for her mother as a birthday present when she was in the third grade. "It's my favorite, and I'm gonna put my favorite girl in it." Two minutes didn't pass before Marcia hurried and grabbed a picture of Robin. She pushed it inside the frame, and, stepping back, she smiled hard at the picture and the frame.

Robin shook her head and whispered, "A time that seemed so long ago." She turned the frame over and stared at its front. Tears pooled in her eyes when she stared at the picture it enclosed. Sonia. She couldn't have been older than three months in the picture. Fat chubby legs and that little, button nose. She looked at her baby sister while she listened to the song on the radio. It was an old song by The Carpenters. *We've Only Just Begun.* Allowing herself to weep freely, she returned the frame to its original location then she ran her hand along the base of the shelf. She remembered an old Bible her mother kept next to the radio years ago. She would pull it down while she was bathing Sonia. Robin would be standing at her side singing to Sonia along with the songs on the radio. Marcia would read from the Bible and tell Robin how important it was that she obey God and grow up and become a good woman. "Only good women are allowed to marry good men," she would tell her. "No man wants a woman who's been used before. Keep yourself pure. Live right and God will bless you with a wonderful family just like he did me."

Flipping to the back of the Bible, she pulled in her bottom lip and read her mother's handwriting. "September 8, 1963, Robin Marie Carlile born to Theo Allan and Marcia Elizabeth Carlile at St. Mary's Hospital in Johnson City, Tennessee. Weighed 7 pounds and nine ounces. Twenty-one inches long. Healthy." Scanning down the Bible, she read, "December 23, 1969, Sonia Elizabeth Carlile born to Theo Allan and Marcia Elizabeth Carlile at St. Mary's Hospital in Johnson City, Tennessee. Weighed 4 pounds and 6 ounches. Sixteen inches long. Under observation." Robin started to cry again. Closing the Bible she couldn't forget the last inscription. "December 25, 1973, Sonia Elizabeth Carlile is pronounced dead by Dr. Henry Washington at St. Mary's Hospital in Johnson City, Tennessee. She took all that is Marcia Elizabeth Carlile with her."

Turning the radio up and climbing into the tub, she lowered herself into the warm bubble bath, and, parting the curtains she stared out the window. She tried to remember a time when, for her, life was easy. To do that, she kept going back to when she was younger than ten years old.

When Sonia was just a few weeks old, she used to stand over her crib and tell her how much fun they would have after she learned how to walk and talk. "Hi, little Sis," She'd coo into Sonia's smiling face. "I can't wait until you grow up. I'm gonna teach you how to dance. We'll dress up in Mama's clothes and pretend we're Gladys Knight and Aretha Franklin singing a duet. I'll write the best stories and read them all to you first. After it rains we'll run outside and make mud pies. I'll push you when we go to the park and play on the swing set. Nobody will be able to out double dutch us. You and me, Sonia, we're going to be the best sisters ever."

A news piece went across the radio and interrupted her thoughts. The Dow Jones had dropped ten points. Chuckling at the urgency in the DJ's voice, she dipped her head beneath the bath water. Cool air went around her shoulders when she sat up. Hearing her father's voice, she turned and looked at the door.

From the basement, Marcia listened to Theo walk inside the dining room. When she heard his feet still, she knew he was placing mail on the dining room table. "Theo!" She walked to the foot of the basement stairs, shook the wet bedspread she carried in her arms and peered all the way up the steps. She refused to use the washing machine pushed next to the basement's tan dryer. Keeping her mother's ways, she pushed her family's laundry up and down a splintered scrubbing board. Had she not whined and begged Theo for the washer and dryer, she wouldn't feel guilty each time she descended the basement steps and looked at the two appliances. "Theo!"

An amazingly beautiful woman, only family and close friends knew Marcia was in her mid-fifties. Everyone else thought she was thirty years old. The white shorts, yellow tank top and leather, strapped sandals she wore accentuated her heavy, firm bosom, tight thighs and round behind. "Theo!" She called again.

Dropping the last piece of mail on the dining room table, he frowned and walked inside the kitchen. "What? What do you want?"

"Come get a towel, and take it to Robin."

"Where's the towel?"

Rolling her eyes, she answered, "In the basement, Honey."

"Give me a minute."

"Just come get the towel."

Slowly he walked halfway down the basement stairs and ducked his head beneath the low ceiling. When he glanced over his shoulder, she tossed him a pink towel. It almost struck him in the face.

"I didn't try to hit you," was the first thing she said when she turned away from him and faced the clothes floating in the metal tub.

He sighed, "Yea," before he turned and climbed the stairs. It was 1:30. "Where's Rob?"

"Why don't you go see for yourself? What am I, the gatekeeper?"

"I just asked."

"Do I have to do everything around here? I don't suppose it's enough that I keep this house you live in clean enough to eat off the floors of."

His voice lowered. He shook his head and walked away from the basement door. "Never mind."

Her hand fell against the rim of the tub. She tried to curb her anger by talking out loud to herself. "Calm down, Marcia." She coached herself while she took in a deep breath. A second later, she climbed the basement stairs and walked in his footsteps. She called, "Theo? Theo? Theo, Honey? Baby? Theo?" while she walked

Halfway up the living room stairs, he stopped and answered, "What?"

Before he could turn around, she had one hand on his shoulder. "I'm sorry for being short with you. I'm sorry, Honey. Please forgive me." She looked down at her hands. "Do you forgive me?" She raised her head, put her arms around his shoulders and pecked the nape of his neck. "Forgive me?" When she stepped back, she was smiling.

Stifling a chuckle, he told himself, *"We've been here a thousand times before, and she always wins."* Then he nodded into, "Yea." He took her hand inside his, gently pulled it over his shoulder and kissed her mouth.

She returned him his smile. "I'm sorry."

His smiled widened. "Apology accepted." He pecked her mouth again.

The kiss warm on her mouth, she turned her head away from him and called out, "Robin!"

"Good morning, Dad!" She answered, splashing her torso with water.

"Are you almost finished splashing around in that tub?"

"Mama, I haven't been in here that long."

"Nearly an hour!"

Theo turned and faced the bathroom door. "She's been in there almost an hour?"

"She certainly has." Marcia answered, planting her hands on her hips.

He turned the knob back and forth teasingly. "Come out of there, Girl. This ain't no mansion. We've only got one bathroom."

"Just a minute, Dad. I need a towel."

"Is that why you've been in there all this time and still aren't finished taking a bath?" He paused. "Longer than an hour, I'm sure. I know how you like to soak in the tub." A second later, he tuned Robin out, looked down the hall toward Marcia and his bedroom and asked, "What are we going to do today?"

Marcia shrugged. "I don't know." When she turned and saw his lips pursed, she raised her voice and offered, "How about going out to eat at a nice restaurant, catching a show and taking a walk? I heard there's a good play downtown at that theatre. You know the one that was renovated. What's the name of it? Do you know the name of it?" She turned and walked into the closet. "And, what am I going to wear?" She faced her bedroom dresser. "Well, Honey, do you know the name of the theatre I'm talking about?"

"Manhattans?"

"No. The theatre's downtown. I don't know what I'm going to wear." She slapped her thigh and frowned when she heard Robin call her.

"Mama?"

"What, Robin?"

"Mama?"

"Here." She walked passed Theo who stood beneath the arch of their bedroom door and tugged on the towel in his hand. "Give me that towel, so that child'll stop hollering." She walked away from him and stood outside the bathroom door. "Robin?"

"Un-huh?"

"Crack the door. Here's a towel, and it's clean."

Grabbing the towel, Robin met her glance and tossed her head back. "Thanks, Mama."

"Yea. Finally, huh?"

"I wasn't in that big of a hurry."

"You never are when you get in that tub." When she stuck her head through the crack in the door again, she asked, "You through?"

"Yes, Mama." She answered, closing the bathroom door.

"Then, come out of there."

"In a second."

"Oh, Girl, will you come on. What do you do in there anyway? Dream. Dream. Dream. If you aren't one dreaming child. That's all you do is dream. Girl, you better start living. You don't have forever. After what this family has been through, you, of all people should know that."

Like a robot, Robin scrubbed and rinsed the tub, threw the floor mat over the edge of the tub and picked her dirty clothes off the floor. After she tossed her dirty clothes inside the hamper, she flossed and brushed her teeth, gargled and wiggled into a khaki skirt and white, cotton blouse.

Marcia's fingers went through the air like confetti when Robin opened the bathroom door. "Finally! I was beginning to wonder if you were ever coming out of there." She stepped around Robin and entered the bathroom. "Child, you've got this bathroom fogged up!"

"It'll clear out, Mama." She blew cool air out of her mouth. "It was hot in there before I started taking a bath."

"I suppose." Marcia reached to the back of the tub. "Help me get this window up."

"Just a second. Let me go put on a pair of socks first." She passed her parents' bedroom before she reached her own. "Dad, you look handsome. That green shirt looks nice on you. Did I get you that for Christmas?"

He tugged on the front of the shirt and peered down at its unique design. "Yea. I think you did get this for me. I like it. It's one of my favorites." He smiled softly at her. "I see you finally dug your way out of the bathroom. The way you go in there and stay, a person would think you were hibernating."

"So, you do like the shirt?"

"Sure. I thought I just said that."

"Yes, Sir."

He waved his hand. "Oh, Girl, go on." He followed her to the edge of her bedroom and stuck his head inside. "Oh, yea, Rob?"

"Yes, Sir?" She didn't turn from pulling on a sock.

"When are you leaving, and where're you headed? You've been travelling so much lately."

"I'm going back to New York. Next month I go to Florida A&M. I'm giving a string of seminars, radio and television interviews down there."

"I'm so proud of you." He wrapped her shoulders inside his thick, warm arms.

She hugged his neck and kissed the side of his face. "Thanks, Dad. That means a lot to me."

Freeing her from his embrace, he stepped back and looked at her. "I tell your mama how strong and positive you are. Of course, she always agrees. I love you, Baby. Both your mama and I do. You keep your faith in God. It shows in your work. I'm so proud of you."

"Dad,   are   you   trying   to   make   me   cry?"

"No. I remember when I read your first play. I was sitting in the recliner in the living room afraid I'd come across a boring part. You know I read a lot. I've read so many books. Sure. I'm prejudiced, but it's not just that you're my daughter." He stopped and chuckled. "After I read your play, I sat back in the recliner and smiled. I was proud. I knew you were a writer after I read that play."

"Thanks, Daddy." She hugged his neck a second time. "Thanks a thousand times."

When Marcia walked behind them wearing a sundress, they turned and   chorused,   "Who're   you   smiling   at?"

"Look at you two. You always were like friends. You tickle me. I think every parent has their favorite child." She smiled.

"What are you going to do today, Mama?"

"Well, I was trying to think of the name of the theatre downtown they renovated, the one that puts on hit plays from the 40s, 50s and 60s."

Robin snapped her fingers. "Oh, you're talking about Headliner."

A grin widened Theo's face. "That's it! Thanks, Rob."

"What's showing there?"

"I'm not sure," Theo answered.

Robin turned from him to Marcia. "Where's the paper?"

"Un-un. You're not going. Do you want her to go, Honey?"

"No." He answered matter-of-factly. A crooked smile shadowed his answer.

"I know I'm not going, Mama and Dad." She said, turning and looking at her mother. "I just want to know what the name of the show is."

Marcia looked over her head at Theo. "I think the paper's downstairs on the kitchen table. Is that where you put it last, Honey?"

"That's where I put it."

She turned to Robin. "The paper's on the kitchen table."

"Are you two on your way downstairs?" Robin asked.

"Sure. Are you hungry?"

"Yes, Mama."

"Tell you what, Robin. Let's go out for lunch, since you got out of bed so late. Then we can come back to the house, so you can hang out with your friends. You can have the Buick today. When did you say you were leaving?"

"Mama, are you two trying to get rid of me so you can spend more time alone together?" She turned from her mother to her father. She smiled and winked at her father.

"No." Marcia answered, "I just want to know when you're leaving, so I'll have enough time to work hard to get something special together with family and friends before you go."

"Mama, you don't have to do anything special for me."

"Sure. You say that now."

"No. Really."

"Robin, we both know if I don't go out of my way and make you stand out you'll hold it against me for the rest of your life. I can hear you complaining to Leslie already. I went home and my mom didn't do anything for me."

Bowing her head, she stared at her hands. "No. Really."

Marcia tried again. "So, when are you leaving?"

When she looked up, she met her father's glance. He looked at her and mouthed the words "It's all right." A second later, inhaling deeply she teased her mother with, "You really are trying to get rid of me. You haven't fallen helplessly in love with Dad again, have you?"

"Oh, Girl." She lowered her hand. "Falling in love is for young folks like you. Your dad and I have a family now, however small it is."

****

Dinah accompanied her boss to Miami, Florida to close a 120 million-dollar contract. Loretta was in Knoxville at the University of Tennessee meeting with the Dean of Arts and Sciences. She wanted the dean to approve her proposed curriculum for her freshman Algebra winter quarter classes. Until temperatures rose Betsy was grooming and training horses in the lower elevations of the Smokey Mountains. Robin was in New York City. Soon she would be in Jamaica visiting an old friend, a musician she kept in touch with mostly by mail. His name was Mark. He was a success in Jamaica. His popularity continued to grow in the United States. It was Mark who loaned her the money she needed to get her first play, *On Your Feet*, marketed. Four years ago when Mark needed someone to keep his house while he washed cocaine out of his system at a detox center, she flew to Jamaica and stayed at his house during her entire summer break from NYU.

Michael's deep voice would come into all of her conversations on this trip. Her heart skipped at that fact.

Michael. He looked forward to sharing his days and nights tucked inside Robin's love.

It was February 15. That gave Robin and Michael two weeks to pack for their visit to the island. Michael imagined only good things when he thought about the trip. In his dreams, he saw natives, their dress colorful and rich with texture, performing local dances. He saw himself walking the crowded streets listening to the smooth sounds of reggae. Each time Robin dreamed about Jamaica, she saw Michael's face. She heard his voice racing. She saw herself introducing him to Mark. The two men were the best of friends in her dreams.

Until Michael and she flew to Jamaica, she busied herself editing a play she adapted from a newspaper article. It took her three weeks, but she finally came up with a title for the play -- *Funny Thing*.

Funny Thing's main character was a college co-ed. Full of wit, she was well liked on campus. Her parents lacked the knowledge that she suffered through stages of depression. They thought she was the perfect daughter until their attempts to contact her by telephone and mail at Florida A&M, where she labored feverishly to maintain a 4.0 grade point average, failed.

****

Old Florida newspapers cluttered the living room floor. Most of the newspapers were 1974 editions. The O'Jays, Teddy Pendegrass, Earth, Wind & Fire, Stevie Wonder and Peabo Bryson hits spun, one after the other, on the phonograph. Old *Ebony*, *Essence* and *Life* magazines piled in the love seat.

Leslie tripped over a stack of Stevie Wonder albums. When she did, drops of her tea spilled into the carpet.

Robin looked up from her place on the sofa. Spiral notebooks and black and red ink pens surrounded her hips and thighs.

"Well?" Leslie stared down at the top of Robin's head.

Robin narrowed her brow and turned up her nose. "What?"

Leslie's hands went out like a flower in bloom. "Wha-wha-what is all of this . . . junk?"

Robin stood more to stretch her legs than to address Leslie. "Junk?"

"Junk," Leslie said flatly while she stared at the design on the cover of a rhythm and blues album.

Robin pushed her head back. "This is creativity, Girl!"

Leslie rocked her head from side to side. "Well, move your creativity."

"Please," Robin said standing akimbo.

Leslie laughed, just once, so loudly and sharply she sounded like a bird going "Ah-Ah!" "What's got your goat lately?"

Robin arched her brow and stepped back. "Why do you ask that?"

"You're so moody lately."

"Oh, shut up."

"Ooohhh."

"Shut up."

"Well?"

Robin looked at her again. "What's bugging me?"

"Yes."

"Nothing." She took her gaze off Leslie's face and returned to her writing. A second later, she threw the pen she wrote with against the spiral notebook she was writing in and leaped to her feet. With a furrowed brow, she stomped across the living room floor and swept the newspapers she used to research *Funny Thing* into her arms and pushed them against her chest. She plopped on the sofa, the newspapers still in her arms, before she stood again and stomped to the spot on the floor the albums covered. She took in a deep breath, bent her knees and scooped the albums into her arms, and, wobbling across the floor, she placed the newspapers and albums on top of the coffee table.

Leslie sat on the sofa and peered at the albums and old newspapers. "Heavy?"

Robin worked to catch her breath.

Leslie sat against the back of the sofa. When she did, tea sprinkled her pant leg. "What are you researching . . . writing this time?"

"I'm doing research for a play I'm working on."

"Oh, nooo."

"Oh, yyeess." She wiped her brow and tossed her head back. "I'm ttiirreedd! I'm tired. I'm tired. I'm tired."

"Then rest. Most people rest when they get tired, but, not you."

"Yea."

"Yea." Leslie chimed, mocking her. "Come. Sit down."

She walked to the sofa. Shots of pain pierced the backs of her thighs while she walked. "Thanks."

Leslie slid down the sofa and gave her more room to sit. "Sure."

"I need to rest. I'm pushing myself too hard." She released a deep breath. "Yea. I know. I know I push myself too hard. I can't stop though. I'm compelled. Sometimes it makes me angry . . . my drive, but I can't stop. I don't know why. I've always pushed myself hard."

"Ummm."

"Ummm?"

"Hmmm."

"Hmmm?"

Leslie looked her squarely in the eye. "Well, you said it all. I was waiting to hear why you drive yourself so hard."

She sighed, "Yea."

Knowing her quest for a direct answer would go unmet she quickly changed the subject. "The Islands . . . Jamaica is gorgeous."

"I know. I was there four years ago."

"What am I gonna do while you're away having fun?"

"Have fun here."

"You gotta be kidding."

"Well, you've got the movie you're working on."

She crossed her legs and sipped her tea. "That's right. You have been out of town at home in Tennessee. You don't know I finished working on the set."

"How did it go?"

"All right."

"When did you finish shooting?" She asked, sneaking glances at the old newspaper headlines.

"Almost a week ago."

"How do you think the movie'll do?"

"I think it'll do all right. The screenplay was excellent. If it doesn't do well at the box office, no one can lay it on the screenplay, but people will. I had a stomach virus for two weeks while I was working on that movie. Something's missing from the movie. I don't know exactly what, just something. I've spent a lot of time wondering if I should have taken the movie Leonard Jones, Leontynee, the choreographer . . . you know Leontynee, don't you?"

"Yes. She's very good. It's always good to see African Americans in positions in Hollywood that are historically predominated by Caucasians. You know, much of Hollywood operates as though Jim Crow were still law."

"That's true. Leontynee's husband's a producer, one of the money bags." She chuckled. "You know producers only put up the money to make the movie and do the director's dirty work." She stopped and chuckled again. "They were having dinner at a restaurant in Manhattan." She tossed her hand through the air. "I forgot the name of the restaurant. When I came in, Leonard invited me to their table. While I ate dinner with them, he tried to sell me to the movie. Another bad decision on my part. I think Leonard's movie'll do better than the one I just finished acting in . . . a lot better."

"Leonard's finished shooting his movie?"

She dropped her gaze to the sofa. "I suppose."

"You're depressed."   Robin glanced up from scanning the newspapers. "You're drinking tea. Funny how your drinking always starts with you on the health nut wagon." She smiled softly. "Trying to stimulate your psyche?"

Leslie turned the mug her tea warmed in circles. "You're right."

"I know I am."

"I know you know you are. You know so much about me, and I know so much about you." She stopped turning the mug and sipped her tea. "The woman who always wanted to be perfect." She smiled softly at Robin and let the heat from the mug warm her hands.

Robin stole glances at the pile of newspapers. "Yea."

Leslie sipped her tea.

Robin's tone was casual, but her thoughts were riddled with guilt. "We all want to be innocent, Les."

Leslie kicked her feet up and laughed. "Nope. Not me."

The word dragged off Robin's tongue. "Well."

"What are you doing now?" She asked, talking to the back of Robin's head while she shuffled through a stack of cassettes. She pulled out her favorite Aretha Franklin and Reverend James Cleveland recording. When the music to *Amazing Grace* came into the living room, she returned to the stack of newspapers.

"I already told you. I'm working on a play."

"Oh. Now I remember."

"Um-hmmm. Bored, Les?"

"Now--" She lay the mug on the coffee table. "That's a definite understatement."

She chuckled and scanned the newspapers.

She was still chuckling when Leslie pushed off the sofa, reached to the coffee table, picked up her mug and walked into the kitchen. She talked to her while she filled her mug with more tea. "As busy as you stay, you probably never get bored."

She shouted from where she sat on the living room floor next to the sofa. "I'm a writer!"

Leslie watched the tea darken as it filled the mug. "Yea."

Robin sprang to her feet carrying a newspaper and an album by Earth, Wind & Fire. "Writers are always thinking of something to write about, so we never stop working."

Leslie returned to the living room, her mug full and hot. "Play some Al Jarreau. It'll make me feel better."

Robin rolled her eyes when she heard Aretha Franklin croon, "I once was lost, but now I'm found." She knew Leslie knew how much she enjoyed listening to Aretha Franklin belt out *Amazing Grace.* "Where are my other albums?"

"Where are they usually?" Leslie asked.

"In your room."

"Your albums are in your room. I didn't move them."

"Then, go get an Al Jarreau cut out," she suggested.

"All right." Leslie said while she walked away from the sofa. "Be back in a minute."

She talked while Leslie looked for the album in her bedroom. "What's wrong? You've been mopping in and out of different rooms in this apartment for the last two days."

"Nothing. Just that I stopped living when my acting career took off. I miss not having a normal childhood. Sometimes I wish I could do it over. You know, really enjoy life, without having to pretend so much."

"This is the life we both chose."

Returning to the sofa with the album, she sat forward and sighed. "Yea. It might kill us, but here we are."

Robin frowned. "Why do you talk about death? Sometimes you talk like you think we're both going to die tomorrow. Is there something you need to tell me?"

Leslie shook her head. "No. No." She raised then lowered her shoulders. "I don't know anything that you don't."

Robin laughed. "We're both going to live to be old, gray headed, wrinkled women."

Leslie sat back on the sofa and bit her fingernail. She chuckled dryly. She thought about the letters. Two so far. Another one came today. She was glad she was always home when they came. "Rob?"

"What?"

"You still got that old, blue typewriter or did you finally give it away?"

Robin chuckled. "What do you want with a typewriter? You don't even know how to type."

"Just answer the question. Please."

"I moved it under my bed."

"Has it always been there?"

"Leslie."

Leslie balled her hand into a tight fist. "I'm just asking! Can't a person ask a question around here?"

Chapter Ten

Three large suitcases and one travelling bag were pushed next to the apartment door. Leslie was in London acting in Leonard Jones' latest movie, *Mrs. Smith's Accident*. Ten mornings ago when Leonard's executive secretary telephoned and informed her she was selected to be the female lead in *Mrs. Smith's Accident*, she jumped so high on her bed, her elbow scraped the ceiling. When she came down, she screamed until her throat grew sore.

Robin reached across her bed and grabbed a sweat suit and a third pair of sneakers. She stuffed them inside one of the suitcases before she turned and looked down the hall toward the front door. She listened to the speaker bell ring, then she zipped the suitcase closed, and dragged it and the other two suitcases across the floor. The suitcase corners banged the insides of her calves while she hurried to the elevator. When she reached the main floor, her breathing was labored and her forehead pricked with sweat.

Michael was curt. He threw a flat "Hi" at her when his gaze fell across her face. Flipping his wrist, he glanced at his watch and added, "I've been waiting for nearly half an hour. I thought you said you would be down here by ten."

"I know, Baby. I got held up packing."

"Well, I got a ticket."

"Why didn't you park in the lot?"

"Because you said you'd be down here waiting by the time I pulled up when I called you earlier."

She lowered her head and pulled her ponytail inside her jacket collar. Wind thrashed the shortest parts of her hair and pushed her clothes against her skin. "Sorry."

He sat behind the steering wheel and stared blankly through the windshield after he pushed the suitcases inside the trunk. She sat silently beside him in the Honda Accord he rented earlier in the morning. When he turned and saw her staring blankly through the windshield, he told himself she was thinking about meeting Mark. Twisting his mouth, he worked to silence the sea of jealousy that raged inside of him. He glanced at her and almost shook his head she was so beautiful.

After she pulled strands of hair off her forehead, she leaned forward and laid her brush on the dashboard.

He tapped the accelerator. The brush fell to the floor.

She giggled into, "Ump! Michael."

"Umm." Was the most he responded.

She picked her brush off the car floor before she turned and asked, "What's wrong?"

His voice softened. "Sorry, Sweetheart. I've just got something on my mind."

She arched her brow. "Care to share what it is?" When he didn't answer, she smiled and asked, "Well?"

He chuckled when she leaned and pecked the side of his face. Her deep burgundy lipstick left a mark. "You seem distant, like you're thinking about something or somebody." He arched his shoulders then added, "But maybe it's me."

She stared at her fingers. "No. It's me. I'm being distant. I kept you waiting. I've just been rushing around so much. This is the first time we've gone away together. I want everything to be perfect. I want to remember this special time we share in Jamaica together forever. I know I'll never forget it. But I apologize for being late." She embraced the sides of his face before she kissed him again. "I love you, Baby."

A smile made its way across his face.

"That's better. I like it when those pretty brown eyes of yours light up.""

He smiled wider. He rubbed his palms together. When he returned his hands to the steering wheel, he blurted, "Look out, Jamaica. Here come Robin and Michael!"

She sat against the back of her seat and stuffed the brush inside her pocketbook. "Yes! Child!"

The Honda passed a string of restaurants, businesses and residential buildings.

She sat up and pushed her nose close to the passenger window. Half an hour later while she stared at a house sitting up on a long hill, thoughts of Tennessee filled her head. Moments later, she stared at miles of empty road. When another string of restaurants came into view, both Michael and she raised their shoulders. Next to the row of restaurants, was a hotel. Across the street was John F. Kennedy International Airport.

Michael gazed up and down the street until he saw the car rental office where he immediately pulled into a vacant parking space.

The Honda puttered to a stop. He turned and faced Robin before he took the key out of the ignition. "Ready!"

"Open that trunk!"

"You're ready, all right." He opened the door and stepped outside the car.

"Wwwhhheeewww!" Reaching overhead, she took in a deep breath and pulled hair off her face. "Am I ever."

Five minutes later, after he turned the keys to the Honda in to the car rental office, his eyes swelled when he neared the car. "When are you going to get out?" He asked while he watched her pull her brush outside her pocketbook.

"As soon as I do something with my hair and get my pocketbook up on my shoulder, so I can grab some of those suitcases."

"Hair. Purse. Hair. Purse. If you don't come on, we're going to miss our plane."

Exiting the car with her pocketbook and travel bag over her shoulder, she grabbed one suitcase then hurried to catch up to him. "Coming!"

"You can see the parking lot's packed." He talked while he walked, his shoulders jerking forward with each step, away from the rental car and closer to the airport.

"Yea." Her breath thickened. "I see."

He moved his body closer to the airport terminal in long strides. "So, you know it's packed inside."

She tripped over a crack in the pavement. "Probably worse." Then she took in a deep breath. "More people than cars."

He didn't stop moving or slow down. "Exactly. So, come on. Hurry. Let's go."

She almost stopped, her back hurt so badly. "Listen to you."

He chuckled.

"Listen to you." She said, repeating herself, this time with a tight brow.

He smiled when he looked up. "Come on. I'll hold the door open."

"Good." She let her shoulders go down. "My hands are full, and I'm almost out of breath."

"I carried most of the luggage. You and your heavy suitcases."

"Just hold the door."

"Ladies first." A second later, he watched her walk through the glass airport entrance door, the wheels to the suitcase she carried scraping the floor behind her.

Panting more than talking, she pushed a long, thick, "Thanks," out of her mouth.

He chuckled and withdrew his foot from the door.

"Sure." Extending her legs, she huffed her way beyond him. "Now we have to hurry to the counter. So, you better hustle. Pick it up."

"Thank God for wheels." He said while he bent and grabbed the strap to his travel bag and the handles to three suitcases. Pain raced from the center of his back to the nape of his neck with each step he took. "Rob," he called over his shoulder.

"Go on." Again behind him, she stood and waved her hand. "I'm right behind you."

Moving in short, choppy steps, he hurried to the ticket counter, then he returned to her side and took the suitcase she struggled to pull across the floor away from her with a bump of his hips and a jerk of his arms. "Give me this. You just carry your travel bag and purse."

She frowned purposely and looked down her nose at the top of his head. "I'm not helpless, Honey."

"I know that. Why do you think you've got all of my heart?" Chuckling he teased, "Huh?"

"Oh. Go on." She massaged her lower back and the arch of her shoulders while she walked to the ticket counter. "My back and shoulders are aching."

"Mine too."

"You should have let me help you."

"Maybe so." He rolled and massaged the nape of his neck. "Let's get our luggage checked in. I don't want to see or think about luggage again until we land in Jamaica."

"Did you bring your dance books and Broadway musicals to study?" Before he could answer her, she looked up and smiled at the US Air attendant. "Hi." She handed the attendant two first class tickets then she turned and faced Michael.

"Yes. I brought all my reading material. I may not get to the books, but I brought them."

"You two are all set." The attendant said smiling at Robin who took the return tickets and boarding passes inside her hand. "Thank you," the attendant said, "Have a pleasant flight and a pleasant stay in Jamaica."

She returned the attendant her smile. "Thank you. We will enjoy our trip. You have a nice day."

No longer bothered with the weight of four suitcases, Robin and Michael turned and walked away from the ticket counter.

"We've got twenty minutes." Robin said, flipping her wrist over and looking at the diamond Rolex watch Michael bought her for Christmas. "I want the window seat."

She took a stride and stuck a piece of sugarless chewing gum inside her mouth. "You got it."

He took the stick of chewing gum she offered him. "Thanks."

"Are you hungry?"

His gaze darted across the terminal. "I feel like a sandwich. I'm definitely thirsty."

"Good. Me too."

"Where do you want to eat?"

She shrugged. "I don't know." A second later, she decided, "I want fish."

"All right. Anything but hamburger, huh?"

"You got it."

He pointed to a neon sign. "How about McDouglas' Fish and Old Fashioned Chips?"

Her shoulders went up. "Sure." Then they went down. "Why not?"

Minutes later and sitting on two McDouglas' Fish and Old Fashioned Chips' counter stools, their conversation kept pace with their rocking feet. They talked between chewing and swallowing. Nearly half an hour passed before they sat next to one another on US Air Flight 267 and headed for Jamaica.

Trinidad's Piarco International Airport, where they landed February 15, 1989 at 5:03 a.m., is close to San Juan. Trinidad's second largest city and capital is the Port-of-Spain. Robin and Michael's heads teeter tottered and their eyes swelled with amazement the second their plane bumped the runway on the Island, a cosmopolitan society where most its residents are of East Indian or African origin. Looking about, Michael saw a large mix of Syrian, European and Chinese races too. Peering out of the window while the airplane bumped the runway, he twiddled his fingers. He was eager to hear natives discuss Carnival held the Monday and Tuesday prior to Lent. He wanted someone to explain the festive parades where residents dressed in fancy costumes sang calypso songs and dancing bands filled and stomped the walkways. Watching the Creole and East Indians parade in Carnival was a celebration he knew he would never forget.

Flight 267 stopped with a light jolt. As soon as the airplane wheels ceased to roll, Robin and Michael stood from their seats and hunted through the overhead rack for their travel bags. "Here." Michael said when he turned and handed Robin her travel bag.

She strapped the bag over the crown of her shoulder. "Thanks."

For three weeks she studied the history of the Jamaican islands. She knew that when Trinidad and Tobago's petroleum success fell at the end of 1981, the economy of the islands plummeted. That fact and information she gathered during this trip, she planned to use to plot a novel later in the year.

A thick boned Mexican woman wearing a flowered sundress and a Korean couple followed them down the ramp. Robin wondered if the passengers following them knew Christopher Columbus didn't discover Trinidad in 1748 anymore than he discovered America during his third trip to the Western hemisphere . . . natives already residing at both locations when he arrived. Although Jamaica was not her home, it angered her to learn Indian tribes settled in Trinidad before European settlers murdered them, and the Spanish went on to colonize Trinidad in 1592. In 1833 the abolition of slavery swept the British Empire, and from 1846-1915 agricultural workers migrated from India to the Island. In 1962, Trinidad and Tobago gained full independence and joined the Commonwealth of Nations. During her studies, it surprised her to learn that the United States was Trinidad and Tobago's largest trader.

The first thing she exclaimed was, "This is great!" when they stepped off the airplane.

"It certainly is."

"You'll love the dance and music here!"

"Reggae!"

A cherub faced, plum colored girl with tiny braids going all over her head turned from standing just outside the terminal door. She looked at Michael and smiled.

"And pretty girls." Robin added, looking at the top of the small girl's head.

He smiled at the girl's round face. "She's cute."

Robin nodded while she smiled. "She sure is." A second later, she looked intently at the girl and spoke slowly, "Hi."

The girl spoke evenly while she gazed at Robin. "I know what you're saying. I speak English, Spanish and French."

Michael stepped back and chuckled.

"Hi." The girl again silent, Robin tried another approach. "Where're you from?"

"Her parents probably told her not to speak with strangers," Michael offered.

"This isn't the United States."

"I know, but it's still a safe practice."

She conceded, "Yea," with a slow nod. "The world's such a busy, crowded place, everyone's becoming a stranger."

"Hi." The girl raised her head and smiled up into Michael's face.

Robin's gaze followed the young girl's smile. "I think she likes you."

Peering at Robin, he bent his waist. "Does she want me to pick her up?"

She shrugged. "I don't know. Why don't you ask her."

He took his face close to the girl's face and spoke in slow, broken English. "Want me to pick you up?"

Not once -- not even for the time it would take her to pop out a quick "Hi" to Robin -- did the girl turn away from looking inside his tootsie roll brown eyes. "I told you I speak English. I understand you, and, yes, I want you to pick me up. But, I'm too big. I'm eight years old."

Robin smiled at the girl who continued to ignore her. "Oh, she is cute."

He planted a kiss on the girl's jaw. "She is, isn't she?"

Tapping his forearm in jerky motions, Robin, her brow heightened and her shoulders back, watched a shadow approach, loom and darken about her. "Michael, don't. Michael, maybe you better not be so friendly. Michael? Michael?" She fastened her eyes on a mahogany-skinned man while she continued to tap his forearm. "Michael, I think the little girl's father is coming and he is not smiling."

He looked up and sputtered, "Oh, oh," then he backed away from the girl.

The man was grim until he came face to face with them, until he passed them and the girl.

He took the girl's hand. "Come on. For a minute there we thought that man was your father."

The girl's feet were planted.

He tugged on the end of her hand. "Come on. We'll take you to the security desk."

The girl turned and looked over the arch of her shoulder. "Can't. Here comes my mama. But--" She pulled a wrinkled map out of her pocket. "I'll sell you this for one dollar."

Robin threw her head back and laughed. While she laughed, she laid her head on the flat of Michael's shoulder.

After he gave the girl a dollar, he pulled on the strap to his travel bag and waved good-bye to the girl. Then he faced Robin and said, "Come on, Baby. Let's go have a good time."

"Do you have the map?" She arched her brow. "The one we brought with us."

"Let's get our luggage first."

Ignoring his side stepping her question, she blurted, "That's right. Most of it's mine."

He winked at her. "It is."

She chuckled dryly. "I know most of the luggage is mine, but I don't care. I'm happy to be here." Her arms moved in long fluid motions while she walked. "This weather is beautiful. I just love it here. I'm looking forward to seeing our suite. Didn't it look gorgeous in the brochures? We can go swimming and take lots of pictures. I tell you, Michael, Jamaica is absolutely gorgeous! Tomorrow we go on our boat ride." She squeezed his shoulder. "We're gonna love our stay." Her gaze going to the side of his head, she spoke to his quiet thoughts. "I know the boat ride we scheduled isn't a cruise ship, but I'm really looking forward to it. I've never taken a cruise before." She smiled. "My parents have taken two cruises. They say, aboard ship, the ocean is like a giant carpet. The water is still, and doesn't seem to move. I'm looking forward to experiencing anything like that." She released his shoulder and pressed her palms together before she lowered her arms to her sides. "I'm so excited!"

He smiled so hard claw-like marks formed on the outer corners of his eyes. "I see."

Turning and gazing inside his eyes, she softened her voice and asked, "Aren't you?"

"Yes." His gaze darted from her face to the pavement. His thoughts kept going to Mark. "Yes, Baby."

The longer she looked at him the thinner her smile became. "When do you think we should leave for the boat ride tomorrow?"

A hope went with the turn of his head. "Around ten," He answered while he wished they would forego meeting Mark this trip to Jamaica.

She tried to smile again, but she couldn't. "Yes. Early."

"Come on!" Tugging on the end of her fingers, he skipped once and hurried into a trot. "We can get on that van to go get our luggage."

The wind at her back, when she stepped into her run, this time she smiled with energy. "You're right!. Let's make a run for it. The van looks like it's about to take off."

He pointed at the van driver while he ran. "Wwaaiitt!"

The driver stretched his neck until he could see around the steering wheel. Every seat on the van was taken. Many passengers stood. Babies and toddlers sat on women's rocking laps. Adult conversations mixed. The talk was loud and non-stop.

Robin slowed her pace from a run to a jog. "The driver's waiting for us."

"Yes, and the van's packed, but, let's go."

"Maybe we'll strike up one or two friendships. The riders look friendly. Who knows? Maybe some of them are going on the boat ride."

"Come on." He reached for her hand. "Let's run faster. We don't want to keep the driver waiting."

"Oh. Don't worry." The travel bag slid down her arm the second she stepped in front of him. "I can out run anybody when I want."

He extended his stride. "Nnaawww."

They raced to the van running mostly side by side. Everyone on the van turned quiet when they reached the base of the steps that led into the van. Their tennis shoes smacked the pavement loudly and sounded like wet flip-flops going across concrete until they stopped running.

Robin pulled on the strap to her travel bag, and climbed inside the van in front of Michael who steadied her back with the strength of his hand. "I've got 'cha!"

"You better have me." She said, working to catch her breath and trying to gain firm footing.

He chuckled. "I do." A moment later, he stood next to her on the van. They held the overhead rail. Looking around, he was surprised to find an array of races and nationalities looking back at him.

He nodded at an elderly Chinese man.

The man nodded and answered him with, "Hi."

Michael's body shook like jello while the van made its way across the airport wing. "Where're you from?"

"New York."

Though he bowed his head, Michael couldn't conceal his laughter.

"No joke."

"For real?"

"For real."

"If it ain't a small world. I'm from the city too."

"Yea?"

"Yea. Vacation?"

"Yes." Suddenly the man's eyes bulged. "Watch your head! Here comes a bump!"

Michael grabbed the man's hand. Using his other hand, he gripped the overhead rail.

The man grinned at the strain on Michael's face. "I saw it coming. We've hit enough of them. I'll be glad when we reach the baggage claim area."

"Me too."

"Sir?"

Michael turned and faced an overweight, Italian woman.

The woman pushed the back of his thigh. "Move over, please."

"Oh, of course," he said stepping to the right.

The driver announced, "Here we are!" when he put his gaze into the rearview mirror.

All the passengers stood.

"Am I blocking your path?" Michael asked a tall, dark Cuban man who stood in front of him.

The Cuban man didn't turn to face him. "I can wait."

He waved the man onward with, "Go on," then he pulled in his buttocks and stood stiffly with both his hands on the overhead rail. The Cuban man grabbed he and his wife's bags and inched his way off the van. Less than a minute later, Robin waved to Michael, who was still on the van, from her place on the pavement.

He said, "Nice people," to her after he stepped off the van.

She went to her toes when he neared her side. "I'm so glad we came here!"

Lowering his head, he looked inside her eyes. "Give me your hand."

Extending her hand, she blushed and said, "Be my guest, Handsome."

They walked hand in hand, their fingers entwined, the sun melting into their naturally darkened skin. Michael located their suitcases and pulled them off the conveyor belt. "All set?" He called over his shoulder to her after he placed the last of their suitcases on the floor.

"I'm all set, Baby."

"Good! Let's go find that hotel."

"First, I want something to drink." Her face tightened. "My throat's dry, and the flight upset my stomach."

"Plane rides always make you nauseous. You took those motion sickness pills I gave you, didn't you?"

She nodded.

"They didn't help?"

She shook her head. "They didn't help."

"Okay. After we get you something to drink, let's find a phone booth and call a taxi."

"That sounds good. I know you're tired of lugging those suitcases around. I'm only pulling this one suitcase, and my shoulder's throbbing."

"You said it. Tell you what. Give me some change. While you get something to drink, I'll call a taxi."

"Okay." She combed through her purse until her hands filled with coins. "Here're eight coins. I'll be right back. I'll leave the suitcases with you."

"All right."

"I'll be right back."

He called out, "All right," before he turned and dropped the coins inside the mouth of the telephone.

Fifteen minutes later, she returned with a large orange juice. She turned the Styrofoam cup the orange juice filled upside down and took a long swig before she dried her mouth with the end of her tongue and asked, "How'd the phone calls go?"

"Taxi should be here any second."

"Mmmm."

He pointed to the Styrofoam cup in her hand. "May I have a sip?" When she extended her arm and gave him a sip, he took the cup inside his thick hand, smiled softly inside her eyes and asked, "How about a kiss?"

She called him to her with, "Come here, Baby." Seconds later, she stepped back and ran the point of her tongue across her mouth. Her tongue was hot, and her mouth was tender where he kissed it. "Mmmm."

"Yes, Ma'am." He leaned forward, cupped the nape of her neck with his hand, and kissed her full on the mouth before the taxi inched along the curb they stood next to. The driver honked the horn.

She was silent while she stood outside the taxi's passenger side door. She listened to the new song the secret parts of her body sang while Michael helped the driver load their suitcases in the trunk of the cab. "Come on, Baby. Let's go." He said when he returned to her side and took her hand inside his.

She slid across the cab's back seat and looked at the back of the driver's pointy-head. "What are your rates?"

"Where are you going?" the driver asked after he glanced in the rearview mirror.

"Michael, where's that brochure?"

Instead of digging through his travel bag, he pushed close to the taxi driver's ear. "We're going to the Club Jamaica."

"That's right." Robin confirmed, sitting against the back of the seat.

He turned and faced her. "Let's go to the hotel first."

Her eyes swelled. "Yes."

"We can relax and enjoy a meal before we visit Mark and his family."

"I'm with that." She stopped. Her next words came out slowly. "You didn't want to go straight to Mark's, did you?"

He almost shook his head. "No. I didn't."

She pushed her back against the seat again. "Neither did I." A second later, she moved her shoulder close to the open window, just behind the driver's ear. "Where's the Club Jamaica?"

"On the other side of the island."

With that, they smiled teasingly at one another, moved so close to each other their thighs touched, then turned and looked out the window closest to them and watched palm trees speed passed.
****

Their adjoining rooms were large and elegant with a marble shower, tub, full kitchen with both conventional and microwave ovens and floor length refrigerators.

Michael stood with his room's satin, peach colored curtains between his fingers. He gazed down on the sidewalk sixteen floors below. Bright colored shirts, pretty thin, loose skirts, sandals and big floppy hats filled the busy thoroughfare.

Montego Bay, its people friendly, its rhythms melodic and its beauty breath taking, proved itself the heart of the Caribbean Islands. A symphony of heavenly music rushing down its famous waterfalls greeted Robin and Michael the second day of their visit. Their hearts throbbed and quickened at the site of the tall palm trees and mountain foot horizons at sunset. Walking about the sandy shores, fingers entwined, Montego Bay delivered them sweetly into the arms of the world's most potent love gods. Sea breeze sprayed their skin and hair at midnight while they sat on the balcony of their exquisite, luxury resort. For the first time in months, Robin relaxed and indulged herself in different island recipes. Site of a garden of tropical plants and flowers brought tears to her eyes. When she wiped the mist away with her fingers, Michael hugged her waist. Beneath his gentle embrace and standing among the bright array of colors the tropical plants and flowers brought, her body stirred and warmed. As if commanded by the clear blue, still waters, she lost control of her emotions and fell helplessly in love with Michael.

A history buff, in the afternoons she left Michael in the company of Mark and sauntered off down the narrow passageways in search of historic homes and landmarks.

Upon first greeting, Robin and Mark laughed and guffawed while they shared highlights of the last four years of their lives. Michael stood by idly marveling at the depth of their friendship. For half of that first day, he felt ill equipped to share the joy of their long awaited meeting or offer insights he gained from his own life experiences. Before the day deepened with the going down of the sun and unwilling to make himself a stranger, Mark pulled Michael to the side and assured him that Robin and his was but a friendship.

That evening, the trio embarked upon a horseback ride through the majestic mountains. Time seemed to stand still as they ascended the rugged mountainside, their three stallions' hoofs beating into the rocky clefts. They drank up the darkening sunset and allowed themselves to be enchanted by the sounds of nature when they tugged on the reins of their horses and headed down the mountain.

Two days later, Robin and Michael familiar with the Island and alone took a torch lit canoe ride along the Great River. Chasing sexual escapades and tasting the sweetness of one another mouths, tongues and bodies, the transparent waters and nearby mountains called to them. Distant sounds of Calypso rocked them. A golden sunset enchanted them. It was morning before the spell released them.

Mark rattled the doors of Michael and Robin's resort at 10 a.m. the following morning. With a sweep of his arm, he bid them to accompany him on a walk through the market where vendors sold goods out of old, wood pushcarts and chatted with natives in a language neither Robin or Michael understood, but he smiled and laughed at. Reggae music pulsing in her ear, Robin found it hard to resist the temptations of local women encouraging her to allow them to read her future, which they claimed was written in the palm of her small hand.

The third day of their stay, Robin, Michael and Mark took a helicopter flight to Falmouth and Runaway Bay. There Robin marveled at the Georgian architecture and especially enjoyed their visit to the home of the great poetess, Elizabeth Barrett Browning on Market Street. Influence of the powerful family infiltrated all of Market Street. Robin claimed to feel the presence of the great writer hovering over her shoulder the entire time she tiptoed through the massive rooms of the mansion. The feeling both frightened and exhilarated her. It frightened her because she believed in ghosts. It exhilarated her because it gave her the promise that, should a great writer care to brace her with her ghostly presence, she must be destined to be an equally powerful and eloquent writer. The following morning, after dining at the Rafter's Village, the three companions toured the Safari Village, a place that intrigued Michael and Mark more than Robin who kept thinking about the previous day's visit to Elizabeth Browning's house.

Late that afternoon, Mark borrowed a friend's jeep and sped, sand and dirt whirling high off the ground about the sides of the jeep, to Rock where Robin, Michael and he, their feet clad in local sandals, raced to a small white house at the side of the beach. Inside the small house, he presented identification and rented a boat. Robin, Michael and he spent the remainder of the day snorkeling, water skiing and boat riding.

It was Michael who insisted they spend morning and afternoon of the following day toeing through some of the island's massive caves. The trio walked with hushed voices and pounding hearts while they investigated the walls of the caves and listened to foreign cries of faraway animals and roaring waves.

They spent the last days of Robin and Michael's ten-day stay visiting sectors of the busy island. At Port Antonio, once the banana capital of the world, fear and excitement gripped Robin's chest when they boarded a river raft and whipped in and out of the Rio Grande's currents. The trio topped the evening with a visit to the Athenry Gardens, an explosion of colors and sweet fragrances.

Before returning to the resort in Montego Bay, they drove to Kingston, Jamaica's capital city, and visited the Crafts Market and the National Gallery. Hours later, at her strong request, they headed for Caymanas Park. The sports woman in Robin took great delight in watching horses rip around the circular rail trying with great desperation to out run one another. Though Mark's frequent trips to the betting office tempted her to put money on a favorite horse, she held the rein to her religion and gambled not.

That night, Mark stayed with a lady friend who tempted him with the delicacies of a woman's touch; he gave in easily. Robin and Michael, resting side by side beneath the moonlight on a deserted beach, spent the night exploring one another's bodies. It surprised Michael when Robin allowed him to visit places before she always limited with a sturdy 'no'. While they enjoyed one another, he promised himself to bring Robin back to Jamaica one day.

Michael turned when he heard the door close. He walked from the curtains to the center of his room with his arms open. "Hey, Baby!"

Robin smiled before she wrapped her arms tightly around his shoulders. She stepped back and looked at him before she kissed him fully on the mouth. "Mmmmm."

"Good morning, Baby."

"Good morning, Baby." She repeated, lingering in the tenderness of his kiss.

"I really enjoyed my stay here, Baby. Mark's a good brother. I like him. I hope he checks us out in New York sometime."

"Me too."

He chuckled heartily. "I know you do."

"This time we spent together was so special to me, Michael. I love you." She reached for his bottom lip with her tongue while she stroked the side of his face.

"I wish this wasn't our last day here." He turned until his shoulder brushed hers. His arm was still draped around her waist when he looked out the window. "I loved it here. This island is beautiful. I have a feeling the government ushered us into the more lucrative parts of the island. Next time, I'd like to explore the Jamaica tourists prefer not to frequent. I really want to get to know this island and its many, different people." His free hand fell limp against the side of his thigh. "I really enjoyed being here with you, my lady. Being with you made Jamaica a very beautiful place for me."

She caressed the side of his face in long, slow strokes. "Oh, Michael. I love you so much. We have to come back."

"We do." He pecked her mouth. "What time is it?"

"Seven-thirty."

"What's up for this morning?"

"That's right." She stopped stroking his face. "We said we'd spend this morning alone on the beach and this afternoon we'd spend with Mark and his friends."

He kissed her mouth softly before he responded, "Yes. We did." He rocked her in his arms. "Baby?"

"Yes?"

"Do you know anybody from Jamaica besides Mark?"

"No. Why? Thinking about making Jamaica your second home?" He laughed. "No."

She waited.

Silence.

"Michael, don't do that. You know I hate when somebody does that. Start talking about something, then just stop. Just like that. Just stop."

"No. It's no big deal." He shook his head. "It's just that. Well. When I went to the hotel lobby this morning to get a cup of coffee, this guy stopped me. Gave me a picture of a red headed woman and told me to be sure to tell you to have a nice day." He nodded. "A very nice day. That's what he said. Told me to tell you to have a very nice day."

She stepped back. "What?"

"He knew you. He knows you."

"I don't know anybody over here except Mark. What are you talking about?"

"I don't know the dude. He knew I knew you though. You must know him."

"Michael, I don't. Maybe Mark knows him."

"Well. You can best believe I'm going to ask Mark about this guy as soon as we see Mark. Because I want to know who this guy is. Why we don't know this guy but this guy knows us."

Chapter Eleven

The sun beamed in the sky. Its rays pointed toward the apartment's living room window and sent orange and yellow hues over the sofa, love seat and walls. Sandal clad foot walks along the Atlantic shore, horseback rides through the Poconos and Saturday afternoons spent frolicking at Coney Island was the way Robin spent the bulk of her summer. Michael accompanied her on all of her getaway excursions. Weekdays, they critiqued their latest work. She nodded and applauded when he showed her his latest dance steps. He read her screen and stage plays with an aura of disbelief. He considered her life, at best, sheltered. Yet, in her writings, he found deep spiritual, sexual and tragic truths. The findings shocked him. Finished reading her work, he pondered the delicate nature of the woman he had chosen to love nearly four years ago. There seemed to be so much about her he was yet unfamiliar with. For him, she remained a challenge, though not nearly as pleasant a conquest as she once was.

Leslie worked away from New York for nearly two years. Contractual obligations on the set of *Dancing In The Dark* took her from California to France. While in France, she shopped like a mad woman. She hunted and bought original paintings, gold picture frames, antique chairs, gold book ends, extravagant, designer suits and dresses and jewelry. Before she returned to the States a week ago, she shipped her newly purchased goods back to Apartment 1201.

Prior to her return, Robin and Michelle organized three rummage sales. Those three Saturdays, portraits of young maidens sitting against New England backdrops lined the floor. A set of china, half of the dishes chipped, porcelain dolls wearing stained, satin gowns, disco albums and forty-fives, car cellular telephones, a walkie talkie Robin spent two days convincing Leslie to let go of and scores of paperback novels piled high on folding tables Michelle borrowed from Mavis'. Total collected from the rummage sales was $2,056. Robin and Michelle hand delivered the money to the homeless shelter serving the Harlem borough.

High on the success of *Dancing In The Dark*, Leslie bathed in the attention her adoring fans heaped upon her. Senior editors at top international slicks, television anchorwomen and radio talk show hosts faxed Donald requests for interviews with her. Again under good working agreements, Donald and she focused their thoughts on steady work and future successes. Last summer, she reinstated the services of two of her four attorneys. The other two attorneys she never did get along with, and, at Robin's advice, felt it a waste of money to re-hire.

Because of Robin's prodding and because she knew Robin was right, Leslie telephoned her mother once a week, usually on a Saturday night. The breadth of their conversations limited since Leslie's childhood, they never took their discussions beyond the status of Leslie's career, the depth of her relationship with her "new" beau, the cost of her wardrobe or how Robin was faring.

Gossip columnists dared not stroke her fire. In and outside of Hollywood, she was treated as if she were a delicate china doll. Her financial and career mistakes and her tantrums no longer haunted her in the eyes of movie critics and Hollywood executives. To their great surprise, she found her niche.

"Leslie Fletcher is back!" Leslie couldn't count the number of magazines that title headlined. Her face was everywhere. *"Just What The Doctor Ordered For Hollywood: Leslie Fletcher"* aired internationally July 26, 1990. Leslie, afraid she looked fat because she gained three pounds munching on bread sticks while in France, didn't watch the hour-long biography. That same evening Robin sat cross-legged on the love seat nibbling popcorn. From her bedroom, every five minutes, Leslie called out, "What are they saying about me now?"

She gave in to Leslie's pleas for "more information". She knew the pain of feeling fat. Twice when Michael and her relationship was iffy she became a borderline anorexic. As if the cooling temperatures were affecting Michael and her relationship, once again she rarely ate.

Because she suffered through a string of failed romances, Leslie cringed while she watched Robin and Michael visit the beach, amusement parks, sporting events and the theatre in the hopes of restoring excitement to their relationship. She rehearsed different ways she could warn Robin that Michael and she were growing apart. Yet, each time she went to talk with her about Michael, she waved and told her, "Everything between Michael and me is okay. We're doing just fine."

While she struggled to hedge Robin away from the breakage in Michael and her relationship, she found herself busy giving a round of interviews. "Hollywood's a reflection of society at large," she answered Susan Burns, senior editor of *Epik* magazine after she asked her for the fourth time what it was like to live with an African American.

"What do you mean?" Susan asked.

Pursing her lips and tilting her head back, Leslie gritted her teeth and said. "What do you mean by continuously asking questions that point toward race? Robin's a writer. I'm an actress. If you simply want to write about a black and a white woman who are living together, go knock on somebody else's door."

Despite Leslie's sarcasm the questions and the headlines continued. One tabloid printed, *"Robin Carlile and Leslie Fletcher Prove Blacks and Whites Can Get Along."*

"Leslie and my friendship just happened. We didn't plan to be friends. This is the most unlikely friendship ever. You can take that to the bank. We definitely didn't start off as friends. Neither of us worked to get to this place of love and trust. With each other, we share our deepest secrets. We respect one another's craft. We critique one another's work, and we spend hours sharing the highs and lows of our love affairs," Robin told Robert Browning of BDS News during a late night interview that aired in May.

"What did you say?" Leslie asked her the second she walked through the door after doing the interview. "What did you tell that Browning guy? You know. The part about us talking about our love affairs." Then she tossed her hands up and laughed. "You. Robin. You. You keep all your secrets to yourself. You don't tell anybody anything. Since the end of summer, you and Michael hardly see each other anymore, and every time I go to talk with you about it, you shut me out."

"I'm busy. I've got speeches to get ready for at SUNY campuses. Three months of speeches, Leslie. It's not like I have time to chit chat. I'm busy. Can't you see that?"

"And so you're still not going to talk about Michael?"

Paulette Jones, a tall, slender, cinnamon colored woman, a Broadway dancer and one of Diane Armstrong's girlfriends drove to Michael's flat an hour after the sky darkened. Diane introduced her to Michael one afternoon at the end of summer. Michael was boarding the elevator to visit Robin. As soon as Diane saw him, she ran up to him. Pulling Paulette by the arm, she nearly pushed them into each other while she extended her hands and said, "Michael, this is Paulette. I told her how much you want to make it as a dancer. Paulette has connections. She's an established Broadway dancer." Then she turned and said, "Paulette, this is Michael."

Six weeks passed. It was Friday when Paulette drove to Michael's flat. She dashed up the back steps to the red brick building his sparsely furnished flat was housed in. Robin was out of town delivering motivational speeches to a group of freshmen drama majors at Spellman College in Atlanta, Georgia. Michael set his answering machine to pick up on the first ring. That night, Robin called six times. Lonely in a strange city, she did hear Michael's voice, but all it said was, "Hi. You have reached 555-2244. This is Mike. I am unavailable right now. Please leave your name, number and the time that you called, and I'll get right back to you. Peace."

Paulette spent hours easing him into his own king-size waterbed. Once there, she unleashed each of his sensual desires for a woman, all the desires Robin curbed and imprisoned. Saturday morning when he turned to his side in bed and saw Paulette laying next to him, her arm stretched across his bare chest, he blinked. He pushed off his bed and hurried inside the bathroom. Guilt crushed him and sent him to the floor. When he rose to his feet, he stared through his mirror and saw Robin's face, sunken and pale, staring back at him. That same night sexual hunger returned him to Paulette's warm embrace. While he rocked in delicious rhythm to her yearnings, he forgave himself for disturbing Robin's fantasy. All that night and the following morning, he gave in to Paulette again and again. Their bodies exploded in ecstasy.

Robin caught a red eye home Sunday night, her heart longing for Michael. She thought about him endlessly. Her emotions badgered her to alter her romantic habits. All the hours she spent in Georgia, she thought of ways she could insure his love. She shopped for tight knit dresses and revealing pant suits she could purchase and parade her firm, curvaceous body in front of him in. She imagined her body softened in pretty, silk lingerie. She rehearsed lines of sweet nothing when she was alone in her hotel room. She teased strange men with seductive glances while she shopped at the mall or dined at a restaurant and marked their responses so she could determine which moves were best to use on Michael.

It was sprinkling on August 12, 1990 when USAir Flight 287 landed at John F. Kennedy International Airport. Leslie drove to the airport and picked Robin up. Though she talked nonstop during the drive home, Robin sat next to her mute. Thoughts of Michael filled her head.

■■■
The building's entrance door was unlocked. Robin climbed the cement steps. She pulled a door key out of her purse and unlocked Michael's front door. She laid her hand against the door and pushed. The door opened with a slow yawn. Her brown eyes looked into another pair of brown eyes. It was Paulette. Thinking perhaps Michael had moved and forgot to tell her, she turned sharply on her heels and raced down the building's cold, cement stairs, her own apologies to Paulette trailing her.

"I've seen that woman somewhere before. She looks just like Diane's friend, but I know Paulette doesn't know Michael. I mean. What would she or any woman be doing at Michael's at eight in the morning on a Sunday?" Over and over she repeated the question to Leslie as soon as she returned home. An hour later when she returned to Michael's flat and again unlocking the door, found Michael and Paulette lingering in the taste of one another's passion, the answer came to her.

She sought solace in work. She leaned over her word processor banging out sentences into the wee hours of the morning. Lovelorn songs and short plays canvassed her bedroom floor. She complained to Leslie about a tightness in her chest and a sore throb in her left arm. "Go to the doctor," Leslie screamed, her face red and her hands shaking. She lost sleep worrying about Robin. She wasn't one for courting fear, but when Robin's weight plunged to a meager 88 pounds, she panicked.

She allowed another week to pass before she took matters into her own hands. Hurrying across the living room floor and grabbing her keys, she announced, "Come on, Rob. Let's go shopping!"

She looked up misty-eyed. When she turned away from Leslie she nibbled her bottom lip and returned her attention to the romance novel she was reading.

"You know they've got some slamming Labor Day sales going! What would we look like missing a good sale? That's not us!" She turned. "Rob?"

She closed the book and stood from her bed. "All right. All right." She dragged her feet across the floor. "I'll go with you. I don't really feel like going out, but I know how you are. You won't stop until you get what you want."

"It's not about me getting what I want. I just want us to get out and have some fun. Don't you want to get out and enjoy this nice warm weather? It's gorgeous outside. Have you looked out yet?"

Standing at the front door with pursed lips, she answered, "Let's go. You want to go. We'll go. Come on."

Leslie took charge of the entire afternoon. She had to. Robin followed her moping in and out of different stores, hardly speaking. Other shoppers looked at her and turned quickly away after she met their glances. The pain in her eyes attacked their joy.

"Where are we headed now?" she asked while Leslie crossed the street and moved toward a row of designer clothing stores.

"Come on." She held the entrance door open so Robin could pass through. "Let's see what they have in here. These are supposed to be some of the nicest designer stores in Midtown."

"Okay. If that's what you want." An hour later she placed a stack of shirts, dresses and suit pants on top of a clothes rack. She turned to Leslie and said, "I've got to go to the bathroom. Watch these clothes. I'll be back. Shouldn't take long."

The first two bathrooms she approached were crowded. Lines went down the hall and halfway around the nearest corner. Without a second thought, she turned and started walking from store to store. She almost smiled when she saw a door marked "Ladies Room". There was no line.

She pushed the heavy restroom door open and breathed in the thick odor of mildew and urine. Walking slowly she peered beneath each stall.

Soon she discovered that she was alone with her fears about public restrooms. Tragic newspaper headlines pushed to the front of her memory when she inched inside the stall closest to the restroom's entrance door. She grabbed the strap of her pocketbook and pulled it close to her breast. She pushed her jeans down and squatted.

Her jeans straddling her thinning hips, she snapped, "Stop it!" when she felt sweat prick her forehead. "Stop it. Have faith in God!" she shouted a second time to the empty bathroom when she felt the sweat trace the side of her face. She clutched her heart when its pace quickened. Control was her strong suit. It angered her that she couldn't stop shaking, couldn't make her heart stop pounding. Not until she heard urine splash the commode's brown water did she realize that she was peeing. She pulled her jeans down until they hung around her ankles. A second later, she looked toward the ceiling and whispered, "Thank you, God," when she saw that she barely wet her pants.

Twenty minutes passed before Leslie realized that she had not returned to the ladies department. Clothes and one fedora hat caging her feet, she arched her brow. Her eyes swelled. She called out, "Rob? Rob? Robin?" In another minute, she stood in the security office. "Page my friend."

"What's her name?"

"Robin Carlile?"

"Were you two supposed to meet somewhere?"

"No."

"Why should we page her then?"

"We came here together. Look. She went to use the bathroom minutes ago. She hasn't come back. I'm worried. This isn't like her."

"Are you sure she's not on her way back now?"

Between clenched teeth, she growled, "Just page a Robin Carlile, will you?"

A minute later, she raced outside the security office screaming, "Rob? Rob? Robin?" She hollered down every corridor until she came upon a quiet restroom, alone in the row of stores with its foul odors. When she pushed the door open, the hair on the nape of her neck rose and stiffened.

The door squeaked to a close. Robin froze.

"Rob?"

Her feet straddling the top of the commode and her arms wrapped around her shoulders, she "ssshhhed" herself.

"Rob?"

She tightened her grip around her shoulders and mused, *"Mama's the one who created this fear in me. Ever since Sonia died, she's told me not to trust people. Said those doctors could have saved Sonia. Could have arrested the disease that challenged her life. Told me to stay away from disease and filth. Told me disease and filth live in hospitals and public restrooms. Help me, Jesus."* She peered toward the ceiling and wept, "Oh, Mama, why did you do this to me?"

Leslie stopped. Her gaze darted from the door to the stalls to the window at the back of the restroom. "Rob?"

Her voice shook and cracked, "Les?"

"Rob? Where are you?"

"I'm in here."

She pushed against the door of the first stall.

"Just a minute," Robin said while she climbed to the floor.

"What are you doing in there? Do you have diarrhea?"

"No."

Leslie pried the worn lock on the stall loose and pushed the door open.

Chapter Twelve

"*President Ronald Reagan winds down a second term,*" newspapers reported the night Robin drove her sorority sisters to NYU. The prior weekend the women were together in Silver Springs, Maryland. Sigma Gamma Rho was holding its regional conference. The fall conference saw a record turnout. At twenty-five years of age, Robin felt old when she moved alongside other Sigmas and started stepping. Moments later and stepping with 500 of her sorority sisters from across the country, she worked her legs and arms into a hard rhythm. Her voice squeaked, and her brow was wet with sweat.

History was her strong suit at the conference. She won every quiz, and after the Grand Basilius expressed to her the importance of being prepared to speak for and about your people at all times, she led two group discussions.

"True. We are proud members of Sigma Gamma Rho Sorority, Incorporated, but we are not a separate entity. We need the Zetas and the AKAs. We need Omega Psi Phi and the Kappas. We need those not committed to a sorority or fraternity. We are a people more than a sorority. We are a proud and strong people. Let's have fun at Greek Show competitions, but let's not forget that we are a people. We are one. Only then will we be strong and we ought to be strong. God created us to be strong." She concluded the last of her half-hour group discussions on the second day of the regional conference.

One weekend later at NYU's 1990 Fall Greek Show competition, she forgot every word she uttered at the regional conference. Fiercely loyal Sigmas, her sorority sisters never took the words to heart.

"Go ahead, Sigma!" Trish shouted.

Sharon cupped her hands around her mouth and boomed, "S G Rho!"

Across from her a competing sorority undergrad called out, "Zetas are the best! Step! Zetas, step!"

Next to Robin a woman clapped her hands fast. She stomped the floor alongside four other woman and chanted, ""AKAs! AKAs! Show 'em up, AKA! Show 'em up! Get it, Girls! Step! Step! Step!"

A high pitched scream went through the crowded room at the student center. Then Robin, Betsy and Loretta screamed, "Go, Sigma! Go, Sigma! Go, Sigma! Go, Sigma! Show those AKAs and Zetas how to step! Go ahead! Go ahead! Go ahead!"

Ten loud minutes passed before Anna raised her hands and screamed, "We won! We won! We finally beat the AKAs!" As if high on the recent step show success she talked about the victory while her sorority sisters and she made their way out of the student center and into the night. After they climbed inside Robin's car, Anna resumed her conversation.

Robin kept glancing in the rearview and side mirrors while she drove away from the student center to Club Nubia. She looked for a police cruiser hiding along the darkened interstate shoulder or parked with its headlights off in the grassy medium creating an illegal speed trap. Seeing no police cruiser, she put more weight on the Z's accelerator and watched the mph gauge race to eighty. "I didn't think we'd win," she said glancing into the rearview mirror. "Trish, move your head to the side just a little, please. I can't see out the back window."

"I would if I could, Rob. Girl, I can hardly move it's so packed in this car."

Sharon said, "I didn't think we'd win either."

Betsy asked, "Why not?" while she leaned forward on Loretta's lap.

"Because. Well, you know Linda, president of the undergrad chapter? Well, she told me the new sorors were weak. She said they weren't like us. You know how we talked back and gave quick answers when they tried us with questions? Linda said the new sorors were boring." Robin laughed. "Linda said the new sorors were scared all the time." Her mind returning to her days on line, She tossed her head back and laughed again. "And you know Linda. She likes the pledgees when they get fresh. Big Sisters laugh about the fresh things pledgees say when the pledgees aren't around. You never know that stuff until you're a Big Sister yourself." She smiled into, "Remember how we were with our first pledgees?"

"Pledgees?" Trish chuckled. "Girl, what are you talking about? Remember how we were with our first rushees?"

"Hey, Rob!" Betsy piped wrapping her arms around the back of the passenger seat head cushion and pulling herself forward. "Take that left! You were supposed to take that left!"

Anna looked out the window. "You were supposed to take that left turn back there! You missed the turn, Rob! Tell you what. Take the next turn. I can get you from here to Club Nubia. Don't worry, ladies. We'll get there. And I'm sure there will be plenty of good looking men waiting for us when we get there." She smiled behind the thought.

"Speaking of men, Rob. Have you met any fine men lately?" Trish asked.

"I hear you, Trish." Anna added. "I know Michael wishes she'd ask him back. What a loss he took messing around and losing Rob."

"I know, Anna. Who'd have thought it would have turned out this way? I thought Rob was as good as married the way Michael and she hung out there for awhile." A smile on her face, she turned and stared at the crown of Robin's head.

Robin lowered her head sheepishly. "Oh, go on. I wasn't anywhere near getting married, and you know it. You know I've always been a one man woman. I've never dated a lot. You all dated a lot in high school and when we were at NYU. I never did."

"I know," Trish offered. "To tell you the truth, you had me worried there for awhile, Rob."

She arched her brow, "Why's that?"

"Because I didn't think you would ever open your heart and let a man in. I didn't think you would ever let yourself fall in love or even come close to falling in love."

She stared at Trish. "What?"

"I thought you would be too scared—"

Her eyes ballooned. "Scared?"

"To let a man get close to you." Trish looked away from her and stared into the starry sky. "And speaking of being a one man woman, a lot of people who aren't monogamous only aren't because they're afraid that if they are faithful and put their all into someone else, they'll get hurt."

"I never was scared to fall in love."

Chuckling, Trish smiled and said, "Rob."

"But I do know what you just said about many people is true."

Trish nodded at her. "Most people are chickens when it comes to love." She smiled at the stars. "Men are more afraid of love than women are. I think that's the reason they use sex and lack of communication to keep women at bay. Men use cheating and lack of communication as weapons against women, weapons to keep us from getting too close to them, weapons to keep themselves from falling in love and possibly, just maybe, getting hurt."

"That's what I think is wrong with some men," Betsy offered. "And I said some – not all. Some men grow up in homes without a father. I really think they resent not having a father. A mother and a father are a child's greatest loves. When a parent deserts a child, I think that sends a strong message to the child that they are not loved. So, what do some men do? They make sure nobody gets as close as daddy once was as long as they live. They won't suffer another loss like that ever, if they can help it. And I agree with you, Trish, girl. Men use cheating as a way to keep women at bay. It's sad. It's a cycle I wonder will ever be broken."

Sharon crossed her legs. "Some man, some woman, has to have the gut, the courage, to take the chance on romance. Yea. Heartbreak might be at the end of that road, but so might true love."

Insects filled the night with music. Anna squinted and pointed until Robin pulled the Z inside Club Nubia's parking lot. Row after row of compacts, luxury and sports cars filled the lot.

"Look at this parking lot!" Betsy said, pulling up on the headrest. Loretta pursed her lips. "It's packed in here."

"I knew it would be," Sharon said reaching for her purse.

Anna added, "I did too." Then she pulled down on the hem of her leather skirt.

Slowly turning the steering wheel while she glanced down the parking lot rows, Robin was silent. When Club Nubia came into view, its white paint fresh, the glass of its entrance doors shiny, her stomach turned. She bit her bottom lip and prayed for "no empty parking spaces". She was only going to the club because Dinah and Loretta made an issue out of all the sorority sisters partying together.

"So what we haven't seen each other in nearly a year," she pleaded hours before she drove to the student center. "You know I feel uncomfortable at clubs. Club Nubia is always packed. I can hang out with you all later. Go without me. Have a good time. We can hang out tomorrow. We'll all be in the city for the weekend. It's only Friday night. There's a lot of time for us to do fun things together." Less than two seconds later all the sorors shot down her pleas. Badgering her with "Stop being a loner," they gave her no choice but to join them at Club Nubia for a night of dancing and carousing, two things she was painfully inept at.

Dinah pointed and called out, "Pull in there, Rob."

Without a word, she shifted the 280ZX into first gear and parked next to a Pontiac Sunbird.

The sorority sisters hurried out of the Z. Robin pretended to hunt for her purse.

Sharon hurried her with, "Come on, Girl! Let's go party!"

Raising her head, she whispered, "I'm coming."

Cigarette smoke choked her as soon as she walked inside Club Nubia. She started blinking. Anna ran her hand across her nose, as if that would screen the thick smoke. Trish squeezed her buttocks in and excused herself while she inched beyond three tables of huddling, drinking men and women. The couples peered up and nodded and the other sorority sisters followed Trish to a long, empty table.

"Rob!"

The familiar alto voice took the shaking out of her hands. She turned quickly on her heels and smiled into Aretha's face. When she saw the gloss in Aretha's eyes, she lowered her head and said, "Hey, Aretha."

Kathleen and Bertha followed Aretha's footsteps.

After she brushed her hands over the lap of her pants, Robin sat. She looked up and pushed her chair close to the table. "Go ahead, Kathleen. Say what you were going to say."

"I can't believe you came out."

She drew her hands into her lap and folded them there. She met Kathleen and Aretha's glances. "Yes. I'm here."

"I didn't mean it like that, Rob."

"No need to offer apology, Kathleen."

"Rob, I didn't mean it like it sounded. I didn't mean it the way you took it."

"No need to apologize, Kathleen."

"I didn't mean it like that, Rob."

She laughed until she saw concern wash off Kathleen and Aretha's faces. "It's all right. Really. It's all right."

Aretha smiled softly. "Rob, you know you're my girl."

She glanced at the end of Aretha's nose. "I know."

"Look at her gloating," Aretha teased.

"If you turn your head, you'll gloat too."

"Wha-wha-wha—" Aretha stuttered. Then she turned her head and followed Robin's pointing finger.

She stared at the tall cocoa-colored man dressed in stripped baggies. "Yea. He's nice, but he's not my type."

Robin chuckled, shook her head and prayed forgiveness upon Aretha's soul.

Trish fastened her gaze on the man's handsome face. "Catch you three later." She walked onto the center floor and mixed in with a crowd of dancing couples.

Chuckling, Robin called out, "Don't fall in love in the first two minutes you're on the floor!" to Trish's moving back.

Turning, Trish winked at her. "Don't worry. I won't fall in love unless I run into Robin Hood." Then she headed for the dance floor.

Aretha leaned across the table Kathleen, Robin and she sat at. "Want something to drink?"

"I'll take a beer," Kathleen answered.

Aretha nodded. "All right. Rob?"

"I'll take an ice water."

Two song and dances later, Loretta walked away from the center floor and returned to the table. "What are you three doing over here?"

"Ordering drinks."

"Good. I need something to drink. I want a Tequila Rum."

Robin stared at Loretta while she worked to catch her breath. "What brought you back so soon?"

"Can't stay out there on that floor forever. It gets hot out there dancing after awhile."

Another voice came up behind Loretta, "It sure does."

"Betsy."

"Hey, Rob." Then Betsy asked, "Aretha, do I see you taking orders?"

"Yea."

"I'll take a strawberry daiquiri." She glanced over her shoulder when she felt a wall of heat behind her. "Dinah?"

Robin's gaze went across the table. "You all came back?"

"Everybody except Trish," Dinah answered. "She's still out there dancing cheek to cheek with that gorgeous man."

Betsy and Dinah started to laugh as they pulled chairs away from the table and sat.

"What do you want, Sharon?"

"A Tom Collins."

"Anna?"

"Scotch."

"All right. Rob?"

Her brow went up. "Water. I already told you that. I want ice water." Her brow lowered, "Please."

Anna almost stood. "Rob!"

"Lower your voice," Aretha directed.

"Take it easy, Aretha," Robin said. "I'll have a glass of ice water." Then she turned and faced Anna. "You know I don't drink."

Her gaze going from Dinah to Betsy, Anna nodded slowly before she turned to Robin and said, "I know."

Turning away from Anna's glance, Robin stared at a dark spot on the wall where a fly was splattered. Not until a petite, ebony skinned waitress neared their table, did she turn away from staring at the wall.

"May I take your orders?"

After she handed the waitress the napkin the orders were written on, Aretha sat back and offered, "I'm sure everyone came here to have a good time. Let's enjoy our drinks and do just that."

Loretta added, "After we get a few drinks in us, we can get loose."

Aretha chuckled. "Sounds like there's gonna be a party going on over here in a little while."

"Yes, Ma'am," Sharon enthused. "All I need is a little more rest, then I'm getting back out on that dance floor."

Chat circled the long table. Five minutes passed before Dinah broke the talk up with, "Here come our drinks."

Kathleen blurted, "Fast service," into the waitress' round face when she arrived with their drinks.

"Kathleen," Bertha called. "Club Nubia always has good service . . . best waitresses in town."

145

Sharon chuckled dryly. "Except when they wait on college students."

"It's as if they knew we were in college a few years ago the one or two times we came in here together." Robin said, sitting against the back of her chair and chuckling. "College students." She shook her head. "They knew we didn't have any money. They knew we were broke."

Sharon crossed her legs and sipped her Bloody Mary. "Say that, Rob."

Leaning forward, Loretta asked, "And just what do college students look like, Rob?"

Her shoulders rocked when she laughed. "Like po' folk."

Dinah said, "If you ain't telling the truth," before she raised her glass of Tom Collins and took a sip.

"Say that, Dinah," Sharon added.

"And if you're a Sistah," Dinah continued, "You know you're going to have those days when you don't have money to go to the hair dresser and get your 'do' right. That's why all the Sistahs have a pretty ribbon or ol' trusty hat or scarf."

Loretta laughed and tapped the top of Dinah's hand. "Shut up, Girl."

Anna pursed her lips. "I never wore a scarf."

Betsy said, "When I ran out of money and couldn't afford to get to the hair dresser, I always braided my hair."

Robin grinned like a fox while she patted the back of her head, one long braid reaching down to the end of her spine. "Me too."

When the table grew quiet, Loretta injected, "Shortest debate I've ever heard Rob engage in."

Dinah took a long swig of her drink.

"That's the truth," Sharon added with a chuckle.

After Dinah took another sip of her drink, she stood.

"Going to show those folks how to dance?" Loretta teased.

Before Dinah answered, she turned and finished her drink. "I sure am. Somebody get me another drink, so I'll have it when I get back. Thanks."

Anna extended her hand. "Dinah, take it easy."

Her back moving away from the table, Dinah talked over her shoulder. "Keep an eye on me, Anna. And you too, Rob."

Anna stood, pressed her palms on the table and shouted, "I don't know about Rob, but every now and then, I'll be shooting a glance in your direction."

Dinah didn't look over the top of her shoulder when she called out, "I want you to. I need you to, because I'm really going to let my hair down tonight." A second later, she let an athletic looking man take her hand inside his.

Aretha stood with a raised hand. "Wait, Dinah! I'm coming too!"

Loretta finished her drink. "Let's go, Anna and Rob. Let's go show Aretha and Dinah how to dance."

"Rob," Loretta said, "Come on, Girl. Let's go show these folks how it's done."

Robin smiled and shook her head. "No. I'm going to sit this one out."

Tilting her head, Loretta smiled softly at her. "All right."

"Rob?" Anna called back to the table.

"What?" She scarcely peered up.

"Watch my purse."

"Oh, Rob might get up," Aretha offered.

Robin smiled softly while she looked at her friends standing on the dance floor. "Sure, Anna. Aretha, I'll watch your purse too."

Aretha cajoled, "Oh, Rob."

"It's okay."

"Sure?'

She nodded. "Sure."

"Well," Aretha said turning toward the dance floor, "Okay then."

Robin took her gaze away from the dance floor and stared at the top of the table.

Sharon's voice was loud. "Come on, ladies! Let's get out on that floor. The DJ's got the music bumping tonight."

Loretta rocked her hips. "Sure, Girl. If these men have good sense, they'll ask us to dance."

"Say that," Betsy added. "They'll realize what they're missing."

"They're some cute guys in here too," Anna offered while she stood next to Loretta and scanned the dance floor for handsome, available men.

"Hopefully none of them are married. The first guy Trish met was married."

Betsy turned and looked over her shoulder at Sharon. "How do you know he was married?"

Loretta pushed her shoulder into Sharon's. "Look at that, Girl." Both their heads turning, they smiled while they watched a stocky man strut in front of them.

Sharon chuckled while her gaze went from the crown of the back of the man's head to his round, tight behind. "Loretta, you always did have a good eye for men."

"I know."

"Betsy likes 'em in suits and ties," Dinah said before she turned and followed a light skinned man as he walked to his table and sat.

"I do too," Loretta said.

"Suit and tie men fool Betsy every time."

Dinah asked, "How's that, Loretta?" but she was more interested in the man sitting three tables down from where they stood.

"They're never rich."

Her chest shaking from hard laughter, Betsy patted Loretta's forearm. "Look. Look."

A smile went across Loretta's face. "Eww, Betsy, you do spot them." Leaning close to her ear, she whispered, "He's so fine."

With a twisted mouth, Betsy whispered back, "Why do you think I told you to look? I know a fine man when I see one."

Dinah leaned passed her and looked at Sharon. "So how do you know the first guy Trish met here tonight is married?"

"Some lady here's a good friend of his wife's."

Loretta pursed her lips, "Trifling."

"The other guy must be single. I haven't seen Trish in over half an hour."

"I know, Sharon," Betsy agreed. "Trish always meets someone, someone who has as much interest in her as she has in them when we go out."

Loretta added, "It's that long pretty hair of hers."

"I know, and those long legs," Dinah said, lengthening the portrait of Trish.

"Let's face it. Trish's a poster girl."

Dinah agreed with several quick nods. "She is."

"Look, ladies."

Dinah giggled. "I want the tall one."

"Good," Betsy announced with authority. "I want the one wearing the GQ tie."

Loretta's gaze went to the side of Sharon's head. "And?"

"I want the one with the suit on."

An hour passed. Robin turned down a fifth request to dance. She lowered her gaze and pushed her chair so close to the edge of the table her stomach hurt. A second later, she pushed away from the table and took her thoughts outside the club. She thought about games Dinah, Betsy, Loretta and she played at the park in Johnson City when they were little girls. They always took their baby sisters to the park with them on Saturday mornings while their mothers stayed home and cleaned house. Wherever she went at the park, Sonia held her hand. She squeezed Sonia tightly and kissed her face after she looked up at her and mumbled, "I wuv you, 'ob. I wuv you."

A woman laughed and squealed at the side of her head, and she turned her thoughts away from Sonia. The point of her elbow ached. She spent half the night with her chin tucked in her palm. Though a cute college student, his eyes dark brown, his lashes long and thick, sat two tables away from her peering at her, she was bored. Before the sun yawned in the sky, she promised herself to ask her sorors how much fun they had. At least a dozen times she asked herself what she was doing in the club, why she even came. It behooved her that after five years she felt it necessary to prove to her Sigma sisters that she was fun to be with. Except for the college student sitting two tables from her, she was the only person at the club who hadn't danced. Amid the loud crowd, she felt debased. "I deserve this," she scolded herself. "It's punishment. I know better. I shouldn't have come here. I shouldn't have come. I'm a wallflower. All night I've been nothing but a wallflower." She ran her hand across her face and told herself she had no one; she was alone. "All the sororities and fraternities must be here tonight. What a night for me to decide to let the gang drag me to a club. I know I look like a pitiful wallflower." Her elbow slipped. She caught her head before it fell against the table. A second later, she peered up to see if anyone noticed.

Two more hours passed. The college student was gone. She jerked her head up and peered into all corners of the club. A sinking feeling came over her. The college student was her only company most of the night. Locked away in her fear and shyness, he would always be a nameless face to her.

Raising her head, she surveyed the club. "Everybody's probably gotten tired of looking at me sitting by myself as much as I'm tired of sitting here by myself."

If she was not the night's driver, she knew she would be on her way home. A moment later when Dinah returned to the table, she asked, "Do you all have a way to get home tonight?"

Dinah smiled and nudged her elbow.

Turning, Robin glanced at the man standing in Dinah's shadow. She greeted him while she shook his hand loosely. Then she returned her attention to Dinah. "Well?"

Dinah nodded.

"How about the others?'

"They all have rides."

"Dinah, come here."

She pulled close to Robin's ear. Her companion stepped away from the table and turned his head, a sign to Robin that he had obvious manners.

"Make sure you go back to your hotel in, at the very least, twos. You don't know these men. Promise me you'll be the one to make sure you go home in no less than twos." She searched Dinah's face. "Promise me."

She nodded slowly. "All right, Rob. I promise. I promise."

Fifteen minutes later, a green traffic light shined in her face as she drove through quiet city streets then over the bridge and into Manhattan. Her eyelids were heavy. She stretched her neck, leaned into the headrest and widened her eyes. It took her half an hour to reach 22nd Street. The 280ZX slowed to a crawl when she pulled into the high rise's parking lot. Most of the spaces in the lot remained vacant.

At the entrance door, she nodded at the night shift doorman.

The lobby was empty. The elevator doors opened before she pressed the 'up' button. She almost smiled. She stood with her back pressed against the elevator wall. The ride to Apartment 1201 was long. The higher the elevator ascended, the tighter her head became. She had her keys in her hand before the elevator doors parted. Inside the apartment and without forethought, she kicked off her shiny, black pumps, climbed out of her pants and blouse and pulled down her stockings. She fanned her bosom while she walked across her bedroom floor and switched the air conditioner on low. She didn't notice the breakage at the side of the front door. For the first time in many nights she didn't check to insure that the safety chain was secure before she went to bed.

The air conditioner humming, she walked inside the kitchen and poured a glass of orange juice before she returned to her bedroom and sat on the bed. Taking down the Bible, she read the twenty-third division of the Psalms. She drifted to sleep with the Bible atop her stomach. When she woke, her heart raced. She stared into the hall. A shadow passed. She almost called out, "Leslie." Her mind raced. Before she drove to NYU with her sorority sisters, Leslie told her she was going over her boyfriend's and wouldn't be home all night. While she stared into the hall, she knew she was not alone.

Chapter Thirteen

The faint sound of footsteps sent a chill up Robin's spine. Pulling the blanket around her shoulders, she gazed across the room. A shadow moved close to her door. She held her breath. Sweat dotted her forehead. She swallowed hard and stared into the darkness. Silence. The shadow turned. Footsteps. They neared Leslie's bedroom then they moved forward. Slowly. Slowly. She inched onto her back and closed her eyes. Sending a chorus of prayers toward heaven, she begged God to keep her safe. Whoever was in the room bumped against a corner of Leslie's bed. Seconds later the sound of papers being slung across Leslie's dresser scared her until her shoulders shook. Time seemed to play a trick on her as she lay in her bed. A moment became eternity. Fear took hold of her back and seemingly froze it to the mattress. The sound of papers falling to the floor. Hurrying feet. They grew loud. Then Leslie's room grew silent. Scurrying footsteps. A bump in the hallway. The intruder stared at the lump in the bed her body formed. The shadow loomed over her. She held her breath. Whoever was in her room had stopped moving. They hovered over her for the longest moment. Then she felt herself breathing again. The intruder had turned away. Her ears working to pick up sound like a hollow cave, she bit away tears and listened while the intruder limped across her bedroom floor, down the hall and out the front door.

Alone in her bedroom she curled on her side and wept. It was a long time before she mustered the nerve to enter the hall and lock the front door. Her hands shook when she reached for the safety chain. It was broke.

Hurrying to the telephone, she dialed 911 and waited.

"911."

"Yes. My name is Robin Carlile. Someone. An intruder has been in my apartment. They just left. Please send someone now. Right away."

The clerk working the 911 line asked her a string of questions. Twenty minutes later she looked up and listened to the sound of fists drumming the front door. It was the police. She told them she was in bed when she woke to the sound of footsteps in the hall. "Yes." She locked the apartment's front door before she went to bed, she told them. "No." She had no enemies that she knew of. She had a roommate. They got along. "No." No one was after her roommate. "No." She didn't want to come down to the station. "Yes." She'd like them to check the stairwells and elevators before they left. "Yes. Yes, please," she told them. "Please notify the front desk and the doorman and have them check everyone's ID before they allow anyone to enter the building for the remainder of the night." And "yes" she'd be all right. She thanked them for coming, followed their precautions then shut and locked the door. When she passed the dining room, she stared at a chair. Pulling the chair by its arms, she pushed the top of its spine beneath the front door knob.

Returning to her bed, she pulled down the Bible and read the twenty-third division of the Psalms again. "The Lord is my shepherd, I shall not want. He makes me lie down in green pastures, he leads me beside quiet waters, he restores my soul. He guides me in paths of righteousness for his name's sake. Even though I walk through the valley of the shadow of death, I will fear no evil, for you are with me; your rod and your staff, they comfort me. You prepare a table before me in the presence of my enemies. You anoint my head with oil; my cup overflows. Surely goodness and love will follow me all the days of my life, and I will dwell in the house of the Lord forever." Her hands still shaking, she turned the Bible to Psalm chapter 34 and read verse four. "I sought the Lord, and he answered me; he delivered me from all my fears." Closing the Bible, she turned and looked into the hall. "You've kept me this far, God," she said. "I know you're not going to let anything happen to me now." Then she stood, closed and locked her bedroom door, turned out the light, and, climbing back in bed, tried to fall to sleep.

An hour. That's the longest she slept before she woke and pulled the blanket around her shoulders again. Her brow arched. The rustling noise silenced. Telling herself her mind was playing tricks on her she lay down again. A moment later she was climbing out of bed. She tiptoed across the floor to her phone. The second she raised the receiver, the console lit up. Her eyes bulged. The living room. Remembering that the console in the living room lit up whenever she used her phone, she lowered the receiver to the cradle and stepped back. She listened with intent. She heard feet shuffling then she heard a moan. She hurried across the floor and reached beneath her bed. Her eyes ballooned. Her mind raced. She couldn't find her typewriter. Crawling on her knees, she peered beneath the bed. Her mouth fell open. Her typewriter was gone. When she heard someone move down the hall, she reached for the nearest object under her bed. A moment later, she opened her bedroom door slowly. Slowly. She stared into the hallway. Her heart beat so hard, her chest hurt. She tiptoed down the hall carrying her skateboard. At the edge of the living room, she raised the skateboard over her head and tripped. Her voice pierced the air with a shrill scream when she landed on the sofa.

Leslie sat Indian Style. Sweat coated her brow. Her back was arched. She was wrapped in a wool sweater and a leather coat.

After she climbed to her feet, Robin surveyed the room. Seeing that Leslie and she were alone, she guessed Drew carried Leslie inside the apartment. Scent of marijuana and cigarette smoke was so strong in the living room, she thought she was still at Club Nubia.

Leslie hugged her shoulders and rocked back and forth. The marijuana scent thickened and Robin pinched her nose.
"Leslie, not tonight," she moaned. "Not tonight. I need you to be strong tonight. Somebody's been here and," Raising her hands to her face, she wiped away a tear, "I'm scared."
Her head resting against the top of the sofa, Leslie looked at her and whispered, "Please. Help me. I feel sick."
"Leslie, don't you hear me? Someone was here. There was a stranger in our house. I had to call—"
Tears welled in Leslie's eyes. Her bottom lip quivered, and she whined, "I'm sick."
"Leslie, please. This has not been an easy night. By the grace of God, we're both all right."
"Rob." Her head bowed and her eyes closed. Her breathing was even until she began to snore.
Taking in a deep breath, Robin moved close to her and said, "Come on, Girl. Let me help you up." She grabbed her shoulders and pulled up. Pain raced up her left arm and created a tight spot in the center of her chest. Without stopping to catch her breath, she continued to pull Leslie up by the shoulders. "Come on, Girl. Let me get you washed up and into bed. You're tired. You need to rest. Come on. Let's get you on your feet and into the bathroom, so I can wash you up. We're almost there. We're almost to the bathroom." Reaching to the bathroom sink, she lowered her shoulders and looked down at Leslie. Her eyes were closed; her head rolled and bobbed. As if a sleeping Leslie would speak back to her, she continued to talk out loud. "Let me put some soap and water on your face." She pushed her knee into her shoulder to keep her from sliding to the floor. "Here we go." She dabbed her face with a wash cloth. While she washed her face she glanced at the walls then again at Leslie. She whispered soft prayers. "Lord, help us all. Teach us to be more thankful for there is so much to be thankful for. Teach us to count our days, dear Lord. Help me to help Leslie. She's my friend. She's special. If she has gotten herself involved in something wrong, Lord, make me willing to be used by you to help set it right. Help me not to be self-righteous or to see myself above or beneath her." She took in a deep breath and tossed her head back. "Lord, Jesus, please help me with my fears and with my insecurities. Thank you, Jesus, for all your help, for everything. When I start to feel anxious, scared and alone, tell me you're with me. Just like your holy word says I am never alone in you. You are with me always. Just like you were with me earlier tonight when someone was in here, you are always with me. Thank you, master. And Lord, please forgive me for sinning and going to Club Nubia tonight. I didn't go there to witness, so I know it was wrong. I put people's judgments, impressions and

thoughts of me ahead of you and your way. I'm sorry, not because I didn't have fun at Club Nubia, but because I went against your Holy Spirit. And Lord, whoever was in here tonight and whatever is going on, keep Leslie and me safe. Please, Lord. Thank you for not letting us get hurt. In Jesus' sweet name. Amen." She rinsed and dried Leslie's face then she said, "Come on. Let's get you to bed."

At the edge of Leslie's bed, she stood and released a heavy sigh. "Finally," she said while she peered down on Leslie who she recently dressed in her favorite silk pajama set.

Since she turned the air conditioner on two hours ago all the furniture in the apartment went cold. Hurrying across the floor, she turned the air off. Cool air pierced her thighs and calves when she turned away from the thermostat. The rising sun was moving an orange glow across the sky. Eager to distance herself from the fear the intruder brought into her life, she thought about editing her latest play. Without turning on lights, she knew exactly where everything was. Her spiral notebook was in the top drawer of the file cabinet closest to her bed. Walking on her toes, she scarcely made a sound. Notebook in hand, she went into the living room and parted the drapes. Though it was no longer pitch black outside, the moon still hovered in the sky. The dawn was clear. She raised her head and gazed up at the moon. She didn't turn from staring into the sky until she heard Leslie's feet scrape the floor.

"Les," she whispered, hoping her ears deceived her.

"Rob-nn. Rob-nn. Rob-nnnn," she cried. She stretched her arms toward Robin then quickly drew them back.

"Leslie," she whispered at the edge of the sofa, her own stale breath rushing up her nose.

"Rob-nn. Rob-nn. Rob-nn. Rob-nnnn. Rob-nnnnn. Rob-nnnnn."

"Leslie, get up." Her mind went to Tuesday when *Mirage* magazine's December 1 issue hit the press. She walked from the high rise and bought a copy at Loew's. At newspaper stands she saw articles headlining Leslie's latest cinematic triumphs. *"Leslie Fletcher. Hollywood's Courageous Actress,"* the *Mirage* cover article read. *"Leslie Fletcher has never been afraid to tell the truth,"* a second article began. *"Leslie Fletcher, how does she do it? How does she keep us asking for more?"* a third article led. *"Leslie, thanks for letting us grow up with you,"* a fourth article concluded. At Loew's and now in the living room, it was clear to her that New York City, with its eight million residents, was anxious to watch her roommate live out the steps to her life. Time and again storeowners told her that slicks featuring Leslie sold out in record time at record numbers.

"Rob-nn. Rob-nn. Rob-nnnn." She shook her head from side to side and screamed, "Rob-nn. Rob-nn. Rob-nnnn."

"Leslie, come on," she pleaded with an outstretched arm. "Take my hand and get up. It's been one rough night. I simply do not have the strength to pick you up off the floor again."

She gritted her teeth and growled, "No." Then she slapped Robin's hand out of her view.

Taking a step back, she snapped, "Then, get up." When Leslie started to cry, she turned away from her and said, "Stay there then. I already told you somebody was here earlier. I could have been killed. And now look at you. You're on your hands and knees again. I just put you in bed. Leslie, please. Please stop."

Her weeping grew loud when Robin neared the edge of the living room.

"Leslie." She placed her hand midway down the room's entrance wall.

"Rob-nn."

"Leslie. Stop it." She shook when she heard herself scream.

"Rob-nn," Leslie called back equally as loud.

Leaving her place at the edge of the living room, she stomped across the floor until she stood inches above Leslie who lay on the floor. "Get up!"

"No. You come down here with me."

"What?"

"Ro—"

"What?"

"Ro—"

"What?"

"Rob-nn."

"What did you say?"

"Rob-nn."

"What did you say to me?"

She buried her face in the carpet and wept.

"No." She leaned over her. "What did you say? I dare you to say it again."

Her shoulders heaved. "I said come down here with me."

Moving her hands away from her hips and turning sharply on her heels, Robin glared at her. "I will never lower myself. Never. Never. Never. You get up." Then she said, "I'm going into the kitchen," and walked away from Leslie.

"Rob-nn."

"Will you let me fix myself something to eat in peace? I could have been maimed. I could have been killed. And all you can do is think about yourself. You always have to be the center of attention. Made me pick you off the sofa and take you into the bathroom. And here you are in the living room all over again. You could have walked into the bedroom before. You just wanted me to shower you with attention. And I always fall for your tricks. After all this time, I still fall for your tricks."

"I was sick. I was not acting. I was sick. Can't you see that? I'm still sick."

Reaching for a spoon, she stirred a glass of tea. "You always have to have things your way. You always have to be the focus of attention. I could have been killed. Right here in this apartment. Tonight. You could have come home to stare at my corpse, but you don't care." She took in a deep breath. "You always have to-"

Leslie listened to the silence coming away from the kitchen before she asked, "What's wrong?"

She sighed. "Never mind. Besides, I don't think you'd hear me even if I repeated myself for the third time."

"What?"

"Never mind. I'm just upset. I'm still shaken. That's all." She tasted the tea before she lowered her voice and spoke evenly. "Someone was here tonight. I was in bed and I saw a shadow. Someone went through papers on your dresser. Then they stood over me. Right over me. I was so scared."

"Did you ca—"

"Yes. I called the police. They checked out the entire apartment, the stairwells and the elevators. They notified the front desk. Everything's okay. I guess. I just don't need any more pressure right now. That's all. And I certainly don't need you acting like you're helpless when you're not."

"Probably a burglar."

"Don't be so sure. I don't think so. I don't think it was. Still it's better to be safe—"

"They won't come back."

"How do you know?"

She shook her head. "I just don't think they will."

"Whatever. I'm tired. I'm mentally exhausted. I'm not going around in circles with you."

"I'm glad you were in bed sleeping when the burglar came. You don't have one mean bone in your body. I can't see you hurting anyone. I can't see you fighting back."

She chuckled. "Don't be so sure about that."

The volume in Leslie's voice went up. "And you mean to tell me after going through an attempted burglary you were going to get up and come in here and start writing?"

"I needed to relax. I still need to relax."

"So you decide to come in here and write?"

"Whatever works. I just had a huge scare." She lowered then shook her head. "It was awful, just awful."

Leslie chuckled. "I don't get you. You're scared. We almost get robb—"

"Why do you keep saying it was a burglary? The cops were here. Nothing was taken. Why are you so sure it was a burglary?"

"Rob, I don't know for sure. I don't know what it was, okay?"

"Well, stop talking like you're so sure. Stop talking like you just know. You weren't even here. I was the one who was here. All alone. I could have been killed. I don't care what you say. I could have been killed."

"So you get up, come in here and try to write? You're a nut."

"At least I don't have people rumbling through my papers."

Leslie leaned forward. "Is that what happened?"

"I already told you that. I just told you—" She waved her hand. "Never mind. Whoever it was. I heard them in your room. Turning over papers. Looking for something." She narrowed her brow and pointed it at Leslie. "You aren't into anything, are you?"

The veins in Leslie's temples bulged. She shouted, "I have nothing to do with what happened here tonight. Don't you dare. Don't you dare try to say I caused this. Don't you dare. I'm as scared and upset as you are."

"Yea. And you're also a very good actress."

Her bottom lip dropped. "Wha-- Apologize. Apologize to me right now. Right now. I mean it, Rob. Apologize to me. That wasn't fair, and you know it. I don't know what's gotten into you. You must have really been shaken by the burg—"

"There you go again, trying to cover it all up by calling it a burglary. I told you nothing was taken. The police checked. Do you hear me? Nothing was taken. Hence. It was not a burglary. Not. Not. Not a burglary."

She pursed her lips and stared at the floor.

"And about me coming in here to write. At least I'm not too drunk to walk across the floor without leaning on someone. I see you. You're not the least concerned about what happened here tonight."

"I am!"

"You don't even know what it is to live anymore. You're losing your grip on what's real and what's make-believe."

"Do we hav--."

"Acting is a mad profession. I'm convinced of that. After living with you I am thoroughly convinced of that. A person can't be all there to want to live through and act out other people's pains and confusion. Then again, maybe that's why you chose the profession." She stood at the edge of the living room. She was surprised to find Leslie sitting on the sofa. "Like I said earlier, you weren't near death sick after all."

"My head's spinning."

"When are you going to learn to stop making yourself sick?"

"My eyes hurt, and my stomach's turning."

"I get so tired of you driving yourself to desperate places. Living with you, I have to learn how to protect myself."

"So   long   as   you're   not   still   mad   at   me."

"I was scared from seeing that shadow. Whoever it was. Living in the city has numbed me to crime a lot but not to the point where being alone with an intruder doesn't scare me."

"Yet, you're always so sensible. Only hours after an attempted burglary, look at you. Cool and calm."

She nibbled her bottom lip. "I'm not cool and calm. What happened tonight scared me real bad. Real bad. I do trust that God will take care of me. And besides, I don't see you shaking."

Laying her head against the back of the sofa, she said, "Rob, I'm stoned. You're not."

She sat next to her. "Oh, so that's what it is."

"It doesn't matter what happens to you or when it happens. You're always cool, calm and collective. Think that doesn't get on my last nerve? You're always breaking your neck to put your best foot forward. You never let your guard down. I wonder if you've ever really been you instead of this woman you think everybody else thinks you're supposed to be."

"This is who I am. I'm always being me. Whether you like it or not, this is me. You and I are different, that's all."

"Is that what it is?"

"That's what it is."

"Well, it's too late anyway. You're stuck with me.'

"Think so?"

"And I'm stuck with you."

"Now you're defending yourself."

She cradled her stomach with her hands until a wave of nausea passed over her. "No. I'm telling the truth."

Robin watched her face contort. "Feeling sick again?"

She moaned and laid her head against Robin's shoulder.

"I don't know why you alcoholics and junkies insist on making yourselves sick. Could be what the intruder was after. Money to buy drugs with. Probably was stoned when they came in here. Guess that's why they didn't find what they were looking for. Probably too stoned to know the floor from the ceiling. I don't know why you people insist on ruining your own lives, the only life you'll ever have. You're not getting another life, Les. You're not getting another one. This is it. So, you better do something with it."

She stared at the blank wall and shrugged.

Robin pursed her lips and shook her head. "You don't even know. You just don't get it."

"It's a part of who I am."

"No, it's not." Leaning close to Leslie and lowering her voice she asked, "Why were you on the floor crying earlier?"

Chapter Fourteen

Leslie broke her vow not to attend or watch an award ceremony and flew to Los Angeles. It was Robin. Late in February she came into Leslie's bedroom, stared at her and pleaded, "Go with me. Michael's dancing in the opening number. I want to see if we can talk and work things out. I haven't seen him in nearly two years. I need you there with me to do this. Please."

Sitting cross-legged on the bed she shrugged and waited for Leslie's answer. Despite what she told Leslie and her sorority sisters she couldn't get Michael out of her heart. She hadn't stopped thinking about him since they broke up.

Shaking her head, Leslie told her, "I don't know why you're putting yourself through this. I may as well tell you now. I never liked Michael. He never was your type. Michael's a ladies man. You deserve so much better. You're a first class woman. You're going to make some man very, very happy. I just don't think that man's Michael. You can do so much better."

"I appreciate your honesty, but you know how much Michael means to me."

"Yea." She kicked her feet out. "He was your first love. You're never going to forget him."

"How do you know he was my first love?"

Tossing her head back, she gazed at the ceiling and rolled her eyes. "Well. I don't know for certain that Michael was your first love. Then again," she raised her shoulders. "Maybe I do. I've never heard you talk about any other man in the five years we've been living together."

"Maybe that's because Michael was and is very special."

"Maybe that's because Michael is the first man you ever allowed to get close to you."

Turning away from her, she said, "You always think like that." Then she faced her again. "Will you go with me? Please?"

"Rob, look at me and tell me not once did you notice how selfish Michael can be. Sure. You're into your writing like I'm into acting, but Michael – he's only about making it to the top."

"What's wrong with wanting to excel, wanting to make your dreams come true? I think that's a very good quality in a person. And Michael doesn't think about dancing and success all the time. He's a very well rounded person. I also never knew you had such a dislike for him."

She chuckled. "You're my best friend. I know I can be obnoxious, but I'd never hurt you like that. I toed the line. I kept my feelings and thoughts about Michael to myself. I'm only telling you now because you two are no longer together."

She looked at her and smiled. A second later she lowered her head.
"You knew, didn't you?"
"How do you think Michael will react to seeing you again?"
"Answer me, Les. You knew. You knew didn't you?"
"Knew what?"
"Knew Michael was seeing Paulette?"
"Rob."
"No. Answer me."
"What's it matter at this point?"
"I want to know."
Straightening her spine, she stared across the room. "I didn't know.
I did hear through the grapevine that Diane intended to introduce Paulette to
him at one of her parties. But I thought she just wanted them to meet since
they both dance. It was all around the same time I was asking you how
Michael and you were doing. I even went to Diane's one Saturday and told
her to mind her own business, not to get Paulette and Michael to talking –
about anything. Not dancing, not anything. Of course, Diane didn't listen.
Even after I threatened to put my hands on her, she still didn't listen."
Robin's eyes swelled. "Diane?"
"Yea. Diane and Paulette go way back."
"I know that, but why would she—"
"You know how Di—"
"That. That. That. Oh. She plotted the whole thing."
She watched Robin's brow tighten. "I don't think so. True. She
had every intention of meddling. She always does. Because of Diane, I'm
not with Drew anymore." She chuckled. "Not that I miss him." Leaning
back on the bed, she laughed outright. "I think Diane and Paulette are like a
tag team. And the games those two play."
Lowering her head into her hands, she said, "Diane never liked me.
She's never liked me. Ever since I turned down her drugs. She hates my
belief in God. She hates the way I live my life. And isn't that stupid? I've
never done one unkind thing to her. Not once have I been mean to her.
Since those early parties when I told her I didn't do drugs, she's been out to
get me. I don't know why I never saw it coming."
Leslie gazed at the side of her head.
"I know. I know," Robin said nodding. "You think I'm too nice."
"You didn't hear me say anything."
"Well. I know what you're thinking."
"This one time there's a very good chance that you do."
Tears pooled in her eyes. Mills. Jamaica. The arts. Late night
conversations. Candle light diners. The beach. The Theatre. Christmas.
New Years. Birthday celebrations. Long walks through Central Park.

Warm kisses that linger. Valentine's Day. She missed Michael. She ached to hear his voice croon out "I love you" while he looked deeply inside her eyes.

Releasing a deep breath Leslie extended her hand and asked, "Where are the tickets?"

Pushing off the bed, Robin left the room and rounded the corner. She walked to her own bedroom dresser. When she returned, she extended her arm and handed Leslie four tickets.

Leslie arched her brow while she read the wording on the tickets. Finished reading, she raised her voice. "You're sitting on the second row. You must be a winner!" She turned the tickets over twice. She shook her head. "You have to be a winner."

Robin shrugged and twisted her mouth.

"Did Michael tell you he was dancing or did—"

"I found out through the grapevine."

"Rob," she waited for Robin to face her. "Do you still love him?"

Turning her back to Leslie, she asked, "Who?"

Leslie lowered her arms to her sides. "Don't be coy. You know exactly who I'm talking about."

Facing Leslie again, she shrugged.

Leslie walked to her dresser and laid the tickets down. "So?"

Lowering her head, she stared at her hands. "I suppose I do."

She gazed hard inside Robin's face. "You suppose you do?"

"Yes."

"When do you think you'll know for sure?" She chuckled. "Michael and you dated for nearly three years and you're not sure if you love him or not?" She threw her head back and laughed.

Robin's brow narrowed. "Yes. I love Michael. You know I love Michael. I always have."

No longer laughing, she leaned forward and stood erect. "And when do you suppose you'll stop?"

"Loving Michael?"

She smiled like a fox. "Is there an echo in here?"

Taking her gaze to the ceiling, Robin rolled her eyes. "No. There's not an echo in here." Then she took her gaze off the ceiling and stared at the wall on the other side of the bedroom. "And what a wack question." She faced her. "You obviously don't know what love is." She laughed. "After all this time, after all the relationships you've been in and out of, don't tell me that you, Leslie Fletcher, do not know what love is. Please don't tell me that. If you knew what love was you wouldn't have asked me that question." Her laughter subsided. "You love people for life. Once you start loving a person, nothing they do or say can make you stop loving them. You may love them in a different way, but you never stop loving them."

"Well. Let me rephrase the question." She stared blankly at her. "Are you still in love with Michael?'

Painful memories snaked around her thoughts. She bowed her head and looked at the floor. Her bottom lip went inside her mouth. She nibbled on it. Then she shrugged and peered up.

"Well?"

She stared at her hands as if they were filled with right answers. "I'm not sure."

"Do you think Michael is still in love with you?"

Another shrug introduced her answer. "He could be. Who knows?"

"Rob, he hasn't called you in more than a year . . . nearly two years."

"Everyone needs their space, Les."

"No one needs, wants or will tolerate two years of space when they are in love, not from the person they are in love with. Now you can stand over there and play that shy, innocent girl role, but I know you know that. That much I know you know."

"I know," she said while she nodded. "Michael and I love one another."

Walking in her footsteps, Leslie crossed the floor. "That's not what I asked you."

She released a deep breath. Then she lowered her hands. "You wouldn't understand Michael and my relationship."

"What do you mean I wouldn't understand Michael and your relationship?" At once, she turned up her nose and pursed her lips. "As many times as my heart's been broken and you say something like that to me? I'm standing over here trying to figure out how you could say something like that. I, Leslie Fletcher, queen of failed romance, understand every conceivable relationship. You know how many different men I've tried to love, how many men have come in and out of here only to break my heart. How many broken promises have come my way. You can't stand there and say something like that to me." She sighed. "I wouldn't understand Michael and your relationship." Tossing her hands into the air, she turned her gaze toward the ceiling and rolled her eyes. "I don't understand Michael and your relationship." She stuck her finger against the center of her chest. "Rob, Michael's a player, and you're a practicing Christian."

Robin crossed her arms. "Christian men are players too." Rolling her eyes, she continued with, "In case you didn't know."

"I know that," she answered with a dry chuckle.

"Christians are only sinners saved by God's grace."

"Rob, I know. You've told me a thousand times."

Going to the bed, Robin sat. The mattress squeaked when it caught her weight. When the bed settled, the space around her hips caved in.

"Has it ever occurred to you," Crossing the floor taking long strides, she stopped inches in front of Robin. "That Michael and you have less in common than you ever thought?"

Robin gazed at the blank wall across the room.

"Michael is like most men, Rob. He's not down for being in love with a woman who wants to wait until she's married to go to bed. Like most men, Michael follows the pulse of his hormones, not the beat of his heart. I admit most times that's unfortunate, but it's true. I've never lied to you, and I won't start now. You are better off with Michael out of your life. I know you don't believe that right now, but it's true." She nodded. "Yes. Yes. I believe Michael once was in love with you. However, I also believe he has fallen out of love with you. Michael's not in love with you anymore, Rob. No. No," she said shaking her head. "Michael has gone one hundred percent Hollywood. Michael is in love with his career. Working with all those Pop and Rhythm and Blues acts, he's become more of a choreographer than a dancer. He's getting paid now, and I do mean paid. He goes back and forth from New York to California now more than I do. All the acts he's worked with this past year, I know he has to be putting in sixteen and eighteen hour work days. He must only work, eat and sleep. As much work as he's doing, he certainly doesn't have time to do much else."

Robin dropped her gaze and watched her fingers move while she twiddled them. "Have you ever seen Michael with anyone when you were in California?" She shrugged. "Or here in the city?" When she peered up, she hoped Leslie would answer 'no'.

Seconds passed before Leslie stopped turning Robin's question in her head. For the first time in many years, she gave lying a great deal of consideration. She waved her hand and answered, "Oh. It doesn't matter. That's not important."

Robin twiddled her fingers. She stared into her lap. "You saw him with somebody else."

"Did I say that?"

"No. But you didn't deny it either."

She cocked her head to the side. "Rob."

Tears pooled in her eyes. "You just don't want to hurt my feelings."

"You never hurt mine."

"Les."

"Friends don't hurt each other's feelings . . At least not on purpose, they don't."

"Les?"

"Yea?"

She raised her head. ""I am still in love with Michael."

She sat next to her. "It's okay. Other people do it all the time." A soft smile on her face, she added, "But Michael's not marrying material, and whether you admit it or not—" Her smiled widened. "You want to get married."

She turned and faced her. "I do not."

She leaned her shoulder into Robin's. "Yes, you do." They swayed from side to side while they leaned into each other's shoulder. When they stopped moving, they laughed for a long time.

Two days later Robin helped Leslie pick out her gown, and Leslie helped Robin pick out her pant suit. Not even a week passed before Wednesday, February 21, 1991 rolled onto the calendar. It was the night of the Grammy Awards Presentation. In Los Angeles at the Shrine Auditorium, Robin sat next to Leslie. Leslie sat next to her date, Frank Brown, an electric guitarist. With his long, black curls dipping over his forehead, Frank, dressed in a white tuxedo, took Leslie's breath each time she turned to look at him.

During Michael and his dance company's routine, Leslie glanced at Robin. Each time she did, Robin turned away. Whenever Leslie looked at Michael dancing across the polished stage floor, Robin peered at the side of Leslie's head.

In his hip-hop style, Michael mastered the stage. His choreography was riveting. Because he danced mainly center stage and smiled while he popped, spun and tapped, Robin, sitting cross-legged only feet away from the stage, thought he was looking and smiling at her. His dance number finished, the Shrine Auditorium grew loud with the noise of thunderous applause. Soon the audience was on its feet. Tears pooled in Robin's eyes while she watched Michael blow kisses into the air and bow. Emotions rose and tugged at her insecurities until a knot formed in her stomach. She closed her eyes and rolled forward. She wanted to toss her head back and scream, "Michael, I'm ready to be loved. Even if it means I might lose someone close to my heart the way I lost my baby sister, I'm ready. Even if it means the object of my affections might be deeply hurt at some point in life and reject me the way Mama has, I'm ready. I'm not scared of love anymore. I want to be loved." But, she didn't. Instead, she bit her bottom lip, locking in her emotions, stood erect, opened her eyes and stared at the stage.

Moments passed before the audience returned to their seats. Crossing her legs at the thigh, Robin leaned back in her chair and pulled down on her suit jacket. The knot in her stomach moved into her throat. Balling her hand, she brought it to her mouth and bit down on her knuckles. Michael and his dance company exited the stage. Replacing them was Linda Mason, an internationally acclaimed gospel singer. She presented the award for Best Female Gospel Singer. "Ladies and Gentlemen, these next ladies are some of the world's greatest singers," Linda said.

Robin didn't hear her. She waited for Michael to leave the backstage area and return to the auditorium. Nostalgia clouded her thoughts. She couldn't stop thinking about the first time Michael and she met at Mills Clothing Factory. So long ago, and she was still in love with him.

A shadow interrupted her memories. It was Michael. When he rounded the corner and entered the auditorium, she fastened her gaze upon him and followed him to his seat. The knot in her stomach returned. This time it stabbed at her love for Michael and made her heart ache. Next to Michael sat a wide-eyed, long legged dark skinned woman. Although Robin never saw the woman before she created a list of reasons she should choose not to like the woman. A moment passed. She turned away from staring at Michael and the woman. She gawked at the stage and blinked back tears.

Leaning in front of Frank, Leslie tapped her forearm and whispered, "Rob?"

She darted her gaze. It finally fell on Leslie.

"You okay?"

Rolling her eyes and swallowing hard, she pulled down on her suit jacket and turned away from Leslie.

"Rob?"

Pursing her lips, she lifted her head and stared at the ceiling.

"Rob?"

She turned her head slowly. "What?"

"You okay? You all right?"

While she leaned back in her chair, she nodded and said, "Yea. Yes. Yes. Yes."

With that, Leslie leaned against the spine of her own chair with a twisted mouth.

A raspy voice interrupted her thoughts. "Should we announce the winner?" The woman, a satin jacket warming her shoulders and a long, ankle length gown covering her thin frame, worked to interest the audience in the next award.

Her male companion lengthened the tease with, "Aw, who wants to know?"

The female presenter extended her hand and said, "The envelope."

"Yes, Ma'am."

"Thank you, kind gentleman."

A snicker rose from the audience.

The microphone echoed the crackling noise the opening envelope made. "And the winner is—"

"Wait."

The male presenter asked, "Now what is it?"

"Were you nominated this year?"

"Come to think of it, I wasn't."

"If it helps, neither was I."

The audience chuckled lightly.

"Guess we best announce the winner."

"Or the audience will attack us."

The audience's chuckle thickened and became laughter.

Pulling their heads together, the two presenters chorused, "And the winner is!"

At the conclusion of the 31st Annual Grammy Awards Presentation, Leslie folded her program and placed it in the seat of her chair. Down from her, Robin folded her program and stuffed it inside her pocketbook. Before Robin closed her pocketbook, Leslie looked at her and asked, "Ready?"

With a nod she followed Leslie and Frank backstage. Midway backstage, Leslie stopped walking.

Sensing that Leslie and Robin wanted to be alone, Frank whispered, "Catch you later, Baby," in Leslie's ear, then he walked on.

As soon as Robin neared her side, Leslie asked, "Are you sure you want to do this?"

Ire pulsed in her and darkened her skin. She narrowed her brow and stepped back.

Leslie lowered her voice, "Sorry."

She was quick. "I'm absolutely sure that I want to do this."

Turning they resumed their walk backstage.

Television screens, print and radio reporters, cameramen, musicians, soloists and their invited guests crowded the backstage area. Badges went around the performers' necks like long, ugly jewelry. Leslie's gaze darted like radar while she walked inches in front of Robin. Though she searched for Michael, the first person she saw was Amanda Gaynor. When she glanced at Amanda's date, she clucked her tongue. Tom Jackson, her own boyfriend six years ago, stood beside Amanda meeting her requests like he'd been born to serve her. If not for Robin breathing down her neck, Leslie would have laughed outright. She found her thoughts going to Frank. She wanted to pull him to her side, show him off. He was much better looking than Tom ever was, ever would be. She peered at Amanda out of the corners of her eyes. Amanda wasn't aware but she knew about her attempt to contact Frank for a date by telephoning his publicist two weeks ago.

Her gaze falling on Frank, Leslie smiled. Three friends surrounded him. They laughed and talked until their voices rose and fell like roller coasters. Although she hoped to spend the night alone with Frank sipping wine and listening to old Charlie Parker cuts, listening to the laughter, she entertained the notion of spending the night partying with Frank and his friends.

"Looks like Frank's having a good time."

She almost gawked at Robin. "So you decided to talk." She chuckled. "Yes. Frank's with his crew."

"Are you two going out to eat?"

She stopped walking and stood next to a local affiliate television station's crew. She turned and faced Robin. Before she could answer her, one of the station's roving reporters stuck a microphone below her mouth.

Leslie stepped back. Her brow narrowed and rose. Her nose flared and her mouth tightened. The lack of grace over anxious reporters displayed when they requested an interview amazed her. "This money thing is a two way street," she remembered shouting at Donald one day two years ago. "You spend too much time telling me how the media holds the keys to my success. Reporters only interview celebrities who are good copy. Money. Money. Money. Good copy spells money. So, don't come off to me with some failed line about how I owe my career to some celebrity reporter or tabloid photographer. If what you say is true, some of them owe their career to me."

Before Robin ducked behind a group of lead singers to avoid the reporter's stare, she glanced at Leslie. While Leslie answered the reporter's questions, Robin chuckled and shook her head.

Working with the reporter and the cameraman the reporter called to her side, Leslie was a picture of skill and manners. Not once did she swear or make impolite inference to people in the industry she didn't like. The interview lasted two minutes.

The reporter finished with her, Leslie pointed her gaze into the corner Robin hid in. Waving her hand, she called out, "Come on. Let's go grab Frank and his partners and get out of here."

Robin jerked her shoulders back, away from her. The corners of her mouth turned down. She patted the ends of her long, curly hair, then she pulled her pocketbook against her stomach. "I came here to see Michael, and I'm going to see Michael."

She gawked at her the way her mother gawked at her when she was an unruly child living at home in Connecticut.

"I came here to see Michael, and I'm going to see Michael."

"But, Rob—"

A sinister grin widened her face. "I know. I saw him with his luscious date."

Shaking her head, Leslie rolled her eyes.

"Oh, Les. Stop," she said.

Leslie met her glance.

"You've done many more gutsy things where the men in your life were concerned, and you know it."

The night she poured a gallon of water into a former boyfriend's gas tank again familiar to her, Leslie smiled when she said, "That's true."

"Oh. By the way," Robin said, moving in front of her. She approached a circle of rock and roll drummers. "I'm no longer in love with Michael. Seeing him with that woman tonight did it. I just want to step up to him, and you know I hope his lady friend is with him when I do. I want to make him more uncomfortable than he's ever been."

Drawing one side of her mouth down, Leslie gawked at her. "Looks like I've rubbed off on you a little."

She tapped Leslie's forearm.

While she followed Robin's gaze, Leslie turned slowly and peered over the crown of her shoulder.

As if she was a mime, Robin moved her lips, but she did not utter a word. She almost pointed while she mouthed, "Here comes the gossip queen of America."

Scarcely giving Leslie time to turn and monitor how close Rita Wallace was on her heels Robin called out, "Les." A dynamo Hollywood columnist, Rita knew so many celebrity secrets, big names in the industry labeled her, "Peeping Rita."

She yanked the end of Leslie's free hand and pulled her around the nearest corner. Concealing their laughter behind the palms of their hands, they rocked their shoulders while they watched Rita walk back and forth down the open passageway a few feet in front of were they stood. "Rita didn't see us," was the first thing Robin said when Rita walked to the end of the backstage area and ended her search for the popular roommates.

"Is it safe?" Leslie asked while she peeked around the corner one last time.

Stepping completely around the corner, Robin waved her forward. "She's gone. Come on. I still have one thing left to do before I'll ever allow this night to be over for me."

"Why, Robin Carlile. I do believe you are angry."

"Oh. Shut up, and come on."

"And you never tell people to shut up."

With a wave of her hand, she dismissed the words. "Oh. I've told you to shut up a thousand times. You just never heard me. I always only said it in my mind, but did I ever want you to shut up." She walked further down the backstage area. "And I'm not angry. I just want to get even with Michael."

"But that's not what you came here to do."

She turned and gawked at Leslie.

"Well. You didn't."

Trading glances, they worked their way through a throng of singers and songwriters.

"You didn't." This time Leslie gawked at her.

"I changed my mind."

"The way you didn't take your eyes off the stage, I didn't think you saw anything except Michael. I thought you forgot Frank and I were sitting next to you."

"I didn't forget about you, Les. And," she turned. "Where is Frank?"

She stopped and looked over her shoulder. "He's still back there clowning with his partners. Tell you what. Wait here while I go tell him to meet us at the main entrance in half an hour." She arched her brow. "You do think you will have found Michael and said what you made up your mind to say, don't you?"

'Half an hour?"

She chuckled. "Rob, the last week you've been repeating what seems like everything I say. I keep thinking we're in a cave."

Releasing Michael from her plot of revenge, Robin laughed.

"So, stop repeating me. Please."

When she stopped laughing, she caught her breath and said, "Okay."

"Half an hour?"

"Half an hour."

"Good. Stay here while I go tell Frank. When I come back we'll take off on a serious hunt for Michael."

With a smile, Robin nodded and said, "Okay."

Leslie no longer at her side, Robin watched a string of songwriters, musicians, producers and record company executives saunter in front of her. Several R&B vocalists, most of them male, nodded at her while they passed. A few songwriters stopped and chatted with her. Mere associates, the bulk of their conversations were filled with empty praise. Keeping to her manners, she nodded gracefully while the songwriters complimented her recent stage play. She trusted none of their well wishes. She heard the gossip, the lies they created about her being a self-righteous right-winger. She knew they were jealous of her success.

A moment later, she grinned when she looked up and saw Leslie and heard her say, "I told Frank."

"Hi, Leslie," Brenda Day, a multi-talented songwriter turned from Robin and said.

Leslie smirked before she faced Brenda. "Hi."

Brenda extended her hand. She looked at Robin while she did.

"Leslie, this is Brenda Day. And Brenda, this is Leslie Fletcher."

Brenda and Leslie shook hands.

"I saw your new movie. Oscar material."

"Thanks," Leslie said with a nod. "I saw you won a Grammy tonight."

"Yes. My third one."

Leslie's eyes swelled. "Tonight?"

After she took a step back, Brenda chuckled. "No. In my twelve year career."

"You look young," Robin injected.

"I am young, Robin. At least I think I am. I'm only twenty-eight years old." She shrugged. "I think that's young."

"I'm a year older than you are," Leslie offered. "So you're a spring chicken. Just a baby."

Brenda laughed.

"It's just that when you said you were in the business for twelve years . . . well, that's a long time. I thought you were in your forties or something. But, don't get me wrong. You don't look it. You look twenty-eight."

Brenda chuckled. "Thanks."

"And anyhow, most child stars are into acting. You're a songwriter. Most of you folk," Leslie paused and looked slowly over her shoulder at Robin. She grinned softly when she met her gaze. "Get to live normal lives. You get to stay at home and work out the skill to your profession. You can raise your babies free of nannies. You don't have to do your best at living out the life of a child while you grow up on a movie set. You writers are normal people." She smiled softly at Robin again before she turned and faced Brenda. "Know what I mean?"

Brenda nodded. "I know what you mean, and I think you're right."

"I know I'm right."

All at once, Brenda turned and faced Robin. "I thought you were nominated for a Grammy?" Then she turned and faced Leslie to make sure she hadn't overstepped her bounds. When Leslie didn't say anything, she continued. "Weren't you?"

Robin nodded. "Yes. I was nominated."

"Did you win anything?"

"Did you see me walk onstage? Did you hear me give a thank you speech?"

Leslie arched her brow when she looked at Robin.

Brenda stepped back. "Sorry."

Robin raised her hand. "No. I didn't mean anything I said sarcastically. What you said didn't hurt me. My feelings weren't hurt. I didn't mean it the way you took it."

"No. It's okay."

Leslie extended her hand. "It was nice meeting you, Brenda."

Taking Leslie's hand inside hers, Brenda said, "It was nice meeting you." Before she walked away from Robin and Leslie, she turned and waved at Robin. "Bye, Robin. I'll see you again sometime. Take care of yourself."

Robin returned Brenda her wave. "You take care too. I'll see you around. Besides. I heard you were trying to break into the movie writing business." She smiled.

"Yea."

Leaning forward, she shook Brenda's hand. When she stopped shaking her hand, she cupped it inside her own. She tapped the top of her hand and said, "I wish you the best. It's not always nice out here. Very, very competitive."

"I know."

"Later." Then she released Brenda's hand.

Leslie waited for Brenda to walk out of earshot before she turned and waved over her shoulder. "Come on. Let's go find that ex-boyfriend of yours."

"Yea. Let's go. We only have twenty something minutes before we have to head to the main entrance so we can meet with your present day beau."

"Rob."

"Sorry."

"Just because—"

"I know. I know. Just because Michael and I split doesn't mean I have to throw who and how many men you date in your face."

Bumping her shoulder, Leslie moved ahead of her. After Robin caught up to her they laughed, their shoulders rocking and bumping against one another, while they walked further down the backstage area. "Enough about me and my men."

"Frank's cute though."

"Rob," Her eyes swelled. She lowered her hands to her sides. "Where is all of this coming from?"

She turned her palms up. "I don't know." She sighed. "Maybe I'm tired of being nice and polite when so few people return me that same measure of respect."

Nodding into her response, she said, "I knew it. I knew it. Being in this business is changing you. It's making you hard. Don't feel bad. Sooner or later, it happens to everybody. You were such a nice person; it just took longer for the business to get to you."

"I haven't hardened. I serve God, not Hollywood. I serve God alone. I don't have one, two, three, four gods. I serve one God, God all mighty. God all mighty is the only god there is. Hollywood hasn't hardened me. No. That's not what it is. I haven't hardened. I've wised up."

"One and the same thing. One and the same thing. The wiser you get, the harder you become."

"No. I don't think so." She shook her head. "When you put your trust in God, you can go through anything. God gave me this wonderful talent to be a writer, this marvelous and wonderful talent. I'm grateful to God for the talent of writing, for each talent that God gave me. God's talent comes with no burden, no yoke. It's a free gift. I have a joy the world cannot take away. I have a joy that is within. Hollywood cannot change me. We all have the ultimate power at our disposal, and it's always at our disposal. We have the power to choose. I choose not to be hard." She shook her head again. "No. I'm not hard. I'm just wiser, and they are not the same thing."

"No?"

"No." She allowed a moment of silence to fall between that and her next words. "Hard people lose their zest and their thirst to love other people. People who are hard don't weep when children suffer or animals die. I'm not hard. God's given me too much wisdom for me to choose to be hard. Life is about choices, Leslie. I keep telling you that. When you look back over your life years from now what you will see will be a series of choices that you have made. I mean. Granted. There are some surprises, but for the most part our lives are the total sum of the choices, whether conscious or unconscious, that we make." Raising her shoulders, she sighed. "But back to the business and what people want. I'm telling you, most people want you to be downright ignorant." Her brow arched. "You know?"

"That's true."

"Most people want you to be ignorant so they can mistreat you, step all over you free of retaliation. In this business, ignorance is at a premium. The millions and billions of dollars spent on ads prove that too many people believe what they hear, trust what they see time and again. Why do you think," she spread her hands. "We're all famous?"

After she tossed her head back, Leslie enjoyed a long, loud spasm of laughter. "You're right. You're right," she said while she laughed. "You're exactly right."

"I know I am."

At once Leslie stopped laughing and leveled her head. "Rob?"

"What?"

She pointed. "Look over there."

The second her gaze crossed Michael's eyes and mouth, she pushed down Leslie's hand and snapped, "Don't point. It's not nice."

"Sorry."

"Wonder where his escort is."

Leslie chuckled. "Don't know. Maybe he shook her so he could chase somebody else."

Turning slowly, Robin glared at her.

"Sorry."

"Come on," she charged, her voice inches above a whisper.

Standing center of a huddle of dancers, Michael followed Hollywood protocol for new acts. While his companions circled him, he smiled and nodded. He moved with the turn of roving cameramen. He laughed each time a camera bulb exploded in his face. A quartet of R&B female singers winked at and blew him a flurry of kisses. Award winners, nominees and their guests milled about the backstage area in loud throngs. Television programming over, pandemonium reigned at the Los Angeles Shrine Auditorium. Michael turned and looked over his shoulder each time someone approached him. Talking loud and non-stop, he worked feverishly to gain the attention of prominent music industry executives.

Six months remained on the contract he performed Broadway stage shows under. The contract with MegamMix, a music and theatre firm out of Syracuse, New York, was his first. He signed with MegamMix two weeks before Robin and he broke off their relationship. Handling Broadway musicals, a few Rhythm and Blues vocalists and promising new dance artists, MegamMix saw Michael through a variety of dance performances.

Under MegamMix he cut two albums. His first album made it into the Top 100 album sells of the year. His second album, which sold well below 10,000 units, was an embarrassing failure. Attributing all his successes and failures to the barometer of his entertainment deals, Michael claimed MegamMix's advertisement and distribution policies were the cause of the demise of his second album.

Hoping to salvage remaining bits of his self-esteem, he turned to cocaine. J. T., a singer and his homeboy who grew up in the same borough he grew up in, introduced him to the drug. Constantly referring to Michael as his "closest friend", J. T. took Michael to every plush party he was invited to while he was in California. Album covers spread across the room, Michael beamed at J. T. each time they turned and looked at each other. He was proud of J. T. and the release of his first album titled *J. T.'s Hype*. The album was released in June of 1989. By December of that same year, *J. T.'s Hype* held a sturdy twelve on *Step* magazine's Top Twenty Albums list.

Although he was familiar with the pulse of the street and the trappings of the drug trade, Michael not once considered J. T.'s erratic behavior to be the result of narcotics. He believed each excuse J. T. used to cover his mood swings. "It comes from growing up poor. Having to hustle just to survive starting at a very early age. You know how it is, Man. It's just the way I am. It's a part of me. I'll never change. I was born this way. Everybody in my family is crazy." Michael even believed the excuses after J. T. shot a round of bullets into a wall through the 45 magnum his uncle gave him.

As it was with Michael, so it was with J. T.

J. T. had no idea his uncle trafficked illegal drugs on the streets of New York City. He desperately wanted to believe his uncle when he told him the money to pay cash for his Jeep, his 1988 Mazda and his Porsche came from the salary he earned working as an accountant for an investment firm. J. T. was shocked the day he walked up the front stoop to his mother's brownstone to be pushed out of the way by a pair of plains clothes policemen.

His uncle active in his life since the day his father died, he adored his uncle. His uncle was his hero.

J. T. was only four years old when his father was gunned down outside a corner gas station over a one-dollar loss in a crap game. As if he was born to be a frightened child's stand-in father, J. T.'s uncle stepped in. Early Saturday mornings he drove to J. T.'s mother's brownstone and picked J. T. up. When the sky was clear and the air was warm, he would hoist J.T. atop his broad shoulders and walk him to the park. At the park, nephew and uncle ran through the tall grass, played on and around the squeaky sliding board, and, chasing each other, pretended to be detectives and criminals while they played an energetic game of cops and robbers.

J. T. couldn't bring himself to understand his uncle's demise. His uncle was busted for carrying half a gram of crack. A small sale, J. T. found no error in the transaction. To him it wasn't wrong. It didn't bother him that the woman his uncle took the twenty dollars from then handed a plastic sandwich bag of rock cocaine was in the prime of her life, shamelessly attractive and seven months pregnant. "I don't make them take it. I never made one junkie. I don't make people take drugs." His uncle rationalized the first time J.T. visited him in jail. "I never put a gun to a junkie's head, forced them outside and made them hand me twenty dollars for a bag of crack. I don't advertise. Liquor makers do all the drug advertising. Drugs of choice in the burbs probably come from pharmacies more than from any other source. Every bad drug ain't illegal. A lot of prescription drugs do major damage, addict a lot of people too. And I don't ship the junk into the country." With pursed lips his uncle continued by saying, "So called chic guys in expensive designer suits breed and ship that junk. The higher you go in this business, the more quote, unquote professional people you see. I know what I'm talking about. Drugs ain't a black crime. It's all about money. I know people who'd kill their own mother for the right amount of money, and most of them ain't black." J. T.'s heart raced while he listened to his uncle. "Come in all shapes, sizes and colors. I see it everyday. I know what I'm talking about. Use drugs to put a Brother on lock down when the establishment knows full well a lot of folk in the drug business live in the burbs and go untouched, without being harassed, unscathed. But a Brother, now he's going to jail, and he's going to do twice, if not three or four times, the amount of time a white guy dealing in drugs will do. And folks get mad when you stand up and say that's not fair." Shaking his head he concluded his take on America's drug situation by saying, "Common sense answers that question every day."

Six months after the party to celebrate the release of J. T. 's first album, cocaine became Michael's closest companion. He spent so much time thinking about it and shoving it up his nose. After using cocaine for more than a year, he became a disheveled addict. He stole money from business associates and friends. He took his grandmother's floor length television set, and, driving it to the nearest pawnshop traded it in for fifty bucks. J. T.'s party stretched into a two-year nightmare for Michael. If not for J. T. hurrying to his Manhattan high rise a year ago, Michael would be dead. Spread across his own bathroom floor while his head banged the door and his body convulsed, he would have become another O. D. statistic.

One day later he started on his first of two stays in a detox center. During the second stay, grace moved closely around his life. Unlike J. T.'s father, Michael survived.

Robin heard about his visits to the detox center from Diane. Despite her efforts to avoid her, Diane managed to make herself seen. It was cold and snowing outside on the day she raced around a corner of the high rise lobby. Hurrying up to Robin she asked her, "Have you heard what happened to Michael? Maybe you should go see him. He always did respect you. Paulette's trying everything she knows, but he's just not coming around. I don't think he sees how addicted to coke he is. This level

Michael is on is scary." Before she turned to leave, she smiled softly and told Robin, "Paulette really would appreciate any assistance you could offer. She's about to pull her hair out. You know how much she loves Michael. She's tried everything. Maybe seeing you will work . . . as a last resort."

Days later whenever Robin thought about Michael, she prayed and fasted feverishly. She wanted Michael to stay clean. She wanted him to be happy.

Backstage at the Grammy's, Michael went unaware of her love for him. Backstage at the Grammy's only ire pulsed in her while she gazed across the room at him.

Leslie stepped back and hovered over her shoulder while they approached Michael and his huddle of friends. Inches away from Michael, she glared at Robin and waited for her to speak.

Robin drew in a deep breath.

As if sensing the presence of an ex-girlfriend, the dancers circling Michael stepped back until their circle broke up and Michael stood alone.

Michael turned his head in the direction of his friends' gaze. His eyes ballooned when he saw Robin. The suit she wore, its jacket short and snug against her hips, caused desire to swell in his pants. Keeping to his street schooling, he worked to lower the rise in his pants with the flat of his hand.

Anger filled Robin's eyes and turned their tint red. She stared across the room at him.

He glanced at her narrow brow. Her emotions always able to do something for him he couldn't do for himself, he took his hand away from the crotch of his pants and shook his head. He felt flush. He knew his blood pressure was peaking. No longer sexually aroused, he enjoyed the taste of his newfound anger and refused to speak to her until she spoke to him first.

She almost turned and looked at Leslie, but, pressured with the need to prove the thoughts filling her head were her own, she didn't.

Standing behind Robin nibbling on her bottom lip, Leslie couldn't count the times she wanted to sit Robin down and tell her that Michael wasn't right for her.

Robin crossed her arms. "What's up, Michael?" First words spoken, her mind raced.

He shoved his hands inside his pant pockets. He tossed his head back "What's up?"

A member of his dance troupe met Leslie's glare. He pursed his lips when Leslie started rolling her eyes.

Robin arched her shoulders then lowered her arms to her sides. She swung her arms loosely in effort to calm her nerves. "I'm all right, and what's up? Same ol', same o'. You know how it is."

He nodded, "Yea."

She stopped swinging her arms and pointed at him. "How about you?"

"Trying to get it right. Know what I'm saying?"

"Yea."

"Yea."

"I see you've got yourself a new dance company."

"Oh. Those fellas." Turning slowly from side to side, he spread his hands and waved his dance troupe into full view. Robin followed the movement of his spreading hands and smoked his dance crew over. "This is," he called out names. "These are my hommies."

She closed her mouth slowly. "Oh."

"We've been dancing together for nearly six months."

She arched her brow. "Oh, yea?"

He nodded, "Yea."

"So, now you're dancing at award ceremonies?"

He chuckled, peered down and kicked his foot back and forth across the floor.

"Hmmm."

Leslie looked for Frank out of the corner of her eye. She grit her teeth while she listened to Robin make small talk with Michael. "Be careful, Rob," she mused. "With this slow and easy approach of yours, if you don't watch out you're gonna grow weak and find yourself wrapped up inside Michael's arms again."

"Well?" Robin asked while she patted her foot.

Michael's smile burned into her heart. "No. Not really."

"Not really?"

"This and The American Music Awards."

She smiled softly. "You're getting there, Michael."

"I thought I already was there."

She shrugged.

"I thought I was."

She nodded. "You're getting there."

"I'll take that. It's better than nothing."

"Of course it is."

"So, how have you been?"

She nodded again. "I've been okay."

"Still writing the way you used to?"

"Yes."

"Still staying up into the middle of the night pumping out those plays and stories?"

She smiled softly. "Yes."

"I saw one of your plays."

"As long as you've known me, you've only seen one of my plays?"

"Sorry."

"Sorry?"

"Yea. I said I'm sorry."

"Michael."

"You never would let me go to a play you wrote with you."

"Because if you didn't like what you saw I didn't want to know about it."

"As good as you are?"

Lowering her head, she turned away from him. "Go on."

"No. Really."

Facing him again, she said, "Whatever."

"You are good, Rob, and you know it."

"It's a talent from God. God is so very good. I give God all the credit for these wonderful talents and gifts that I have."

"True."

"So is your dancing. God gave you that talent too."

"I know that."

"So, how have you been dong outside of dancing?"

"All right."

"Sure?"

He was quick. "Sure."

"Sure?"

"I've been clean for nearly six months."

"I heard."

"In this business, I'm sure everybody has heard."

She chuckled. A second later she thought better of it and apologized. "Sorry."

"That's okay."

"Well, it's good to hear you're really doing okay now. Honestly."

"It's better to be doing good. I'm going to stay clean this time."

"I'm sure you will. Just put your trust in God. Trust, obey and serve God. He will make sure you stay clean."

"Drugs are a Hollywood vice."

She turned and stared at the top of a photographer's head.

"I forgot. You wouldn't know about that."

She faced him again and said, "One of those times I'm glad to be a square."

He chuckled.

"Are you still singing?"

"A little. You?"

179

She pursed her lips. "Pplleeaassee."

"Well. Are you still trying to sing?"

"You know I am."

"You never know, Rob."

"I know." Her voice fell flat. "We all know. Everybody knows."

"So, I see you were nominated for a Grammy."

"Yea."

"How's it feel?"

"I didn't win."

"That's not what I asked you."

"I know."

"So?"

"It feels good. God has been so very good to me. God has blessed me in so many ways. I couldn't do anything without God."

"Yea."

"Yes."

"I knew."

"All the nominees do."

"I think the winners do too."

He shook his head. "No."

"Sometimes they do. They don't always come off as surprised when they win."

"No. I don't think the winners know. You can see the losers trying to play off their disappointment when their name is not announced."

"That's true."

"I bet you were surprised when you found out you were nominated."

"I was. When I first read the letter, I flipped."

"Yea?"

"Yes. I was fooling around when I wrote that song."

"Yea?"

"Yea."

Leslie tucked in her knees and pushed them against the backs of Robin's thighs.

Robin turned and narrowed her brow. Certain that Leslie noted her anger, a second later she returned her undivided attention to Michael. "May we speak alone?"

Rolling her eyes, Leslie clucked her tongue and looked away from Robin. Her gaze fell upon Amanda Gaynor. She turned up her nose and laughed.

Amanda snapped, "Hi, Leslie," while she hurried beyond her.

Laughter was the most she returned Amanda's greeting. She stared at a throng of photographers circling Amanda and Tom.

For the second time, Amanda called out, "Hi, Leslie." When Leslie parted her lips to speak, Amanda turned and grinned coyly at the photographers. She spread her hands and arched her shoulders. "Guess she doesn't want to talk to me. Guess she doesn't want to be polite. Don't know what's going on with that."

Though she knew pictures of her backstage at the Grammys and nasty made-up stories would cover next week's tabloids, Leslie looked away from Amanda and faced Robin's distant back. Leaning to the side, she glanced at the side of Michael's head. Would that she could see his face, monitor his emotions. She hated him for the pain he introduced to Robin's life.

While she watched Robin and Michael talk, she thought about the last conversation she had with Bertha. They were standing in the apartment lounge when Diane strutted passed them. She grinned and tossed them a curtly wave. No sooner did she pass than Leslie raised her voice and said, "Michael knows Robin can't handle this type of indiscretion." She clenched her teeth. "He knows Robin trust him as if he was a saint. Michael knows Robin loves him. He knows she's deeply in love with him. Theirs isn't a mere friendship. He knew having an affair on Robin – and with Paulette of all people – would devastate her. He knew that. I don't care what anyone says. He knew how deeply he was hurting Robin. He knew only Robin's love for God kept her from having sex with him. How could he do something like this to my best friend? If he had done it to me, I'd just have whipped his behind, but not Robin. She fights differently. Well. I'd have whipped his behind or laid his best friend. Either way, I would have evened the score."

Leslie shook her head while she watched Michael gently tug on Robin's forearm and guide her further away from her.

"Thanks for stepping away from your hommies so I could talk to you privately," was the first thing Robin said to him. "I wouldn't bother you. I know this is your night. But to put our relationship fully to rest I have to know some things. Will you please answer a few questions for me? I don't have many."

He scratched his nose. "Yea. All right. I'll answer your questions."

"You don't mind?"

He shook his head. "Nah. No. I don't mind."

She took in a deep breath. "Michael, did you ever love me?"

He turned away from her. He clucked his tongue before he answered, "Yes, Robin. Of course, I loved you. How could you ask me something like that?"

Because she resented the tension in his voice, she lowered her own voice and lined it with ire. "How could I ask you something like that?" Forever concerned with what others thought of her, she crossed her arms and looked from side to side. Seeing that Michael and she were a safe distance away from everyone else, she lowered her arms and continued. "How could I ask you something like that? How could you do what you did to me?"

He sighed. "Robin, I didn't do anything to you. I didn't do anything to hurt you. You sound as if you think I was attacking you. I wasn't attacking you. You sound as if you think I wanted to hurt you. I never wanted to hurt you." He turned and looked further down the backstage area. "I don't see how you can stand those few feet away from me and ask me something like that . . . as long as we were together."

"That's exactly what I'm talking about, Michael. As long as we were together, and you do something like that to me."

"I just finished saying I didn't do anything to you. Robin, I wasn't trying to hurt you."

"But you go sleep with a – with Paulette. Paulette of all people. It would have hurt me bad enough to walk in on you with any woman as much as I loved you, but Paulette! Michael!"

"It wasn't something I planned."

"Maybe not, but you sure eased yourself into Diane and Paulette's trap."

"Stop thinking like that. You don't even know Paulette. I know Diane stays in the mix, but Paulette's not like that."

"Whatever."

"Yea. Whatever."

"And we're not talking about Paulette, that tricky, conniving – we're talking about you and me. Paulette." She turned in a half circle. "What were you trying to do to me?"

"I was trying to be a man."

"Cheating on the woman you supposedly love is being a man?"

He parted his lips, but she didn't give him time to answer.

"Having an affair on your girlfriend, that's what you call being a man? Michael, I was always there for you."

"Don't try to turn this into an I was there for you when no one else was there for you then when you made it you left me deal. Don't do that. I won't let you do that."

"I'm not trying to say you loved me until you made it. I know that's wrong. I wouldn't do that. And I don't appreciate you implying that I would either."

"Then why did you say you were always there for me?"

"Because I was. Don't you think so?'

"Robin, we had a good relationship, but all relationships don't last."

"What did our relationship mean to you, Michael? Was it just something to pass the time or to keep you from feeling lonely?"

"Pass the time . . . keep me from feeling lonely? You have to be kidding. You must be kidding. Pass the time . . keep me from feeling lonely? Robin, I did feel lonely in our relationship."

A lump formed in her throat, and she swallowed hard. "Why didn't you ever tell me?'

"I tried."

"Oh. You mean I didn't satisfy you sexually?"

"There was no sex in our relationship."

"That's not true, and you know it."

"Robin, there was very little intimacy in our relationship."

Forgetting her whereabouts, she stomped her foot and raised her voice. "Michael, that's not true and you know it!"

"Stop and think of all the times we were intimate. I always had to work hard to get you to relax and open up. Getting you to warm up to me sexually was a job."

"Do you have to say it like that?"

"That's the way it was. How else can I say it?"

"Michael." She lowered her shoulders and gazed at the floor. "That hurts."

"I don't mean for it to, but it's true."

Cocking her head to the side, she lowered her voice and whispered, "I loved you."

"I know that. I know that. I know that, Robin. I know you loved me. Don't you think I knew and still know that?"

All at once, her eyes became slits. Her chest went up. She shook her head. "No. No. I'm not in love with you anymore."

"I didn't . . . you misunderstand everything I say."

Glancing further down the backstage area, she was glad that they were so far away from the press. "No, I don't."

"You are right now."

"I'm angry."

"When are you going to stop being mad at me for being a man? I haven't done anything out of the ordinary. Many people want to have sex.

It's a very normal thing. God invented sex, and I refuse to believe it's just for making babies."

"There you go, throwing religion in my face."

He hung his head back and laughed. "Throwing religion in your face? Throwing religion in your face? Yea. Right."

"You resent my faith, my belief in God."

He shook his head. "No. I don't."

"My devotion to God's word. My desire to live the way God, in the Word, says I should live."

His head continuing to shake, he repeated, "No. I don't."

"Yes, you do. If you didn't, you wouldn't have said what you just said."

"Robin, where is this conversation going? We're only arguing. We can do that anytime. When you called me over here, away from my friends you obviously had something you wanted to say to me. I don't think this is what it was."

"I asked you a question when we first came over here. The answer is very important to me, but you never answered the question."

"Oh. Yea. Right. Did I ever love you. I did answer your question. I told you, of course, I loved you. But you didn't believe me. That's the problem, Robin. You don't think anyone loves you. You think if a man loves you, he won't want to be intimate with you. You and your rigid, unbreakable rules. You're going to die a lonely woman if you don't adjust the rules you guide your life by."

Extending her neck until her face neared his, she jabbed her finger against the center of her chest. "They're not my rules."

"Oh, that's right. I forgot. The Bible."

"Michael, I can't live my life for you, be what you want me to be."

"I never asked you to. I wouldn't want you to. I wouldn't respect you if you did, and I not only love you, I also respect you. I respect you a great deal. I'm sure you know that. You'll give me credit for that, even if you are pissed off. But, you know, Robin, I can work to understand you, but you don't seem to be able to want to work to understand me. It's either your way or no way." Before she could part her lips, he rushed into, "And don't give me that religion and Bible stuff. I could have gone without sex, but very little to no intimacy. You simply asked too much of me."

"But, you don't understand."

"I do understand. I understand your religious beliefs, and I respect them. I have the same beliefs myself which you already know. I don't live by them as rigidly as you do, but I believe in God. I go to church. You know that. I love God. I worship God. I'm grateful. I count my blessings. I just don't believe that God considers sex taboo or evil."

After she lowered her gaze, she shook her head. "I don't either."

"What you don't realize, is the way you currently live your life, when you do get married, and I see you married with kids one day – you'll be so rigid sexually, your husband, though he may be faithful, will be frustrated. You're going to be so accustomed to turning your sexual energy off and ignoring and denying your sexual desires, even after you get married and everything's official, you're going to be rigid. You need to loosen up. And no, I'm not saying go get laid. I'm saying, open up. Let a man love you in more ways than talking about your latest play, his career, the Bible, your families and how much you love people and love helping people. You need to learn to recognize that men and women have physical desires, and that there's nothing wrong with that. You need to loosen up. You need to loosen up your mind. You're never comfortable around a crowd of people. It's like you're paranoid or something. When we went out I always felt guilty when I left you sitting at a table by yourself or standing alone in a club, because you didn't talk to people on your own. You didn't mingle. Talk about hurting you. I felt like I was hurting you when I took you out. Like it was a challenge for you to mix it up with other folk. You always seemed scared. You get too comfortable holed up in that apartment sometimes. You're going to fool around and miss out on a lot in life. And if you're not happy, you can blame your mother for the cold way she brought you up, but you also have to blame yourself. You're a grown woman. You don't live at home anymore. You know how to take control of a situation. You know how to take control of your life. You don't have to be alone. And sure, you'll make a good wife. Your husband won't have to think twice about you fooling around. You'll be faithful and caring. You'll love your man with unbreakable, deep down, soulful love. But, if you don't learn to loosen up, you'll be rigid, and your man will get bored and become frustrated." Taking a step forward, he moved closer to her. "Just like what happened to you when you were a kid growing up in Johnson City, Tennessee is still with you, what you put yourself through now will be with you years later. You can't change what happened to you when you were a kid, but you most definitely can do something about what's going on with you right now."

"I know that. And I'm not as rigid as you think I am."

"I have my ideas about that, and you have your ideas about that."

"I recognize that I have sexual desires. I've told you that. We've talked about that before. I've never denied that. I never denied that I wanted you. I never told you that I didn't want you."

"But, Robin, it was hard work just to get you to open up and kiss me passionately."

185

"You mean to tell me that you didn't enjoy kissing me? You never enjoyed when we held each other? You never enjoyed the time we spent together? Is that what you're telling me, Michael?"

He bowed his head and kicked his foot back and forth across the floor. "No. That's not what I'm saying. I enjoyed everything we did together. What I said was that it was hard work getting you to open up."

She crossed her arms and swallowed hard. Her gaze darted while she looked for passersby. Seeing that Michael and she were still standing alone, she blinked hard several times. Then she said, "Oh."

"Oh."

"So, now I'm a terrible kisser. I guess I just can't do anything right when it comes to satisfying a man. I might as well just give up. I might as well just resign myself to spending the rest of my life alone." Pausing, she peered into his eyes. Then she arched her shoulders. "I guess."

"Don't be dramatic."

"I'm not being dramatic."

"Yes, you are."

She raised her voice. "Well, that's what you're saying. I'm helpless. I'm hopeless. I'm so much hard work, no man will want to take the time to teach me how to make love."

His eyes swelled. "The kind of man you want will be a virgin. He won't be able to teach you anything. You'll both struggle through somehow. Don't feel bad. A lot of people do."

"A lot of so called experienced people struggle through."

"That's true. Robin, it has nothing to do with being a virgin. It has to do with opening your mind. Your mind is closed airtight. You probably confess after you have a sexual fantasy."

"Oh, Michael."

He smiled like a fox. "You do." Widening his brow, he leaned close to her. "You do."

"Shut up, Michael."

His smile turned into a chuckle. "You do."

She whispered, "Sometimes."

"I don't believe this."

"Why is that so hard to believe?"

"Robin! You're in trouble. Your husband's in deep, deep trouble."

"Well, I'll work at opening up then."

"Promise?"

"I promise."

"Good." He stuffed his hands inside his pant pockets. "You know, I've learned a lot of things from you. Our relationship was good. We gave each other a lot. We learned a lot from each other. . I don't regret having loved you. I'll always love you. We'll always be friends. I'll always consider you as someone I can go to if I need to talk to someone. Because one thing is certain, you're an excellent listener. And you can always come to me if you want to talk."

Pulling her bottom lip inside her mouth, she peered at him and asked, "But, it's over?"

"Between us?" He waited until she looked up and met his stare. "Yes. It's over between us. We're too different. We don't belong together. We'll always be friends. We did love one another, and we always will. It's just different now."

"You got tired of trying, of waiting?"

"I didn't get tired of waiting, because you sure are worth the wait. I did get tired of trying."

"Thanks for being honest. I'll have to work on being more open."

"I think you should, because you're better than gold as a woman. I don't think . . . I know I won't meet a woman who'll surpass you, few who will ever equal you. You're a thoroughbred, Robin. You should never feel like you're less of a woman because you're a virgin. Don't believe the hype. Having sex does not make men of little boys or women of little girls. No way. You're for real. You believe in people. You help people. You consciously support our businesses and teach the generation coming up behind us. You don't forget where you came from. You reach back. You're a good person. You're a good woman. You're an unsurpassable woman. You should know that."

A smile went across her face. "I do know that."

"Hearing another person say it adds something good to your life though, doesn't it?"

"Yes."

"It should."

"Well, Michael—"

"Any more questions? You said you had a few."

"No more questions. That's it."

"Well," Grateful for the exchange, she peered around. Certain that no one was watching them, she opened her arms and invited him inside. "At least I know you loved me. And that's very important to me, more than you know. I love you too." Closing her eyes she wrapped her arms around his back. Heat from his body pushed against her chest and caused her heart to race. "I love you too." She stroked his spine while she held him. After she whispered, "I love you too," a third time she stepped back. Her eyes were misty with regret. She scolded herself for not embracing him more those few years ago.

He gazed softly inside her eyes. He smiled at her and took her hand inside his. "I love you, Robin," he called out while he allowed his hand to slide to the end of her fingers.

Chapter Fifteen

In an effort to engage Robin's interest, Elizabeth leaned forward on the sofa and talked about hit movies, the top ticket sellers at the theatre and road racing. Disregarding her attempts to bridge the gulf of silence that separated them, Robin pursed her lips and stared across the room at a blank wall.

After she crossed then uncrossed her legs for the fourth time, Elizabeth chuckled into, "Patricia and Robert are having an affair." A crooked grin widened her face. "Peppermint caught them. She was in the cloakroom putting on her jacket when she heard a noise coming from Patricia's office. The door was cracked. When Pep went to check the noise out, she said what she saw shocked her." No longer spewing ten words a second out of her mouth, she chuckled. "Robert had his tongue stuck so far down Patricia's throat, Pep said she wondered how Patricia kept from choking." Without looking at Robin, she tossed her head back and laughed. When her laughter subsided, she leaned forward on the sofa and laid the cup of apple, cinnamon tea warming her palms on the living room coffee table.

Robin turned her cup of apple, cinnamon tea in her hand, sat against the back of the sofa and muttered, "Yea."

A Grammy nomination, a Tony award and numerous state, university and city awards found Robin psychologically unprepared for fame . . . found her choking for self-confidence. To avoid the unexpected rush of strangers, people she didn't know, people she never saw before, people who knew her parents' names, people who knew she was an only child, people who knew her address and the low down on Michael and her relationship, people other celebrities called fans, Robin started shopping through catalogs. Mavis', its food still stove cooked and fresh, the atmosphere still quaint, casual and friendly, no longer provided her a haven from the walls of loneliness that started forming around her one year into her celebrity. Fans, managers, publicists and other celebrities engulfed her. If the telephone at the side of her bed wasn't ringing, she was shuffling through a stack of mail. Seldom alone with her thoughts, she marveled at how lonely she felt. On cold nights when she was alone in the apartment and she knew Leslie was out with Frank, she thought about picking up the telephone and dialing Michael's number. Desperate nights . . . laughing and chatting with her girlfriends no longer did the trick. Settled into a life of misery as if misery was a warm, milk bath, she hushed Elizabeth's voice out of her thoughts.

M. C. Rocket's *Rock EM* spun round and round on the phonograph. While the rap artist sang a remake of *Look At Her*, Robin, a sleek 105 pounds, worried that her thighs and butt were too big. Between that thought and hearing Leslie open the apartment's front door and call, "You're so sweet. I'll call you later, Baby," to Frank, Michael invaded her mind. Although angry with herself for lacking control over her thoughts, her mind wandered into places she preferred not to venture, places that were her gardens of pain.

"Damn it!" She heard a voice familiar to her own shout. When she looked up and saw Leslie and Elizabeth gawking at her, then looked down and saw her fist balled and fitted into the palm of her hand, she knew the voice belonged to her. Embarrassment darkened the color in her face, and she almost covered her mouth with her opened hand.

Leslie stared at her and worked hard to recall any other time that she heard her curse. When the answer 'never' came to her, she asked, "Rob, are you okay?"

Nodding more than speaking, she lowered her gaze and mumbled, "Yea."

A tap from Leslie to the side of her thigh pushed her further down the sofa. "Scoot over."

She crossed her legs and pointed the crown of her head in the direction of the apartment's front door. "That was Frank?"

Leslie smiled softly at her. "You know it was."

She arched her shoulders. "I guess."

"Rob, did you hear anything I said? I must have been talking for half an hour." All at once, she stopped and stared into Robin's eyes. "Have I been talking to myself all this time?"

When she looked at Elizabeth, her eyes were sheepish. "Yea. I guess."

"Ggiirrll."

"Sorry."

She raised her hand. When Robin raised hers, they slapped palms. "It's all right."

Leslie sat against the back of the sofa. "Rob, what's been eating at you lately?"

Elizabeth looked at Leslie before she turned and looked at Robin.

"Fame is too much for me. I can't handle it."

Leslie shook her head. "Yes you can. You're strong."

"I don't know. It's starting to get to me. It seems like everywhere I go there's a photographer, a reporter or a gossip columnist. When I think no one's watching while I'm outside minding my own business, I pick up the paper a few days later and see a story all about me splashed across the gossip column or the entertainment section. Things I tell people I think I can trust turn up in the paper or on a TV celebrity program. My life's not my own anymore." She spread her hands. "You know I need my anonymity. I never asked for this fame. True, I wanted to be a great writer. I wanted people, a lot of people, to pay for tickets to see plays I authored, but, I never wanted to be famous."

"Did you really think you could write hit plays, have two top selling Broadway plays open within eighteen months of each other, be smart and quick, not to mention your looks, and not become famous? Did you really think you could pull that off?" She leaned so close to Robin, her breath brushed the end of her nose and tickled. "Really?"

Leslie's question echoed in her ears. Rather than answer the question, she wished she could walk into her bedroom, close the door and be alone.

"I mean, I know you didn't wish for the fame, but you're talented. And though you never use it, you are very pretty. You're the only woman I know who is one hundred percent for real. Through and through, Rob, you're for real. Who else can honestly compliment another woman and mean every word of the compliment? Not once have I heard you be catty. Rob, you're not every day. You're for real. Girl, you were going to the top in something in life, and, being who you are, you were bound to make noise." She rocked her foot before she smiled teasingly. "You might as well get used to it, Girl. And you ought to be glad I help keep so many men at bay." This time she laughed outright. It wasn't long before Elizabeth looked at her and started laughing too. "If I didn't, you'd be in trouble, Girl."

She didn't so much as smile. Instead, she crossed her arms.

"Rob?"

Her words were thick with frustrated gasps. "What, Les?"

Leslie sat against the back of the sofa and gawked at the woman sitting to her right. "Girl, something is eating at you. What is it?"

She let out a deep breath. "I told you."

"You know you're not going to stop writing."

"No."

"And you're damned good."

She turned and looked at the side of Leslie's head. "Les."

She covered her mouth. "Sorry."

Robin stared into her lap and started shaking her head. "I never should have gone to the Grammys."

"Ah . . . Michael."

"No, Elizabeth."

"Then, what is it?" Leslie asked for the third time.

Ire took the volume in her voice up. "I already told you. All this," she paused and spread her upturned palms, "Attention. It's just too much for me. I can't go anywhere in peace. I can't trust anybody. Seems like everybody I know turns out to be a, quote unquote, very reliable source a newspaper can't identify. People I thought I could trust are getting paid tens of thousands of dollars to send stories about me to the tabloids. My life's an open book. I no longer have any privacy. I'll have to become a recluse to have an inch of life I can live outside the public eye."

The musical cue that Side One of M.C. Rocket's *Rock EM* was at its end took Elizabeth's, an avid M. C. Rocket fan, mind off Robin's troubles. She left the sofa and walked to the stereo system covering the wall adjacent the new wide screen television set Robin bought from Music City six months ago. She turned the album over, and *Dance All Night* blared in the living room.

Because she wanted Robin to focus on a solution to her situation, while she stood in front of the stereo, she asked, "Speaking of your sorors, when's the last time you saw Sharon or one of your partners?"

"About six weeks ago."

Her eyes ballooned. "Really?"

Leslie was equally as disbelieving. "That long?"

She nodded slowly. "That long."

"Ggiirrll, you're just drying up in this apartment."

Robin arched her brow when she turned and looked at Elizabeth. "Who're you telling?"

"Why don't you give Craig a chance?"

She turned up her nose before she lowered her hand. "Pplleeaassee."

Leslie thought about Craig Morton, a confirmed womanizer, then tossed her head back and enjoyed a spurt of laughter.

"He sleeps around." Her nose was still upturned. A vision of Craig, a singer from Brooklyn, entered her mind's eye. She waved her hand and shook her head. "All those skirt chasers are the same. The only difference between them and the everyday Joe is what they do for a living and the money that lines their wallets. They aren't all that. Craig doesn't have it going on. He's weak."

Leslie nodded. "I know. Those male singers get me . . . giving themselves to a different woman night after night."

For the first time since they started trying to pick her brain, Robin felt someone understood her. "Then you read an interview one of those skirt chasers gives in *Our Community* or *Soar* magazine where they say, 'I'm lonely. I wish I could find a nice woman to settle down with.' Liars. Some of them even have the nerve to do that type of interview in *Mahogany* magazine." She stopped and waved her hand again. "What some men won't do to get thirty minutes of sex." She pursed her lips. "If it last that long."

Leslie's shoulders jerked and shook. She had a hard time controlling her laughter.

Robin shook her head. "Dumb women fall for those smooth games time after time."

Elizabeth leaned forward and ran her hands over the tops of her knees. "A lot of the women who run behind those guys wouldn't give those guys the time of day if their names weren't high up on the record charts."

Leslie's shoulders stilled. "That's true. I know more than a few lead singers who have horror stories of their own. Now, Rob, you know women manipulate men too. Don't try to make it a one sided story."

Elizabeth's head bobbed to the beat of *Hope*. "That's true."

"But take," Robin walked across the room and picked up the jacket to M. C. Rocket's album. "This album. Listen to the titles." She read the titles of the songs slowly, then she commented, "Now Rocket seems to be positive, but he advocates having a good time sleeping around. That's one thing a whole lot of men will never learn."

Leslie chuckled. "But I still say women are just as guilty of that as men are. Take a woman who prostitutes herself or a woman who is whorish then becomes angry when, after having sex with a man she hardly knows or a man she fully knows is not monogamous. I mean. A lot of women know what type of man they are with before they take their clothes off. Then days, weeks, months, whatever after the sex when the man doesn't make her his one and only or ask her for her hand in marriage she cries foul. I'm a firm believer that no one does something for nothing. A lot of women want money in a relationship. A lot of women want a trade for sex. A nice home, a man who earns a nice salary. You know. It's like a trade for a lot of people. In my book, if a woman screws a man for money, prestige or to be able to live in a beautiful home with a wealthy man and the man turns around and emotionally screws her, that's an even break. They both got what they wanted. The man wanted sex but no emotional attachment, so that's what he gave. The woman wanted a trade for her sex. She wanted to trade her very own body for a wedding band or economic clout. If a woman wants a man to truly love her, sex is not the key to any man's heart. I say that you better know where you want to end up before you start walking, before you take that first step. If you want true love, keep your clothes on." She laughed. "Of course that doesn't apply to me. I know what I'm doing. I enjoy sex but I don't have sex because I want something from a man. I know better than that. I know much, much better than that." She shook her head. "Some people really are fools. I don't think a person can uplift his or herself by blaming all their bad decisions on other people. There comes a time when a woman has to take responsibility for her own life. Rob, you know you have to get mad at women too. Women shouldn't be so catty and competitive, so insecure. You know there are actually women who don't think they are a woman unless they have a man to climb in bed with at night.

There are women who have no plans to ever have a career of their own. Their career is trying to turn a man out sexually to the point where the man will become their sugar daddy. I've seen enough to know. I've been around enough to know what I'm talking about."

"That much is true." Robin nodded into her response. "Insecure women need to constantly have a man up in their face, and insecure men need the same thing from a woman."

"Then, women are equally as much at fault for what's going on as men are." Elizabeth injected.

As much as she hated to concede defeat, Robin found herself nodding. "I suppose that's true. It's just that a man has full choice whether or not to cheat on or be faithful to a woman who's being faithful and good to him. Men don't have to cheat on good women, but they usually do. And one thing's certain. Men grow up thinking having sex with women is no more than engaging in a series of sexual conquests. This isn't the jungle, and we aren't animals. We're human beings. Women are raised that in order to be good and worthwhile it's important to remain a virgin until marriage. So, husbands, who're nice enough to teach their wives how to satisfy them sexually, because real men lose their virginity before they turn eighteen, or so the unspoken law goes – are former players. And you know what they say . . . sex is the poorly educated man's recreation."

"Rob. Where have you been all this time you've been working in the entertainment industry? Do you know how many tall, slender, beautiful call girls work Hollywood, work the government area of Washington, work foreign officials, work top level corporate executives and attorneys? You don't know what you're talking about right now, Rob. I'm sorry." Leslie dropped then shook her head. When she raised her head again, she looked directly at Robin. "I'm sorry. But, you don't know what you're talking about this time. Wealthy men screw hookers before they hurry home to take care of their doting wives and children. Girl, where've you been? Living in a cave? The only difference between a poor man and a rich man is the same difference between a poor woman and a rich woman. Poor folk can't afford to sale their children, go to other countries to birth babies they later tell the world is their niece or nephew. Poor folk birth their babies in front of the entire world. Rich folk hide their sexual indiscretions. Rich folk go deep-deep in debt just to keep up appearances that they have something then they file bankruptcy time and again and let the same people they sneer at pay their bills. Poor folks live on the street and go about begging. They don't have enough money to even file for bankruptcy. Rich folk hide their dirt. They abuse alcohol and narcotics at the same rates poor folks do. They just know how to hide their abuses. There is no difference between poor folk and rich folk. People are people. I don't care what anyone says. There is no difference. If you ever plan to get ahead in this world, Rob, you better start seeing what's happening right up under your nose. Hearing you talk tonight, Girl, if you don't wise up, you're going to get burned something awful out here."

Warm air rushed over Robin when she looked at Leslie. All of her life, poor people was another way of saying African American. She'd seen enough African American ghettos to know that not even rural white America suffered the emotional, financial, psychologically and physical costs African American ghettos did. The one time a friend drove her through North Philadelphia when she was speaking at Temple University, she kept turning and asking her friend if he was sure they weren't in the middle of a war zone in a third world country. Instead of waiting to see pigtailed girls and little boys sporting fades dash back and forth across the streets, she kept bracing herself to see a shower of bombs fall from the sky. Her gaze still on Leslie, she said, "I didn't say poor. I said poorly educated. And sex is a power tool. You should know that."

Leslie's brow and voice went up. "Why are you so certain I know that?"

She spoke evenly. "You know sex is a power tool."

Elizabeth moved her head from side to side, turning from Robin to Leslie, whoever was talking. "How did we get onto this subject?"

She looked Elizabeth in the eye then she raised her shoulders. "We were talking about men."

"Oh." Leslie moved to the back of the sofa. "That's right."

"We were talking about Craig."

Robin turned and looked at Elizabeth. She wished she would be silent.

Elizabeth denied her wish. "And how all men aren't low down. How men aren't any more low down or manipulative than women are."

Robin was quick. "I'm not down on men. A woman's father is her first impression of a man. My father is an excellent father. My uncles are good, hard working men. I can't get down on men. No one should be stereotyped. But too many men will mistreat a good woman." She lowered her head and shook it. "I don't understand that."

Leslie pursed her lips when she turned and looked at her. "What about Kenneth?"

"What about Kenneth?"

"He was nice."

Robin waved her hand. "Oh, Leslie, Kenneth was boring."

Leslie's eyes swelled. "Bingo!"

Robin stared at her palms and chuckled in spite of herself. "Yea. I guess good men and good women are boring."

With that, the three women leaned against the back of the sofa and laughed loudly. M. C. Rocket's *Together We Can* came to an end. Robin bobbed her head and made drumming noises with her lips when the song *I Love Your Smile* came on.

Elizabeth said, "He's positive." A smile widened her face, and her finger pointed at the stereo.

Though Robin, every hip hop or rap artist reminding her of Michael, was down on dancers, she had to agree with Elizabeth. Besides, M. C. Rocket and The New York City Crew were the only rap artists she bought CDs from.

Sitting on the sofa next to Robin, Leslie thought about a television station president who insisted upon courting her. Her thoughts dripped with guilt. She scolded herself for giving her thoughts to Bob when two months ago it was Frank who escorted her to the Grammy Awards Presentation.

Frank was an experienced lover. Leslie couldn't recall the last time a man paid so much attention to her body. From the first time they were intimate, Frank never minded when she took his hands inside hers and guided them to her body's secret parts. His tongue always waited for her to invite it to enjoy the warmth of her mouth. He was patient all the times they undressed their passion for each other. It was as if he thought they had forever to unlock their bodies, to stop molding one another's hips, backs and thighs into pleasant contours. Everything he did while he touched the secret parts on her body, he did in slow motion.

Then there was Bob. A forty-eight year old entrepreneur, Bob enchanted her with his dark, brown eyes that saw everything, especially the way they made her smile. She admired the zest Bob held for life. Her eyes softened and her heart raced each time she arrived home at the apartment and found a bouquet of assorted flowers placed on the center of the dining room table -- flowers sent from Bob.

Bob was always cordial. He was always thoughtful. He was always affectionate. He was always a gentleman. When he escorted her to expensive restaurants, the theatre or to a sporting event, he was careful to open doors for her. He not once pressured her to submit to his insatiable sexual appetite -- not physically, not verbally. He stroked her long, blonde hair slow and methodically while he whispered, "I love you," softly to her the few times they were intimate. Though she tried, she couldn't recall him taking in her countenance free of complimenting her. He preferred her natural, because, as he was quick to tell her, she was a beautiful woman, a woman who didn't need cosmetics to conceal flaws, a woman who didn't need make-up to enhance her baby soft, silky smooth skin.

A consummate businessman, BCA was the first television station Bob purchased in his long, lucrative, communications career. Based in Sacramento, California, under Bob's aggressive leadership, the popular, local television station soon gained a large regional audience. Four years after he purchased BCA, Bob flew from New York City to Houston, Texas and bought SCC, a dying television station with a majority Mexican audience.

SCC did well on the stock market, most investors relying on Bob's performance in Sacramento. Eight months after he became the sole proprietor of SCC, he purchased television station ICZ. Because ICZ had a large African American audience, Bob found himself challenged to gain African American advertisers. Within two months of purchasing ICZ, he settled into several lifetime relationships with Houston's African American community. ICZ was the most watched television station by Houston's African American community. As if to pad his expanding financial horizon, SCC held the number one spot for Houston's Mexican population. When his oldest communication purchase, fifteen year old radio station WBPP, a major pop music medium with large Caucasian, Hispanic and African American audiences was brought into view, Bob was seen as one of America's wealthiest and most influential entrepreneurs.

Perhaps because Leslie was an established actress who enjoyed her share of around-the-world getaways -- perhaps because Leslie owned a vast array of expensive jewelry and designer clothing, Bob spent more money on Leslie than he did on any other woman he charmed with his wit, wisdom, his precise, exact attention – his smile.

Because he feared Leslie spent nights wrapped in the thick arms of a nameless man whose body looked as though it was sculptured into shape, Bob started lifting weights at the membership only health spa he attended. Monday, Wednesday, Friday and Saturday mornings, he donned his sweats and ran a brisk two miles through the East Coast upper class neighborhood one of his three homes was located in. While he ran, he looked at the celebrity mansions lining the street he lived on. Oak trees and a rising sun made for an enchanting landscape. The brisk morning runs provided him a needed chance to relax. Despite what became of Leslie and his relationship, he coached his will to refuse to part with the morning runs.

Following hours of passionate sex, he normally fell into a long, deep sleep. Yet, he not once drifted off to sleep after having sex with Leslie. She excited him. She put him on edge. He never felt certain of her love, that she would always be in his life. He attributed the insecurity to the difference in their ages. Though he was certain Leslie thought he was an excellent lover . . . her deep, grunted moans and high pierced screams, her fingers clawing at his back while their bodies pushed together beneath his satin sheets . . . he pushed himself to prove his feelings for her. When he was on the West Coast at his office headquarters, even after working sixteen hours at his ocean side complex, he telephoned Leslie as soon as he walked through his front door. He never returned the receiver to its cradle before he asked her, "Would you like to spend the night tucked inside my love? I can fly my private jet to Jersey and be at your front door before midnight."

Robin pried upon Leslie and Bob's relationship through the peephole in her imagination. She seldom questioned Leslie about the progress of her romance with Bob, primarily because she didn't think it was her business, partly because she didn't want to risk revealing her true feelings about Bob to Leslie.

Without so much as a frown from Robin, Bob concluded that she wished he would disappear. Her shoulders heightened and stiffened when he drove by the apartment and popped in just to say, "I love you," to Leslie. Robin also had a bad habit Bob suspected she knew nothing about. When he graced one of the rooms with his presence, she cut her conversations short and excused herself from the apartment. Wanting to please not only Leslie but her best friend as well, he watched Robin like a hawk studying prey. Her dislike for him frightened him, and he worried that, in his absence, she would caution Leslie against loving him.

After courting Leslie sporadically for four months, Bob grew impatient -- aggressive. He popped in the apartment at least once a week. He telephoned Leslie from his office and left notes with Annette. While at his penthouse in Manhattan, he drove directly home after work and telephoned Leslie. While he was cooking dinner, he asked her to come over, and, his parental instincts taking charge, he advised her to pack an overnight bag "in case" she wanted to spend the night. He called business associates and asked them about the latest musicals, concerts and restaurants he hoped Leslie hadn't been to. At the end of the week, he beamed while she chatted excitedly when they sat across from one another at a favorite Hollywood restaurant, a hideaway place Leslie hadn't heard of or dined at before. For the first time in his life, he didn't keep a mental record of how much money he spent on a date. Though Leslie continued to see other men and though they never called their outings "dates," Bob drunk with emotion, was convinced that he was in love with Leslie. He refused to part with her.

Robin stared out the picture window while she listened to Elizabeth.
"I wish M. C. Rocket, Rapper Delight and The New York City Crew would do a concert together. Can you imagine how many people would go?"

She chuckled when she turned and glanced at her. The anger she felt seconds earlier disappeared inside Elizabeth's smile.

"Don't you?"

Robin turned toward the window. "What?"

"I said, don't you wish M. C. Rocket, Rapper Delight and The New York City Crew would give a concert together?"

She continued to smile.

"You avid M. C. Rocket fan!" Robin screamed. "Goodness forbid that they would perform in concert together and you'd win a backstage pass." She bumped Leslie's elbow. "What do you think?"

She nodded. "You know it." A thought came to her. "Rob, we need to introduce her to some of our celebrity friends so she won't be so star struck." Crossing her legs, she turned sideways on the sofa and faced Elizabeth. "Half of your favorite celebrities would shock you if you saw them without their get up. Without that oil paint on our faces, we don't look so beautiful, and, goodness, what computers don't do to touch up our bodies and faces. No amount of diet, exercise or facial cream can catch up to those trusty ol' computers." Imagining what she looked like when she crawled out of bed in the morning, cursing as she went, she threw her head back and laughed.

Robin pursed her lips. "Tell the truth, Girl."

"Say what you want, you two. I still would pay good money to see that concert."

Robin and Leslie turned and faced one another. "Sure. Right."

"I would."

Robin turned to Leslie again and chuckled. "We know, Liz. And you'd die to get a backstage pass or have one of the lead rappers use a member of their entourage to call you onstage so you could dance and cuddle with the rapper."

"So."

"Ain't nothing like being with a celebrity."

Leslie chuckled. "They're the most faithful lovers."

Elizabeth waved. "Oh, stop it."

"Oh, we know, Liz. Les and I know you only want to see M. C. Rocket in concert because you're a fan of his rap style." She stopped and popped her fingers. "Oh, that reminds me, that conniving ex of mine is performing on Broadway this weekend."

"In what?"

"A musical."

Leslie lowered her shoulders. "I figured that, Rob. What musical?"

She arched her shoulders. "I don't know."

"And you don't care."

199

She turned toward Elizabeth. "Oh, Liz, you're such a genius."

Leslie added, "She is. She's just not smart enough to realize most celebrity men are more selfish than the everyday Joe. Girl, you don't need to get involved with a famous singer. Most of them go from road show to road show screwing different girls. Girls, I say, because a real woman wouldn't sleep with a man she knew she wasn't going to see again. Not even I have done that."

Robin pursed her lips, as if she could work the distaste for Leslie's dialogue out of her mouth. "Score a point for Leslie."

"Oh, Rob, stop being a prude."

"I liked the true love part you were talking about earlier. That sounds so much better to me than coupling for sex and money."

"It does." She nodded. "It does, but it's not the norm from what I've seen. Exit your fantasy world. Most men just want to get laid and a lot of women want a man who has long money. A few rare couples have been trying to change that for years. Seeing that we can't, I say trade off without whining and complaining."

Michael's face pushed its way to the front of her mind, and, kicking her legs up, Robin leaned against the back of the sofa and laughed for a long time.

The Grammy award nomination brought Robin a stack of movie offers. Not only did industry executives see her as a creative writing genius, they sensed that she had the potential to be a star actress.

Though she leafed through the unsolicited movie scripts, she snubbed the offers. Despite her desire to keep her feet firmly on the ground, pushy motion picture executives had articles printed in tabloids and legitimate slicks. *Line After Line* magazine, *Reaching Out, Writer's Forum, The Writer Tools, Track and Cross-Country* (Robin continued to subscribe to the magazine considered the sport's bible), *Publishing Today, Mahogany, Black Woman Today, Entertainment Hits,* and *On Top Of The World* all headlined articles detailing her obvious talent for writing and presumably also acting.

She screamed, "I've never acted in my life!" at Leslie the first week after her Grammy award nomination. "Where are they getting this stuff from! I don't want to be an actress! I'm a writer! I live with an actress! I see how crazy acting makes a person! Goodness, no! I don't want to be an actress! I'm a writer!"

Hours of conversation with Leslie provided her the outlet she desperately needed. In the two months that followed the Grammys, she came to understand Leslie's dislike for autograph seekers, something she swore with religious fervor she never would. Besides the discomfort of having to stop her normal routine to fulfill unexpected requests, she came to dislike the personal questions the same autograph seekers hammered her with. Following each attack, as she came to refer to the requests, she returned to the apartment and complained bitterly to Leslie, the walls when Leslie was absent from the apartment, that, as kind and patient as she was, autograph seekers treated her more like a number than a person.

Leslie watched in wide-eyed disbelief as she transformed into a bitter, professional writer. Hoping to encourage her to regain the warm spirit that once filled and strengthened her naturally sweet disposition, she told Robin her fans adored her. "They want to get to know you better. That's the reason they've started asking you so many personal questions. They respect you. You're a wonderful person. Show a little of yourself to your fans. They'll back off and give you your space. Fans of writers know they need their alone time to work. And they want you to work, because they love your work. Your plays help your fans to get through their own troubles. They don't want you to stop writing, to stop working. Do a couple of in-depth interviews and leave it at that. The time has come when your fans want more than just your plays. They want a part of you now. You're making it, Rob."

"Yea. Right." Was the most she ever returned Leslie's comments. If she couldn't venture outdoors free of reporters, photographers, gossip columnists and autograph seekers stepping in her shadow, she threatened to purchase a large estate, and, therein, bury herself. "All I want to do is write. I don't want to do interviews and make my personal life an open book. I put enough of myself in my plays. Writers display more of themselves than any other group of artists. All of my so-called fans . . . I don't like that word. I never did . . . have to do is read and watch plays I author. They'll find more of me in them than they'll ever find in a thirty-minute magazine, radio or live television interview."

Across from her, Leslie nodded into a frown. She considered the change in Robin's lifestyle and attitude a mean twist of fate. Whereas she would curse and glare at photographers and gossip columnists who interrupted her while she was dining or shopping, she knew Robin refused to equip herself with such weaponry. All the world could open ammunition on her, demanding that she make her life privy to them, and she wouldn't return attack.

The times Robin left the apartment, fear tugged at the corners of Leslie's mind. *"What will happen to Rob if the world does open ammunition on her? What will happen to her if the same press that's now building her up, one day tears her down? What will happen to her if men hunt her like a prized animal only to have bragging rights to say they were among the first* who laid her then left her to herself, a filthy stock of sexual rumors gushing her back?"

Questions filled her head. Those times, working as sentry for Robin's well being, she thought of ways to protect her. She was willing to make a fool of herself to protect her. She endured criticism from the press, the public and her family so many times the thought of public disapproval gave her no fear.

Robin found her thoughts going to her mother a lot the last two weeks. "Sonia dying took Mama's chance at a perfect daughter away," she thought to herself. "Then again, no one's perfect. If Sonia had lived, maybe Mama wouldn't have loved her so much either." While sitting in the apartment she couldn't stop herself from wondering why she allowed her mother to mold her into a woman who worked to please everyone. She tried so hard to be perfect, to pull off the impossible. "It's Mama. It's Mama," she mused with tears in her eyes. "She always made me fight so hard to avoid making a mistake, to keep from saying or doing anything wrong. Even when Sonia was alive I had to be the perfect big sister."

She stared at her feet. She was wearing a pair of high priced sneakers. She turned her feet in circles. She was six years old when she started dressing up in Marcia's shoes and letting Sonia stick her tiny feet inside her sneakers. Holding Sonia's soft hand, she would sing songs and walk in and out of different rooms of their parents' house on warm summer afternoons. Sonia would wobble, fall, laugh, stand back up and walk further down the hall. Marcia knew. Sonia and she laughed so loudly and made so much racket marching across the floor, Robin was certain Marcia heard them. Yet she hollered at her until veins pulsed at the sides of her head the afternoon Sonia started screaming. Robin had to pee, so she raced to the bathroom. Before she left Sonia alone in the middle of the hallway she was careful to shake her finger at her and tell her, "Don't move. I'll be right back. Don't move."

Leaning over, Sonia laughed and patted the floor while she looked up at her big sister. Because she wanted to hear every move Sonia made, she peed with the bathroom door open. She wet her pants when she heard Sonia scream. Pulling her pants up while she ran, she raced into the hallway. When she didn't see Sonia, her eyes ballooned. Her heart raced and she hurried toward the stairs. Marcia was standing in the center of the stairs holding Sonia. When she looked up at Robin, her eyes were narrow slits. "How could you? You know she's sick."

She opened her mouth, but Marcia refused her utterance. "Just walk off and leave her so close to the stairs."

"But, Ma—"

"Shut up! You are so thoughtless! She could have been hurt badly! She fell halfway down the stairs before I caught her! You're her big sister. You told me you would watch her. I was in the kitchen. If you didn't want to watch her, you should have simply brought her to me. You didn't have to leave her so close to the stairs."

Tears pooled in her eyes. "I didn't try to hurt—"

"Forget it. I just know I'll never leave you alone with Sonia again." Then she turned and walked down the stairs.

Robin stood on the top stair watching her mother and baby sister move away from her. She bit back tears.

From that day forward she vowed to never hurt anyone again. She didn't care what it cost her. When life's pains pressed tightly about her or when she sat in a dark room and thought she heard Sonia calling out to her, she pulled on a pair of earphones, turned the music up loud, reached for the light switch and wrote.

On a stormy night after the Grammys and because she didn't have anything better to do, she wrote the theme song to two blockbuster movies. The hit songs brought her a flux of newspaper and magazine interview requests. Directors and producers wrote her personal letters asking her to try her hand at screenplay writing. The letters poured in. Those and letters addressed to her from devoted theatre goers, over flowed in the sturdy mail bag the postal carrier left with Annette each Monday morning. After receiving the bag of fan mail for months, she flew home to Johnson City. She longed to insulate herself in the warmth of real love. She wanted to be around her father. She wanted to hear his deep voice say, "I'm proud of you." She wanted to laugh with him, catch fish with him and trade tall stories with him.

Home for the first time absent the company of Betsy, Anna and Loretta, she spent most of her time outdoors. Theo worked long hours and was unable to walk through the front door before the sun lowered behind the Great Smokey Mountains. During the day and away from home, she breathed in mountain air and contemplated her future. A few lazy afternoons she packed a bag of fruit, cheese and crackers and went hiking in the higher elevations of the Smokey Mountains. While she trudged up the mountainside, her boots pushing against the rock and dirt, dreams flashed like movie scenes in her head. The dreams nudging her to create, when she returned home, she found herself dusting cobwebs off old ideas. Sitting at the table in her parents' spacious kitchen with her shoulders hunched, she put the ideas on paper. When Marcia asked, "Why are you writing? I thought you came here to rest . . . to get your mind off of work. Can't you stop writing just for once? Is writing all you can do? Is it all you ever want to do?" She answered, "I know I came home to rest, Mama. I am resting. I am relaxing. I sleep until noon every day. And, no, Mama. I don't only want to write, but you already know that. Before you used to tell me that I gave too many speeches. Now you're telling me I write too much." Then, turning away from the ruled notebook pad and facing her mother, she added, "Besides, writing isn't work to me. It's doing all those interviews that's work to me."

It was a time in her life when regardless of how she struggled to avoid emotional and mental pain heartache found her. Fans constantly asked her about Michael. Tabloid reporters telephoned her and pleaded with her to tell them when Michael and she were going to patch up their relationship and get married. Avid theatergoers wrote and mailed her letters of advice. They told her what type of man was best suited for her. Many asked her for her hand in marriage. A rare few wrote her religiously and told her they shared a spiritual past together. These letters she shipped off to her attorney as a trail of evidence should one of the fans begin to stalk her. No longer finding solace in the mounds of letters, she came to view the letters as too much work to shift through and read.

"What you need is a good man who's in the business. You need someone who will readily understand you. It takes an artist to fully and truly understand another artist. Famous people marry famous people," Leslie often told her when the issue of men, dating and romance rose between them, which was less frequently than five years ago.

Much of Africa-America wrote television executives and newspaper and magazine editors and informed them that she "wasn't really black". They wrote that she wasn't dark enough and that she didn't possess sharp ethnic features. After two years of fame, Robin stopped counting the times someone sharing her heritage stopped her on the sidewalk, while she dashed through John F. Kennedy International Airport or dined with a friend at Mavis' and asked her if she was half black/half white. A long, wide nose, naturally long, wavy hair and almond colored skin marked her and made it nearly impossible for her to go unnoticed. Hungry for acceptance from her own people, when she looked in the mirror sadness came over her. She wondered why her skin wasn't darker and why her nose didn't look more like it belonged to an African American.

"It's almost like Robin wishes she were someone else," Theo told Marcia late one night while they were in bed. Down the hall from them Robin sat in her bed watching a PBS program.

Marcia asked, "Why do you say that?"

"Because she's always asking me why she looks like she does. Sometimes I think that girl studies so much on our family tree because she's trying to find out if there are any white people in our tree. Sometimes I don't think she likes the way she looks or something. If it's not her weight, then it's her nose. If it's not her nose, then it's her skin tone. One thing or another, she just doesn't seem happy to be the woman who she is. I don't know what to do."

"I'll talk to her tomorrow," Marcia offered. "Don't worry. Now turn over and go to sleep. It's getting late."

The following morning, she pulled Robin aside. She pressed her hands firmly against her hips and stood akimbo.

Robin was pouring herself a bowl of cereal.

"What's wrong with you?" She asked without giving Robin time to answer. "You are the only daughter I have. You are my only child." She dropped her hands off her hips and walked toward her. "You are my only chance for a future. I don't have any other children. You are the only child God allowed me to see grow into a woman. I mean. I know I'm not always as warm and mushy as you probably want me to be, but that's not my style. Life hasn't been easy for me. You know that. Losing Sonia and all. Sonia meant so much to me. I'll never recover from losing her." She shook her head and gazed at the floor. "Never." When she raised her head, she looked Robin squarely in the eye. "I don't spoil you like your father does. He gives you far too much attention, but you are important to me. You are my only child. Your father told me he thinks you don't like the way you look or something. Said you're always asking about our family tree. I think I know where all that is coming from." Shaking her head, she grinned. "I read those magazine and newspaper articles. I know what those people are saying about you." She stopped smiling and looked up at her. "Well, girl, let me tell you, you are black. Your father is black. I am black. Whatever color could you possibly be? Don't believe that talk about your not being black enough, about your not behaving black enough, about your not writing black enough in some of your work." She stood akimbo again. "And tell me. What is black enough? I didn't know you had to act a certain way to be black. Pay all of that talk no mind, Robin. You pay too much attention to what people say about you. You are black. And you know your father and I didn't raise you to put emphasis on color. I don't care if most of the rest of the world does. You were not raised like that. Color means nothing. It has about as much relevance as the size of the shoe you wear. People walk around talking like they told God what color to make them before they were ever born. Like they told God who to make their parents. Like they told God what city, hospital, date and time to have them be born in." She shook her head "Don't let those folks put you in a shoebox then get mad at you every time you want to come out. Be yourself. Nothing you do can make you black or stop making you be black. God took care of that. Being black is not something you got to choose to be, so just be yourself. That you do have control over. Stop thinking you have to act, dress, think, write or look a certain way to be black. Nobody made you black but God. Now who else do you think can turn around and change that? And," she continued with a shake of her head and a cluck of her tongue. "I think other black folk saying mean things about you and questioning your racial identity is racism, as much as some of the ignorant white folk around saying mean things about you because of your skin color." She waved her hand as if by doing so she could brush the accusations posed against her daughter aside, silence them from both of their lives. "Both are racism. People expecting you to act and think a certain way because of your skin color. It's ignorant, and it's wrong. I don't know why you let either upset you the way you do." That said, she hung her head and walked slowly backwards, putting more distance between her daughter and herself. "I don't know why you even let yourself listen to all the things so many people say about you. People say so many things. I don't know why you don't just shut all of their voices out of your head. You should just shut all of their voices out of your head. That's what you do, Robin. Just silence all of those people . . . people who don't even know you. Just don't listen to them. Don't pay any attention to them. That's the only way to shut them up, at this point." Then, she shook the end of her skirt. Turning, she walked to the refrigerator, pulled out a can of soda and walked into the living room, leaving Robin alone with her thoughts and her bowl of cereal.

Robin waited until she returned home to New York City to flirt with anorexia nervosa again. Grabbing a roll of measuring tape she purchased in Johnson City, she wrapped the tape around her thighs, hips, buttocks and stomach. She logged the measurements on stapled sheets of notebook paper she hid at the bottom of the last drawer of her bedroom dresser.

The few times Leslie was at the apartment and not with Bob, she teased her about her obsession. "Rob. As skinny as you are. I can't believe you actually stare at yourself in the mirror then turn away and whisper that you're fat. Please don't tell me that you're trying to lose weight again. You can't possibly be trying to come down another dress size. I can't believe you, Rob . . . trying to lose weight. You've got to be kidding. You have to be kidding. How much do you weigh anyway? About 95 pounds? You're a pee wee."

Despite Leslie's concern, Robin forced herself not to eat. Without the advice of her father or the love of Michael, for the first time in her life her moods swung. She snapped at jaywalking pedestrians while she drove through the city. She honked her horn at elderly drivers and wished them off the road. In the grocery store checkout line, she shifted her weight from foot to foot, rolled her eyes and complained that the cashier was too slow. When Annette read her messages to her, she snatched the papers out of her hand and told her she'd read them later herself. She cringed when she walked in front of mirrors. She was never pleased with the woman she saw gawking back at her. When a play she wrote closed early, she complained bitterly to Derrick for long hours on the telephone. She accused him of being incompetent and not looking out for her best interest.

Michael kept up-to-date on the latest details of her career and as much of her private life as he could gather via information he obtained from Derrick, Robin's dual hatted manager/publicist. When Derrick told him her weight was dropping rapidly, Michael rang the apartment. Leslie answered the telephone. Although she was curt during the brief conversation, he made her promise to keep a close eye on Robin. Not until he said, "Watch her. Promise me that you'll watch her, that you won't let anything bad happen to her," did it dawn on Leslie that Robin had dropped more than ten pounds since she returned home from Johnson City three short weeks ago.

"It's her mother," Leslie said trying to put him at ease. "Rob always comes back feeling dejected after she's been home for longer than a weekend. I don't know why she went home anyway. I know she wanted to see her father but being around her mother for a long time always upsets her. Rob knows that." Moments later, she returned the receiver to its cradle. Staring at the ceiling, she worked to devise a plan to get Robin to start eating again.

Unaware of Michael and Leslie's telephone conversation, Robin maintained her grueling work schedule. Saturdays, she continued her timed runs at the track and field. Times she felt dizzy while she ran she called on internal fortitude and told herself to open her stride while she circled the track. She blamed the tightness in her chest and her light headedness on the weather. Busy with work and her unforgiving exercise regimen, she didn't allow herself the time to think about her lackluster social life, the increasing strain in her relationship with her mother or her obsession with her weight. When Leslie told her that Michael was concerned about her weight loss, she grew sad. The longer she thought about Michael only asking about her because he thought she was too thin, the sharper her sadness became. Within a matter of weeks the sadness deepened and became a hard depression. To escape the truth Michael's concern embodied, she wrote feverishly. Wanting to avoid the stares of onlookers and the lens of suspecting photographers – everyone whispered that she was too thin – she seldom ventured outdoors. She avoided telephoning her sorority sisters. She didn't even take the time to call or visit with Trisha who lived a mere one-hour drive away in upstate New York. Guilt and shame for not chatting no longer coached her conscience where her friends were concerned. She wasn't bothered that she hadn't spoken with them in months. She missed them but not enough to keep in touch.

****

The last two years Theo used the same phrases of hope when he ended his telephone conversations with her. He told her, "You are important. You shouldn't need anyone to tell you that you're somebody. Take time out for yourself. Relax. Life is short. Make sure you take the time to enjoy life." While he talked with her on the telephone, Marcia sat across from him in their living room. She frowned and clucked her tongue while he talked into the receiver. Though she kept her feelings to herself, she gathered, particularly through interviews, that Robin held her at fault for her lack of trust of strangers, her fear of public rebuke.

Gone unspoken in all of their telephone conversations was Theo's longing to see her returned to Michael's warm embrace, and, in Michael's warmth, find the ability to free herself from her fear of strangers, her heightening distrust of other people. To his disbelief, Marcia also, prayed during Altar Call in church on Sunday for Robin to meet a nice, Christian man, fall helplessly in love and marry in a large, Baptist church.

Until his requests were answered and Robin's life was filled with the joy of his answered prayers, Theo thanked God for Leslie. Though he realized the roommates were as different as they were alike, he knew how important Leslie was to Robin. He chuckled when he recalled the times Leslie performed in a hit motion picture. While the box office tallies went up-up-up, Robin called home. Her voice rose, fell and raced like a gazelle across the telephone wire while she told him, "Les is doing great! She's one of the highest paid actresses in the industry! She's tearing up the box office! I can't believe the roll she's on! Hit after hit, she just keeps getting better! I'm so happy for her! She deserves this. She's worked so hard."

Listening to her shout excitedly into the wire, he sat in his favorite chair in the living room in Tennessee. He shook his head. Her enthusiasm was contagious. It worked a smile onto his face, but it failed to harness his worry that she was spending too much time alone. It pained him that a generation ago she would have been deemed "an old maid". He wrestled with himself to find a reasonable answer for her being single. She was intelligent, independent, attractive, gentle and caring. When he asked her if she ever wanted to get married and she just turned and stared at him, he wondered if something could be wrong with her. But, "no, no," she assured him. She was fine. She wasn't sick. Nothing was wrong with her. That said, she dropped the subject, smiled at him and asked him what he thought her favorite football team, the Pittsburgh Steelers, chances were of winning the Super Bowl.

While in New York, Robin and Leslie spent late nights talking about men they found attractive, intriguing. Leslie did most of the talking. Across from her, Robin relived the bulk of her few romantic relationships within the confines of her mind. Next to her, Leslie rambled for two to three hours while she recanted memorable times she shared with Drew, Bob, Mark, Jerome, Chris, Doug, John and Frank, men who shared their affections with her during different points in her life. At the end of their late night discussions, Robin concluded that the only man who really loved her was her father. Certain that her romantic liaisons had all been a trick, she concluded that men, regardless of their age, race or color, took more from than they gave to the women in their lives. She pent her emotions inside her heart. Turning to anger, she placed the blame for her pent up emotions on the men who gawked at her when she passed them on busy thoroughfares. She was angry for not having a successful relationship. She knew it wasn't her. She told herself she was a good catch. Women's magazines headlined articles that made it clear to her that she had all the inner workings of a woman a good man would want to call his own. Yet, she was alone. With each passing year her fears mounted. She started to wonder if she would always be alone, single, solo, going it on her own. Yet, when Leslie turned with an arched brow and asked her if she ever contemplated giving up on love because she feared heartache, she answered flatly, "No. I stay in control of my love life. I don't monitor my happiness by what's going on with a man and me. I'm too smart for that."

****

"Rob! Rob! Rob!"

Elizabeth's rising voice startled her. She stopped gazing at the *New York Post*. Turning and facing Elizabeth, she arched her shoulders. While Elizabeth talked at the side of her head, she thought about a conversation she overheard while eating a late lunch at Mavis' two days ago.

A balding, Caucasian man with a double chin and a thin, gray haired woman she assumed to be the man's wife, were talking at Mavis' then . . . two days ago. She didn't notice them until the woman taped the man's forearm, titled her head in Robin's direction and asked, "Isn't she that feisty actress' writer roommate?"

When the man looked in her direction, breadcrumbs sprinkling the bottom of his chin, she lowered her gaze and pretended to return her attention to the *New York Post*.

The man leaned close to the woman and whispered, "Leslie Fletcher is the actress' name. Isn't she dating that Tycoon, Bob Long?"

The woman sat back. "Bob Long?"

Her brow didn't lower until the man pressed his finger against his lips and said, "Sssshhhh, Honey."

The woman sat back with obvious surprise. "Bob Long." They both whispered now. "Bob Long's in his late forties."

"Heard he's getting in the movie business."

"Yes."

"Hmph."

"They make movies here too." The man said, amid the choke of his own laughter. "Why, with not having to pay to use City Hall, for police help or for parking, it's no wonder Hollywood doesn't pack up and move to New York City. I knew I should have taken up acting or directing."

The woman smiled at him. "Oh, yeah?"

He turned his own words recently spoken about Hollywood in his mind. Then he shook his head. "Naw."

The woman echoed, "Naw."

"Wanta know why?"

"Yeah."

"Sure?"

"Tell me."

"I--," Pausing long enough to smile, he reached across the table and took her hand gently inside his own. "Wouldn't have met you."

She smiled wider. Her gaze lowered to the table.

Listening to the sound of their own laughter, the couple peered inside each other's eyes. They didn't turn when a man bumped their table and nearly upset their pitcher of water.

Robin followed the new customer with her gaze. She squinted and told herself she saw him before. He sat behind the elderly couple with his hands stuffed in his jacket pockets. Robin took in a deep breath when a waitress approached his table. The second he turned, Robin's eyes ballooned. She stared at the butt of the gun in his pocket. Fear cleaved her tongue to her mouth. She told herself to stand and wave her hands, point and draw attention to him, but her hands wouldn't stop shaking.

The older woman took her eyes away from her husband and smiled into, "Leslie. She played in this hit series when she was a kid. She was around twelve. I forget the name of the series. She was real cute then." She chuckled. "You know how kids are cute. It was a pretty good series."

Her husband widened his brow. "Wait a minute. We used to watch that show after I came home from work."

The woman's mouth opened into a slow, "Ahhh."

The man laughed out the words, "That was a good show."

The woman smiled at his laughter. "Yeah. It was. Leslie's grown into a beautiful woman. She's a looker, but I've heard she's had a tough time growing up on so many television and movie sets."

Robin's gaze went from the couple to the man sitting behind them. She glanced at his pocket. The gun was gone. A knot formed in her throat. When a waitress passed her table, she tugged on her uniform. "That man has a gun," she whispered.

Leaning close to Robin's shoulder, the waitress asked, "What?"
She moved so close to the table, her elbow slipped off the edge.
"That man has a gun in his jacket. I saw it. In his pocket. That man. Over
there. Behind that couple."
After she followed Robin's gaze the waitress stood and laughed.
"Oh, him. He comes in here quite a bit. Usually early in the morning. I'm
talking early. In the wee hours of the morning. That's Jack. He's
harmless."
"But I know what I saw. Sure you don't want to check it out?"
"I can't just go over there and ask a customer if he has a gun in his
pocket. Are you kidding?"
Robin brought her hands together. "True." She nodded. "True.
That's true."
"Besides, Jack carries this cell phone with him nearly everywhere
he goes. That's probably what you saw."
Robin started to laugh. "You're right. You're absolutely right. I
forget about those things. Don't see them much."
"Another toy for the rich."
She eyed the waitress suspiciously.
"And you know," scratching her head, the waitress added, "Come
to think of it. Jack talks about you and Leslie. Sure you don't know him?"
"No." Moving to the back of her seat, she made a mental note to
ask Leslie about a man named Jack. A second later she found herself
eavesdropping on the couple's conversation again. It upset her that they
seemed to know more about Leslie and Bob's relationship than she did.
"Hollywood's a hard life. The work to stay on top is endless.
There's no time for rest. It's a constant struggle to keep your name before
millions of moviegoers." The man raised his shoulders. "A hard life.
Wouldn't want it for all the money in the world. I'd rather be happy living
the simple life God's blessed us with."
"Bob probably loves all that Hollywood game. That man sure
fights like mad to stay on top. He likes to be seen." The woman laughed.
"Wonder if he was born with a spotlight shinning on him. He just seems so
out of place when he's not center of a loud crowd."
The man sipped his coffee. "He's always stepping on every and
anybody's feet."
"Ain't that the truth." The woman turned her coffee cup in her
hand. "He sure lucked out to land a looker like Leslie. He's getting kinda
old to still be pulling beautiful woman to his side." Chuckling, she placed
her cup on the table.
"Yeah. I was just getting ready to say Bob must be turning on all of
his charm. Yeah. Years ago he could fool around with the big shot beauties,

but that was years ago. He's older now. Goodness. He has to be almost old enough to be Leslie's father." He spread his hands and arched his shoulders. He chuckled. "Then again, when you think about it, all the girls every other guy wants, Bob's already had. That man just has been around."

"True. . . . Dirty old man."

The man raised his hand. "Ah. Ah. Ah. Never an old man."

"And why's that?"

"Because Bob's younger than both of us. Put some good radio and television stations together too, especially some good talk shows."

The woman waved. "Oh. Who cares."

After he stabbed his poached egg, Jack turned and glanced at Robin. She was eating a piece of ham. He ran his tongue across his mouth and bit into his egg.

"I know one thing. If Bob put a movie out this year, you'd be excited to go see it."

The woman waved again. "Ahhh."

His mouth full of eggs, Jack glanced out of the corner of his eye at Robin. Yes. She was the woman he saw with Leslie shopping at Loew's two weeks ago. He also recalled seeing her at the park across from the high rise Leslie lived in.

Robin looked up from her plate of ham and eggs.

Jack turned and stared at his table. He raised his hand and placed it against the side of his face. He grinned while he listened to the elderly couple discuss Leslie and Bob. It tickled him that Leslie had no idea what she was getting herself into. Bob Long. Jack didn't know him personally, but he'd heard about him. Cold as a snake. That's what Jack heard Bob Long was. Cold as a snake and not above operating his businesses outside the law. He almost turned and winked at the elderly man when he heard him praise Bob's business savvy.

"Oh, come on. You know a studio wouldn't have to spend a lot of money to advertise one of Bob's movies." The elderly man filled his coffee cup then reached for the sugar container. "Lines would form outside movie theatres with just the mention of Bob's name."

"Ahhh."

"Long lines."

"Ahhh."

"Without advertisement. Let Bob, with his powerful radio and television following, put a row of commercials out to advertise a movie he produced, and, there you have it, Bob would have another blockbuster on his hands."

"Ahhh."

"Tell you what."

"What?"

"How many movies in the top all time top 100, all time I'm saying, has Bob helped fund or had an affair with the leading lady in?"

"Okay. Okay. Okay. All right. All right. All right."

"In the top 100."

The woman chuckled. "All time top 100, right?"

"Oh, Baby, come on."

"I don't know."

"Yes, you do."

Listening to the couple, Jack couldn't help but think about Arnold. Mellford residents talked about him the way the couple were talking about Bob. Mellford adored Arnold. He was one of their heroes.

Jack ate more of his poached egg. He almost sat back and sighed. Nearly twenty years passed since he first met Arnold. He did a good job meeting Arnold's request. His brow tightened. "I'm losing my edge," he thought to himself. Crucial information he couldn't get straight in his head. Important facts he was forgetting more and more. Like where he buried that red head. He needed to know the location of the woman's body. It was his winning point to use against Leslie. It was all he had to corner her with. And. He lowered his brow. He couldn't remember. He just couldn't remember. When he raised his head, he heard the couple talking. Gritting his teeth and balling his hands, he told himself not to jump from his table and scream, "Shut up!"

"Haven't all of the women Bob's had affairs with gone on to be big name actresses, and I mean, big name actresses, some of the biggest in the business?" The woman asked.

"There you go."

"Little Miss Leslie's getting her piece of the pie too, then."

"For sure."

"Go ahead, Leslie. That's being smart. Break even."

"You forgot one very important thing."

"What?"

"There's no way a person can break even when they're using someone else."

Recalling the night Arnold contacted him and told him about his girlfriend threatening to tell the police he knew more about a Mafia crime he was prosecuting than he let on, Jack nodded and smiled like a fox. It was dark and cold that night. Arnold kept pulling up on his coat collar. A thick fog clouded their vision. They squinted, turned and looked over their shoulders each time they heard a rustle in the wind. The only other thing Jack remembered about that night was that Arnold and he were standing in what seemed the middle of no where. Not one house or car was in view. He remembered that he took a narrow, winding road to reach the site. An eerie feeling came over him as soon as he stepped out of his car. The hair on the nape of his neck rose. Pride kept him walking. He was a man who took risk. Glancing back at his car, he told himself to go forward into the night and to perform a good job at whatever it was Arnold wanted him to do.

****

Elizabeth looked at Robin and chuckled with misgiving. Robin's level of emotional control amazed her. She recalled how Robin didn't flinch the day she told her she broke up with Michael. She kept waiting for tears to pool in her eyes while she recanted the events of Michael and her breakup. "I told him it was over, and that was it. I mean. There wasn't anything left to work with. I couldn't possibly go back to him after I caught him in bed with Paulette. Paulette. Paulette." When Robin's eyes ballooned, Elizabeth bit her tongue. "No," she said to herself. She couldn't ask Robin if she was more hurt that Michael chose to be with another woman instead of her or if she was more upset that Michael slept with Paulette.

Robin didn't give her long to think. She quickly told her, "The night I broke up with Michael can you believe I called my mother? Of all people, I called my mother for advice. I think I hoped that since I was hurting she'd comfort me." She looked across the room at Elizabeth. "After I told her about finding Michael with Paulette, do you know what she said to me? She told me to stop crying the blues. She told me not to feel so hurt and cheated. Then just before I hung up she said, 'After all, Michael made you feel.' And that I will never forget."

"Well. How are you now?"

She looked around Mavis'. She was sitting at the same table she was sitting at when she thought she saw that man carrying a gun in his jacket pocket two days ago.

"Rob?"

She glanced across the restaurant. The table the man with the gun sat at was empty.

"Rob?"

"Yea? Sorry. I was thinking about something."

"I was asking you how you're doing with what your mom said about Michael and Paulette and all."

"That was years ago."

"I know, but – Do you recover from everything so quickly?" She chuckled while she searched Robin's face for a hint of pain.

She raised then lowered her shoulders. "What's not to recover from? I can't walk around in a stupor. I have to live. Michael's going on with his life and he's not with Paulette anymore. They broke up more than a year ago. I didn't think they'd stay together. Paulette's a player. Men are like toys to her. Not that I feel sorry for Michael. He walked right into Diane and Paulette's trap."

"Yea." Elizabeth sipped her soda. "And how are you and your mom?"

"The same." She turned and looked out the window. "Let's change the subject."

"Sure." Elizabeth sipped more of her soda. "If that's what you want."

She was quick. "That's what I want."

"So, how's Michelle getting along these days?"

"Michelle's doing good. She still wants to break into acting. Leslie offered to help her get her foot in the door, but she turned the offer down. She's about as proud and independent as I am, and that's not always a good thing. I tell you, Liz. One thing I've learned since I started having my plays produced is that you can't be a success all by yourself. Every successful person has advisers and people who support them. I tried to do it all by myself when I started out, but I soon found out that I couldn't. There simply isn't enough time in the day for anyone to cover all the bases by herself." She shook her head. "I don't know what I would do without Derrick. He's like my right hand, and I'm not just saying that. He really is."

"I'm glad to hear you learned that no one is an island."

She chuckled.

"When you started working at Mills you definitely didn't think like that. Remember that time you got behind in folding and boxing all those shirts?"

Leaning back in her seat and shaking her head, she laughed. "Do I ever."

"I kept offering to help you, but you kept telling me you were okay. You kept saying you could do it all by yourself. It was almost like you were offended to have anyone ask you if you needed help."

"I did used to be that way. That's what I was talking about. I'm not that way anymore."

"Not as much as you used to be anyway."

"Liz."

"No, Rob. You still have a ton of pride."

She grinned. "That's true. But I'm not as bad as I used to be. I think I would have gone nuts by now if I was as proud as I used to be. Sometimes a person can be so independent that they become foolish. Do things that just don't make good sense. It's all right to ask for and accept help. A hard lesson for me to learn, but learn that lesson I did."

"Michelle used to tell me how she used to have to talk you into letting her help you. She seemed to know how to go about doing that."

"Michelle and I both felt out of place when we first came to the city. We're both from the South and from small towns at that. New York City was brand spanking new for both of us. I think we were glad when we found each other. I'll never forget the day we met. I came in here hungry for my favorite ham and egg dish, and there was Michelle. She looked sad the first time I saw her. She wanted to be an actress so bad."

"Shame on Michelle for not letting Leslie help her get a start at a acting career. Leslie could have saved her a lot of time."

"And heartache."

"Michelle that set on being an actress?"

"Girl, where have you been? Acting is about the only thing on Michelle's mind these days. I admire her desire to make it on her own without soliciting help from Leslie. I think Leslie respects her for that too. Not that she wouldn't respect her if she accepted her offers for help. It's just that after awhile you like it when people don't come around you asking for something. So many people do."

"I really don't see what's wrong with that so long as you don't make a pain of yourself. You know ask the person for favor after favor."

"There's nothing wrong with asking someone successful to help you get your foot in a door. No. That's not what I'm saying. It's just that it gets old after a couple of hundred people ask you to help them."

"Then I think the thing is to spot good talent and know when a person will do well with a little support. I mean. No. You can't help everybody. Some people just want to be a celebrity or wealthy. I wouldn't help someone just for those reasons. But if I spotted true talent, I'd definitely put a good word in for a person."

"Yea."

"Are you and Michelle still visiting children's hospitals and convalescent homes?" A second later, she added, "I don't know why I asked you that. Of course you're still visiting hospitals and nursing homes. Why wouldn't you? You're the woman who helps more people than anyone else I know."

Robin laughed. "Michelle enjoys helping to lift people's spirits as much as I do. You ought to see her with the kids at the hospitals. She always makes them laugh."

"I don't see how you do it."

"Do what?"

"Visit those sick kids at the hospitals."

Turning away from Elizabeth, she stared out the window. "I always will."

"Don't they remind you of—"

"Yes. Sometimes they make me think about Sonia. Actually, many, many times they make me think about her. Sometimes I think I see her in their faces, especially the really small kids, almost babies. I think it's my way of reaching out to Sonia. My way of showing her how much I love her." She faced Elizabeth. "She'll always be my sister, you know."

"Of course."

"And you and all my good, good friends are like sisters too."

Tilting her head, Elizabeth smiled softly. "You're just a sweetheart."

"Not as cool as I used to be though."

"Oh, Rob."

"Oh, Rob, nothing. I've changed."

"You've been under so much pressure. Is your play doing any better?"

She shook her head. "This new play has been the hardest piece of art I've ever stood behind. Regardless of what I do, it just won't sell. You know I thought after I had a couple of hit plays out, I would be set. Wrong. Every new work is just that. New. And the hard-hard work of selling the piece starts all over again."

"Well. You're dealing with it fairly well. Are you working on anything else?"

"Yes. If I wasn't I probably would be one of the meanest women in the city."

"No."

"Yes. I put a lot into my work."

"What artist doesn't?"

"I know. It's just that I am very attached to my work. As a writer, I think it's hard not to be. My work is my baby from start to finish. But, with this play--" She gazed across the table at Elizabeth. "Do you know that I actually check the *Times* to see how the play is doing? I check the editorials, and I've never done that before. I hate doing that, but it's almost like I can't stop. I have to know what people think about this play. Of course, if it was doing well at the box office I wouldn't be doing this. I'd already have my answer." She stopped and waved her hand. "Liz, don't say it. Don't even say it."

"What?" She leaned forward and chuckled. "What was I going to say?"

"That I already have my answer. I mean. If people aren't going out and buying tickets to see the play that alone tells me what they think about the play."

"Not necessarily. Maybe you just aren't advertising it enough or maybe you're not advertising it in the right circles."

"The right circles? Liz, we're advertising all over the place. Magazines. Newspapers. Billboards. Radio. Television. Are you kidding? That's what makes the slow sales so hard to take."

After she pushed hair off her forehead, Elizabeth chuckled and said, "Know what Leslie told me?"

"No. What?"

"About the play?"

"No, Liz. I don't know what Leslie told you. Tell me."

"You're not going to like it, but knowing you, I know you'll laugh. You're a doll."

"What? What are you talking about? What did Leslie tell you?"

"She said you drive to Broadway and check how long the line to the play is."

Her face grew long.

"Sorry."

"No."

"I thought it was funny, but, maybe—"

"No. I guess it is funny. In a way. In a way it isn't. I just put so much into that play. Watching it do so poorly is not easy in the least. It's like my heart becomes an open book each time that play opens. When few people show up I feel like theatre goers are breaking my heart."

"So long as you don't give up."

She shook her head. "I'll never do that. Besides, living with Leslie taught me that it's possible to come back after a hard fall. I watched Leslie's career resurface after a long hard slide to the bottom. She couldn't find work anywhere when we first started living together. Now she gets more movie offers than she can possibly accept. She's proof that a good career is never over unless the artist chooses to quit. And I'm not a quitter." She shook her head again. "Um-um. No. Robin Carlile does not quit. That's one thing she definitely does not do."

****

Robin hurried across the living room floor. "Les turned the volume on the phone up again. That girl must be death as loud as that phone is ringing." She lifted the receiver out of its cradle and pressed it against her ear. "Hello?"

"Is Leslie Fletcher there?"

Turning her gaze toward the ceiling, she rolled her eyes. "Bob, is this you?" A second later when she heard only silence she asked, "Bob?"

"May I speak with Leslie?"

She clucked her tongue. "Bob, I know this is you. I know your voice. Leslie's not here. Do you want me to take a message for her?" She gritted her teeth when she heard the connection die and the wire buzz. With a shake of her head she dismissed the telephone call and rounded the corner. Going further down the hallway, she entered the bathroom and stepped inside the shower. She wasn't in the shower five minutes when she heard the telephone ring. While she lathered her rag, she waved her hand and said, "Let it ring." Half an hour later she was standing in front of her bedroom dresser trying to decide what to wear. After she pulled out a pair of jeans and a yellow blouse, she crossed the floor and sat on the edge of her bed. She only had one leg in her pants when the telephone rang again.

The telephone rang four times before she stood and went to pick it up. "Hello?"

"May I speak with Leslie Fletcher please?"

Clucking her tongue, she narrowed her brow and said, "Bob, please. Just leave a message with me. I'll give it to Leslie. I don't keep her messages from her. I give her all the messages you give me when you call."

A thick sigh crossed the wire. Then she heard, "Well."

"Tell you what. Let me get a pen and a piece of paper. When I get back, you can give me the message."

"All right."

She walked to her file cabinet and pulled a notebook and pen off the top. "I'm back."

"Thanks, Robin. I know you think I call too much."

"I never said that."

"It's just that Leslie and you have lived together for so long, just the two of you."

"Bob, I'm not threatened by Leslie and your relationship. Les and I go way back. We're tight. Besides," she added with a smirk, "I never had a problem getting along with any of Leslie's other boyfriends."

"That's not what I meant."

"Well. The message?"

"Tell Leslie I called. I'm in the city. Tell her I'd like to get together with her and take her some place special. She really is a special lady, you know?"

She nodded. "Yep. That I do know. You don't find a Leslie Fletcher every day. She's definitely her own woman. No doubt about that."

"Yes. I'm so fortunate to have her." The volume in his voice increased. "And you know. I really want us to get together and have dinner sometime. The three of us. I'd like to get to know you better too."

"Just let me know when."

"Okay. I'll have to run it by Leslie and see when's a good time for her."

She smiled tautly. "You do that."

"All right. Well—"

"Les has the number where you are?"

He chuckled. "Well. Of course she does."

"Oh. That's right. I'm sorry. I just thought maybe you were staying in a hotel or something since you said you just happened to be in the city."

"Leslie didn't tell you I have a penthouse in Manhattan?"

"I don't know. She might have mentioned it. Les tells me so many things. I just can't remember it all."

He chuckled dryly. "Well. She has the number. She knows where to reach me anywhere in the world."

"I'm sure she does. Okay. So, I'll give her the message."

"Thank you."

"Bye."

"Bye."

She returned the receiver to its cradle slowly. Already she missed Leslie. She spent so much time with Bob, she hardly saw her anymore. She told herself to ask her if she wanted to fly to Paris for a weekend of shopping and site seeing as soon as she walked through the front door. Until she came home, she sat in the dining room looking at pictures. Nostalgia created a lump in her throat while she browsed through old magazines and newspapers. Leslie was featured in them all. She chuckled at a few of the articles. Leslie was so skinny in many of the photos. Young at twelve years old and a superstar already, for the first time in months she wondered how Leslie found her way through the maze of celebrity at such a young age. She lowered and shook her head. "Les, just doesn't have any quit in her," she said to the empty room. She sat at the dining room table for an hour before she drifted off to sleep. When she woke up Leslie was standing over her.

"Girl, look at you," she said while she placed her hands on Robin's shoulders. "You're getting to be as bad as me. Falling to sleep in all kinds of places."

"I just took a shower not too long ago," she said while she raised her head off the table. "I can't believe I fell to sleep like that."

"Keeping too many late nights with all that writing you do. You better learn how to relax and put your feet up every now and again." She smiled. "I would say learn to let your hair down, but I know you aren't about to do anything like that." Then she laughed.

After she returned Leslie her smile, she said, "No."

"So, what have you been doing besides sleeping?"

"Nothing much." She raised her voice. "Oh. Bob called. He wanted to know if you wanted to go some place special tonight. He said you would know where to reach him. I asked him for a number, but he said you wouldn't need that."

"I have told Bob about that time and again. He has two apartments in the city. One in the burbs. One downtown. Now how am I supposed to know which one he's staying at this time?"

She raised then lowered her shoulders. "I don't know. He said you'd know."

"That man is so hard to keep up with sometimes."

"He told me how special he thinks you are."

"Yea?" Giggling she added, "But you told him you already knew that. Right?"

She smiled. "As a matter of fact I did." Peering up at her, she asked, "So are you going out with Bob tonight?"

"I don't know. I might."

"Have any special plans for the weekend?"

"Depends. What's up?"

"Thought maybe we could catch a flight to Paris and catch some mad sales."

"This weekend?"

"Yea."

She shook her head. "Can't this weekend. Got plans."

"Bob?"

"Yea. Why do you say it like that?"

"He just wines and dines you so much. How long do you think that'll last?"

"You sound like my mother."

"Well." She spread her hands and turned her palms upright. "Think about it. How long can anyone maintain the incredible level of romance Bob is winning your devotion with? Certainly you don't think he's going to pamper you like this for years and years. I just don't think that is humanely possible."

"You sound like you think Bob's trying to trap me or something."

She was silent.

"Bob likes you, Rob. He thinks very highly of you."

"What's not to like?"

Leslie laughed. "Living with me has done you good, Girl."

"And living with me has done you good. You don't curse half as much as you did when I first moved in here."

"That's true. About Bob. He's had his heart broken so many times. You have to understand that he is incredibly wealthy and you see for yourself how handsome he is. Women around the globe throw themselves at him. I mean. Really. Bob could have any woman he wanted. Any woman. It's not like he's desperate."

"I know that."

"Well," Pulling out a chair, she sat next to Robin. "That makes it clear that he is not trying to trap me. Why is it so hard for people to see that Bob and I love each other."

"Les."

"No, Rob."

"Just last month alone he took you on a cruise, bought you that diamond broach, offered to buy you a restaurant in the city, and bought you all those expensive gowns and dresses. Tell me that's normal."

"What you don't get is that Bob's lifestyle is not normal. This is a multi-millionaire we are talking about here."

"Les. I know long money. We both do. The way Bob is showering you with gifts and attention just is not normal, and you know it. Deep down in your heart I know you know it."

"Bob says you're jealous because—"

"Jealous?"

"Bec—"

"Jealous!"

"Because you're used to—"

"Jealous! I am not jealous! Jealous of what?"

"Rob, you've had me all to yourself for more than six years."

"So? You think that's so great?"

"Admittedly it hasn't always been." She laughed. "But we've grown into a cool groove and you know it."

"Yea."

"Our relationship is not going to change just because Bob and I are getting closer."

Robin was quick. "Are you in love with him?"

"Rob?"

"Answer me."

"Yes."

"You two have only been together for six months."

"I know that."

"Don't move too fast. That's all I'm saying. I'd hate to see you do something that you would spend years of your life regretting. Remember both of our parents. You don't want to rush into a marriage where you stay together with someone who makes you miserable just so the neighbors won't talk and so your kids won't have to grow up in a split family."

"Who said anything about marriage?"

"Les, I'm just saying."

"I know, but Bob and I haven't discussed marrying each other."

"You're out to his mansion in California so much."

"So?"

"You're out there enough to be his wife."

"We can afford to fly from coast to coast like that. We take advantage of it. What's wrong with that?"

"Nothing. I'm happy for you. I'm glad that you met someone you can groove with. There's absolutely nothing wrong with that. I'm happy for you. I just think you should be careful. That's all. Bob is like a charming prince right now. I have never met a man who doted on a woman so much. He's amazing. Maybe he's real and just incredibly romantic."

"Rob, I told you that Bob's had his heart broken so many times that he wants to build the foundation to a strong relationship that will finally last. We both have been in the arts for years. We know the business inside out. We understand fame. We support each other. We encourage each other. We love each other. Bob's not trying to win my affections. He already has my affections. He's the first man to call me every single day. Not a day goes by that he doesn't call me twice. He really cares about how I'm doing. We share so much of our day with each other. We're both only children, and our families are a lot alike. I mean I know I've been spending a lot of time with him lately, but think about my past relationships. You know what all I've been through. Bob's not the only one who's had his heart broken. I've had my heart ripped to shreds too."

"So have—"

"I never thought I would meet a man like Bob. I never thought a man would love me just for me. You even said it yourself. For so many years I thought I had to perform. With Bob, it's not that way. You don't see us when it's just the two of us. If Bob was pretending or trying to trap me into marrying him or something, he wouldn't be as loving when we're alone as he is when we're out in public. People who pretend drop their guard sooner or later, and usually it's sooner. Bob and I are just grateful that we found each other. We are soul mates as much as you may not want to believe that."

Robin waved her hand. "Forget it."

"No."

"You're taking what I'm telling you way out of context. I'm not saying that Bob and you don't care about each other. I'm telling you to be careful. You're so eager to settle into a long relationship with a man who really cares about you, you might make a hasty decision."

"And?"

"And just make a hasty decision."

"I already told you that Bob and I aren't talking about getting married."

She glanced at her watch. "Let's change the subject."

"You still have that watch I bought you from Tiffany's the first Christmas we spent together?"

She smiled while she peered down at the watch. "Yea."

"Diamonds are a girls best friend."

She chuckled. "That's what they say." Then she leaned forward and looked up at Leslie. "But really a girl's best friend is just another good friend."

Their gaze met and they smiled at each other.

"Tell you what," Leslie said. "I'm gonna call around and find Bob. After I do, I'm gonna tell him that we can get together tomorrow. Tonight me and you are gonna have a good time. And I'll take you up on that trip to Paris. Just not this weekend. Like I said earlier, I have something else I have to do."

"Bet." While she watched Leslie walk toward the edge of the room then around the corner, she thought about Bob. Admittedly he was one of the most handsome men she had ever seen. He reminded her of Richard Gere with his salt and pepper colored hair. Bob was suave. He was refined. All his clothes hung on him with a custom designed fit. His shoes always shinned. His moustache was perfectly trimmed. He was a man who carried his age with so much grace he looked twenty years younger than he actually was.

Lowering her chin into her raised palm, she sighed. She recalled the last time Bob visited Leslie at their apartment. He was stopping over on his way home from his office in the city. He carried two dozen white and red roses through the door when she stepped back and ushered him inside the apartment. After he spoke to her he quickened his pace and walked toward Leslie. She stood at the edge of the living room. As soon as she saw Bob she hurried toward him.

"Hi, Baby," Leslie cooed.

"Hi, Love," he said while he pulled Leslie toward him. They kissed without shame. Robin turned away from watching them and walked into her bedroom. Although she turned the television on, she could still hear their voices coming away from the living room.

"How was your day, Sweetheart?" Bob asked.

"Pretty good. I met with Donald. We went over a string of motion picture contracts."

"Did you finish reading that script I gave you?"

"Oh, yes! Bob, where did you get that?"

"A good friend who looks out for me."

"Well your good friend unearthed a gold mine."

"So, do you think you'll act in the movie?"

"Of course, I will. Good scripts like that one are good for any actresses' career. I don't need to tell you that. I'm just glad that you showed it to me. Thanks again, Baby."

The living room grew silent. Robin sat on her bed with her lips pursed. She guessed that Bob was kissing Leslie passionately again.

The following six weeks Bob worked at his office in New York every day. Leslie spent all but three nights with him at his penthouse. When she did come home to the apartment, she told Robin that Bob cooked for her nearly every night. She told her that Bob even took her clothes to the cleaners when he dropped his suits off before he drove to the six-story office complex he owned in the heart of Manhattan.

****

Robin and Leslie never made it to Paris. After Leslie committed herself to working on the movie Bob told her about her spare time filled up. Yet, regardless of how tired she was when she climbed in bed at night she always found time to make love with Bob. A whole month passed before she found herself sitting in Apartment 2101 again. Elizabeth was visiting.

She leaned into Elizabeth's shoulder while she looked at Robin. "What do you think goes on in that head, Liz?"

Elizabeth grinned when she glanced at the side of Robin's head. "No telling."

"No telling."

Elizabeth shook her head. "Ump. Ump. No telling."

Robin still mute, Leslie pursed her lips. She looked at Elizabeth and changed the subject. "So, Liz, how's work at Mill's coming?"

"Same ol'. Same ol'. Fold. Stuff. Box." She shook her head and chuckled. "There are a lot of clothes out there, Les."

Pursing her lips again, Leslie glanced down the sofa. "Rob still not saying anything."

"I know."

"She's sweet, though."

"She is."

"She sure is."

Robin sat forward on the sofa. "You two."

"Oh. You like it." Elizabeth offered.

"And you know it." Leslie added.

Robin rolled her eyes and clucked her tongue. She drew her hand across her face and tried not to blush.

"Enough," Leslie said. Then she paused and added. "Guess what great happened to me?"

Elizabeth accompanied her guess with laughter. "You're engaged."

Leslie shook her head. "No, Liz."

"You're married."

She thickened the tension in her voice. "Liz."

"You're pregnant."

"Rob!"

"Well," she said, lowering her shoulders and sighing, "We guessed."

"Oh, Rob. I might as well spill the beans."

Robin echoed, "Might as well."

Leslie took in a deep breath before she blurted, "The movie's up for an Oscar!"

Worry lines cut across Elizabeth's forehead. "What movie?"

"Make Up. The movie Bob pulled strings to get me to co-direct! But--" Raising her hand, she pressed two fingers against her mouth. "That's our secret. We won't tell anybody." Then she leaned against the back of the sofa and laughed.

"I thought you told me you were—"

She nodded at Robin. "I did act in the movie. But this time I got to do a lot more than just act. It was so excit—"

"You co-directed this movie and you didn't even tell me?"

"I wanted to surprise you, Rob?"

"That you did."

"The cast is fabulous!"

"Ever since you started dating Bob, you've been a bag of secrets."

"No, I have not, Rob. Can't a woman surprise her good friends?"

Her brow tightened. "Yea. Right, Les."

Leslie's eyes swelled. "I oversaw a lot of the casting. I'm excited about this movie, but," she paused to arch her shoulders. "I think you both already picked up on that. The premiere showing for Hollywood's finest and most critical, or, should I say, cynical, is tonight at eight. I want you both to attend. I think you'll be surprised. I know you'll be delighted. You'll really like the movie."

226

Robin leaned into the spine of the sofa. Her heart raced. "Tonight? At eight? Why didn't you say something before?"

Pulling down on her blouse, Leslie peered at the floor. "Umm. Ummm. I don't know."

Elizabeth stood. "Tonight at eight!"

"Tonight at eight." Leslie repeated flatly when she looked up.

Robin scooted to the edge of the sofa and smiled faintly. "Congratulations." Then she stood and hugged her. "Anyway, I'll be there." She turned and looked at Elizabeth.

"I'll be there too. I'll ride with Rob." When she stepped around the back of Leslie, the three women embraced.

"What are you wearing, Les?" was the first question Robin filled the room with after Elizabeth and she moved away from Leslie.

"A green, silk dress good enough?"

Elizabeth lowered the point of her head and drug out, "Ummm-hmmm." Then she nodded and asked, "What do you think, Rob?"

"Good, by me. And what are you wearing for this last minute invite, Miss Liz?"

"How about an off pink, satin gown? It's the same gown I wore when your first play opened on Broadway."

"Go ahead, Girl. I hear you, Liz. That gown is never going to go out of style. That gown is sharp." Robin didn't stop smiling until she raised her hand and connected it with Elizabeth's palm.

"And you, Rob?"

"Oh, Liz. I think I've got something in my closet."

Leslie greeted her answer with a snicker.

Elizabeth turned. "Does she, Les?"

"Where do you think I get my clothes from?"

"Oh." Elizabeth chuckled. "I'm surprised. Rob's either in jeans, a jogging suit or a pair of shorts."

"That's true, Rob." Leslie stated matter-of-factly. "You can't deny that."

"I suppose you both are right, but," Raising her finger, she assured them. "Tonight's going to be different. I'm going to dress to the nines tonight."

"Rob." Leslie teased.

She waved. "Les."

"Go ahead, Girl."

"Oh, Liz. I'm going ahead, all right."

Leslie dragged the word off her tongue. "Well."

"Les, did you invite Aretha, Kathleen and Bertha?"

She shook her head. "No, Rob. Haven't seen them."

"Those three. I haven't seen them hanging out in awhile either."

Leslie gazed across the room. "Don't even see them around the apartment building anymore like we used to."

Robin stared directly ahead. "No. We sure don't."

"Word'll get around about the premiere. I'm not going to worry about it. I'm sure those three still go to Diane's parties, and I know Diane knows."

She looked at Leslie. "Must you bring her name inside our apartment? Besides, why would Diane know? We didn't. Did you tell her?"

"No. Rob, you know Diane."

She almost released a deep breath. "Yea. I know Diane. It's just that if there isn't a catch to something, she's usually not that interested."

Elizabeth's brow went up. "Aretha?"

Robin turned and faced Elizabeth.

"I've seen her."

She smiled at Elizabeth. "Ever talk with her?"

"No."

"Aretha's a nut. You'd like her. She's real friendly." All at once, her smile thinned. "You've seen her?"

She answered with a nod. "Yes."

"When?"

"I saw her. I said I saw her."

"I know, but you're not saying something."

"Well," Elizabeth was hesitant. "The times I saw her, she looked sad, depressed, wiped out."

"Dragging her butt home in the wee hours of the morning half dead?" Leslie concluded the thought with a menacing chuckle.

"She must be a sad person . . . real sad."

"Why do you say that?" Robin refused to end her quest for information until she knew exactly how Aretha was faring.

"She looks so out of it every time I see her."

"Do you see her a lot?" Robin asked. "She gets that way Friday through the weekend."

Elizabeth faced her. "Really?"

She nodded. "Really."

Elizabeth lowered then shook her head. "She looks so sad."

"She's just getting loose. That's Aretha. That's just her. That's the way she is." The words came easily to Leslie, as though they were sitting on the arm of the sofa waiting for her to pick them off. A moment later, after she envisioned the serious threat of drug addiction, she pursed her lips and said, "So, you saw Aretha messed up, Liz?"

"Messed up. That's the truth."

"Late at night . . . early in the morning . . . when?"

"All times, Rob."

"Really?"

"Really."

"Well, Rob," Leslie sat back on the sofa. "Looks like Aretha's having problems again."

Robin was mute.

Leslie tried to excuse Aretha's behavior, since she had no answer for it. "Aretha grew up a hard life, Liz."

"Oh."

Leslie offered, "Aretha's a fighter, though. Most people would have crumbled under the home life Aretha grew up in. She can tell some sad stories. She doesn't think she's as tough as she is."

"Aretha is tough." Robin met Leslie's stare. "But she needs Jesus. She needs to give her life over to Christ?"

Leslie arched her brow and pinched her lips to trap her laughter. "I thought she already did? Remember that day you gave her all those pamphlets when we bumped into her outside Mavis'?"

"Then, why is she always stoned?"

"Not always, Rob." She stared across the room and recalled recent days when she stumbled home in a drunken stupor herself.

Elizabeth twisted her mouth and grunted.

"Exactly when do you see Aretha, Liz?"

She threw her hands up. "All the time, Rob."

Robin tried again. "I mean, day or night?"

"Day and night."

"That's what I'm saying, Les." She continued with a narrowed brow. "You see getting stoned as fun, but Aretha has a problem. She is soul sick. She needs help. She thinks she needs whatever she takes for stimulation. And it's not funny. It's not something to laugh about. Aretha has a serious problem."

Leslie's mouth swung open. "I wa--"

"And if anyone . . . not only you . . . anyone . . . and that includes me . . . cares about her, we'd spend some time with her. It's a way to love and help her. We all get weak and need a helping hand. She needs prayer and she needs good friends around her, supporting her, not talking about her and laughing at her."

"I didn't mean to give the impression that I thought Aretha's addiction was funny. I wasn't laughing at her. And besides, you're the one who has spent more than five years denying that she was a drug addict, not me."

"I still don't think she's a drug addict. I'm telling you. It's her soul. Her soul is what needs fixing. She only takes drugs because she is hurting on the inside. And call it what you want, Les. You still shouldn't laugh at her."

"I wasn't laughing at her. I already told you that."

"You're laughing with her then, huh?"

She shook her head. "No."

"Well, Les, it's not funny."

"I know that, Rob."

"Nothing about Aretha's problem is funny."

"I know that, Rob." A thought came to her. "I wonder if she still has her apartment."

Robin bit her tongue. "That's what I'm saying."

"Out near the business district, out where I work, I've seen her standing in the drug line as much as seven times in one day," Elizabeth offered.

"Rob?"

She didn't answer Leslie.

"Rob?"

"Huh?"

"I wonder if she does still have her apartment. She's got a good job, but coke's not penny candy."

"I know."

"What if she's living on the streets?"

"She probably doesn't have the apartment anymore."

"Wonder if she still has her job."

"Les, I hope so."

She dropped her gaze to the floor. "Who're you telling."

"We've got to help Aretha."

"I know. But, what can we do?"

"Let her live with us."

A silence not unlike death enveloped the living room.

****

While the credits to *Make Up* rolled up the wide screen, the audience stood and clapped until applause resounded in the theatre.

At the front of the theatre, Leslie pressed her hands together. The harder she pressed her hands together, the faster her hands shook. She lowered her hands to her sides. A second later she rolled her eyes. Her hands shook until they tapped her thighs in quick spasms. She told herself not to look over her shoulder at the milling audience. Her hands didn't begin to still until she glanced out of the corners of her eyes and saw Bob; he was beaming. He puckered and blew her a kiss when she returned him his smile.

Dressed in a black tuxedo and newly shaved, Bob, with his piercing sea blue eyes, was threateningly handsome. The longer Leslie looked at him the weaker her resolve not to fall helplessly in love became. She felt drunk with emotion. Darting her gaze about the theatre, she searched for a place to sit down. Her heart raced each time she looked at Bob. Pulling her purse close to her stomach she told herself not to grab his hand, hurry back to his penthouse and make passionate love with him.

He winked at her. He knew she was poised to enjoy a third massive explosion on the silver screen. He saw fight, persistence, determination and passion in her. Circling his mouth with his tongue and shoving his hands inside his pant pockets, he stared at her with desire. He wished he were younger. He wanted to tire her with hours of intense lovemaking. He wanted to leave her in the fire of ecstasy night after night. Though he tried to bury himself in work, he was unable to control his feelings for her. She consumed his thoughts until he lost both his appetite and much needed sleep at night. He fantasized about growing old with her, starting a family with her. It reached the point of disturbing his work.

Cool breezes touched Leslie's face like peppermint on hot, dry breath. New York City's Broadway was heavy with traffic. Weary with smiling, nodding and shaking hands, she was glad to be standing outside the theatre.

Next to her, Bob stepped back and allowed a boy riding a skateboard to push his way beyond the theatre. Couples squeezed their way through the crowd to Leslie's side where they smiled, extended their hands, and shouted, "Congratulations!"

Bob leaned his head to the side, watched Leslie interact with her greeters and smiled. While he watched a string of celebrities parade around him and his new love, he reminisced. He recalled the first time Leslie brought a suitcase to his ranch. She wore peach scented cologne. Her hair was loose and curling over her shoulders. His smile widened. He could still see her hanging her clothes in his bedroom closet.

She reached out and shook a prominent independent television producer's hand.

Bob almost chuckled. She filled his closet with so many clothes that first day he scarcely had room to hang his newly cleaned suits. She had more clothes and shoes than any other woman he dated. Yet she complained that she lacked decent clothing.

Finished greeting her fans and peers and emotionally drained, she walked next to him and squeezed his hand. A smile broadened her face. "Come on, Baby. I'm ready to go."

He parted his lips and pulled on the end of her tongue. He kissed her with longing, then he winked at her and said, "Movie's going to be a big hit, Sweetheart."

Chapter Sixteen

"Les-lee!"

Turning toward the stairs, she called back, "Rob?"

Joyce threaded the eye of a needle. "Leslie!"

She turned away from the stairs and lowered her voice. "Mama?"

"Come here please."

She turned and walked to the sofa where her mama sat with her wedding gown covering her lap and feet. Straight pins were clasped between her teeth.

"Here I am." She stood in front of Joyce looking into her lap.

"So you are." She said, raising her hands to Leslie's thinning waistline. "Turn around."

"Yes, Ma'am." She refused to defy her mother on this, her wedding day.

"Oh, stop. You haven't called me ma'am before one day out of your life."

"Les!" It was Robin. She stood at the top of the stairs holding the hem to her own dress in her hands.

She turned away from her mother and looked toward the stairs. "Rob?"

"Come here a sec."

"Mama's got me right now."

"Oh, all right." She turned toward Leslie's childhood bedroom.

"Can she keep me?"

"For awhile!"

Joyce mumbled. "Don't see why you want to go and let some fifty year old Bob Long keep you for the rest of your life," was all Leslie heard.

She turned partway toward her mother. "Excuse me?"

She pulled a straight pin from between her two front teeth. "Never mind." Then she shook her head as if she could shake away the sour taste thoughts of Bob put on her tongue.

The volume in Leslie's voice went up. "No. No, Mama. Tell me."

She shook her head again. "I said, never mind."

Her bottom lip dropped. "You said something about Bob."

She pulled another straight pin from between her teeth, and, bending over, she pushed the hem to Leslie's white, lace wedding gown closer to her knees. "Right. I did."

"Something negative, no doubt."

"I just don't see why you won't open your eyes."

"What is it now, Mama?"

"He's fifty and you're thirty."

"Age is a state of mind, Mama."

She freed her mouth of the last few straight pins she held between her teeth. "No doubt Bob told you that."

"No." She shook her head and stared at the top of her mother's brow. "I read it in a book."

"In a book a fifty year old man wrote."

"Mama, Bob's a loving man, and he cares for and about me. He doesn't marry as a habit. He loves me."

"He's been married nine times."

"Mama."

"Nine times, Les."

"Mama."

"Nine times!"

"But, compared to--"

"Compared to nothing."

"When you consider his level of power and influence, one has to expect that."

"Leslie?"

"Many women want to marry him for his power and influence, his money. Most of his former wives didn't love him . . . perhaps none of them did."

"Why do you think he, any man, any woman, would get married nine times?"

She arched her shoulders.

Joyce lowered her hands. "Oh, Leslie."

"Mama."

"Let's just drop it, Sweetheart."

Leslie's eyes dampened. Her gaze went toward the floor. "No."

"Why not drop it? Your mind's made up."

She looked up. "I can't back out now, Mama."

With a raised brow, she asked, "Why not?"

"Because if I backed out now, it would really hurt Bob, and he's been good to me. I wouldn't be where I am now if it wasn't for Bob. He could have taken full credit for the success of *Make Up*. He helped a lot with the direction of *Make Up*. He loves me. He wouldn't do the things he does for me if he didn't love me. He knows a million beautiful women, but he makes me feel like I'm the only woman in the world. Mama! Bob does love me!"

"All right." She reached for Leslie's hand. "Baby Doll, if you say so."

After a moment of silence, she stood and stretched her arms over her head and massaged her lower back. She peered out of the corners of her eyes at Leslie when she lowered her arms. She told herself she loved her, the woman standing in front of her she spent thirty years praying over. If she could find the words to express her deep-seated fear about a life spent with Bob to her, she would. She knew it was more than a rumor that Bob crushed the hopes of doting young women by way of mental and physical abuse. She knew his romances brought many flourishing careers to a hurried end.

"I love you, Baby." Was the most she could say when she turned and faced Leslie, her eyes pink and her face tight with fear.

Working to dismiss the truth in her mother's accusations, Leslie walked across the room and whispered, "I love you too, Mama."

She pulled Leslie's face close to her own. "Be careful, Baby." Her hands cradled Leslie's shoulders.

Leslie took one cautious step backwards before she slipped her arm around her back. "I will, Mama."

She smiled when she said, "I mean it."

Leslie nodded thoughtfully. "I will."

She lowered and narrowed her brow. She looked hard into Leslie's face. "Promise?"

"Promise."

She tugged on the hem to Leslie's wedding gown. "You're getting married in four and a half hours."

"Thanks, Mama."

She looked up. "For what?"

"For making my dress and at the last minute. I know. I know. I could have spent thousands of dollars to have an expensive seamstress design my gown, but I wanted you to do it. I kept switching back and forth. Telling myself that I should get a big designer to make my dress. That I should ask you to do it. Then I told myself that this was one of the most important days in my life. Sorry it was a last minute notice." She looked softly inside her mother's eyes. "It hasn't always been easy between you and me, but I could only wear a wedding dress you made. Really."

Running her palms down the front of her skirt, she handed Leslie a container half full with safety and straight pins. "Here. Hold this." After she stood, she gave Leslie her gown. Then she extended her hand. "Okay. Now give me the pins back. Put your gown on. I want to see how it looks on you, so I can see if I need to do anymore work on it." Five minutes later, she took short, quick steps to the other side of the living room. While she stood next to the color television set she examined the gown. "I don't see why you want the lower back so snug."

"Be--"

She waved before she said, "But, if that's the way you want it."

Leslie smoothed the back of her gown with her hand. "Mama."

"Then, that's the way you'll get it."

A smile returned to her face. "Thanks, Mama."

Robin screamed, "Leslie!" from the center of the kitchen where she went, taking the house's back stairwell, ten minutes ago. She struggled to hold the top on a blender. "Mrs. Fletcher!" Vanilla pudding poured down the sides of the blender and oozed across the counter top. "Leslie! Mrs. Fletcher!"

"Okay. Okay. What?" Joyce called out while she walked across the living room floor. When she stood just outside the kitchen doorway, it took her less than a second to scream, "Rob!"

Her gaze darted to the counter top. Her feet went with an equal amount of speed to the kitchen sink spigot and the striped rag that draped the spigot. She scoured the counter with the rag. The vanilla pudding disappeared quickly. Behind her, leaning against the kitchen door archway, Leslie stood with her gaze cast to the linoleum floor. The hem of her wedding gown was tucked in her hands.

While Joyce cleaned up the mess in the kitchen, Robin stared at Leslie. She thought her face was placid for a bride. She stared at her and thought her face was long. Her eyes were sunken. Robin raised her brow while she watched Leslie's face tighten. Leslie kept pushing her hands up and down the front of her wedding gown. She kept rolling her feet from side to side. Robin stared deeper into Leslie's face, and noticed that her eyes were taking on a reddish hue.

Befuddled by Leslie's dour expression, Robin turned away from her and rushed to Joyce's side. "Mrs. Fletcher, I'll wash out the sink." She opened her hand and prepared to receive the rag. "Thanks."

Joyce dropped the rag inside Robin's opened hand. "All right, Baby. Thank you."

Then she peered inside the blender. "What were you making, Sweetheart?"

Moving her hands across the counter top, she found the 5 X 8 index card Theo wrote the recipe on, and, wearing a lopsided grin, she lifted the card by its corner and turned it until her father's familiar handwriting faced Joyce.

"Why were you making pudding? Bob's catered at least five thousand dollars worth of food."

She glanced at Leslie. "It was for later when Les and I got together one last time before she moved in with Bob."

Joyce chuckled. "It's not going to seem right. You two girls not living in that apartment together."

While Joyce read the recipe, Robin asked, "Finished with Leslie's gown?"

She nodded. "Yes."

"So, in less than half an hour we'll be out of here?"

She turned and looked at Leslie who continued to stand in the doorway. "You got it."

Leslie tried to smile, but her mouth only went into a crooked line. "That's right."

While Joyce prolonged her view of Leslie, she told herself the most she could give her was what her mother gave her on her wedding day over thirty years ago – her prayers. She dared not to tell Leslie that she suspected her motives for marrying Bob involved the progress of her career. While she looked at her, she couldn't stop thinking about the times she called her after Bob and she had a fight. "Bob's an egomaniac," Leslie told her repeatedly. "That's what's wrong with him. He has to be in the spotlight."

When Joyce summed Leslie and Bob's relationship, she was wanting. Looking at her daughter, she wished she'd realize that it wasn't too late to excuse herself from her impending wedding and all its pageantry. A second later, images of Leslie bearing and caring for Bob's children stabbed her imagination, and she blinked.

Chapter Seventeen

Leslie smiled so hard her face hurt. She squeezed Bob's hand and hurried out of the cathedral.

Bob tugged on the ends of her fingers. "Come on, Darling. We don't want to be late to our own reception."

After she cooed, "I love you, Honey," she kissed his mouth and nodded. "You're right. We better get going. We don't want to keep our guests waiting." Fifteen minutes later they were on the opposite side of the street dancing to loud music. More celebrities came to their reception than attended their wedding ceremony. The hall was noisy with well wishes. Crystal vases filled with red and white carnations decorated tabletops. At the front of the hall, near the guest registry, a pair of caged white doves fluttered their wings. A five-foot long floral arrangement took up most of the space at the head table. Waiters excused themselves while they eased in and out of the crowd. They carried silver platters lined with chocolates, caviar, shrimp, and miniature wedding cakes. Shouts of "Congratulations!" went like a siren into the air. Each time they did, corks flew off bottle tops. It wasn't long before the wedding guests intoxicated themselves with wine and champagne. In the bathrooms, couples smoked joints and snorted cocaine. People who hadn't spoken to each other in years kissed the sides of each other's face in passing. Though merriment filled the air, when Robin turned and looked at the drinking, laughing people surrounding her, she shook. An eerie feeling crept up her spine. She toyed with the ends of her hair and wondered at the hint of misery she saw in the smiling faces milling the hall.

She looked across the room at Leslie. Since she pulled her close over an hour ago and held her for a long time thus concluding her duties as her maid of honor, she hadn't spoken to her alone. Constantly, there was someone at her side. Already she missed her, and they hadn't even spent an entire day apart.

Leslie looked up and met her glance. She smiled, waved then winked. After Robin returned Leslie her smile, Leslie turned around and gently rested her head atop Bob's shoulder. She couldn't stop giggling each time she turned and looked at him. Throughout the afternoon despite her mother's watchful stare, she brushed her hips against his.

Arnold smiled while he stood next to Joyce creating small talk with a string of young actresses. He liked Bob. He was pleased with the business possibilities he believed Bob would bring to him. It delighted him that Bob was at Leslie's side each time he looked across the room.

Joyce stood behind Arnold holding her purse against her stomach. She wondered why more people didn't talk to her. After all, she was the mother of the bride. Not once during his lengthy conversations with the young actresses did Arnold pause and introduce the women to her. It wasn't until she tapped his forearm and asked, "Doesn't that man look familiar?" while she pointed to a bald headed man standing next to the refreshment table that Arnold stopped talking to the actresses.

He froze. He stared across the room in amazement. A moment passed before he whispered, "Jack." Then he grabbed Joyce's hand and hurried out of the hall.

"Arnold, who was that man?" she asked while she skip-walked next to him.

He shook his head. "I-I don't know. Never saw him before. But it's getting late. These folks are getting tanked. I want to get out of here before it gets too late and we find ourselves on the road with a slew of drunks."

"But—"

"We'll call Leslie from the house. She knows we wish her the best."

"But we should at least tell her and Bob that we are leaving."

He pushed the hall doors asunder and walked into the cool late noon air. He hurried down the sidewalk until he reached his car. Putting his hands on the hood, he turned and looked over his shoulder. They were alone. He breathed deeply. "Okay," he said taking the car keys out of his pant pocket. "You go back inside and tell Leslie and Bob that we're leaving and that we wish them the best. I'll pull the car up to the front door while you go inside. That way we can head for the interstate as soon as you come outside the hall."

She arched her brow and answered, "Okay." Then she crossed the lawn and went back inside the hall.

"Rob?" she called.

Robin smiled when she saw her. "Mrs. Fletcher."

"Hi, Hon. Where did Les go?"

She turned and pointed. "She's over there by the door with Bob. I think they're getting ready to leave." Turning her wrist over, she glanced at her watch. "It's getting late."

"It is. Well. Let me go say my farewells to my baby girl and her husband. Arnold's out front waiting on me."

"He didn't come back inside?"

"No. He got in a hurry all of a sudden. You know how that man is."

She chuckled. "I know. You never know what family's gonna do. My dad wanted to come, but my mom told him she wasn't feeling well and that she needed him home with her."

"I'm sorry they couldn't make it, Honey. I know Les would have loved to see them. She thinks the world of you."

"I know," Robin said while she nodded. "You already know the feeling's mutual."

She tapped Robin's forearm. "Well. I better get going. Arnold's not going to wait long."

"Okay. Tell Mr. Fletcher I said good-night."

"I certainly will."

"Take it easy and before I forget – You look great in that dress. It's you, Ma Fletcher. That dress is you."

She chuckled. "Thanks, Sweetie." She reached out and they embraced. After they patted each other's back they stepped away from one another with a wave.

Joyce walked down the hall. She stared at the back of the bald man's head when she neared the refreshment table. "No," she told herself. "I don't know him." She passed the man, turned and glanced over the top of her shoulder. There was a long scar above the man's left eye. She shook her head. "Never seen him before."

Leslie saw her coming. "Mom." She looked next to her then she looked behind her. "Where's Dad?"

"He's in the car. He's waiting out front for me." She pulled her purse to the top of her stomach. "Honey, I came back to tell you your father and I wish you and Bob the very best."

Bob turned and smiled. "Thank you, Mom."

She peered up at him and forced a smile. "We love you both. You make such a lovely couple. You have many good years ahead of you. Bob, it's gonna be great having you in our family. You two have a blast on your honeymoon. If you need anything you know to call us." She leaned and kissed Leslie then Bob. "I love you both. God bless you! Arnold and I wish you all the best, the very best! You deserve it!" She squeezed Leslie's hand.

"I wish Dad had come back inside, Mom. One of the waiter's said there was a man here asking around for him."

Joyce narrowed her brow. "A bald man?"

"Yes." Leslie stepped back. "You know him?"

She shook her head. "No. No. No, I don't know him." Then she waved her hand. "Oh. It's nothing."

Bob took Leslie's hand inside his. "That's right." Winking at Joyce, he added, "It's nothing."

Before Joyce turned to leave, she smiled and waved at Bob and Leslie. Each time she thought about Bob's wink, a chill went up her spine and she lowered her head. "Something's going on," she whispered to herself while she left the hall.

Moments later, Bob turned to Leslie and asked her, "Ready to go to Acapulco?" Outside temperatures had cooled and the sun had tucked itself behind the row of trees on the street St. Mark's Cathedral was located on.

"Yes, Baby." She chuckled and pushed her shoulder against his all the way out of the hall, all the way down the hall's main sidewalk. She blushed while she pulled her dress around her hips and climbed inside the limousine. When Bob joined her inside the limousine they entwined their fingers and waved out the windows at their ogling wedding guests.

Although they both visited Acapulco before, they laughed when wind tossed their hair while they rode horses bareback down the sandy shores. They nibbled on each other's ears and whispered, "I love you" while they shopped at the most expensive stores and dined at outdoor restaurants. When they weren't at the beach, shopping or dining, they lit scented candles, played soft music and made love in their honeymoon suite. Weeks later the effects of their honeymoon lingered.

The first week home from Acapulco, Leslie familiarized herself with the full layout of the ranch, the responsibilities of each employee and where major shopping marts where located in the neighborhood. At the end of the week she introduced herself to her new neighbors. It surprised her to discover that only the men in the neighborhood worked. Each of the wives was president or secretary of some club. None of the children attended public school. All the lawns in the neighborhood were cared for by a lawn service. No one mowed their own lawn or trimmed their own hedges. She thought more than a few of the wives had their noses stuck in the air. Walking back to the ranch from each of their houses, she told herself to mind her own business and keep to herself.

"How was your day, Baby?"

She hurried down the stairs and ran to the front door. "Bob." Wrapping her arms around his neck, she kissed him. "You're home early."

"Yea." He circled his mouth with his tongue after she kissed him. "I got us tickets to the opera."

"Really?" Her eyes ballooned. She told herself to be excited. She had never been to the opera before. She'd never wanted to go. "That's great, Honey. I can go get dressed. What time does the show start?"

"In a little less than two hours. We'll make it. But first—" Reaching inside his briefcase, he added, "I have a surprise for you."

She grinned shamelessly. "Another surprise. Honey, you're spoiling me."

"You bring me so much joy," he said while he placed a small box inside her palm. "These gifts are merely a token of my love. For the first time, my life is good. It's really good, and it's all because of you. I cannot thank you enough, Darling." He leaned and pecked the crown of her forehead.

"A diamond pendant! Oh, Bob!"

"Here. Let me pin it on you."

"Oh, Honey. I'll wear it tonight."

"I'd like that."

"Oh, Bob." She moved inside his embrace. They held one another and kissed passionately.

On the way home from the opera, she asked, "Honey, if you're not too tired there's a script I'd love you to look at. Just briefly. I know you've had a busy day. Donald sent it to me this morn—"

"How about some other time, Sweetheart."

Pulling her coat collar around her neck, she nodded into, "Okay. Okay. All right. I know you're tired."

He leaned across the seat and kissed her fully on the mouth. "I'm not that tired."

She giggled and moved closer to him. They spent the night tucked inside each other's love. When she woke the following morning she was alone. "Bob? Honey? Baby?" she called. Then she looked at the clock on the nightstand. It was seven o'clock. She turned away from the clock and sighed. "He's at work." Even though it was early and the neighborhood mothers hadn't backed their luxury cars out of their side driveways to take their children to the private schools they attended, she pulled back the bed covers. While she climbed out of bed she thought of ways she could busy herself throughout the day until Bob returned home from work. After she showered she heard the telephone ring. "Who was that, Theodore?" she called out to the dayshift butler.

"MacMillan Furniture Company. They're on their way with the new living room sofa."

"Oh," she said while she walked to the closet and stared inside. She never had so many clothes. It took her half an hour to decide what to wear.

"Morning, Theodore," she said when she walked into the kitchen.

"Good Morning, Mrs. Long. Coffee?"

"Yes, and two boiled eggs."

While she waited for her breakfast, she skimmed the newspaper. Halfway down the second page she placed the newspaper on the table and stood. "You can place my breakfast on the table, Theodore. I'm going to make a phone call."

"Should I let the furniture men in when they arrive? The store's not far from here."

"I know. It's practically around the corner. I don't know why Bob didn't just put that sofa in the truck when I picked it out last weekend." Then she nodded. "Yes. Yes. Let the men in. You know where to put the sofa."

"Okay, Mrs. Long. I'll have the men put the sofa by the window if that's all right with you."

"Fine with me. Thank you, Theodore." Halfway up the stairs she lowered her voice and said, "You know more about what goes on around this house than I do. Put the sofa where you want." She went straight for her purse when she entered the bedroom. Her fingers crawled over a tube of lipstick, eyeliner, loose coins, a roll of dollar bills, a stack of gold credit cards and her personal phone book. Grabbing the phone book she closed the purse and sat on the edge of the bed closest to the telephone. She dialed 555-2222. Then she crossed her legs and waited.

"Donald Rigg's Office. How may I help you?"

"Hi, Paula. This is Leslie. Is Donald in?"

The volume in Paula's voice went up. "Les! Hi. How are ya?"

"I'm getting along."

"How's married life treating you?"

"Good. Good. Bob's a dream, just a dream. He's spoiling me. I'm telling you. The man is spoiling me. We've got a gorgeous new sofa coming this afternoon, and Bob's always taking me somewhere or buying me gifts."

"He's so in love with you, Les. You are so fortunate. What a lucky, lucky lady you are."

"I know. My life is perfect except for one thing."

"What's that?"

"I'm ready to get back to work."

"After only six months?"

"Yes. Never thought I'd miss a movie set, especially with all the on set waiting, but I miss work. I don't miss waiting on the set. Please. It's the work I miss."

"I understand. My sister said the same thing after she got married. Never thought she'd miss being a secretary, but she did." A second later she said, "Hold on. I'll buzz Donald. And hey, Les."

"Yea."

"Sure is good hearing from you again."

"Same here."

A moment later Donald's voice crossed the wire. "Leslie!"

"Hi, Donald. How are things going for you back at the office?"

243

"Busy as ever. Scripts are coming in left and right."

"Well, why haven't you called me?"

"I wanted to give you time to settle into your marriage. Plus, I thought you were taking a break from acting after you turned down the last script I gave you."

She sighed. "I know, but Bob didn't think it would be good for my career. He's been at this so long, I trust his advice."

"I also read the trades. I know Bob's keeping you plenty busy with all the social engagements he makes."

"Yes." She looked down at her hands. "We're always going somewhere. I never knew there were so many charity and award events." She chuckled. "Sometimes I think Bob tries to make them all."

Donald laughed.

"So," she asked, "Any of those scripts that are coming in left and right sound suited for me?"

"Are you kidding?"

"What does that mean?"

"At least three of the scripts are perfect, just perfect, for you!"

"Well. When are you going to get off your duff and mail them to me?"

"I'll send them out as soon as I get off the phone with you. I'm really kind of surprised that you called. I tried calling you a few times, but I always got Bob or the butler."

"Bob answered the phone when you called?"

"Yea. A couple of times."

"Really?"

"Yea. Why?"

"I mean. I just never knew—" She pulled her bottom lip inside her mouth and narrowed her brow. "Oh, nothing. It's nothing. Send me the scripts today. Send them express mail. Overnight. Okay?"

"Sure thing."

"Thanks, Donald." After she returned the receiver to its cradle she stood and walked to the dresser. She gazed at her image in the mirror. While she looked into the mirror, she rehearsed the speech she promised herself to give Bob when he came home. "So, Bob. Why didn't you tell me Donald called?" She shook her head and stared at the mirror. "No. No. That doesn't sound right." A second later she tried, "Bob, I spoke with Donald today. He's found three scripts that he thinks are perfect for me. I can't wait to read them. It's gonna be good getting back to work. Oh, and Bob. Have you spoken with Donald since we married?" She shook her head again.

That night when Bob walked through the front door she was sitting on the new living room sofa. She smiled when he rounded the corner. "Hi, Sweetheart." She didn't stand. She knew he would come to her. He kissed her lovingly before he sat next to her. "I see we got our new sofa."

She patted the sofa. "Yes. It's even more gorgeous in our house where it belongs than it was when I first saw it in the showroom."

"It is." After he kissed her again, he asked, "So how was your day?"

"Good. Very good."

"What did you do?"

"Nothing special. I helped out around the house, and I planted two flowers out back."

He smiled softly while he gazed at her. "Really? What did you plant?"

Her mind raced for the names of two popular flowers. "A bed of petunias and a row of tulips."

He sat back on the sofa. "A whole bed of petunias?"

She waved her hand. "It wasn't too much. I like working out in the yard. And you know how nice it was outside today."

"I know. I'm glad to see the temperatures rising. There's nothing like spring and summer."

"As long as it doesn't get too hot."

He reached out and wrapped his arms around her waist. "Honey, it can never get too hot."

She giggled while he nuzzled his nose against the side of her neck.

"What are we gonna do tonight?"

"I don't know. Something special. Something fun. Let's really enjoy each other tonight. Tomorrow I'm gonna spend the day reading screenplays."

His eyes ballooned. He leaned against the spine of the sofa. "Screenplays?"

"Yes. Can you believe Donald found three screenplays that he thinks are perfect for me?"

His brow went up. "Donald called you?"

"No. No. No, he didn't. I called him."

"Why?"

"Well, Bob. I've only spoken with Donald twice since we got married. I wanted to see how he was doing."

"And he just told you about the screenplays?"

"No. I asked him if he had come across any good screenplays lately. He just answered my question. That's all. Is there something unusual about that?"

"No. There's nothing unusual about it. I just thought you wanted to get to know the neighborhood better. You know. Get more acquainted with the other wives in the neighborhood. Settle in around the house. This place is so big. There's so much to do around here. I don't want you to over extend yourself."

She strangled a chuckle. "Honey, I'll be just fine. I promise that I won't over extend myself. I won't overdo it. I love keeping busy around the house, but I need to get back to work. Acting is in my blood. You know that."

"I also know that you were tired of the games and the endless promoting."

"What endless promoting?"

"Pushing movie after movie that you act in. Going on one TV show after another. All the interviews."

She chuckled. "Now that I don't miss. You're right about that. I don't miss promoting my work, but I do miss working."

"Those long waits on the set."

"I know."

"Hours and hours of waiting."

"Honey, I know."

"I never understood why directors make actresses wait for hours between takes. It seems like such an awful waste of time."

"I know. I wish there was some other way."

"Sweetheart, you really don't have to work. You know that. Whatever you want I'll see that you get it. You don't have to wait or want for anything. Not anything."

"I know, Honey, and I appreciate that. You are so good, so very good, to me. I love you. I appreciate everything that you do. I just want to get back to work. It's not a matter of money or wanting anything. It's just a matter of getting back to work."

"Work just to work?" He laughed. "What good sense does that make?"

"Acting is not work to me, Honey. Perhaps I used the wrong word. It's in my blood. I have to act. I love acting. Acting is not a chore. I need to connect with an audience. I need to either be on a stage or in front of a camera. Not to show off or to be seen. I really think it's the characters. There are so many excellent characters out there. So many stories that are yearning to be told. They call out to me. I just need to get back on set, Honey. That's all."

"Well." He lowered his voice and combed his fingers through her hair. "How many more movies do you think you have to act in before acting gets out of your blood?"

She turned and looked at him gape-eyed.

"Well." He said while he stood from the sofa. "We can talk about this later." He glanced at his watch. "We don't have long. We have guests coming."

Her eyes swelled. "When?"

"At nine."

"If you knew we were having guests why did you ask me what we were going to do tonight?"

"Sweetheart, don't be silly."

"I'm not being silly. I just wonder why you asked me that."

"We still have two hours Les-lee."

"But that's not a lot of time when you consider that we have a house full of guests coming. Like you said, nine o'clock is only two hours from now."

"I know, Sweetheart." He leaned and pecked her forehead. "We don't have much to do. The staff will handle most of the work." He stood and turned his back to her. "They always do most of the work around here. Honey, you know that."

Two and a half hours later she stood next to him facing the front door. They extended their hands and greeted the last of their guests. "Hello, Margaret."

"Why, hello, Leslie," Margaret, wife of Dwight Gooding, a Printise Movie Company Executive, said. "How are you and Bob doing this evening?"

"We're good." She nodded so perfectly she felt like the Queen of England. "Thank you for asking."

"Bob." Dwight stretched forth his hand.

He met Dwight's stare. "Come inside, you two. Do come inside. It's nice to have you join us this evening. Most of the other guests are in the dining room. Come on in. Let us go join them."

Leslie and Margaret walked next to one another. Behind them Dwight leaned close to Bob and snarled, "Why did you tell us dinner was at nine thirty?"

"Dwight, dinner hasn't been served yet."

"Well, why is everyone else already here?"

"Everyone else isn't already here."

Dwight pulled down on the hem to his suit coat. "Good."

"One of the maids is running late."

He glared at the side of Bob's head while they entered the dining room.

"Nice of you to join us, Dwight," Matthew Crane called out from across the table when Bob and Dwight entered the room. Before Dwight could respond, Matthew added, "How do you get anywhere on time, Margaret? You're probably always late arriving anywhere when you take that husband of yours with you." While he stared at Dwight, he sat back in his chair and laughed.

"We're not late," Dwight said through clenched teeth. "According to our invitations dinner didn't start until nine—"

Bob waved his hand. "Everything's fine. Everything's just fine. Leslie and I don't mind it when guests arrive late. Let me just go check and make sure dinner is ready. If it is I'll have dinner served now."

Leslie tugged on her blouse collar while she sat. Her gaze circled the table. She'd seen each of the guests at the table before she married Bob. She simply never chose to keep company with them. Looking at them it seemed odd to her that Diane wasn't present. The guests seemed more to her liking – gossipy and untrustworthy. She stared at the clock on the wall until Bob returned to the room.

Two butlers and one maid accompanied him when he returned to the dining room. Straightway they busied themselves serving the guests. Protocol was the order of the evening. Couples were seated according to their level of influence in the industry. The less powerful and those with dying careers were seated in front of the window. It didn't bother Bob to know that it was cool at the back of the room. He knew the sill was not tight. As if money were a measure of human worth, he felt it right to sit the less powerful of his guests closest to the night air, inches away from a chill.

"So, Bob," Leonard Davis sipped on white wine. "Did that deal go through?"

Dwight glanced down the table at Leonard. Then he peered at Bob.

"Yes. I didn't have any trouble getting Keith to sign the papers. In fact, he understood my point readily."

Leonard nodded while he swallowed the wine. "Good. Very good."

"So we can move forward?" Jerry Smith, owner of CVA Television asked.

"Move forward on what?"

The men turned and gawked at Dwight.

Bob broke his dinner roll in half. "If you had made it your business to attend our last meeting you would know what we were talking about, Dwight."

Dwight swallowed hard. "I told you my son was sick."

"Ever heard of a nanny?" Leonard asked with a chuckle.

Dwight gritted his teeth. "Sometimes a parent has to be with their child, Leonard."

After he stuck a piece of the roll inside his mouth, Bob said, "That's what a wife is for."

Leslie coughed then she cleared her throat. She almost choked on her wine. After she wiped her mouth with her napkin she glanced at Bob. He didn't return her glance. Instead he lengthened his discussion with the men at the table. It wasn't until she heard the name Jack that her interest returned to the conversation.

"Did Jack call the banker or did you?" Jerry asked Bob.

"It doesn't matter who called. Everything's set to go." Then Bob stuck the last piece of roll inside his mouth. He sipped his wine and looked up at Jerry. When he tightened his brow, Jerry sat back.

Except for a short debate about the year's best selling movie, the remainder of the evening proved long and dull for Leslie. That night while she lay in bed next to Bob questions filled her head. "Honey, who is Jack?" she finally asked.

"A very important man. And now," he rolled to his side. "Come on." He wrapped his arms around her shoulders. "Let's not talk about work. You're my wife, not my business partner."

"I know, Honey." After she moved her head until it rested against his, she added, "I just wanted to know who Jack was. I keep hearing that name."

"Really?" Raising his hand, he combed his fingers through her hair in long, slow strokes. "Where else have you heard the name Jack?"

She raised then lowered her shoulders. "I don't know. I don't remember for sure. I just know I've heard the name before."

"Well." He laughed. "One thing's certain. Jack is a very common name. It's not like only one man on earth is named Jack."

She chuckled. "You're right. You're right."

He stuck the tip of his tongue inside her ear. "It's not like his name is Bob or anything."

She laughed. When she turned, they took their time undressing one another. That night started a routine. For the first time in her life Leslie didn't feel she had to fight the world alone. Each night after Bob came home from work and the streetlights came on and stars shined in the sky, they snuggled and talked in bed. They shared their deepest secrets, laughed, cried and often made love until the wee hours of the morning. The long hours of intimacy were freeing episodes for Bob.

"Darling," Bob whispered.

"Yes, Sugar?"

"I'm so glad I have you."

"Oh, Baby," she said while she kissed the side of his face.

He lowered his head and nuzzled the tip of his nose against her neck. "I can tell you anything. Talking to you helps me deal with so many things. You always listen." His voice quaked. "Honey."

"No. No. I want to talk. I want to say this. All my life I have kept so much to myself. People assume that life has been easy for me. But it hasn't. It hasn't. It really hasn't. It just hasn't."

"Honey, maybe people think life's been easy for you because you've been so successful. They don't pause to realize that success takes hard work. Persistence. Courage. Iron will and an amount of determination few can imagine putting to use."

He shook his head. "No. That's not it. I mean. I understand what you're saying. You made a very good point, but that's not it. Everything I have I got on my own."

"But, Hon—"

"I know no one is an island. I'm not saying that. I don't mean that absolutely no one ever helped me. Along the way many people have helped me in one way or another. What I meant was that the people who should have helped me the most never did. And even with the bits and pieces of help I received from people in business, I gained most of what I have on my own. I'll never forget the time I worked two jobs and went to high school."

"You're kidding."

"Wish I was. I went to school. Walked to my first job as soon as school let out. Worked there four hours, then I walked to my second job. Didn't get home until after midnight. Can you believe my dad didn't come and pick me up from work once?"

"Why? Did your father work more than one job too?"

He chuckled into, "Are you kidding? My dad was absent from his one job what seemed like half the time. He was always sick. Hung over is more like it."

She lowered her voice. "Your father had a drinking problem?"

"Alcoholic is more like it. My dad was an alcoholic. It's that plain and that simple."

"And your mom? She seemed such a caring woman each time I met her. Crazy about you." She laughed. "I can tell she doesn't think any woman is suited for her son."

"It just takes her awhile to warm up to people."

"Is that what it is?"

"That's what it is." He sighed then added, "My mom's just not the idea mother or mother-in-law."

"Honey, don't say that about your own mother."

It was his turn to laugh. "As if you've never said one unkind word about your mother."

After she poked him teasingly in the side, she said, "Let's leave my mother out of this. Everybody who knows her knows she lives for my dad. Can't say I didn't grow up in a dysfunctional home."

"Funny thing about that term dysfunctional. More than half of America probably thought they grew up in a normal home until that term rolled onto the scene. I know I thought I had a normal childhood and a normal family until I started meeting more kids and finding out that some of the things that went on in my home didn't go on in theirs."

She stretched an arm across his chest. "Like what?"

"Like how my parents disciplined me when they said I was misbehaving."

She chuckled. "You never misbehaved, Bob?"

"Now, I didn't say that."

"No. You didn't, but you implied it."

"I wasn't a perfect angel. I'm not saying that. It's just that my parents, especially my mother, were always accusing me of doing something wrong. I can't tell you how many times I wondered if they regretted having me." He chuckled. "If they had a wealthy relative in another country, I bet they would have shipped me out of the U. S. in no time at all."

"Bob."

"I'm serious."

"No."

"They put on a show for you, Les. You don't really know my parents."

"Well. I have picked up a few things."

Pulling away from her, he asked, "Like what?"

"Your mom seems to think no woman is good enough for you. Like no woman will ever measure up to be suited to be your wife and her daughter-in-law."

He laughed. "Like I told you, it takes her awhile to warm up to people. Besides. If anything. It's probably more like she thinks no one is good enough to be her daughter-in-law." His laughter silenced. "My mother beat bruises on me when I was a kid."

She pulled on his shoulders until heat from his body warmed her chest. "Bob, Honey, tell me you aren't serious. The mere mention of child abuse frightens me. I remember the times my dad struck my mother. I spent more than a few nights with my fingers plugged in my ears." She sighed. "I wish people would find other ways to deal with disagreements, their frustrations and life's mean setbacks."

He was silent.

"You are nothing like that." She pulled him closer. "We always talk things out. And Honey, I must tell you, even with your hectic schedule, you always find time for us to talk at night. Like you, this is the first time in my life that I've had someone special to talk with the way you and I talk. I mean. I have Robin, but she's a girlfriend. It's different. It's just different."

"How? How is it different?"

"Robin's a woman. It's that simple."

"She's your closest friend, isn't she?"

"We didn't start off that way."

"I think a husband should be a wife's closest friend."

"You are my best friend, Honey. I love you dearly."

"You just love Robin more?"

"I love Robin differently."

"Well. At this juncture in my life I suppose any type of real love is better than what I've been getting all the rest of my life."

"Honey, why do you talk like you feel sorry for yourself?"

"Because everybody who claimed to love me didn't. And of course, I didn't find that out until my heart was severely broken."

"As handsome as you are I'm sure you've broken your share of hearts."

"I'm not talking about women right now, Leslie. I'm talking about my mother."

"Was she that awful?"

"What do you think about a mother who locks her son in the closet for something—"

"It doesn't matter what a child does. No one should be locked in a closet. I don't care if they're trying to burn the house down."

"Well. I wasn't trying to burn the house down."

She sat up. "Your mother locked you in the closet?"

"At least once a week."

"For how long?"

"Had to have been five to seven years."

"No. That's not what I meant. How long did she lock you in the closet for each time she locked you in the closet?"

"I don't know, Leslie. There wasn't a clock in the closet."

She lay down again. "Sorry."

He clung to her. "I shouldn't have been short with you. It's just that looking back on my childhood brings me so much pain. You know. For so many people – I'm talking millions and millions of people – thinking back to their childhood brings them happy feelings . . . good memories, but not me. Not for me. My mother saw to that."

"What did your father do when you told him your mother locked you in the closet?"

"I never told him."

"You're kidding."

"My dad was gone a lot. He didn't love my mother. We were just there. Like pictures on a wall to bring a room out a bit."

"Bob."

"Don't scold me."

"I'm not. I'm just saying that your childhood couldn't have been that loveless, that cold. Someone loved you."

"You don't think she locked me in the closet, do you?"

"Honey, I'm not say—"

"You don't believe me."

"Did your mother have problems?"

"What kind of problems?"

"Mental problems."

He raised then lowered his shoulders.

"Oh, Baby," she said while she stroked of side of his face.

"And why couldn't my childhood have been loveless and cold? Why do you say that?"

She kissed him softly before she answered, "Because you turned out so well. You have accomplished so much."

"You know I bet she kept me locked in the closet for an hour at a time. I used to stand in there and sweat, cry and count my fingers over and over and over again."

The summer was hot and long. For the first time in many years Leslie was glad when she looked out the living room window and saw trees turning bare. "Oh, winter," she sighed while she waited for the telephone to ring. "I need a change."

The telephone rang and interrupted her thoughts. "Rob. Where are you? You were supposed to have been here an hour ago?"

"What? You still want me to come?"

"Yes. Why would you think that I wouldn't?"

"Well. When I called last night, Bob told—"

"What?"

"Never mind. Never mind. I'll tell you when I get there."

It took her two hours to drive to the ranch. Her shoulders lowered and she released a thick breath when she pulled inside the long driveway.

Leslie opened the front door and hurried outside before she could open her car door. "Hi, Girl. How're you doing?"

"I'm blessed," she enthused. "And you're looking good. Feeling better than you were the last time I talked with you?"

"You don't visit like you used to."

"And you didn't answer my question."

"Well. Come on in. We can go in the den and talk."

"Got any fruit?"

"You know we do. Bob has the staff keep the refrigerator stocked. What do you want?"

"A bowl of cold, juicy grapes."

She smiled at her. "Coming right up."

Robin followed her inside the kitchen. "So why did you have Bob call and tell me you were busy the last four weeks? Why didn't you call yourself? Are you that busy all of a sudden?"

She froze. She stood with the refrigerator door open. "What?"

"You heard me."

"Rob, stop playing."

She chuckled and moved passed Leslie. Reaching inside the refrigerator she grabbed a bowl of red seedless grapes. "I'm not playing. Bob has called me every Tuesday for the last month and told me you said you couldn't meet with me because you had things to do. When I called you and called you and called you, you never came to the phone. You can't imagine how that made me feel, but I prayed to God for guidance. I knew I had to keep trying to get in touch with you, and so here we are."

When Leslie closed the refrigerator door and turned she frowned. "I didn't tell Bob to call you. I never even gave him your new phone number. Bob and I were doing so good. We were talking. He even started trusting me with some very deep secrets. But these last couple of months he's been strange."

Robin's brow arched. "How?"

"Well. He's started drinking quite a bit. He stays out late, and sometimes he's mean."

"Mean?"

"Screaming and hollering, cursing, swearing." She shrugged. "You know."

"He screams and curses at you?"

"He works hard. He works very, very hard."

"Leslie, everybody knows that. I'm asking if he screams and curses at you?"

"Who else would he be screaming and cursing out. It's just the two of us here."

"I'll keep you in my prayers. God will work it out. I don't care what the problem is. God will work it out. You should trust God. Trust God with your life, with your soul, with your mind. Trust God totally. Life will never be right until you trust God completely, one hundred percent."

"I do trust God, Rob. I'm just not a saint like you are."

She laughed. "I'm not a saint. I have more than my fair share of faults. You know that. You don't have to be a saint to trust God fully, completely, without reservation, without so much as a hint of doubt."

Leslie smiled into, "You talk about God like God's a good friend you met in Manhattan."

Robin chuckled. "Not Manhattan. Tennessee."

They leaned their shoulders together while they laughed.

"And this woman who met God while she was still living in Tennessee sure has missed her friend she met in New York City."

"I've been here."

"Just unreachable."

"Bob and I have been working hard trying to turn our marriage around."

"You mean to tell me in a little over a year your marriage has experienced that much trouble?"

"It's Bob's job. It's the people he works with. They put a lot of pressure on him to do more, do more, do more."

"But why? All of his businesses are doing well. He's got money coming in hand over fist."

"I know. I also know that a couple needs to spend time together. A couple needs to talk. If Bob's always working we don't have much time to see each other."

"Still having all those dinner parties?"

She rolled her eyes. "Yes."

"Maybe you should ask Bob—"

She waved her hand. "He wouldn't hear of it. He's told me flat out I don't know how many times that he's not going to give up his dinner parties."

"Not even if you sit down and talk—"

She waved her hand again. "I've tried. I've tried. "I've tried telling him how the dinner parties eat up time we could be spending together."

Robin laughed. "What does he do at these dinner parties? Map out the next week of his life?"

"You would think so."

"What I don't get is why he won't stop working long hours or cut down on the dinner parties but tries to stop you from seeing your friends."

She shook her head. "Just don't get it." A second later, she looked up. "Oh. And by the way, that guy stopped calling."

"Let's go in the den." While they walked, Leslie asked, "What did you say that guy's name was again?"

"What guy?"

"The guy who was calling you. You know the guy who was making those prank calls after I moved out."

"Les, prank callers don't leave their names. I don't know what the guy's name is. Couldn't tell you."

"Well. I'm glad he stopped calling."

Robin pulled one leg behind her buttocks then she sat on the sofa next to Leslie. "You're telling me."

"Still don't know how Bob got your new number."

"I never believed you told him to call me and tell me you were busy. We've always had time for each other."

"Not to mention the fact that besides going to Ryan's--"

"Who's Ryan?"

"Oh, Rob. You know. I should just say Cutters."

"Oh, your hairdresser."

"Yea. Anyhow, besides going to the hairdresser, shopping – can you believe I actually look forward to grocery shopping?"

"What?"

"That's how much I have going on in my life right now."

"Les, why don't you just go back to work? Who are you trying to fool? Don't want people to think being Bob's wife isn't enough for you?"

"Shut up, Rob."

"Whew. It feels good to have you get smart with me again for a change. You have become so prim and proper."

"I have not."

"Yes you have." She stuck a grape inside her mouth. "Want one?" Leslie shook her head. "Naw."

"Naw, what?"

"Shut up, Rob."

"You only changed for Bob, huh?"

"Shut up." She leaned a finger against the crown of her head. "Bob doesn't want me to work. I don't care what he says. He doesn't want me to work again – ever."

"What makes you think that?"

"Well. Months ago I called Donald and he started to tell me that Bob had spoken to him. But he stopped himself. Think he wanted to keep me from getting suspicious that Bob might be trying to keep me from acting so soon after we got married. Anyhow, Donald said he had three screenplays that he thought were perfect for me."

"Great."

"No."

"They weren't good screenplays?"

"No. That's not it. I never got the screenplays."

"Why?"

"You won't believe this."

"Try me."

"When I called Donald back two days later he told me that Bob called him."

"So."

"Rob, Bob told Donald not to talk to me anymore. He told Donald not to send me the screenplays."

Robin lowered her leg and sat forward on the sofa. "What?"

"Yes."

"Les."

"That's what I'm saying, Rob. Bob is monopolizing my life. He wants me to be his wife and that's it. He doesn't want me to work again. He doesn't want me to see you. He wants to pick and choose my friends."

"You know I never thought anything of it until you said that." She raised a finger. "I ran into Bob when I was at the store last week."

"Where was this?"

"At Murray's."

"The grocery store?"

"Yes."

"What in the world was Bob doing in a grocery store?"

"I know. When you stop to think about it, it is the oddest thing, isn't it?"

"Yes. It is."

"But in the grocery store he was. Banged right into my cart."

"No."

"Girl, yes. Would have thought he was blind. Acted like he didn't even see me until I looked up."

"Go on."

"Yes. Asked me if I had seen you lately. Didn't even apologize."

"Mr. Manners?"

They sat back on the sofa and laughed.

"Then what happened," Leslie wanted to know.

"I told him that I had been out of town. That was when I was at Spellman."

"Did you deliver the commencement address there again this year?"

"No. I was down there doing a workshop."

"You always did know how to keep your life on track."

"The good Lord guides me. God'll guide you too if you'll allow Him."

Leslie grinned like a fox. "How do you know God is a man?"

"He's not. I just say He. God is a spirit."

"On that religious principle we agree."

After she smiled at Leslie she said, "Good."

"So after Bob ran into you at the store what happened?"

"He told me you hadn't been feeling well lately because you were over extending yourself. He told me you liked me so much that you didn't know how to tell me you wanted to spend a few weeks by yourself."

"So you stayed away?"

"No. I called you every day just like I always have."

"When did you call? I mean, what time of day did you call?"

"Around. I don't know. Around one or two in the afternoon."

"Oh, Rob. I was at Ryan's then. I go to Ryan's around one."

"Oh."

"But nobody answered the phone?"

"One of the butlers or maids always answered the phone. They said they'd give you the message." All at once she lowered her voice. She glanced at the corner of the room. "Do you think we should go somewhere else and talk?"

Leslie turned and glanced over her shoulder. "No." A second later she stood and walked to the edge of the den. When she didn't see any of the staff in the hall she returned to the sofa. "They can't hear us. They're probably in the other kitchen preparing dinner or upstairs cleaning the linen."

"Are you sure?"

"Yes. I'm sure. Rob, you don't trust anybody around here, do you?"

She looked at her gape-eyed. "Do you?"

She folded her hands inside her lap. "Oh."

"Bob still buying you all those gifts?"

"Rob."

"I'm not saying he doesn't love you. I'm just asking you a question."

"He still buys me nice things. Not as often as he used to, but yes. He still buys me gifts."

"Well. How have you been feeling lately?"

"Oh." She sighed. "That's why I called you last night before Bob came home." She pursed her lips. "You won't believe this."

"What?"

She stared at her hands. "I'm pregnant."

Robin stood and opened her arms. "Congratulations!"

When Leslie stood she placed her head against Robin's shoulder. "Thanks."

"Is Bob excited?"

"He doesn't know."

"Les!"

"No."

"You told me before you told Bob?"

"You know you're my best friend."

"But Bob's your husband, the father of your unborn child."

"Yes. But best friends are more important."

"That's not what you should be saying right now."

"I've never been good at saying what I should say. You of all people should certainly know that."

"If I didn't know any better I would say that you don't look too happy to be a mommy."

Her voice was flat. "I'm not."

"Les!"

She shook her head. "I don't want this baby."

"Why not?"

"Things just aren't right."

"What? Is it because you're not working? You want to get your career going again before you have a baby?"

"No. It's not that. It's not that at all. I'd love to have a baby. Just not now and not with Bob."

"Bob's your husband."

"We all make mistakes."

Robin ran her hand over the top of her hair. She looked at Leslie with intent. "What's going on?" When she leaned forward, she placed her hands over the tops of Leslie's hands. "What's really going on?"

When Robin drove away from the ranch that afternoon she knew her suspicions about Bob were on target. The entire drive back to Apartment 1201 she prayed to God for the strength not to hate – the strength not to hate Bob.

Leslie allowed an entire week to pass before she approached Bob with an old question. They were resting in bed. It was early in the morning since Bob didn't come home until two o'clock. "What do you think about me going back to work, Honey?"

He belched and rolled to his side.

"Bob? Honey?" She pulled on his shoulders until they rocked.

"Don't, Les. I'm tired."

"I know you've been getting home in the wee hours of the morning lately, but this is very important to me. You know that."

"Can't we talk about this later?'

"No, Honey. I really would like to talk about it now. In a few hours you'll be up and headed out to work again."

"I have to work hard to keep you satisfied."

"You don't have to work this hard."

"And if I don't?"

"Nothing will happen. I'd like for us to spend more time together." She rested her head against his shoulder. "Wouldn't you like that? Especially with our baby coming?"

"You know you've been talking a lot about the baby. You keep telling me how sick you get every day. It's almost like we're living on a ship the way you keep getting sick."

"It's called morning sickness, Honey. A lot of women get morning sickness when they're pregnant."

"I know that."

"Well, that's all it is. That's all I'm saying, Honey."

"I never knew you were so eager to become a mother."

"What's that supposed to mean?"

"Just what I said."

"What are you saying, Bob?"

"I'm saying, I never knew you wanted to be a mother so badly. You never join in with any of the other mothers in the neighborhood. You always keep to yourself. It's almost like you don't want to let your life with your old friends go."

"Friends like who?"

"No one in particular."

She rolled to her back. "Oh."

"And no wife of mine is going to work while she's pregnant. I hope that answers your question once and for all."

"What about all the times I asked you about going back to work before I was pregnant?"

"Leslie, don't turn this around?"

"I'm not turning anything around. You never wanted me to work and you know it."

"I never wanted you to work?" Raising his voice, he jabbed his chest with his finger. "I never wanted you to work? I'm the one who revived your dead career."

"Since when."

He chuckled dryly. "You don't remember when we first met? How soon. How soon she forgets."

"How long and how many times do I have to thank you for landing me that role? And my career was doing very good before we met. Thank you."

"I'm not asking you to thank me for the break I gave you. I'm just asking you to remember. And if you're career was so hot when we first met, I'd hate to see lukewarm."

"I do remember what you did for me in allowing me to direct *Make Up*, Bob. I do remember."

"Well."

"But that doesn't mean that I don't ever want to work again."

"Just don't act like I'm trying to control your life."

"I didn't say that you were."

"Yea. I bet that's what you tell Robin too, huh?"

"How do you know what I tell Rob? You're never here when she visits." She sighed. "You never did like her."

"You know, Leslie. I wish you would just open your eyes for once." He jabbed his chest with his finger again. "I'm not the one who doesn't like Robin. It's more like she's the one who never liked me. She always did see me as the person who was a threat to you and her relationship. Sometimes I wonder if you're the only friend that hermit has."

"Some people don't have a lot of true, good, decent friends, Bob." She stared at the ceiling. "I know what that's like."

"Hmph! You've got Ryan and your slew of friends."

"You know all about my day. It's me who wonders where you are half the time."

"I'm a hard working man!"

"From six in the a.m. until two the following morning?"

"Your taste are very expensive, Sweetheart."

"You don't stay out until the crack of dawn for me, and we both know that."

"Are you implying something, Dear?"

"No. I'm just making a statement."

"Because as hard as I work--" He sat up. "I don't need a slut like you telling me that I'm fooling around."

Tears pooled in her eyes. She swallowed hard. "Is that how you see me?" Her voice cracked. "As a slut?"

"I call it straight from the hip."

"So you think you married a slut?"

"I call it straight from the hip."

She squeezed her eyes closed. "Can't you just be direct with me?"

"Okay." He turned and faced her. She was looking at the ceiling. "I'll be direct with you. You refuse to be neighborly. You keep to yourself all the time. You make our guests—"

"Our guests?"

"Yes. Our guests. You make our guests—"

"As I recall it, none of my friends have ever been over for dinner."

He returned to his back. "It's impossible with you." Then he sat up again.

"Where are you going?"

"Into the bathroom."

"What for? I don't mind if you call your girlfriend from our bedroom."

He stood and pulled on the waistband to his boxers.

"Not going to deny it this time."

He walked around the corner of the bed.

She turned from staring at the ceiling and watched him move through the dark in the bedroom. Her heart raced when he neared her side of the bed. She didn't speak again until he stepped away from the bed and started walking toward the bathroom. "Don't you dare call that hussy from this house!" She sat up. "I mean it, Bob! I'm serious. I mean it!"

He pushed the bathroom door closed so gently she didn't hear it shut. Knowing she was alone, she lay down on the bed and wept softly. A moment later, she turned to her side and looked at the telephone on the nightstand. Her eyes ballooned when she saw the first line lit up. "Damn it," she whispered to the room. "He's on the phone with her. I know he is. I just know he is." Then she lay down again and wept. She lay in bed crying until her cheeks grew sore, then she turned and glanced at the telephone again. The console showed that the first line was still in use. Sitting up and pushing off the bed, she hurried across the hall. She pounded on the bathroom door. "Open up, you sorry excuse for a human being! Open this door! I'm tired of your games! Call yourself a man! If you ain't screwing some other woman, you're having an experimental rendezvous with one of your male clients!"

"Let me call you back," she heard him speak into the phone. Then she heard a click.

The door flew open. He grabbed her neck so fast she lost her balance and fell to the floor. Keeping one hand on her neck, he reached out with his other hand and grabbed a chunk of her hair. He twisted and pulled her hair until she started to kick and scream.

"Let me go! Get your hands off of me! You're hurting me, Bob. Stop! You're hurting me. Stop!"

He pulled her hair with so much force, her waist rocked and her legs careened into the wall. He kicked her. Then he reached down and punched her face. "Now, you're sorry. You ungrateful slut! I'm gonna show you the difference between a good life and a bad way to live. You've enjoyed the good life long enough." While she squirmed, flinched and screamed, he ranted into, "I don't care what I do. You're never grateful. I can never do enough for you ungrateful whores. Never enough. I give you money. I give you clothes. I buy you shoes. I buy you jewelry, furniture. I give you my credit cards and let you max them out. And what do I get in return. Some whiny late night nonsense from you. Do you know how many women are begging to be in your shoes? Do you know how many women want to be my wife? But you, you ungrateful slut, you can't see a good thing when it's standing in front of your face. You stupid piece of trash!"

She tried to raise her hands, tried to loosen his grasp. "Let me go! You're hurting me!"

"You're not hurt. You aren't even bleeding."

"Please, Bob," she whimpered. "Please stop. Just let me go. I'll leave tonight if you want me to. It's obvious that this isn't working. I'll get out right now if you just let me go."

"Let you go. Are you kidding? You must be joking. You're my wife. You are not going anywhere. You're going to honor your wedding vows. I'm tired of you whores backing out on me."

"Bob, please just let me go. You are really hurting me."

With one last pull, he yanked a clump of her hair until it filled his hand. "Now you're hurt," he said while he stepped back and laughed robustly, laughed like a comedian just told a hilarious joke.

"I've been hurting since you grabbed me," she said while she crawled on the floor and worked to gain her footing.

"No. You're hurt for sure now," he said with a chuckle. "Your head's bleeding." Then he stepped back until his shoulders touched the wall. He lowered his arms to his sides and laughed. He laughed until his stomach hurt.

She stared into his face while she lay on her side on the floor. She narrowed her brow and vowed to get even while he bowled over in laughter.

Moments later, with one arm, he scooped her off the floor. He pushed her hair off her face. "Come on," he told her. "Let's go to bed."

He spent the night holding her. "Stop crying, Love," he whispered in her ear. "You'll be okay. I didn't mean to hurt you. Don't ever push me like that again. Okay?" Then he wrapped his arms around her shoulders and rocked her until she drifted off to sleep.

Hours later a blaring car horn woke her. She sat up slowly. A ray of light came through the drapes. She returned to her back and placed her hands against her eyes. At once her hands then her shoulders shook. Her face was puffy. It took her a long time to swallow. She almost screamed when she lowered her hands to her neck. Her mind raced. With each act of abuse Bob heaped upon her last night she was certain that he had not tried to strangle her. In fact, he rocked her to sleep. She remembered. Though her legs and arms were sore in the spots where he had kicked and punched her, she sat up then scooted off the bed. She shuffled to the mirror. Her knees quaked the second she looked inside the mirror. She shook her head and cried, "No." Then she stepped back and allowed the pent up emotion she felt to work its way into a pool of tears, tears that streamed down the sides of her face.

She didn't leave the house. She didn't part the drapes.

Theodore called up the stairs and asked her, "May I prepare you breakfast and bring it up to you, Mrs. Long?"

"No," was the only reply she returned him.

The telephone rang throughout the day. While she sat on the edge of the bed watching one soap opera after another, she glanced at the different telephone numbers that came up on the Caller ID box next to the telephone. Ryan. Her mother. Christine Simpson. Ryan. Ryan. Teresa. Jerry O'Flax. Ryan. Her mother. Her mother. Her mother. Robin.

"Hello."

"Les?"

Though she pursed her lips and swallowed slowly, she started to cry. Her shoulders shook. Tears slid down her face and bounced off the end of the telephone. "Rob."

Silence was all that came back to her.

"Rob?"

The silence in the wire stiffened her spine. She wiped her eyes with the back of her hand. "Rob? Robin?"

Robin's voice was flat. Her words came out like bricks falling on the ground. "Leslie, what is going on over there?"

A moment passed.

"Leslie." The volume in her voice went up. "Answer me. Leslie, answer me. Answer me now. I'm on my way over. That's it. I'm coming over right now. You better answer me, Les. I'm going for my car keys. There's my jacket. Hanging on the door knob. I'll get it, Les. I don't care if Bob is home or no—"

"He beat me," she sobbed. "He beat me. He—"

"Les-lee," she stood. Her eyes ballooned and her heart raced. She placed her hand against her chest and worked to even her breathing. When she felt a sharp pain go into her chest, she sat on the living room sofa again.

"He kicked me." She started to scream. "He punched me. He hit me. He hit me. He hit me over and over and over again. And, then," her voice trailed off. "And then." She started to cry again.

Robin gripped the receiver. "Les, what is it? Tell me. You can tell me anything. I don't care what it is. You can tell me anything."

"And then."

"Les, please. Just say it. And then what happened?"

"And then he picked me up off the floor."

She gasped while she threw her hand over her mouth.

"He took me into the bedroom."

"Oh, goodness, no."

"He layed me down on the bed."

"Stop. Stop. I can't take anymore." Turning her gaze toward the ceiling, she mouthed, "Help us, God. In Jesus' mighty name, please help us. Go see about Les, dear Lord. Don't leave her alone. She needs you right now, Lord. Right now. Show her your wonder working power. Please, Lord, please. Show her you're God."

While she prayed, Leslie raced through, "He told me he loved me. He said it over and over again. I think he told me he loved me more times than he punched and kicked me. He stroked my hair. He kissed me. He held me. He told me he was sorry. He told me how awful he felt. He asked me not to push him to hit me ever again. He told me he just felt awful. Then he wrapped his arms around me and rocked me to sleep."

Her gaze no longer toward the ceiling, Robin returned her attention to the telephone. "What? What?"

"He wrapped his arms around me and rocked me to sleep."

"What?"

"He rocked me to sleep, Rob. He told me he loved me, then he rocked me to sleep."

"What!"

"He said he loved me."

"Bastard." A second later, Leslie heard, "Oh, Lord. Oh, God, please forgive me. I didn't mean to curse. I didn't mean to swear. Please forgive me holy God, in Jesus' mighty name. Lord, please do forgive me."

"Rob? Are you there?"

"Yea. Yea. Yes." She looked across the room at her jacket. "I'm coming over. I'm coming right over."

Leslie took in a deep breath. "What time is it?"

"Two o'clock."

"Hurry." Then she hung up the telephone. She hobbled inside the bathroom where she washed her face, neck, arms and legs. Then she limped back inside the bedroom, grabbed a pant suit and a gold Master Card. She nearly fell down the stairs she moved down them with such haste. To avoid the peering eyes of the staff, she went outside and sat on the front porch. She didn't smile until Robin's Benz bumped its way up the driveway.

She reached the side of the Benz before Robin had chance to step outside the car. "Hurry. Let's go."

Robin's gaze darted from Leslie to the house to her car back to Leslie. "Where are we going?"

"To the doctor's office."

"What?"

"Stop gawking at my bruises and just start driving."

She bit her bottom lip and worked to still her hands. Although she told herself not to, she kept glancing at Leslie's face. A knot formed in her throat each time her gaze went across the black and blue marks on her face. When she looked at her neck, her stomach turned. "Well—"

"Bob'll be home in three hours. I bet he comes home on time today. Probably'll have an expensive gift for me. He feels real bad about last night. He's going to try to make it up to me." Moving her head back until it touched the headrest, she snapped, "I don't care. I'm tired of his gifts. His games. He's such an opportunist, a manipulator."

Glancing in the rearview mirror, Robin backed the Benz out of the driveway and pulled onto the street. She punched the accelerator and sped away from the house.

Leslie stared at her hands. "I don't know what kept me from killing him. I really don't. "I—"

"God is watching out for you. God is taking care of you."

"Then why—"

"I know it doesn't seem like it, but God is. God is."

"Take that left."

"Isn't your doctor's office five miles further down this ro—"

"I'm not going to my doctor."

Turning slowly, she gawked at her. "Then where are you going?"

"I don't want everyone to know I'm pregnant. I'm not even showing yet."

She choked the steering wheel. She leaned forward. "Oh, my, gosh. I forgot. I forgot. I forgot about the baby. The baby." She reached out for Leslie's hand.

Without looking to her side, Leslie moved her hand inside Robin's.

They were at the doctor's office less than an hour. The doctor stood in her office doorway while Robin escorted Leslie down the front walk. "Since you refuse to be hospitalized for observation, call me if you have anymore complications or concerns. I want to see you again in two weeks," she called out.

Robin patted Leslie's shoulders and rubbed her back while she walked next to her down the sidewalk to her Benz. "It's gonna be all right, Les. I know it doesn't seem that way right now, but it's gonna be all right. My mom had a miscarriage before." She bit her bottom lip. "Before she had Sonia."

"I didn't have a miscarriage," Leslie finally said when the Benz neared the ranch. "Bob murdered our baby."

"Les."

"I didn't think I wanted the baby until now. Now it's too late. My child was beaten out of me, beaten away from my life – forever."

The Benz stilled. Robin climbed out of the car and ran toward her. They stood in the driveway holding each other for a long time.

"You better go," Leslie sighed while she wiped her eyes. "I don't want Bob to see you here."

She clenched her teeth. She moved her head back and stood erect. "Go, Rob. I don't want to have a hard night."

"Are you going to tell him about the baby?"

She shook her head.

"Good," Robin said while a grin tugged at the corners of her mouth. "I never thought I'd say this, but I want to see him suffer. Wait as long as you can. Let him warm up real good to the thought of being a father, then tell him you lost the baby the night he struck you."

Leslie chuckled once before she reached out and hugged her. She smiled thinly while she waved and told her, "Bye. See ya. Thanks."

When Bob came home, she was sitting at the writing table in their bedroom.

"Hi, Baby," he said while he stood next to her holding a bouquet of flowers. "These are for you, my special lady, the love of my life."

She didn't turn. She didn't move.

Leaning, he kissed the side of her face. "Here, Baby. These are for you." He tried to push the flowers inside her hand.

She stared at the wall.

"Here," he said putting starch in his voice. "I bought these flowers for you." He placed the bouquet on the writing table, next to her hand. Then he turned and walked toward the closet. He pulled his suit jacket off. "Traffic was awful today. You don't know how much trouble I went through to get those flowers."

Silence.

Turning away from the closet, he asked, "Something wrong?"

She stared at the wall.

"Do you hear me?" He crossed the floor and neared her side. "Are you a deaf idiot?"

She swallowed hard. She choked back tears.

He stroked her hair. He whispered, "Don't you like the flowers, Honey? I bought them for you."

She bowed her head.

Moving close to her, he wet his mouth with his tongue and puckered.

She pulled away.

"Slut," he snapped while he pulled on the ends of her hair. "You stupid slut! I told you I was stuck in a mess of traffic. You cunt!" He thundered across the floor and hurried out of the bedroom.

"Where are you going?" She called out.

"None of your business!"

"Bob, don't you do this." She stood, turned and faced the door. "Don't you do this to me."

He stood in the archway with his brow raised. "Do what?"

"Go see her."

"Go see who?" He walked inside the bedroom. "Who? What are you talking about? Are you losing your mind? Are you going nuts on me?"

"You know who I'm talking about."

Shaking his head, he said, "No. No, I don't. You'll have to tell—"

"Amanda."

"What?"

"I know you've been seeing her. Don't bother lying to me. I know. I know. Oh, yea. I know. I know, all right."

"Who have you been talking to?"

"Don't worry about it."

"Well. Maybe if you'd be more of a wife to me, rumors wouldn't get started."

When he reached her side, she stood and extended her hands. "I'm sorry I wasn't more receptive when you came home." She shook her head. "I'm so sorry." Then she peered up at him. "Forgive me? Please forgive me."

He smiled while he nodded at her. "Okay. All right. I forgive you."

She brushed the back of her hand against his face. "I only want it to be us. You and me. Just the two of us. We can be good. We can have something real good." Rocking her hips from side to side, she toyed with his belt. "You have no idea what you mean to me. You have no idea how I see you."

He smiled while he watched her unbuckle his pants. A moment later, he cupped her chin and kissed her full on the mouth. He moved his hands over her buttocks and pulled her pelvis against his groin. Her nipples hardened when she brushed against his erection. Opening her mouth, she invited his tongue to explore her. He pushed his tongue across her teeth. Then he thrust his tongue in and out of her mouth. Her hands crawled over his back. She pulled off his shirt and moaned while she squeezed the lump at the front of his pants. She moaned and writhed while she backed him to the bed. Once on the bed they pulled each other's clothes off. Climbing to his feet, he stood at the side of the bed and cradled his erection with his hands. He guided his manhood inside her mouth. While she licked, pulled and sucked, he leaned his head back and moaned. Moments later he thrust himself in and out of her mouth. He didn't step away from her until semen poured out of her mouth. "Swallow it," he told her.

She did.

He smiled. Then he walked to the foot of the bed and parted her legs. He stroked her inner thighs until her entire body grew hot. Moving his hands to the tops of her thighs, he climbed on the bed and hovered over her. Sticking out his tongue, he licked her stomach in long, slow strokes. Then he took his tongue down until it rested over her clitoris. She opened her thighs until her legs formed two triangles. He licked her clitoris slowly. She squirmed and moaned. When she arched her back in ecstasy, he mounted her. He thrust himself inside her. She wrapped her legs around his back and squeezed. She turned her head to the side so he couldn't see her eyes. Tears warmed her face while she begged, "Please let me get pregnant. God, please. I want the baby this time. Please, God, please."

Eight months later when her stomach was full with child, she lay in bed next to Bob. She massaged his neck. I'm tired, Sweetheart. Can we cancel tonight's dinner engagement?"

He yawned before he answered, "I wish we could. I'm tired myself. Think I might be coming down with that flu."

She sat up. "I'll go call the guests and tell them we've cancelled dinner."

"No."

"Honey?"

"I never cancel anything. I don't care how I feel. I never go back on my word."

"But, I'm tired, Honey. Sweetheart, I'm so tired." She circled her stomach with her hand. "Our baby is taking a lot out of me. I really need to rest. The last time I visited the doctor, she sai—"

"I don't care what some doctor says. We are not canceling dinner, and I don't want to hear anymore about it."

"Okay, Honey," she said while she pushed off the bed. "What should I wear?"

He chuckled. "I don't know. I don't care as long as it's something that doesn't make you look fat."

Standing in front of the closet, she asked, "How about this blue dress?"

He leaned forward on the bed. "Looks cute. When did I get that for you?"

"You bought me this for Easter. I wore it that same Sunday we went to church."

"It's nice. My secretary really knows what you like." He smiled.

She stared at the dress while she asked, "What are we having for dinner?"

"Baked chicken. That won't make you sick, will it?"

She shook her head. "No. No. It won't. I'll be all right."

"Good. Because I want to have a good time tonight. I don't want to have to cut the evening short just because you're feeling queasy."

"You never have to cut the evening short for me. Honey, you know that. I can just come upstairs an—"

"You're my wife. You'll be with me."

"Of course."

"You know, I've been meaning to ask you. Have you thought anymore about taking those Bible classes I told you about? Nearly all of the neighborhood wives take those classes. I've been very patient with you about this. But it's time you started getting involved. You sit around the house too much. You need to go out a little."

"Bob, I'm fat and pregnant."

He laughed. "I know, but you'll lose it. A friend of mine says you're carrying most of your weight in your stomach."

"Who's your friend?"

"Just a friend. It's nothing important."

"A no name friend?"

He sat up. "I am not about to argue with you. Not now. I'm not. Let's have a nice quiet evening."

"That's what I've been saying. I couldn't agree with you more. Why don't we cancel dinner an—"

"No! I won't hear it. Stop it! Stop asking me that. We are having dinner and we are going to have a good time and that's that. I don't want to hear another word about it."

She toyed with the dress' hem. "Sure, Honey."

He joined her in the shower. He kissed her stomach then he washed her back. When they stepped out of the shower he told her to sit on the bed so he could towel dry her. They dressed side by side then headed down the staircase.

"Your guests have already arrived, Mr. Long. We kept them entertained. They haven't been here longer than five minutes," the maid told Bob from her place at the foot of the stairs.

He nodded, "Thank you." Turning toward Leslie, he said, "Let's go greet our guests, Darling."

The second Leslie rounded the corner, her eyes ballooned and her heart raced.

"Leslie!" Amanda screamed from behind the table. "How good to see you. Come. Give me a hug."

Leslie's feet froze.

Bob pushed her. "Go ahead, Hon. Welcome our guests."

That night Leslie didn't sleep more than an hour. As soon as Bob left the house for work she hurried to the telephone. She dialed Robin's number. She wept when she returned the receiver to its cradle. She let the telephone ring ten times. Robin wasn't home.

Months passed until they stretched into years. Leslie lost Bob and her second child to a hard, painful miscarriage. Robin drove her to the hospital. The blood that oozed out of Leslie's body while her unborn child lost blood, lost oxygen then died chilled her conscience. Somehow she felt responsible for Leslie's growing demise. She told herself to pray harder, to fast, to give herself over to the Lord fully, completely, so that her prayers for Leslie would be effective. As a last ditch effort, she even prayed for Leslie to learn how to appreciate how fervently Bob worked. Yet, there was something in her prayers that seemed artificial to her. When she looked back over the landscape of her own life she recalled how her own father worked what seemed like all the time. He didn't start working long hours until after Sonia died. As a grown woman, she realized that her father worked long hours as a way to avoid her mother, as a way to stay away from home. Just last weekend when she telephoned home her mother told her that Theo was at work. As soon as she did Robin found an excuse to hang up the telephone. She told her she was under contract to finish a play and that the deadline was tight. Then she told her to have a good night and hung up.

Walking into the apartment's living room and opening the drapes, she stared at the sky. She smiled when she remembered how many dreams incubated in her head while she gazed out the living room window. "Be happy, Leslie," she said when she released the drapes and stepped away from the window.

The central air conditioner was on high. Leslie pulled half of the black, satin comforter with her when she stirred and rolled to her side. Facing the bedroom window, she watched sun rays dance over the top of the grass. The longer she lay in bed, the clearer visions and the nearer sounds of children, pretty women dressed in skimpy bathing suits and bare-chest men romping Atlantic City and Coney Island shores came to her. Daydreams. Fantasies that worked like lifeboats that rescued her from an unsuccessful suicide attempt. It wasn't long before she found herself thinking back to her high school days. The year was 1974. She was in the tenth grade. It was summertime, and she was sitting high above an Olympic size community pool scanning the water. While she scanned the pool's clear, cool waters, she sipped iced tea and fulfilled the last of her four-hour lifeguard shift.

Rolling to her back in the bed, she chuckled. It tickled her when she recalled how certain she was that she was grown back then. Joyce and she screamed at one another. Their days were filled with anger and disappointment. As the years passed, they worked to avoid each other. Leslie chuckled. When she was in high school she expected to go and come at will. Her rebellion saddened her family. Her grandparents, aunts and uncles told her parents that she was lost, forsaken of qualities all good girls possessed.

She turned in the bed and nodded. "They're right," she mumbled. "I'm a lost cause."

She stared at the ceiling. With tears in her eyes she vowed not to spoil her children, not to comfort them with toys and designer outfits. She blinked hard. All her life she blamed her mother for her shortcomings. Yet, she knew it was her father who ruined her. She knew if he wasn't badgering her self-esteem by accusing her of being sexually loose, he was handing her a wad of money to go clothes shopping with. He also taught her how to lie. While she watched him lie to her mother and business associates, she came to see the vice as an art form. She spent years practicing it. Since her marriage to Bob, when she talked with her father she was grateful for the lessons. When he asked her how Bob and she were getting along, she lied. "We're fine," She always answered while she was careful to smile.

Her face tightened and contorted. Lies. Lies. Lies. Bob lied to her. Even now he did. She knew he wasn't working late at the office; she knew he was seeing another woman.

She reminisced about the days of their courtship. Moments later she swallowed hard. Ire pulsed in her. Her eyes became pink and damp. "Liar!" she shouted. "Bob, you're such a liar!"

"I vow to love, honor and cherish Bob Long… I do. I do." The words haunted her. Bitter with the frustrations of her ailing marriage, she embraced the ark of prayer. She was desperate for their marriage to work. Dissolving their union would draw negative attention to her career. That she could ill afford, especially since Bob demanded that she put her acting career on hold after he took her as his wife.

She rolled to her side and looked out the window. She was the wife of a very wealthy man. She doted on him when he was home. She longed for him to pursue her again, really love her.

Money was never an issue where they were concerned. When they weren't entertaining guests at their ranch, they were attending suit and tie required affairs. Joyce was right. Invitations to attend charity events, award ceremonies, dinner parties, theatre and motion picture openings flooded their mailbox. The telephone seemed to always ring. She came to hate the sound of bells. Bells signaled the approach of powerful, gossipy men and jealous, vindictive women. They signaled another party, another tiring event where she would be compelled to smile, laugh and feign happiness.

She propped herself on her elbows. Then she let out a deep breath. When she glanced at the radio/alarm clock on the nightstand and saw that it was noon, she dropped her head into her pillow again. This was the first time in many days that she was sober. She'd never slept until noon before when she was sober. Her face tightened. She reminisced until she heard Robin's voice, then she wept. She thought about telephoning her mother, but wiping tears from her eyes, she told herself not to pick up the telephone. She told herself she called home too much as it was – two and three times a week. Besides, she knew her mother would only tell her that her nervous system was out of whack because she was pregnant.

She balled her fists, and, raising her arms high over head, she drummed her fists into her pillow. As much as she hated to admit it, she knew Robin would only echo her mother's sentiment if she called and told her she felt like a caged animal, like she was losing her mind. The last time they spoke, Robin told her, "My father said all women go through periods of depression and anger while they're pregnant. He said it's normal. He said you'll get through it. This isn't the end of the road. You're not losing your mind. Stop saying that. You'll be all right. As long as I've known you, you've been tough. You'll pull through this. You only feel so out of sorts because you're expecting. I know you're in a miserable marriage, but God can work wonders. I'm praying hard for you. I only hope Bob supports you this time. Maybe a child will bring the two of you together. I mean. Well. I can't tell you what to do, but any time a man hits a woman, I think the woman should leave. The first time. But I want whatever will make you happy. I just hope Bob never hits you again, and I mean not one more time. I'm serious. Stone serious. If not. Well. The door to Apartment 1201 is always open. It always will be. I just hope. Well. I mean, if Bob's still mean to you regardless of what happens this time. Well. I wish you'd leave. You know that. You could just leave. I don't advocate divorce, but I definitely don't believe in abuse. And besides. You have grounds for divorce. You know Bob' fooling around. You should just leave. I hate to see you like this. Hurting. I wish you'd just. Leave."

She squeezed her eyes shut. Her head throbbed. She sniffed hard and told herself not to cry.

Though she received a flux of movie offers she hadn't worked since she married Bob. Since she became Mrs. Bob Long so much of her life involved couples. At dinner parties, all guests suddenly became married. She never knew so much of Hollywood was legally attached. She was mute when she realized a few years ago many of the men and women she saw in the company of their wives and their husbands at social functions and at the ranch were the same people she saw keeping company with other women, with other men. The only way she could excuse adultery from these people's lives was to tell herself everyone in Hollywood got married when Bob and she did.

"I'm trapped," she moaned to the empty room. She shivered when she thought about how Bob insisted that she not leave the house alone unless she went shopping, to Cutters or to Bible class with one of the neighborhood wives. She never did attend Bible class. Other than go shopping and to Cutters, she simply stayed indoors until Bob came home. Yet he accused her of flirting with strange men, of spending his money on playboys and gigolos. When she confronted him with bills for liquor at strip joints, he stormed out of the room and shouted, "I have to find a release somewhere." To which she exclaimed, "Wish I could. I don't have a playboy or gigolo and you know it. I hardly ever even leave this house. These are all your bills. Not one of them is mine. And about me having a man – you must be kidding. I don't have a husband."

She gazed at the ceiling. "God, get me out of here. I made a mistake, an awful mistake in marrying Bob. Lord, get me out of here. Please set me free. Please. Please." A second later she smiled. She ran her hand over her stomach. She smiled each time the baby kicked. She dreamed of holding her baby, gently pulling her to her breast and rocking her to sleep while she sang pretty lullabies.

When the baby stopped kicking, she turned away from gazing at the ceiling and looked out the window. Rocking her hips, she struggled to understand Bob. What motivated him. What he was afraid of. What made him truly happy. Why he married her. Why he reasoned that to keep the attention of Hollywood's power brokers focused on him he had to snuff out her career

The nights she ventured with him to clubs celebrity sport and television stars frequented, no one stood and called out her name. Men stopped inching to her table and asking, "Do you want to dance?" Bob never asked her to dance. He said he was too old and he complained of sore limbs brought on by playing too many hours of racquetball. She spent those evenings watching other people live out their lives while she ordered one drink after another until she got drunk.

Pride and ego. They were what kept her married to Bob. No amount of encouragement from Joyce or Robin could convince her that her marriage was worth midnight screaming, praying and endless hours of verifying her whereabouts to an aging possessive, egomaniac . . . worth endless apologizing for falling short of perfection at the hour of her birth. If she went into court and dissolved this union now, people would whisper rumors of an affair, that she only married Bob to further her career, for what use could Bob have of her, what good could she possibly be to him? Fearing gossip and the weeklies, she spent the first half of her days turning in bed. She spent the latter half of her days tending to Bob and his many demands.

Since a hush came around her career, Amanda worked on three record setting movies. Her motion picture career strong and thriving, she even stopped doing commercials to supplement her income to help pay for her Monte Carlo ranch, her mansion in Hawaii, her villa in Paris and her penthouse in Manhattan. Trade slicks depicted her as a heroine, a fiercely independent woman meeting the challenge to alter the course of sexist Hollywood. She was a champion when political and socially arresting films she worked in floundered at the box office. She was a powerful intellectual in all of her public conversations. Fans mobbed her and begged for her autograph. While watching recaps of the autograph melees on the evening news or reading the details in the trades, the *Times* or *Post*, Leslie cringed.

While fans mobbed Amanda, Leslie shopped at the grocery store. Tossing wet lettuce, soft tomatoes and round potatoes in her hands gave her something to do. Grocery shopping made her feel needed, useful, important. The afternoons she returned to the ranch from her grocery outings, she laughed out loud to an empty kitchen. Though she worked hard to be a doting wife, she never learned to cook. On Sunday afternoons while Bob read the Dow Jones, she clipped coupons. The first few times he asked her what she was doing when he heard scissors shredding newspaper and she told him, "Getting some good coupons," he laughed. "Like you could ever help me save money. Those little coupons don't mean anything. Stop wasting your time. You're so silly. Save me ten million dollars, then come and talk to me." Then he shook his head and returned to his newspaper.

When she wasn't shopping, she was often whispering on the telephone to Donald. He kept their conversations short. Shame clouded her thoughts when she picked up the telephone and dialed his number. He always seemed to be in a hurry when she called. She heard him say, "Sorry I'm late for a meeting," more than she heard him say, "I found a great script for you."

"Donald, we both know Bob told you not to contact me about work, but I'm calling you."

"Les, I've been warned."

"What did he say?"

"I don't want to go into it."

"But I haven't mentioned work to him in a long time."

"Maybe not. All I know is every time you call me I somehow manage to run into him. Like I told you, he keeps telling me that you aren't interested in reading scripts. Said you only rehired me because you liked me and didn't want to hurt my feelings by telling me you no longer need my services. Told me that even before you two got married. Went so far as to tell me that you said you thought the scripts I send you aren't meaty enough."

"But I—"

"I don't know, Les. I don't know what's going on over there. You tell me one thing then Bob turns around and tells me something else. All I know is that your husband is a very powerful man, a very powerful man."

To this, she smiled thinly and bowed her head upon bidding him farewell. She knew he was the best agent in town. She also knew how powerful her husband was. If he couldn't get passed Bob, she knew no one could. The receiver returned to its cradle, rage tinted her eyes and turned her entire face red.

At her hairdresser was the place where she laid her burdens down. Ryan Golde owned Cutters for five years. It was a small hair styling salon situated in a better section of North Jersey. Leslie drove from Edgewood to Cutters every Wednesday at nine. She confided to Ryan the troubles of her life. She wept on his shoulder. She got her best cocaine from him.

Besides visiting the local food market and Ryan, she resigned herself to bed. At the close of the day when Bob came home from work he mistook her being in bed for desire. She grimaced while he humped her. While he moaned and grabbed her buttocks and thrust his hips against hers, she sent wishes across the room. She wished he would return to his lovers and leave her alone to grieve the details of their marriage. As if aware of her attempts to thread hope back into her life through the mirage of wishes, he moaned until he shook her thoughts and took them away from the wishes, until a chill went through her.

Empty sex. A ritual. A habit that died hard.

Earlier in the morning she closed her eyes, writhed and moaned when he thrust himself inside of her and asked, "Is it good?" A moment later, she opened her eyes and saw him no longer looking at her. His head was buried against her shoulder. She rolled her eyes. While he sucked her breasts and sent their headboard banging against the wall, she sent her thoughts further into the evening. Before he left for work, he told her they were having a party. A party – yes, and yet she stayed in bed all day. Turning her head, she stifled a chuckle. The butlers and maids would do all of the work. They always did. She merely showed up and looked beautiful.

Of late, while at the dinners, she taunted the guests with her icy stares while she circled the dining room, a drinking glass in her hand. She jabbed at their conscience with her jerky nods. Despite their forced smiles, she knew at one time or another each of them had tried to ruin her career. Yet, she was gracious while she engaged them in small talk. When she glanced across the room she always saw Bob grinning at her. He was pleased with her performance.

The morning after a party when the bedroom was empty and Bob was gone away from the house, she turned to her mother, a woman who never complained, even after she kept her confined to the telephone for two hours in one phone call. Regardless of how long she kept her on the phone, Joyce never introduced her to the errands she had yet to complete for the day. She never allowed herself to be too busy for Leslie even after she spent an hour accusing her of guiding her to this miserable, marital end. She refused to return Leslie her anger or retaliate against her many accusations, because she knew without her listening ear, without her encouraging words, without her fervent prayers, without her mother's love, Leslie would crumble.

Hatred passed through Leslie like too much water on a hot day. She taught herself to accept Bob and all his ways. She couldn't bring herself to respect him. The manner in which he worked to control her nauseated her. She noticed the only time he behaved reasonably toward her were the times she ceased to fight for her independence and allowed him to usurp all her efforts to regain the power in her career, over her life.

Even with her career on hold, six hundred pieces of fan mail was the least amount of correspondence she received daily. Most of her admirers pleaded with her to return to the studio lots. They longed to see her on the silver screen.

Nights Bob came home full of liquor and at the height of his neurosis, he screamed at her that he was the cause of her success, the reason for her fame. Moments later and forgetting the sixteen years she toiled in the business unknown to him, she shrunk beneath the comforter. She prayed that she wouldn't upset him further and cause him to strike her. Then she told herself that he was right. Without him, she had no chance of a career.

The one time she told her father that she was an abused wife, he chewed on his lip. A long moment passed before he said, "You need to see a therapist."

"I don't need a shrink! How would you know anything about mental imbalance? The way you've cheated on, talked down to and beat Mama over the years? You need the shrink! You're the one who's crazy! You and Bob are just alike! Neither of you likes me strong. You're probably the one who has this guy following me around."

"Les."

"Don't act like you don't know."

"Leslie. Listen—"

"Checking up on me," she screamed seconds before Arnold, sensing the threat of her full-blown temper looked over the arch of his shoulder and handed the telephone to Joyce.

Raising to her elbows, Leslie told herself to get out of bed and onto the floor – the thought was birthed from her desire not to be cowardly like Joyce. Because she wanted to escape the demons that tormented Aretha. Because she wanted to give something back to Robin for her unending support. Robin.

"Leslie!"

The second Leslie heard Bob's voice rise from the bottom of the living room stairs, she covered her mouth. Returning her back to the mattress, she sunk beneath the comforter. Before Bob pushed the bedroom door ajar, she pulled the top edge of the comforter against the bottom of her chin. She listened to the hum of the air conditioner while the door opened slowly. A thin, fox-like grin cracking the middle of her dry lips, she promised herself that she would get even.

The door opened, and Bob's towering frame came into view. "Honey?"

She watched him cross the bedroom floor.

Bedside, he leaned and planted a full kiss on her mouth. The kiss soothed the cracked spot on her lips. When he stood and stepped away from the bed, she couldn't help but think that he, tightly muscled and perfectly tanned, was the most gorgeous man she ever saw.

He drew his tongue across the fattest part of his mouth. "Mmmm. That was good."

She arched her brow and looked at him sideways. She smiled in effort to disguise her examination. The change in him perplexed her. Before he slammed the front house door to a close behind him this morning, closing her out of his world, he looked over his shoulder and screamed, "I didn't get married to live with a lazy whore! Get your butt out of bed!"

"Mmmm. Think so?" She added in short exchange.

He walked to the bedroom window and stuffed his hands inside his pant pockets.

She watched his back move. She watched his hands work inside his pant pockets while he rolled coins one over another. "Nice day out?"

He answered, "Yes." Then he arched his shoulders. "A little warm out, though."

"*It's mid-August, Idiot. What do you expect?*" She mused to herself. Outwardly, she puckered her lips. It had been months since she retaliated against his abuses. She thought about the last time she challenged his self-righteous ideology. She almost shook her head. She told herself that she didn't need a therapist; she needed to fight back.

He turned away from the window and faced her.

His shirt buttons popping and separating while he ran his hand down his chest stirred her imagination.

"So." He said, pausing. "What have you been doing today?"

"*You mean, it's not we? It's you instead of we? I'm a you instead of a we? Oh, how perfect! I finally made it beyond we! I'm a you now! Thought everything I did was to your credit. Thought everything I ever had that ever meant anything belonged to you. Thought my very existence depended on you. Thought I was nothing without you. Bob, oh, yes, Mr. Chairman of the Board, I'll show you. In due time . . . I'll show you.*" Cloaked in vengeance, the thoughts drummed inside her head while she lay silently in bed.

He pulled off his shirt and exposed his thick, hairy chest. Soon his shirt covered the ends of her exposed feet. "Hmmm?"

When she detected a smile snipping the corners of his mouth, she shifted in the bed until most of her thigh fell from beneath the comforter. "*You owe me. You just don't know, Darling. You just don't know. You have no idea how good of a day it's going to end up being.*"

"Les?"

She turned toward the bedroom door and called, "Bob?"

"Ready, Hon?"

"Just about."

"Come out of the bathroom for a sec. I want to look at you."

The evening gown she wore hugged her hips but fell down loosely over her stomach.

Upon sight of her, Bob smiled. "Don't you look beautiful."

She turned and winked at him. "You were so good today, Baby. You really stoked my fire."

Pulling her close, he kissed her and pushed his tongue inside her mouth. When he stepped back, he said, "Satisfying you is what brings me pleasure. It's what I'm here for." While he circled her lower spine with his hand, her mind went to the first time he asked her out. That night five years

ago, he smiled into her face, blushed with surprise and asked her if she
would care to dine with him. Her heart raced. She couldn't say no.
Tonight, she, in her gold colored evening gown and polished pearls that
dangled her wrists and neck, and, he, in his beige Perry Ellis suit . . . they
looked to be in love again.

She passed the bedroom mirror framed in dark oak and smiled at
the thought. A second later, a frown tore into her face, and she told herself
to do no less than hammer his ego the entire evening, until the last guest
excused himself from the ranch. After all, she told herself, Bob's recent
kindness was a mirage. She couldn't believe that he didn't know she long
ago stopped believing in the expensive gifts, the tireless nights of love
making or these newlywed scenes that always seemed to take place moments
before dinner guests arrived.

"I know, Babe. And I am ever grateful." The words flew out of
her mouth so quickly she almost turned to see from whence they came.

He turned his back to her and pretended to hunt a pair of cuff links.
When she moved toward the window, he arched his brow. She seemed
somehow odd to him. He thought about apologizing to her for unleashing
his frustrations and anger on her at different times during their marriage. He
wanted to convey to her his disappointment for the many times he came
home falling down drunk and so full of liquor he couldn't maintain an
erection. Not once, even now, did it occur to him that she, ill with the stench
of liquor making his clothes smell stale, was grateful for those times he
suffered impotency, because she didn't want to have sex with him on those
nights.

He wanted to show her that he was a changed man. Even for his
tirade this morning, he longed to express to her his repentance, his sorrow
over his behavior towards her. Although the maids and butlers reported to
him that she often drank throughout the day before he returned home, he
hoped she noticed an entire week passed since he came home from work
drunk. He sipped a few martinis during lunch, but he hadn't intoxicated
himself in one entire week. He used his fear of losing her to explain his
mounting psychosis, the fruit of which he aimed at her. He used the fear to
explain his manipulation. He used the fear to explain his keeping his own
behavior unpredictable, which, in turn, kept her confused and unaware of his
deep seated doubts about his self worth. If she would convince him that she
would love him until death parted them, he knew he would never drink or
strike her again.

Hungry to rid his mind of guilt and to right his wrongs, he longed to
tell her that he loved her, loved her more than life itself, loved her more than
she could ever know.

She turned away from the window and forced a smile. "Thank you for the compliment, Sweetheart. I'm glad you think I'm beautiful."

"You are. You are so beautiful. You really did good with this pregnancy. I don't think you gained more than fifteen pounds."

"I'm so happy that you are pleased. You mean so much to me." After he walked toward her, she leaned and kissed the side of his face.

He gazed softly inside her eyes. "I love you. I love you so much. I don't know what I would do without you. You are my life, my very existence."

"I know, Honey." Then she pecked his mouth and said, "We better get going."

He nodded. "Turn around, so I can zip you up. Are you almost ready?"

"Yes, Darling. Just let me put on my earrings and spray on some cologne."

"Wear that cologne I bought you for your birthday."

She smiled. "You really like that cologne, don't you?"

He returned her the semblance of affection. "Yes. You smell delicious when you wear that cologne."

"Thank you, Sweetheart. Did your secretary pick it out?" She chuckled. "You know how she knows what I like."

He stared at her quizzically before he answered, "No. Uh. No. I picked that cologne out myself."

"Well. I guess you know what I like too, Honey. It's very nice."

He moved toward the door. "I'll be downstairs. Call me if you need anything."

"What would I need?"

"Anything, Hon. You're expecting our child. If you need anything at all, call me."

"I'll be down in less than two minutes, Sweetheart. I'm fine."

The living room stairs heaved beneath his weight. Listening to the stairs grow noisy, she made a mental note to contact Edgewood's most expensive carpenter to mend the stairs first thing in the morning. After she screwed her pearl earring posts in place, she lowered her hands to the dresser and stared into the mirror. She whispered, "I love you," to the woman gazing back at her, then she turned and headed toward the stairs.

As soon as she entered the living room, Bob moved toward her. He kissed her softly. Tugging on the back of her dress teasingly and hurrying across the floor, she told him, "I'm going to check out what's going on in the main kitchen."

His gaze followed her. "Thanks, Baby."

She rounded the corner and entered the kitchen.

"Mr. Long." The butler called over his shoulder before he answered the front door chime.

Bob held his finger mid air. "Thank you, Ralph."

Watching Ralph from where she stood at the edge of the kitchen, Leslie wondered if sixty-two year old, Ralph, would bow to the floor and kiss Bob's feet before he opened the front door.

"Certainly, Sir," Ralph called to Bob in return.

After Ralph opened the door, Leslie stood in the living room foyer beside Bob calling out first names and nodding. As usual, the people behind the familiar names that passed before her were cordial and perfunctory. Their clothes were equally as stiff. *"These high class, rich people are such addicts, they don't stumble behind a fifth of liquor or stutter after snorting a gram of coke."* She mused to herself while she strangled a chuckle before she nodded and called out, "Hi, Vince and JoAnn. Nice to see you two could make it. Do come in."

Leslie rested the point of her left elbow on the arm of the living room's antique, English sofa. Most of tonight's guests were in their forties or fifties. *Too much California tanning*, Leslie mused to herself while she crossed her legs at the thigh and dissected the people milling about Bob and her house, a drink ever in their hand. She shook her head and wondered why Bob bothered to keep company with has beens when Darrell Young, a fifty-eight year old director who had one hit movie in 1980, walked beyond her without nodding or speaking. Besides Darrell, since her marriage to Bob and the beginning of these dinner parties, she saw every major motion picture producer or director pass through the downstairs rooms of Bob and her ranch.

Darrell walked in front of her again, and she thought she had it figured out. Everything Bob did was for business. Though his work was outdated, Darrell kept close ties with Frank Johnson and Calvin Bogg, two of Hollywood's most prominent producers. She sat against the back of the sofa and told herself that Bob married her for business. She told herself that, because she was young, he thought marrying her would put time on his side. She figured he told himself, in his twilight years, he could enjoy success by living vicariously through her.

Fearing the worse, that she was on to his manipulative tactics, she knew he was trying to buy both time and insurance by being friendly with her. Magazine articles detailing the events of their marriage lined bookstore shelves all over the country. She saw the articles when she frequented a nearby drugstore to fill a sleeping pill prescription for Bob.

She jumped when Bob tapped her forearm. "Teresa," he said while Leslie looked up until she and a tall brunette faced one another. "Have you met my wife?"

"No, Bob," Teresa answered, smiling and shaking her head. "I don't believe I have."

Her smile almost made Leslie coil. She turned her head slightly before she returned Teresa her pretentious smile and extended her hand.

When Teresa released her hand, it fell limp inside her lap. She continued to smile and look up at her. "It's a pleasure to meet you, Teresa."

"Same here, Dear. I'll see you around."

She dismissed the fact that she didn't notice Teresa's European accent earlier. She simply told herself, *"Acting has to stop somewhere."*

"Please excuse me while I check on the meal." Leslie heard herself say while she pushed off the sofa.

"Oh. Please do." Teresa stepped to the side and watched Leslie saunter toward the kitchen.

Except for Teresa, she purposely restrained from engaging in dialogue with the guests. In an unanticipated move, she also let the day pass minus her telephoning Joyce or Robin. Making a sudden change from her usually predictable schedule, Robin did not visit the ranch earlier in the day. Because Robin's visits elevated her mood and never failed to thrust her from bed, she knew, upon his entry to the house, Bob was aware that she engaged in no outside conversation throughout the day.

Upon climbing the living room stairs and discovering her chin tucked beneath the comforter, she realized that he knew she hadn't driven to Cutters. None of the people who expressed to her their strong dislike for him spoke with her today. She also knew he took note of the fact that she hadn't recapped the events of Robin and her conversations in two weeks. She smiled. Bob was losing the ability to keep tabs on her.

Teresa asked, "Were Leslie's mother and father married?" after she folded her arms and arched her brow.

He chuckled. "Yes. Mr. and Mrs. Fletcher are still married."

"Hmmm," was the most Teresa responded.

He examined her expression and chuckled again. "Come on, Teresa. I know you have a thousand thoughts on the tip of your tongue."

She returned him his chuckle before she added, "So you and Leslie are going to mimic Mr. and Mrs. Fletcher?" Then she laughed.

When he didn't speak, she asked, "Do Mr. and Mrs. Fletcher have other children?"

To their unawares, Leslie eavesdropped on their conversation from where she stood next to the kitchen's refrigerator. The grin lighting Bob's face almost made her nauseous.

"No. Leslie is Mr. and Mrs. Fletcher's only child." He stuck his finger in the center of his chest. "We're both only children."

"Think that's the problem?"

He laughed with her. He shook his head before he answered, "No." Then he arched his brow and looked intently at her. "You don't like Leslie, do you?"

She was quick. "No." She leaned her shoulder into his. After she chuckled dryly, she asked, "Want me to help you get rid of her?"

He stepped back. "Why, no."

"What do you want from her?"

"She's my wife."

Leslie smirked. Never before did she witness Bob struggling to free himself from the long binding ropes of embarrassment. Although she didn't know the art to Teresa's manipulation or appreciate it since it was aimed at her, she promised herself to acquire the skill.

"Bob Long, what do you want from that pretty, young, talented, determined woman?"

He was hesitant. His shirt collar became a toy. He twisted it between his fingers.

From her place in the kitchen, Leslie watched his fingers and shirt collar move. She concluded that Teresa's name wasn't scribbled on the sheets of ruled paper Bob kept folded and tucked between two pairs of dress pants in the second drawer of his bedroom dresser. Less than a week ago, he boasted that he would have to continue the dinner party list on a fifth page. Before midnight sealed the evening, she was going to search the list for Teresa's name. The events flashing before her told her, ten to fifteen years ago, Teresa was a wielding force in the industry and a tremendous influence on Bob's career. She likely had the power to make or break his career in radio and television. She obviously chose to grant him a break. He tolerated the manner in which she treated him and said nothing of the way she made him to feel. It was clear to Leslie that the break Teresa granted him years ago was so big he felt forever in her debt.

She imagined him walking through Manhattan's Upper East Side in the middle of the day sometime this week when Teresa spotted him in a crowd. She didn't need to close her eyes to see Teresa talking at the top of her lungs to an embarrassed Bob. "I heard you recently married, Bob! Why haven't I been invited to the ranch to meet your new wife?"

"Teresa, I care about Leslie." Realizing that sentiment wasn't strong enough reason to validate cause for marriage, he took in a deep breath, then quickly added, "I love her."

She was yet to be charmed. "And just how many women have you loved?"

"You mean, tried to love? Not every woman will let you love her. Not every woman will allow herself to be loved."

"Hold on." She raised her hand. "Wait a minute. You sound as though you believe that women have abused you. You sound as though you've tried time and again to love hapless women. You sound hurt, bruised." She shook her head. "Sounds like a paradox, Bob. Sounds like a paradox too twisted to be true."

His eyes ballooned, and his throat grew dry. He stared into her face and swallowed hard.

After a moment, his throat cleared and he spoke. "I made a spectacle of none of my lovers. I worked to keep the fiber of all my affairs private."

"Buying a woman jewelry, furs and flowers is not kind, is not love, Bob. Love isn't for sale. It either is or is not in a person's heart. Love never fits in or comes from one's pocket. Besides, for the gifts you give, you expect a person's life in return."

He chuckled. "And just how do I do that?"

Leslie glared at him.

"By requesting the impossible."

He chuckled again. "Such as?"

"Such as a woman's happiness, her career, her mental stability." She let out a deep breath. "By situating your lovers under your feet. By causing your lovers intense pain, then not expecting them to retaliate, to mount a defense. By requesting of your lovers what they are incapable of providing, then punishing them with verbal and physical abuse for disappointing you. Your lovers do try to appease your insatiable appetite, nevertheless. You hurt, Bob. You give the tangible, then demand the intangible."

He laughed outright. "That's what I'm doing to Leslie?"

"That's what I'm doing to Leslie?" She enjoyed mocking him. "Leslie and everyone you invite inside your intimate circle."

He chuckled dryly. "Just what type of person do you think I am?"

"Scared . . . Terrified?"

"Scared of what?"

"Scared . . . terrified of failure. You best make an effort to change. If you don't, you won't need me to cut Leslie out of your life."

Leslie smiled when she heard Teresa chuckle.

285

"Leslie's too feisty to hang around long." She inserted a deliberate pause. "And all the nice things you buy her, she can get by herself."

Chapter Eighteen

"Nooooo!   Noooooo!   Dear   God,
helpmmmmmmmmmmmmeeeeeeeeeeee!" Leslie's skull crashed against the
top corner of the bedroom dresser. The tip of her ear caught on the dresser's
bottom knob when she sunk to the floor. "Oh, God! Noooooooooo!" She
screamed while her head banged against the dresser. Blood, coming through
a gash in her forehead, oozed away from her face and moved across the
bedroom carpet.

Bob had to lean his body toward the floor and aim downward to
land his fists in the center of her nose, mouth and forehead. "Die! After all I
gave you, you decide to try to leave me! Die! Die! Die!"

Ten minutes was too long for Leslie on August 18, 1994.

It started when she raised her voice and said, "Bob, I don't say one
word when you run around with your girlfriends. But flaunting your affair
with Amanda in my face is just too much."

He crossed the dining room floor and walked inside the kitchen. A
moment passed. He didn't respond to her, so she stood from the dining
room table where he spent the last two hours telling her the many places he
scheduled them to vacation before fall came to New Jersey. She followed
him inside the kitchen. "It's really too much, Bob."

Though he ate a taco salad less than half an hour ago, he stood over
the kitchen counter making himself a boiled turkey, cheese and rye bread
sandwich. He kept his back to her.

She opened the refrigerator door, took nothing out then slammed
the door closed.

He placed the top slice of rye bread over the turkey and cheese and
raised the sandwich to his mouth.

She bumped his shoulder with the tip of her elbow. "You would
think that you could have waited until our child was born and we were out of
the limelight before you decide to have an affair with that conniving--"
Seeing to the core of the indiscretion, she raised her voice inches below a
shout. "Maybe that's why her career's been going so well. Every time my
career takes a lull, hers soars. I used to wonder why that was. Now it's
becoming clear to me." Her mind traveled over the last eight years of her
life, and, her blood pressure rising, she felt her face fill with color. "That's
probably the reason you married me. To keep me down so she could
succeed! You've probably been sleeping with her for I don't know how
long! She's not new to your bed! Times I was away at Cutters or out
grocery shopping . . . I used to wonder why you asked me what I was going
to do and where I was going to be everyday . . . you were probably bedding

Amanda right upstairs in one of the room's of our house! Well, let me tell you something, Mr. Bob Long, Amanda Gaynor will sleep with anyone! She probably has! So, don't feel special! You're not special, Bob! You're an idiot! And I'm an even greater fool for ever thinking you were otherwise! I'm a bigger fool than you are for marrying you! I should have listened to my mother! I should never have married you!" She paced the area of the floor that separated the refrigerator from the stove. Her eyes were tiny beads. Her brow was tight. "I never should have married you! And if you think I'm upset because I think Amanda's getting something I'm missing, you're sadly mistaken! You're about the poorest piece of lay a woman could ever have! I don't care how you look at it, a man whose impotent half the time, isn't much of a bargain in the bed! You impotent, selfish, egotistic, psychotic! You're the child of a woman who doesn't even love you!"

He chewed his sandwich as if he was oblivious of her screaming at the side of his head.

"And don't think I don't have friends who don't talk to me! You probably think Robin's my only friend! She can't stand you, and she likes everyone! That's it! That's it!" She slammed her hand against the counter. "You're a nobody, Bob Long! You're a nothing! I mean, because Robin likes everybody! That's why she doesn't like you! You're nothing! You're not even a nobody! You're lower than nobody! You're nothing!" Inching closer to the side of his head, she went to her toes and raised her voice until it shrieked. "You're sick! You're a sicko, Bob! You only married me so you could try to see how long it would take you to drive me crazy like you are! Trying to be your mother all over again, Bob? Poor Bob! His mommy locked him in a closet when he was a little boy! Know why, Bob? Because you're nothing, and your parents didn't want you giving away the family secret! Your whole family's nothing! Your entire family's nothing!" Stepping away from him while he continued to chew his sandwich in slow, methodic bites, she circled a small space on the floor not far from his back. "I've met all your people! You all are the sickest bunch of people I've ever met! I know why you're crazy now! I've been your submissive wife long enough, Bob Long!" She heard herself shriek again. "I've been your kicking post long enough, Bob Long! I can't believe I went around here for five years letting you treat me anyway you wanted to treat me, letting you talk to me anyway you wanted to talk to me! I took all your sickness, and I never complained!" She pushed her hands against her face, and her hands became wet. "Oh, God, what have I let you do to me? What have I become?"

Pushing the last bite of sandwich inside his mouth, he dabbed at the corners of his mouth with the tips of his fingers. A second later he turned, and Leslie's life changed forever. "I'll tell you what you are, and what you're going to be." Without so much as raising his voice, he pulled his hand across his chest and threw it against her mouth.

She backed away from him and made her way into the living room, then she headed toward the bedroom stairs. When she reached the second step, she felt herself fall backward.

"I'll tell you what you are, you conniving, selfish whore! I'll tell you what you are!" He pulled and jerked on her long hair, the same long hair, he once told her he loved to stroke and let fall through his fingers. "You are an ingrate! You are a money loving, ungrateful imp! And if you think you're sorry you married me, you should try and think about how I feel! You're an embarrassment! Nobody wants to work with you! You ought to hear how people in the industry talk about you! People keep pulling me to the side and asking me why I married you, and, understanding that we all make mistakes, they turn around and ask me why I stay married to you! You're the nothing! You're the nobody! A man can't even eat a sandwich in peace without you complaining!" That said, he leaned back, and, with the full impact of his weight, he sent his foot against her hip.

She fell up the stairs. Near the top of the stairwell, she scanned the top floor. Her gaze darted. She tried to figure a way to lock herself inside the bedroom and climb out the second floor window without him reaching her.

"And Amanda . . . Amanda's a lot more woman than you'll ever be! You don't know how I wish I had married her instead of you! You're just another one of those free loading, hustling women!" It was his turn to shriek. "I hate you! I wish you never polluted my life with your presence! I wish I never laid eyes on you! You only went out with me because you knew I had money! You only married me because you thought I could revive that dying, hopeless career of yours! You're finished! Nobody likes you! Nobody wants to work with you! Nobody respects you! Nobody thinks you're talented! Nobody's your friend! And I tried to love you, but what do you give me for thanks? I hate you! I hate you!"

Two steps away from the top of the stairwell, she pulled away from him with so much force, a lump of her hair landed inside his hand.

Just as she reached their bedroom door, he lunged for her ankle and threw her to the floor. It was there that he began kicking her and pounding her face with his fists.

Robin sat up on the sofa with a jolt. She knew she was tired when she lay down twenty minutes ago to take a nap, something she hadn't done since the sixth grade, but she didn't figure on the fatigue landing her in the heart of a nightmare. A second later still seeing blood from her dream dribble into a carpeted floor, she heard herself scream, "Les-lee!"

She stood and ran for the front door to Apartment 1201. She reached her Benz in less than three minutes, then, sitting behind the wheel of the luxury car she drove like a mad woman through Manhattan, across the toll bridge and into New Jersey.

Bob's silver and black Ferrari wasn't in the side driveway when Robin pulled in front of the ranch. For that she turned her gaze toward her car ceiling and whispered, "Thank you, Jesus."

She climbed out of her Benz and ran to the front door. Her heart raced while she banged on the door. Tears pooled in her eyes. "Somebody please open up," she begged while she pounded her fists against the door.

The sound of running feet stole her attention. She looked to the back of the house. "Hey! Hey!" She called out while she ran toward the bald man. "Where are you going? What were you doing in there? Hey! Hey! Hey, you!"

The man sped toward a red Mustang. Within seconds he was gone, a memory Robin would never forget, a figure she was certain she had seen before.

She inched toward the back door. Her shoulders were hunched. Her ears were open for the slightest noise. The back door was ajar. "Leslie! Ralph! Bob." Her lips quivered. "Where is everybody?" She went inside the house. A loaf of rye bread lay on the kitchen counter. Her mind reeled. Her thoughts went like a thousand caged bats, striking out, fighting to get free. Her chest heaved. She heard her own emotions working themselves into tears. "God," she whispered. "God, help me." She balled her hand and pushed it against her mouth. "God, please. Please, God. Don't let Leslie be dead."

Car tires screeched.

She froze. Her gaze darted from the back door to the window to the front of the house.

A dog barked.

"Damn it! Hell!"

It was a man's voice.

She listened. The hair rose on the back of her neck when she heard footsteps near the back of the house.

A dog barked and growled. A shadow passed the kitchen window.

She bent and ducked behind the counter. She stared at the back door so hard, her eyes hurt.

A chain broke. She heard it dragging across the ground. The scraping noise grew loud. Soon she heard a dog's feet racing toward the back of the house.

"Damn it!"

The man.

She stood when she saw the man's shadow move toward the front of the house. The dog was chasing him. Running into the living room, she peered through the curtain. "It's him." That's all she said. She didn't know the man's name, but she knew she'd seen him before. She squinted. The way the man moved, that slight limp, that deep, long scar at the side of his face, that bald head. She nodded while she crouched low at the window. He was the man who was in the apartment all those years ago that night she called the police.

The man sat in front of the house while the dog barked, growled and snarled at the side of his car. Clutching her chest, she inched away from the window and moved slowly toward the telephone. When she took the receiver out of the cradle, she snapped, "I'm calling the police." She dialed 911 and waited.

The dog continued to bark, snarl and growl. Women and children started to open their drapes and peer outside. The man sunk down in the Mustang. A moment later he was gone.

Robin raced toward the back door. She closed then locked it. Turning, she went to the stairs. She didn't get halfway up the stairs before the door chimed. What she saw moments later after an ambulance and police cruiser parked in the side driveway sent a chill up her spine. Although cops and ambulance technicians surrounded her and insulated her with their security and authority, she screamed.

"Do you know this woman?" One of the technicians asked her after he and his co-worker lifted Leslie's naked, blood robed body off the bedroom floor and placed it on a stretcher.

Chapter Nineteen

Five months passed. Happiness continued to evade Aretha. It was like a mirage dancing around her life, tearing at her past, haunting her future – forever escaping her. As if exhausted with the chase, tired of searching for happiness -- Aretha sat cross-legged in a splintered, wood chair reading a popular history magazine. The low, steady hum of a love ballad going around on a twelve-year-old phonograph kept her relaxed.

Muffin, a small shaggy dog she rode the subway to a Midtown pet shop and purchased three years ago, sat at the end of her feet. Off and on throughout the morning, she leaned over in the chair and stroked the fur that coated Muffin's spine.

She turned a page in the magazine and uncrossed her legs. Kathleen and Bertha absent from the studio, too much quiet filled the air. It was so quiet in the studio she thought the lack of noise made a loud, deafening sound. Because it was necessary for her to alter her lifestyle to stay alive and because Kathleen and Bertha weren't convinced they needed to alter their lifestyles, she lived alone the last five months of her life. Her circle of friends was changed. When she fell four months behind in her rent, she was evicted from her high rise apartment. Now her residence too was changed.

Quitting a drug habit cold turkey was yet to prove fruitful for her. Distancing herself from the walls of the small studio and walking to a drug rehab clinic she was certain would prove more profitable socially. The excuse she used to sell herself the theory that going cold turkey in the studio would be more beneficial in the long run as opposed to enrolling in a substance abuse clinic was -- money problems. Sitting in the hard, wood chair, she understood the excuse to be a frightening paradox. She knew money problems never stopped her from buying drugs.

Scrounging New York City's streets and avenues wearing cut off blue jeans frayed badly at the bottom edges, a dingy orange tank top and stained under garments – she -- walking with her head bent toward the ground, hunted pennies. Her eyes ballooned and her heart raced when she found a quarter or stumbled upon a dollar bill. Most of her scant wardrobe she pulled from the bottom of apartment building garbage cans. Sometimes she wondered if the garments' former owners recognized their attire when they saw her on the street. If they did, they made no mention of it to her. The last five months of her life, she felt like a vapor, a mirage, a person who really didn't exist, a person no one saw or cared for.

Two restaurants she frequented in her heyday provided her with apple and tomato juice, hamburger patties, bread and canned vegetables free of charge. Bored with the content of their own lives, occasionally New

Yorkers stopped and watched her move toward the outside door leading to her studio apartment. It was this small, curious audience that encouraged her to continue with her life. Perhaps, she thought, the people staring at her back while she pulled her studio door key from her front pant pocket, feared the problems she possessed were contagious.

The music lulled and no longer scanning the magazine's pages, she peered up. Faded paper strings hung across the ceiling. Their ends fell to the floor where they were stomped on until they broke apart. The walls of the living room were bright green. A one hundred-watt light bulb was screwed inside the living room's only lamp. No shade crowned the bulb. The walls of the kitchen were bright red. The walls of the bathroom were navy blue. All of the rooms in the studio, including the living room, kitchen and bedroom, which could be seen from the front door, sent out too much color. Though despised by Kathleen, the different, loud colors helped Aretha to sort out the source of her many troubles, and, at days end, calm enough to climb in bed and sleep two to three hours at night.

The last time she saw Kathleen and Bertha was at the only party she hosted at her new residence -- Studio 63. Joined by cronies who continued to live in the high rise, the trio laughed, joked, drank wine and vodka and danced until they grew light headed. The smell of sweat, liquor and urine, not flushed and brownish, orange in the bathroom toilet, filled Studio 63. Six party guests slept over that night. First to wake in the morning after the party, when Aretha left her bedroom and walked inside the living room, she stumbled over Bertha and Kathleen's legs. They didn't awaken. They slept soundly on the living room floor with their arms strewn across one another's chest. Broken lasagna noodles, milk, sour cream dip, cottage cheese and bits of fried whiting dirtied the living room and kitchen floors. The party's two male guests, strangers to Aretha, but new friends of Kathleen's, over drank and spewed their evening meal on the living room floor. Their vomit remained on the floor.

A string of rhythm and blues hits put a gentle lace of music across the living room and kitchen. Now morning and yet intoxicated, while Aretha made her way through the studio, guilt instructed her to harness her narcotic appetite.

Learn to appreciate the small things in life. See the good in yourself and in others. Laugh at your mistakes more often. Try to be civil with your mother and father. Those were the things she told herself, if she accomplished them, would make her happy. Having walked into the heart of many of New York City's wealthy, middle class and growing impoverished communities, she lived her life on T level. She tolerated everyone circling her. She tolerated all the events of her day. Nothing garnered great emotion from her. Newspaper articles detailing the plight of the poor and the homeless only thickened the ice in her emotional vein. She turned up her nose when pan handlers glared at her and snarled, "Give me some money."

Weary with her own troubles, she would scream if she heard another complaint from a New Yorker. To her, New York City was an over crowded place where few residents bothered to excuse themselves or try to stop bumping her elbows and shoulders and stepping on the ends of her feet. Their complaints meant nothing to her, because, resigning themselves to mental and physical inertia, she told herself the complainers gave birth to their own problems, incubated their own misery.

Of all the places in New York City she could be each day, more often than not, she chose Manhattan. She cried, laughed, danced, embraced her friends, dined, ached, smiled and loved in Manhattan. Crime rarely distracted her daily affairs, her thoughts, her habits. For all her satire, living in Manhattan was what she liked most about New York City.

She knew she had to get herself together before she could truly appreciate Manhattan, truly love New York City, truly love other people -- love herself. She knew she could get herself together. It was just that the studio was so quiet.

The night of the party, her guests laughed so hard a joyous fever pitched the air. Music blared, and, with people she loved holding their intoxicated selves up against the living room and kitchen walls, Studio 63 fell into a graceful decorum.

Friends visited her at her apartment one to two times a day after she returned home from a full day of work at the post office. Those days, savvy drug peddlers also visited her several times a week. Getting cocaine, and, later, heroine was as easy as going to and from work for her when she lived in a finer part of Manhattan. Most of her friends carried, and, her narcotic appetite screaming to be fed, she never denied a request to indulge. None of her friends wanted to get stoned alone. It seemed to be as Kathleen often joked, "Only junkies do drugs alone."

Crossing her legs at the ankles, she looked at the splintered, wood living room furniture and wondered how the studio managed to shrink in five months -- since the day of the party. She wondered if her friends loved her. They didn't visit or telephone anymore. She wondered if it was the studio. She wondered if, secretly, her friends were members of New York's preppie league. She wondered if her friends were insensitive to her needs. She wondered if her friends were selfish. She wondered if her friends were greedy, people who only came around when the going was good for her. She wondered if her friends wanted too much from her. She wondered if her friends were leeches, people who clung to her closer than her own shadow when she carried potent drugs.

The longer she held her friends up to her own mental examination, the more she realized her friends did turn up their noses each time a kid sporting loose, shabby clothes and a dingy pair of sneakers bumped their shoulder while they chased a crony down 49th Street. For the first time, she realized that Kathleen turned away from elderly women while they pushed noisy, grocery carts down 5th Avenue, all their life's belongings inside.

She uncrossed her ankles.

Bertha dropped and broke all of her drinking glasses. Her mother gave her the glasses. They were two generations old. The night she moved her belongings inside the studio, she took a roll of newspaper off one of the glasses. She raised the glass in her hand and admired its exquisite design.

It took Bertha six, drunken weeks to break the glasses, but she refused to stop visiting until all the glasses were broke.

Despite the broken glasses and the broken promises that they would visit, she missed Kathleen and Bertha. She missed their laughter. She never met a person they couldn't make laugh. For that, she loved them, women she longed for now because she needed to laugh.

She also needed to visit her mama. She knew she owed the woman who raised her and her four brothers and two sisters single handedly more of her time. Her sister, Tamra, had to telephone and ask if she would baby sit her daughters, eight year old, Nickie, and ten year old, Sharlene, before she rode the subway to her mama's brownstone, the place where Tamra, Nickie and Sharlene lived.

She used Sharlene and Nickie as an excuse for not stopping by her mama's more frequently. And though she hated to admit it, even Sandy Johnson, her fifty-eight year old mother, knew the excuse was justifiable. Nickie and Sharlene obeyed no one. They were always into something. Nickie loved to climb. Falling off kitchen counters, down the house stairs and off the tops of large, aluminum garbage cans were things she couldn't get enough of. After each calculated fall, she screamed, kicked, slobbered and bit whoever tried to rescue her. When she wasn't climbing and falling, she was dragging her feet while she walked through her grandma's house, her head hung and her hands slipped inside her pant pockets. While she walked, she spit into the carpet and whined about how bored she was.

Equally naughty was Sharlene. A bona fide tomboy, Sharlene liked to fight, and, being the older sister, she pushed, kicked, slapped, pinched and punched Nickie freely without retaliation. A dubious child, Sharlene also got a hoot out of embarrassing adults.

Company filling her grandma's house with noise and an extra degree of heat, Sharlene went to work. Aretha would never forget the night her sisters, brothers, their girlfriends and she were relaxing in her mama's living room. Besides polluting the air with a thick layer of cigarette smoke her brother, Kevin, suffered from gas. It took two seconds for Sharlene to screech, "Ewww! Somebody farted!" after the foul odor emitting from the rear of her youngest uncle's body whisked up her nose. Tamra shot out of the chair she was sitting in and darted across the living room floor. Upon reaching Sharlene, she raised her hand then sent it against the side of her face. Sharlene's gaze went immediately to the floor, and the living room grew quiet. Five minutes later, when Kevin passed gas again, Sharlene pinched her nose and yelped, "Ewww! Uncle Kevin farted again!" Because she felt guilty for striking her daughter five minutes earlier, Tamra allowed the outburst to go unnoticed. Sensing freedom, it wasn't long before Nickie joined in the tease, and the two girls made a laughing stock of their Uncle Kevin. Working together, they sent laughter booming into their grandmother's living room.

Aretha felt awkward at home. She felt she disappointed her mama, a woman she saw work two full-time jobs to pay the mortgage and feed and clothe her and her siblings. Beyond avoiding her nieces, she stayed away from the brownstone in the hope of avoiding her mama's gossip. Nothing was sacred with Sandy Johnson. She made certain all her family members knew each other's business.

During her last visit home, she sat next to her mama on the back porch swing trying to describe the pain gossip brought into a person's life. "People know when they're being talked about, Mama. Gossip is like a dark rain cloud. You can actually feel it. It never brings anything good in its wake. What grows from it is only more pain."

Not unlike her daughter, Sandy possessed a viciously stubborn streak. She heard Aretha's voice booming at the side of her head, but she didn't hear what she said.

Aretha turned in the chair. While she listened to the wood of the door rattle against the hinges, she wondered who her visitor was. She stared at the door. When she stood, Muffin leaped to her feet. Scrambling close on Aretha's heels, Muffin barked loudly.

They reached the door. Muffin stopped barking, and, tilting her head backward, she yawned until her voice squeaked. Aretha peered down at her and smiled approvingly.

After she opened the door, she stepped back. Her brow widened. Her eyes swelled. Her mouth opened into a small 'o'. At two o'clock on a hazy, Wednesday afternoon, she gawked at Robin and Leslie. Disbelief draped her thoughts. She watched them fan their faces with folded sheets of newspaper.

Then she took a step backward and, "Les! Rob!" hurried out of her mouth.

Robin greeted her first. Beside her, Leslie wrestled with the discomfort of having stayed away from Aretha when she knew she needed company most. When Aretha's gaze went to the floor, she knew that she was equally as uncomfortable with Robin and her unannounced visit.

Robin tossed her hands into the air and screamed, "Aretha!"

She called back, "Hey, Rob, both of you."

"Oh." Robin enthused, "What a good hug," while she pressed her cheek against Aretha's.

Aretha smiled. "It's good to see the two of you."

Robin's smile became diminutive. "How've you been?"

Aretha hesitated. "Oh. Okay."

Leslie peered over Robin's shoulder and watched Aretha and her try to warm up to one another. She twisted her mouth when she saw Aretha wring her hands, turn her tennis shoe clad feet to their sides and twirl the ends of her hair.

During the drive to Studio 63, she complained to Robin that, "The last time we saw Aretha was more than two years ago. The last time we saw Aretha, she was cursing and screaming in a hospital detox ward." Her porsche sped down the interstate. "What do we say when we see her? What if she's embarrassed to see us? We don't know how she's doing. Her personality may have changed. What used to make her laugh may very well make her cry now. People change, Rob. We don't know what's happened to Aretha in over two years."

The Porsche ate up miles on the interstate, and Leslie told herself she was apprehensive about visiting Aretha because she changed herself.

"And you?" Aretha returned Robin her question while she stood in the doorway holding the doorknob.

Craning her neck and peering inside the studio, Leslie wondered if Aretha even wanted Robin and her to come inside.

She glanced at Leslie before she stepped back and waved her hand. "Sorry. Forgive me. Come in."

She turned her back toward the door, and Robin and Leslie entered the studio.

Leslie's gaze darted from the splintered furniture to the loud color on the walls in the living room.

Robin piped, "Certainly. We want to come in. The three of us have so much to catch up on!" to Leslie's hidden annoyance.

Aretha glanced at Leslie.

Leslie met her glance then she lowered her head. A second later, she felt guilty for turning away from Aretha and looked up.

Aretha guided them to the living room sofa. "Have a seat."

Robin sat slowly. "Oh, thanks."

With a wave of her hand, Aretha teased, "Oh, stop being your so nice self, Rob."

She smiled hard. "All right."

Aretha tried to remember the questions she asked her guests when she had money and a nice apartment. "Do either of you want something to eat or drink?"

Robin shook her head. "Not me."

Aretha arched her brow. "Sure?"

Robin nodded. "I'm sure."

"Leslie?"

"No, thanks, Aretha."

Anxiety opened Robin's mouth. "So, what's up?"

"Not much, Rob."

"When'd you move here?"

"Oh, Rob, Girl, I've been here about five months."

Robin sent her head into a half nod. "Yea?"

"Yea."

"It's cute." Robin lied. "I like it."

"It's not so great, but it's enough for me. I'm grateful."

Robin nodded, "Yea," then she leaned forward on the sofa. "Rent's cheap."

She half nodded again. "Yea?"

"Yea."

She worked to keep conversation, however strained, going. "Not twelve hundred dollars a month?"

"No!"

Chuckling, she asked, "Any vacancies?"

"No. I don't think so."

"Leslie and I have been talking about leasing a new apartment."

Aretha sat forward and arched her brow. "Really?"

Leslie joined Robin in her nod. "Yes."

"For your careers and so you can resume sharing your secretary?" She decided to dance around the question she really wanted to ask until Robin or Leslie gave her a suitable answer.

Leslie answered. "That too."

"Oh."

"Les wants to move."

"Hmmmm."

Leslie bent and stroked the crown of Muffin's head. "When did you get your dog?"

"Her name's Muffin. I bought her about four months ago. She's a good dog." She bent and smiled into Muffin's face. "Aren't you, girl?" When she sat upright, she looked at Robin and Leslie and chuckled. "You two haven't changed one bit."

Leslie smiled a crooked smile.

Robin was straightforward. "No."

"Rob, how many plays have you written?"

"Seven."

Her mouth flew open, "Seven!"

"Seven."

"How many books have you written?"

"One."

"Ggiirrll."

"I enjoy writing, Aretha. It's my passion."

She smiled softly. "I know you love to write."

"My passion for the art makes it so easy for me to create stories. I think I have the best job in the world. I'm so glad God gave me this wonderful talent."

"I think I might have to agree."

Leslie spoke up. "I have to agree."

"And, Les, how's your acting career coming?"

"Let's talk about something else."

It was Robin. "No."

Leslie was firm. "Yes."

Aretha looked from Leslie to Robin, then she chuckled.

Robin sat against the back of the sofa.

Leslie crossed her legs.

"What would you two do without each other?"

The living room grew quiet. Following an awkward moment of silence, Robin asked Aretha, "How are Kathleen and Bertha?"

Silence shrouded the living room with discomfort.

Leslie crossed her arms and sat forward on the sofa. She was angry with Robin for asking Aretha the wrong question. After all, Aretha didn't ask her about her marriage to Bob, even after Robin told her they were entertaining the possibility of living together again.

Robin pushed her back into the sofa and scolded herself for veering away from light conversation.

The sofa grabbed the backs of Aretha's thighs and squeaked when she turned and faced Robin. "They're okay." The volume in her voice fell. "I guess."

"When was the last time you saw those two knuckle heads?"
Leslie glared at her.

Aretha raised her shoulders. "About five months ago."

"Have you met any new friends?"

Leslie glared at her again.

"No. I'm cleaning up. To do that right, I figure I need to go solo for awhile."

Robin nodded as if she understood the excruciating pain recovering from a lengthy drug addiction stormed inside a junkie's life. "I see."

"You'll do fine, Aretha." Leslie reached passed Robin and squeezed Aretha's hand. She saw so much of herself in Aretha's eyes. "I remember when I was a kid acting."

They stared at one another. Then Leslie ran her hand over the top of her hair and sat against the spine of the sofa.

After she pulled in her bottom lip, Robin nodded at Leslie to continue.

She leaned forward. "I-I didn't have a desire in the world. Mama and Dad handled the madness of my working contract. I think the public saw me as this easy to please kid. The studio staged photo ops of me doing any and everything from visiting an amusement park with a pack of friends to riding my bike at home. Of course, the pictures showed up in the top selling slicks. People envied the assumed relationship my parents and I shared. They thought ours was a relationship straight from heaven." Thinking back, she chuckled. "You know what they say, pictures are worth a thousand words. This past year, Rob's seen my parents more than I have. I don't like facing them. I never did, but it's worse these days. Can't hardly stand my father, but what's new? Still think he had something to do with . . . I feel I failed my mom because my career's gone into this huge lull. I'm always in the press. You know how it is." She twisted her mouth. "The articles are not flattering. I know you've read the stories. I know you've heard. I know you know. I know you know about Bob and me -- how miserable our marriage was. What you don't know is that I scarcely got out with my life. Rob saw that man running away from the house. I don't even remember him. Bob beat me so badly." She threw her hands up. "Mercy. Why am I here? I'm supposed to be dead. Everybody's heard about how badly I've been doing. I always have to watch my step." She gazed at her hands. "My life's an open book." She released a deep breath. "Mama told me I was making a mistake by marrying Bob. I knew he was having me followed. He's so insecure. But, now I'm hearing that my father knew this guy." She looked up. Then she quickly looked down again. "This man. . . .Mama tried to get me to think." She turned and faced Robin. "Remember the day Mama was putting the final touches on my wedding gown, and you were fixing a dessert in the kitchen?"

She smiled and nodded at her.

Leslie shook her head. "Mama tried to tell me to think about what I was doing. But I didn't want to hear what she thought about Bob and me getting married. I didn't want to hear what she thought about Bob. I didn't respect her opinion about him or our then impending marriage."

"Are you afraid of what your mama thinks now?"

"No. Not anymore, Aretha. You know, sometimes we try to tell ourselves we don't think or feel something if we think the thought or feeling is negative or that it will hurt someone. But, those thoughts and feelings continue to belong to us. They are very real. They may be negative, and they may hurt someone, but they are real. They are true. Denying their existence does not cause them to vanish. Just like what my mama thinks of me as a person is important to me, what your mama thinks about your addiction and your recovery is important to you. I know." She nodded at her. Then she smiled at her. "You love your mama. She's important to you. That's good. That's as it should be. You probably feel like your mama's frustrated with you. I know I was after Bob and my marriage started to fall apart. Your visits with your mama are probably like my visits with my mama. Small talk. You know. That's it. Talk with your mama, Aretha. Let her talk with you. She might want to encourage you. Do you see what I'm saying?"

"Yes. I do."

"Am I right?"

"You're right. But promise to practice what you preach."

Leslie's face softened into another smile. "I promise."

Robin bent, stroked the crown of Muffin's head, then sat back. "You know, I think in this life we must accept help from one another. God makes us stronger when we help one another. That's a fact."

"As much sass as I give Mama, and she's still always there," Leslie paused to chuckle. "I know she's always stood by me, right from the start. Rob's the only person who's supported me equally as fiercely, as sincerely. Everyone's laughing at me now. I know. I was sad for so long. I felt so alone." She shook her head. "I almost died. Bob almost killed me." She nodded. "That's right. He almost beat me to death. And my dad." She shook her head. "I don't know. I wish Mama would step away from that relationship. I wish she would. I know my father is into something. I know now." She nodded. "He doesn't know I know, but I know. That man in the Mustang didn't just show up at the house. I've been followed around for I don't know how long. Every time I think back to when someone told me a guy named Jack was looking for me, it sends a chill up my spine. I heard

Bob talk about a man named Jack. Said he was a powerful man. Got things done. What things, I don't know, but I'm not dumb. Mama said she doesn't know a man named Jack, but my father does. I can tell when I ask him. Just looking into his face, I can see it. He knows. He knows." She took in a deep breath. "And there I was stretched out on a hospital bed alive – alive and wanting to be dead. For me, life was awful for a long, long time. I felt like I was carrying the earth on my shoulders. I suspect I took Mama and Rob's support for granted. I felt I had no one to help me. I felt I had no one to turn to, no one to listen to the cries of my heart, no one to love me, no one to be with whom would see me and accept me as I am. Now, I'm not holy. You both know that."

Robin stared at the wall across the room from where she sat.

"I wanted what I didn't need. I longed for what I didn't need. I've always believed in God. I know God got me through those tough times."

Though the pace of her heart quickened, Robin remained silent.

Leslie chuckled and tossed her head back. "I'm so stubborn and bull headed. I imagine I always will be. But, I do believe in God, and I know God answered my prayers." She turned away from Aretha and smiled at the side of Robin's head.

Aretha chuckled. "You sound like me, Les."

"I was happy when I met Bob. My career was on its second wind. I knew the fame would bring an added dimension of pain and a near total lack of privacy to my life, but, as with the first time fame landed on my doorstep, I didn't care. I knew in order to succeed I had to be responsible, but I didn't care about that either. I knew marrying Bob would bring new pressure to my life, but I figured I could handle the pressure. I've always been good at handling pressure. I guess you could say dealing with pressure is my forte." She pulled loose strands of hair off her forehead. "I was happy with the new fame. It was exciting. I bathed in it. I relished it. It must've reached the point where I thought fame got me up in the morning, because when the fame went away from my life to be replaced by Bob's verbal and physical abuse, I started spending my days laying in bed staring up at the ceiling." She gazed into her lap and shook her head. "I thought marrying Bob would bring so much joy to my life." She pulled loose strands of hair off her forehead again. "I tell you, I was never more wrong. Hollywood's the only place I know of where a person's dreams can go right or wrong in so much as an hour. I've learned to build bridges going from Hollywood to the rest of the world. I learned that in my pain. So many people want to hear my story about what I've been through, but it's never been my life's ambition to deliver a jeremiad. Besides. Ninety percent of the people who ask to hear my story care nothing about me or know much about Bob and me. I've always been cautious. I think I'm even more so now. I know regardless of how much I've been hurt I must go on. I must go forward. I can't go around telling people about my problems. That's reserved for my closest friends."

Aretha looked at her. "You have to press your way."

"Yes." Robin quickly agreed. "God's going to pull you both through. God's going to pull all of us through. I have no doubt. And Aretha -- Kathleen and Bertha will start coming around again. I know why they don't come around now. They don't come around now because you stopped doing drugs, and you're drawing closer to God. Your actions convict them of their own wrong doings and make them uncomfortable. They'll come around, though. I just wish the three of you would give your lives to the Lord and either abstain from sex or begin to practice heterosexuality within the bounds of marriage. After all, you do know that homosexuality is wrong. It's a sin like cheating on your husband or wife is a sin. It's wrong, and you should stop. You really should stop."

Aretha stared blankly at her.

Leslie stared blankly at both of them.

Robin stood.

Longing not to be alone, Aretha searched for ways to keep them at her studio. "I want to spice this place up. After all," she spread her upturned hands. "It's home, and it looks like it's going to be home for awhile. Got any suggestions?" She turned from Leslie to Robin and waited for a response.

Robin offered the first decorating tip. "Try painting your place a light yellow."

Leslie nodded her agreement.

A moment later, they excused themselves to go. The conversation spilled into the hallway.

In the hallway, separated from Aretha, Robin and Leslie turned toward one another, then they turned, faced Aretha, and, nodding, chorused, "A very light yellow."

Chapter Twenty

Kathleen sat across from Aretha twirling a pack of matches between her fingers. She couldn't stop wondering what was keeping Bertha. *3811 Dandridge Drive.* Kathleen stopped twirling the matchbook and stared at the address written with a red, felt tip pen on the matchbook's back cover. Since she climbed out of bed early in the morning, she planned to drive to 3811 Dandridge Drive to see Bertha's new home. When she closed the matchbook and resumed twirling it, she envisioned Bertha scampering from room to room in her new three-story brownstone.

While she sat across from Aretha waiting for Bertha to appear, she recalled a conversation she had with Bertha two days ago. She had just stepped out of the shower. The telephone rang when she ran a towel down her shin, taking drops of water from her skin.

Bertha talked fast. The volume in her voice rose and fell with an excited pitch. "I have to buy bath and dish towels. I have to wash laundry. I have to call my father at the hospital to check on him. He was admitted Monday, you know? He complained of having chest pains. I'm glad Daddy finally got serious about his health. I need to wash my car, and, of course, I have to go to the grocery store. My car is almost out of gas. I made a mistake of going to Low Key Gasoline last Friday." She didn't stop to chuckle, but Kathleen could hear the humor in her voice. "Never before has my tank knocked so loudly, so much. I'm going to spend today and most of tomorrow unpacking. I'm going to be so tired by Monday, it's not going to be funny. Mama and Debra are supposed to come over tomorrow afternoon to help me clean and unpack. I think we'll order Chinese, that or pizza. I might not cook for a week."

Kathleen remembered asking her, "Are Betty and Carolyn coming over?"

"No. I don't want those free loaders over here."

Then it was Kathleen's turn to talk fast and long. "Betty and Carolyn are your sisters. Don't talk that way about them. It's not as though you have a thousand sisters. You only have three. I don't know why you get along with Debra so much better than you do with Betty and Carolyn." She paused and let her own words sink in. "Well, I do understand. Betty and Carolyn won't keep a job longer than nine months. Come to think of it, they do bum money from you whenever they visit." She heard herself laugh. "When they fall out with their boyfriends, now that you have your own three bedroom house, they'll be dropping in on you asking if they can stay over a couple of days." She heard herself laugh again. "And the way you keep your refrigerator and your cupboards stocked with food, they're sure to stop by like never before. Those girls are going to eat you out of house and home. Oh, but, they're still your sisters, and you should always love them. Your mom and dad spent twenty-seven years raising and loving you and your sisters. Remember how you used to tell me your father would get up early when you were growing up in Alabama and chop wood until sweat poured down his face? Remember how you told me your family struggled and how your father was often depressed when he picked up and moved you all here from Alabama when you were twelve years old? Then after living in New York City for two years, your father got a job as a clerk in the loan department of a Manhattan bank? Your mom and dad put a lot into raising you and your sisters."

"Then Dad came home from work one day and started packing." On the other end of the telephone wire, Bertha covered her mouth and lowered her head. She was ashamed to have brought one of the saddest moments of her life to Kathleen. "When I asked Daddy what he was doing, he didn't even look at me. He just threw some words over his shoulder. 'Daddy's going away' are the only ones I remember. Mama cried for days, months, afterward. It was so hard, because I had never, not once, seen my mother cry. To be perfectly honest, I don't think she has ever recovered from Daddy divorcing her. She took part-time jobs. After a little over two years of that, she landed a job at a restaurant. She cooked there, at the restaurant, for I don't know how long. She used to bring loads of food home after work. It got to where I rarely saw her cook dinner at home." She chuckled. "I think that job at the restaurant kept her together on her hardest days." Then she took in a deep breath and let her shoulders drop. "I always thought my parents had the perfect marriage. I had no idea anything was wrong. I think Daddy packing and leaving shocked my sisters and me more than it did Mama. I can still see Daddy packing when I close my eyes. When he still lived at home with us and he wasn't at work, he always spent more time with us than Mama did. He played with us more. Mama was always busy cooking, cleaning or passing out housework assignments for the rest of the family to start and finish. She liked to read a lot too. When she tore off her apron and went to the back porch and sat on that back porch swing, I knew it would be one to two hours before I saw her again. She loved to cross her legs and settle into a good book."

Kathleen chuckled when she heard the smile in Bertha's voice.

The cafe door swung open, and Bertha stepped inside. Upon her entrance, she hunted for Kathleen and Aretha.

Kathleen stood and waving her arms, she hollered, "Over here, Bertha!"

From where she sat, Aretha watched Kathleen's hands and arms move. When Bertha smiled and neared their table, she lifted her glass off the table, turned it in her hand and swallowed hard.

"Hi, Aretha!" Was the first thing Bertha said when she reached the table, out of breath and wide eyed. "What are you drinking?"

She lowered her glass to the table before she met Bertha's smile and stare. "Lemonade."

Bertha's smile grew faint. "That's good." Then she turned and looked at Kathleen.

She offered, "Sit down, Girl. Take a load off. Want me to flag the waiter for you?"

Bertha sat and pulled her chair close to the table. "How's the lemonade, Aretha?"

Aretha's gut told her that Bertha's eyes were asking about more than the lemonade. "I only drink lemonade and orange juice now." Lifting her glass, she took a long sip of the cold, freshly squeezed lemonade. A moment later, she placed her glass on the table, raised her finger and flagged down the waiter.

Bertha gave the waiter her order -- a large lemonade -- and he moved away from the table. "So," Bertha folded her arms and placed them on the edge of the table when she sat down. "What's up, Aretha?"

She shrugged. Her mouth formed a lopsided grin. "Nothin' much. Same ol', same ol'." She raised her glass to her mouth again. Before she laid it on the table, she shoved two ice cubes inside her mouth.

"Still living at Studio 63?"

She nodded at Bertha's question.

Bertha continued to work to catch her breath. "Spruce it up yet?"

"A little bit." She slid the ice cubes to the front of her mouth and sucked them. When she stopped sucking the ice cubes, she continued with, "I put yellow curtains in the living room and kitchen. I have brown curtains in the bedroom. I painted the walls, all the walls in the apartment, off white. I put throw rugs on the floor. I thought about getting new kitchen cabinets, but it's only a studio I'm leasing. Management loved it that I wanted to fix the place up with my own money. When I asked for permission, they almost bubbled out a yes. I think I'll varnish the kitchen cabinets rather than replace them. I want to fix the studio up a little more, since I'll probably be there for at least two more years. When I first moved there, I didn't care what the place looked like. Now I want to go home and be glad to be there. After all, I spend more time at home now than I do any place else."

Bertha looked softly at her. "Are you working?"

She watched the waiter lay Bertha's lemonade on a small, square, white napkin. "Yea."

Bertha sipped her lemonade. "Where?"

"Westminger's Inn."

"What are you doing there?"

She turned and looked at Kathleen. "I knew you were going to ask me that. I'm a desk clerk. I also work in the back office handling reservations when staff is short handed. I like it. There's not a lot of pressure. I like it. People there are nice. I have no complaints."

Kathleen nodded. "That's good. That's good."

Bertha took a long swig of her lemonade before she asked, "How long have you been working there?"

"A little over a year."

From where she sat, Bertha could see out the cafe's front window. Watching teenagers, adults lacking patience and retired, older folk saunter on the other side of the glass window, beyond the table she sipped cold lemonade at, she worked to believe New York City was once different. She smiled after she commanded her imagination to the core of her thoughts, took herself back forty years, and saw Jewish, African American and Italian women strutting from one joint to another, a fur straddling their back and a handsome beau holding their forearm. The streets were more festive than dangerous then, it seemed. Big Band, Rhythm and Blues and comedy acts were both adored and deplored by the world famous Apollo Theatre. Women wore dresses that fit snugly around their hips, dresses with low cut fronts, dresses made for full figured women whom wanted to display their greatest physical assets. Men wore spit shinned alligator shoes. Women covered their feet with shiny, black high-heeled pumps. Music thundered inside juke joints and nightclubs and stormed out into the streets. Taxis zipped up and down New York City's thoroughfares, drivers searching for riders. Late at night on Fridays and Saturdays, the ends of their suit coats flapping in the wind, men walked to the edge of the crowded sidewalks, and, waving and shouting shamelessly, hustled taxis to a stop. Women who tended toward jealousy watched one another saunter up and down the city's walkways. Laughter rang out everywhere. Today's festivities paled in comparison to yesterday's gala when Bertha revisited the most recent parties she attended. Books and television documentaries created ghosts of New York City's earlier residents. Looking back in time filled Bertha with hope that a better day was coming.

They spent the next fifteen minutes updating each other on recent, unshared events of their lives. They didn't look up from their conversation until Bertha, feeling a warm hand pressing down on her shoulder, turned and shouted, "Rob!"

Robin smiled into her face. 'Hey. Hey."

"Hey, Bertha, Kathleen and Aretha."

Aretha nearly turned full circle. "Les."

Leslie stuffed her hands inside her pant pockets. "What's goin' on, Ladies?"

"Aretha's working as a desk clerk at Westminger's Inn," Bertha exclaimed, her eyes wide.

Robin and Leslie turned in their chairs and gave each other a "we know" look before they faced Bertha.

Guilt shadowed Bertha's smile. Soon her smile was no more. "So, what have you been up to, Rob? How's the writing? I heard you finally came to your senses and quit your day job. I know you've come into some long money. I hear Leslie and your names all over the place. You girls are stomping."

Robin chuckled. "I just finished a one woman play. I only have one person in mind to bring it to life. Derrick's handling all the paper work. He always knows how to deal with the legalities. He'll also know about getting the right musicians for the play. Derrick has this unique ability to see to the core of a person's gifts and talents. About giving up my job at Mills, I wasn't making as much money as people thought in the early and middle stages of my writing career." She chuckled. "Very few writers can afford to give up their day job. In the entertainment business, being a writer is similar to being a track and field star, that is, until Carl Lewis came along. That Brother did a sure nuff good business thing for all those whom will come after him. In writing . . . I don't know. In writing, a lot of the powers that be don't think you ought to be properly compensated for your labor, for the many sacrifices that you make toward refining your skill. Many editors think if they give you a byline that's enough. Yet they wouldn't work as an editor for a magazine for free or stop taking in advertising dollars. Go figure. I call it selfishness and taking advantage of the dreams of up and coming writers who want to see their work in print so badly they don't say one word when they are taken advantage of. I don't know one professional writer who hasn't burned the midnight oil for free somewhere along the way."

"I keep forgetting that, by and large, writing is not a lucrative profession," Leslie added. "Unlike one hit movie for an actress, one hit book for a writer rarely means a lifetime of financial security." She laughed. "Even in the motion picture industry . . . especially in the motion picture industry, writers of screenplays or of popular novels adapted to screenplays are rarely acknowledged. Most moviegoers don't know the names of a dozen writers of the movies they see over the course of an entire lifetime." She lowered her head and sighed. "Movies and me." She laughed. "Oh, movies. What they haven't brought into my life. Thank God I got rid of one of those things." She shook her head. "Thank God I broke free of Bob." She looked around the table. Her gaze filled with intent. "He beat me so viciously." She shook her head. "I don't remember much of the last week I was with him." She raised her hands and placed her head between them.

After she lifted her head and peered around the table, she released a deep breath. "I do remember losing the child I thought I didn't want. That was early on in my miserable marriage. I never thought I wanted that child. Rob remembers. I literally tried to starve myself . . . as if I could starve the baby right out of my body." She looked around the table. "I know we all just got back together and I'm spilling my guts, but I gotta get this out." Then she sighed. "I knew I'd leave Bob one day. I didn't want a child to remind me of the greatest mistake I made in my life . . . marrying him." She propped the point of her chin inside the cup of her palm. A chuckle caused the dip in her voice to go unnoticed and she continued with, "I took my beatings like any weak, spineless, so-called good wife would." Laughter escaped her. "For nearly four years I thought that's what a good wife did. Damn. I actually thought that's what a good wife did. That and turning the other way when my husband chose to engage in sex with another woman. I can't tell you how many beatings I took over the years I lived with Bob. One time Rob came to visit me, and, thank God, Bob wasn't there. I don't know what he would have done. He never liked Rob, because he knew we were close. Of all the things I can't remember, I don't know why I can't forget that day. It was the second time I decided to really confront Bob about his many infidelities. It was the first time I told myself to start building bridges and networking to leave him." She sighed. "Thank God I finally made that decision. But, if I had known the beating I was going to get for confronting him, I would have been mute. He beat me before, but never like that. He beat me worse than he did when he came home raging drunk. I can still feel my head crashing against the closest. I can still see the hole my head broke in the wall. I can still see that smirk dressing Bob's face. I'll never forget that smirk. Not as long as I live. Never. Coward. That empty shell of a man. He hit me so hard I lost some of the hearing in my left ear. He hit me and he hit me and he hit me. Again and again. I literally saw stars. I thought I was dead. I was still pregnant, and I wanted our baby." She scanned their faces. "He beat me until I lost the baby. After he left I didn't hear anything, but Rob told me she knocked on the front door. Then she heard footsteps. A man was running away from the house. It wasn't Bob. Oh, no. Not Bob. He made sure he got out of there long before he could get caught. This man Rob saw, he was a professional. A good one." She smirked. "Took me the longest to figure out about that man. Still don't know the full story. I do know that man knew both Bob and my father."

Bertha and Kathleen's eyes ballooned. They leaned toward the center of the table. They gawked at Leslie.

She nodded. "Yeah. My father says he didn't know about Bob until I got engaged to him. He finally admitted knowing the bald man named Jack."

Bertha raised her hand. "He—"

"I know, Bertha. That man came around the high rise looking for me. I never put two and two together then."

"How did he know your father? Jack?"

She looked at Kathleen. "Don't know. Told you I don't know the full story. I still don't. My father is never going to tell me the whole story. That much I know. He won't. I know my father. He's gonna take a lifetime of secrets to his grave with him. My gut tells me that he was involved in something shady. Something shady that had to do with a lot of money and the law firm. What. I don't know." She lowered her head. Then she shook it. "I think that man named Jack did something awful for my father. What. I don't know. Something. I only know it was something. And," She lowered her head. "To tell you the truth. I don't want to know. I really don't. I don't want to know." She shook her head and swallowed hard. "I just want to get on with my life. I just want to live again."

Aretha's brow went up. "But, why would he follow you?"

"That I don't know either. Maybe my father thought I knew what his relationship with Jack was."

"So, he'd have him follow you around?"

Leslie was quick. "Aretha, I don't know. I'm the one who was stalked here. I wish I knew worse than you do." She waved her hand. "It's over now. Whatever was going on has stopped. My father told me not to worry about it. He said I would never see Jack again. Said it's all over."

"Well, what happened to Jack?"

"Bertha, please."

Robin leaned against her chair. "Yes, Bertha. You all stop asking Leslie so many questions, please. This was very hard for her. Can you imagine? Someone your own father and husband knows has been following you for who knows how long?"

Kathleen raised a finger. "Just one more question. Was he a fan?"

Leslie and Robin laughed first. Soon the entire table reeled with laughter. When the laughter subsided, Kathleen reached out and patted Leslie's hand. "I'm glad you made it out. Goodness knows each of us has come out of something. And you know." She nodded. "Sometimes it's good to have a story, to be able to say 'I got hit hard, and I'm still standing'. Or 'I took a hard fall, and bobbed back up to the top'."

"Yes. Yes," Leslie said. "I definitely have a story. What's still odd to me is how Rob just knew, just knew, knew my life was in danger. She was no where near me when she came running out to help me. I hadn't called her. I hadn't warned her about anything. I didn't even know what was going to happen myself. Yet, somehow Rob, in her 'I just know' kind of way, sensed the threat of my life. Like I said, Bob was gone when the police and ambulance arrived. Rob said they tore their way up the staircase. I was near unconscious when they arrived. I heard one of them say something about my pulse. I bled profusely. I felt myself dying. I opened my swollen mouth, but no sound came out. Bob wanted me mute, and that's what he got. I felt my fingers clawing at the carpet, but I couldn't turn. I couldn't get up. I guess everything I tried to do, I didn't do. God used to Rob to save my life that day. She did."

"And how are you doing now?" Kathleen took the sting out of the question with a smile.

Leslie nodded. "I'm doing okay. I'm doing more than surviving. Surviving. That's all I did for years. I never lived my life like that before. I never just survived before. I struggled before. Yeah. I struggled before and I struggled hard, but I always had a dream, a hope, but not then. My dreams were snuffed out those years I lived with Bob, simply snuffed out. Murdered. Bob murdered my dreams. And," she peered at her hands. "I let him." She swallowed hard. "Let me tell you, it's no way to live. There's more to life than just surviving . . . much more."

Bertha folded her arms then lay her elbows against the edge of the table. "How's your career coming?"

She smiled. "Rob and I are working on the play she just told you about."

Kathleen's eyes swelled. "You're writing now?"

Leslie sat back and laughed. "No. Rob's the writer. I'm acting in the play. She created the main character for me." Her smile widened.

Kathleen faced Robin. "When will the play be finished?"

"I'm working on the last two acts now."

Chapter Twenty-One

The New York Challenger, November 14, 1996 - Entertainment - By Susan Lakes
"The lines were long. The expectations were huge. Few plays demand this level of attention. *Pack It Up* isn't another show. *Pack It Up* has been talked about since June 26th. It's author, Robin Carlile, does not disappoint.

It's no secret Leslie Fletcher, now thirty-five years old, is making a fierce come back; so like Leslie. Her thirty-four year old writer roommate, Robin Carlile, has produced plays and television documentaries at an enviable pace. The two women are known for being the two most focused women in the entertainment business. Associates say the two women are planning more joint projects. Ticket prices are unreasonably conservative. I was one of those people who stood outside the theatre trying to block some of the cold while I shivered and waited to near the ticket booth. I stood in line for over two hours.

Once inside, my date and I ceased to complain about the weather and the long line. The cold didn't upstage *Pack It Up*'s opening act. Minutes following the final curtain, my date and I stepped into the cold again, a thunderous applause rattled our backs. This time, my hands stung not from the freezing temperature, but from applauding throughout the performance of the play.

The East Coast Journal, November 14, 1996, by Philip Colins
Robin Carlile, playwright, and Leslie Fletcher, Oscar nominated and Emmy award winning actress, have the hit play of the year. For a mere $25.00, theatre goers can relish Leslie Fletcher's magnificent comeback performance in *Pack It Up*. Housed in the recently remodeled Overton Theatre, *Pack It Up* closed its first performance to resounding applause. As if putting together a play worthy of no less than two Tony awards wasn't enough, Robin purchased the once mired theatre nearly a year prior to *Pack It Up*'s opening. Architectural changes to the theatre were few. When questioned, Ms. Carlile stated that she wanted to preserve the history of the theatre originally built and run by Charles Mendin, an early nineteenth century African American architect. Seating five hundred persons, the Overton Theatre is a beautiful structure, its splendor fresh, its magic strong and new. With the success of *Pack It Up*, the only setback to the theatre may be that it will prove itself to be too small.

Hats off to you, Robin and Leslie. Bravo!

New York's Paper, November 14, 1996 - Entertainment - By Lisa Whittle

Robin Carlile and Leslie Fletcher have done it again. Never before have the roommates worked together, nevertheless their portfolios run long with solid successes. Leslie's fierce, energetic personality ignites the play. Robin's calm reservation gives *Pack It Up* a steady, delightful rolling tempo. *Pack It Up* attracts audiences at record numbers. *Pack It Up* is a delicious treat. I strongly suggest you indulge.

The Los Angeles Recorder, November 14, 1996 - Entertainment
By Deanne Michael

Travelling to New York City? You mustn't miss *Pack It Up*. See it twice if you can. No current plans to traipse one of the world's most famous cities? Make time. Mark a trip to the newly renovated Overton Theatre on your vacation calendar. Go see *Pack It Up* before the final curtain falls. Robin Carlile and Leslie Fletcher have the year's best play securely in their hands.

The San Francisco Post, November 14, 1996 - Entertainment
By Jose Hernandez

If you have never been to the Big Apple, now is the time to go. Robin Carlile, a confessed born again Christian, authored *Pack It Up*, the year's finest play. When and if Ms. Carlile peaks, after seeing the opening of *Pack It Up*, I'm afraid we won't be prepared. Ms. Carlile is once again unique, classy, courageous, witty, patient, and, yes, certainly blessed throughout this, her latest work.

Leslie Fletcher, a feisty, internationally acclaimed actress, is the woman packing it all up in the year's finest play. Ms. Fletcher refuses to peak, even after suffering through an ill fated and oft times abusive marriage and heavyweight contentions with cocaine and alcohol. She shines as she never has before. She sparkles with promise. I eagerly anticipate her next performance.

Robin Carlile . . . Leslie Fletcher, I toss at your feet a thousand red roses.

****

People scampered. A cold wind whistled so loudly in the heavens, its sound echoed in city homes. Santa Clauses, red and green wreaths, and large shopping bags gave Midtown a burst of color. Tinsel hung from storefront windows. Pieces of tinsel that fell to the ground were trampled, and, sticking to the soles of shopper's shoes, pushed inside crowded department stores. So many shoppers filled the wide aisles of Loew's Department Store, the line leading to the gift wrapping counter stretched from the women's hat department to the end of the men's shoe department. Fred's, a national record chain store, slashed sale prices. Stock crews worked feverishly to step around loyal customers while they shelved holiday candy, dining room table center pieces, designer suits, winter snow boots, coats and recording sound systems. Day shift managers paced back and forth in their offices. Suppliers screeched over the telephone wire that they couldn't possibly fill last minute orders. From the windows of their offices, the same managers watched sisters, daughters, mothers and grandmothers scowl, curse and fight over the last dress, skirt or pant suit.

Cameo's appearance sagged under the attack of what appeared to be bus loads of record and CD purchasers. Mavis' Homestyle Restaurant was loud with varying conversation. Men lowered their brow and ogled bashful women. Over a fulfilling entree these couples hoped to fall in love for the first time or to renew uncommon interest in one another. As usual, Mavis' busboys, waiters and waitresses forbid themselves to pry. A quartet of celebrity couples, mostly professional athletes and their wives, dotted the restaurant.

It seemed all of Manhattan, young and old alike, anticipated Christmas Day. From city construction workers to wrinkled grandmothers, everyone busied herself making preparations. An air of excitement hung taller than the long icicles that clung to the tops and bottoms of apartment and brownstone windowsills.

Robin edited the second act of *Pack It Up*. Leslie studied her lines religiously. Ensuring homage to their parents, the duo sent Aretha, Bertha and Kathleen midtown two weeks before Thanksgiving with forty thousand dollars and two long shopping lists.

One week later, Robin telephoned Derrick and requisitioned Leslie's stand in for the week of November 23 through November 29. Instead of travelling home, she spent the holiday talking to Theo on the phone and writing two winter commencement addresses she was requested to deliver, one at Temple, the other at Tennessee State. While Leslie was in Connecticut shopping with her mother, visiting family and rehearsing her lines, Robin tried to relax. Days she wrote the early chapters of her second novel. Afternoons she ran six brisk miles through the Chelsea District. Nights she curled up on the living room sofa and read thick history books that chronicled the many successes of African American, African and Native Americans. She also began to take an unexpected interest in Elvis Presley and Albert Einstein biographies and much of the musician's music and many of the scientist's writings.

Family sat in Joyce and Arnold's living room circling Leslie. While she turned from cousin to uncle to aunt, whoever was speaking to her, Leslie wondered how much her relatives remembered about her; she last saw so many of them when she was ten, during the time she acted on *Gardenia's Life*. She looked hard into their faces. Everyone was smiling, joking or laughing. Her youngest cousin's nose was as narrow as hers was. She saw the same sea blue in one of her uncle's eyes that was banked in her own. Her mother's younger sister had the same robust laugh she did. She looked down the table. Even her father's oldest brother looked like her. All around the room, everyone seemed to have borrowed each other's most poignant features. She almost chuckled. Here he was, her father's oldest brother. His fingers were long and thin just like hers. And yet. She almost shook her head. Except for the heydays during the run of *Gardenia's Life*, these people who looked so much like her had not called, had not written her one letter, had not visited. Even during the last six years of her life, the hardest years of her life, they had not bothered to contact her.

And then there was her father. She promised herself to corner him before the night closed in so tight the sun started to come up in the sky again. She was going to ask him more questions about Jack. She was going to demand that he stop being mean to her mother.

He wasn't home right now. He was at Petry's Florist, the same flower and plant shop he purchased his mistress' favorite yellow carnations from. Pushing his shoulders back, he shouted, "Three dozen red roses!" at the young, Japanese girl behind the counter.

The girl walked behind a curtain, cut and wrapped thirty-six red roses. When she returned, she was smiling, and, the roses bunched in her hand, she extended her arm.

After Arnold took the roses and placed $78.86 on the counter, he turned and waved over his moving shoulder at the girl. Outside on the sidewalk, he wondered at the girl's age and asked himself if the store's proprietors were aware of the country's child labor laws. "It's not even summer," was all he said as he pulled the back of his coat taut around his buttocks and sat, then scooted across the car seat until he was directly behind the steering wheel.

He arrived home to find corn on the cob, roast beef, turkey, ham, dressing made mostly from bread slices, soda, punch and seasoned mushrooms at one end of the table. Taking in a deep breath, he looked further down the table and stared at the brown, creamy gravy, creamed, sweet peas, broccoli topped with melted cheddar cheese, cornbread, hot, homemade, buttered rolls, apple pie with a lattice crust and peach cobbler. When his gaze neared Leslie's heightened shoulders, he saw lemon cake sweetened with a thin layer of icing, sauerkraut, potato and macaroni salad, whipped potatoes and tossed salad pushed close to the center of the dining room table. Before he pulled off his coat and sat down to eat, he walked directly to Leslie and pushed the roses inside her hands.

Leslie didn't look up from staring at the mole on the side of her Great Uncle Willard's nose when she took the flowers.

"Dinner's ready!"

Joyce's call to the table startled Leslie. She stood from her place at the sofa and asked, "Mom, do you have a vase?" until Joyce ran her palms down the front of her apron, stepped away from the stove she was cleaning the top of and answered, "Look in the cabinet nearest to the back door. There should be two to three pretty, crystal vases in there."

Moments later, Leslie shoved the roses inside a tall, crystal vase and wondered if Arnold bought yellow carnations too. She turned and looked at her mother before she left the kitchen.

Arnold bowed his head and recited grace after Joyce untied the apron from her waist and hurried in small steps to the dining room table. Recited, because Leslie heard her father utter the prayer no less than ninety-nine times, once each year during Easter, Thanksgiving and Christmas. She spent an hour after the blessing eating turkey, dressing, whipped potatoes and slices of carrots and celery while she listened to her Great Aunt Ellen's squeaky voice race out sentences.

"Remember that time Zelma got lost in Queens?" Gravy shook when Ellen banged her hand on the table. While gravy poured down the sides of the ceramic serving dish, she grunted and asked, "Hunh? Remember, Letha? Remember, Frank? Remember, Willard? Joyce, Joyce, you and Arnold remember?" She threw her hand down when she looked at Leslie. "Les, you and those cousins of yours are too young to remember." Then she returned her attention to the older members at the table. "That child screamed through that danged phone until I thought my ears were going to pop plum off my head. I kept trying to tell her to calm down, but she wasn't having it. She just knew she was going to get mugged. Why. Every time somebody passed her, she gasped and held her breath. I thought that girl was going to pass out on me a couple of times. It took Zelma twenty whole minutes to listen to me and find her way to the train station. And, wouldn't you know it. Once she got to the danged train station, she rang my phone again. Wanted to know where to get off in Connecticut. I said, get off where you live at, Girl. Frank, Willard and Letha were all behind me laughing and carrying on. Zelma was supposed to have long been at Frank and my house. Joyce and Arnold were on their way over.

They got to our house before Zelma started banging on the front door. Gracious, that girl's hair when she walked through the front door. It was strung all over her head. I laughed until I cried when I saw Zelma. We all did. She was a sight. Gracious, was Zelma ever a sight on that day."

It was almost midnight when Joyce finished washing the pots and pans and shelving the dishes -- hot from the cleaning they received in the dishwasher. Leslie helped her scrub burnt out of the pots and pans before she went to the foyer closet and pulled out her coat. The front door scarcely made a noise when she opened it. It whispered at her back when she pulled it to a close.

"Hi."

Arnold looked up. "What 'chu doing out here?"

"I want to talk to you."

He smiled and stretched forth his hand. "Sure." Then he patted the space on the porch sofa next to him. "Come on over here and sit down next to your father."

She tried to smile. She turned away from him when she sat. "It's not too cold out."

"No."

"When did you start sitting on the porch? I've never known you to do this."

"A man's got to unwind sometime."

"True."

"You look good." He reached for her hand, but she moved it into her lap. "It's good to see you again."

"I'm never far away. And gosh. I haven't seen most of our family since I was a little girl. Forgot how funny Aunt Ellen and Aunt Zelma were. I miss those two. They haven't changed. Some people don't need to. Some people don't need to change. Aunt Ellen and Aunt Zelma are two of those people."

"Yea. Your mother's side of the family always was a little flighty."

"I meant what I said about Aunt Ellen and Aunt Zelma in a good way."

"I'm sure you did, Honey. After all, they are family."

"And so are you."

He chuckled. "What's that mean?"

"Answer a question I have and I'll answer your question."

"You always were so much like me. That's how you've survived. You have so much of my spirit. We think alike. You're not like your mother. You're strong."

"Dad, if I wasn't like Mom I wouldn't have any friends."

He was silent. A car went down the street and turned the corner.
"Are you saying I'm not friendly?"

"Dad, who is Jack? Really. Who is he really?"

"He—"

"And why did you have him follow me for what seems like all the
time I was living in Manhattan?" She gritted her teeth. "He's been sending
me letters, you know. Threatening letters. For the longest time. Ever since
Robin's been living with me. He wants money, Dad. A lot of money. He's
making threats, but I don't think he'll do anything. I think he's just trying to
scare me into giving him the money he keeps asking for."

"Is that why you had Robin move in with you?"

She shook her head and chuckled dryly. "I didn't know Robin
when Jack started threatening me." She sighed. "It was just those phone
calls before then. Were those from Jack too, Dad? All those phone calls?"

"I—"

"And why did Bob know Jack too?"

"Bu—"

"And why is Jack asking me for money? Are you broke?"

"No. I'm not broke. You see how your mother lives. Think she
could live high like she does if I was broke? Being married to her with her
expensive taste, it's a wonder I'm not broke." He nodded. "That's for
sure."

"Then why is Jack asking me for money?"

He laughed into the night. "Well, now, Leslie darling, I'm not
broke, but I don't have as much money as you have, not nearly as much."

"I don't need to know about your personal finances."

"You asked me a question."

She waved her hand and shook her head.

"And I answered it, young lady. But just for the record. Just so
you'll know, Miss know-it-all. Jack used to threaten me for money all the
time. I gave him money here and there. He's another reason I had to work
such long, hard, painful hours. Take on so many cases."

"Launder money?"

He glared at the side of her head. "You watch your mouth, young
lady. You're at my house. This is my house."

"So, Dad. You stop giving Jack money and he comes after me and
you never bother to tell me what's going on. You still haven't told me."

"Les—"

"You also still haven't told me why Jack was running away from
the ranch the day Bob beat me and beat me and beat me until I landed in the
hospital for a three week stay?"

"You said answer one question. That's more than one question."

She chuckled. "No. That's really several questions rolled into one. I want to know what your relationship is with this man named Jack."

"Les, I told you. Jack was an old acquaintance of mine."

"What did he ever do for you?"

"We had a business arrangement years ago. It had and has absolutely nothing to do with you. Honey, I would never do anything to hurt you."

"Why was Jack trailing me?"

"I don't know. How many times do I have to tell you that? You said he was asking you for money. I don't know anymore than you do. I didn't ask Jack to follow you. In fact, I hadn't heard from him in years. I didn't know he was in New York."

"He probably was living right here in Connecticut and just coming into New York every so often."

"Honey, you cannot believe—"

"No, Dad, I don't. I know you didn't send Jack to New York City. But I don't know Jack. I don't think you sent him, but I think something from your past with Jack is the reason he was trailing me. What did he really want from me? Why was he asking me for money? You know him. I don't."

"Honey, I don't know. I wish I did."

"What was Bob's relationship with Jack?"

"I'm not sure."

She rolled her eyes. "Another question then. What exactly is it that Jack did for a living? He didn't look like an attorney to me."

"He's not. He doesn't work at the firm."

"So what does he do?"

He grinned into the night. He knew Leslie couldn't see his face. "He works as a consultant."

"Wonder why I never heard of him before. I've been around. Being that Bob is in the industry. If Jack is a consultant in the industry, think I would have heard of him instead of finding out about him by way of his stalking me."

"Why don't you ask Bob what his relationship with Jack is? Why don't you ask Bob—"

"I don't talk to Bob anymore, and you know that."

"Well, Leslie, Honey. I don't know what to tell you. I do know that I spoke to Jack. He will never bother you again."

"You sure know how to keep in touch with an old, evil intentioned acquaintance, don't you?"

"I—"

"As long as I've known you it's been money-money-money. Sometimes I think you're trying to save up enough money so you can buy your way into hell."

"Leslie!"

Her face was set like flint. She swallowed hard. "Why are you so sure that Jack won't bother me again? Did you hire another consultant?"

He strangled a chuckle. Another car went down the street. "Quiet out tonight."

"It's always quiet in this neighborhood."

"I thought you liked it that way."

"Sometimes I do, and sometimes I don't."

"Yea. Me too."

"So, Dad, is Jack still in the land of the living?"

This time he did chuckle. "Honey, Jack is the type of man who is going to live a long, long time. In fact, he's living about fifty miles outside Mellford right now. He has a beautiful home." He chuckled again. "Bought that house with money he blackmailed out of me. He's married and has two grown daughters and a teenage son."

"Hmmm."

"Wanna talk about anything else?"

"Yes." She turned and faced him. "Since you obviously are not going to give me a straight answer about Jack, do please grant me this much." She raised a finger. "But before you do, I want you to know that I know in my spirit that Jack and you had shady dealings. Exactly what. That I don't know, but it was something. Something bad. Something awful. Something terrible. 'Spose you'll take it to your grave with you, since you aren't one for telling secrets."

He glanced at her. Then he grinned, "And you wanted me to grant you?"

She spoke between clenched teeth. "Stop being mean to Mom. Stop hitting her. Stop screaming at her when things don't go right for you. Stop blaming your problems on her, as if your life would be perfect if you didn't know her. No ones life is perfect, Dad. Even if you didn't know Mom, you'd have problems. Mom's not the cause of your problems. Trouble comes with life. You know, kinda like noodles come with lasagna. It's just that way. And," she raised a finger. "Stop cheating on Mom. Love her for once." She stood.

"Where are you going? You're gonna lay all that on me then just stand up and leave?"

"I didn't tell you anything you haven't had nearly thirty years to think about." She walked off the porch. When she neared her car she pulled her keys out.

He stood at the edge of the porch. "Where are you going? What do I tell your mother when she ask me where you went?"

"Tell her I went for a ride. I'll be back. I'm not going any place particular. I'm just going somewhere to relax and think."

"You can't do that here?"

"Dad, I just want to take a ride, that's all."

He stuck his hands in his pant pockets. "Okay. All right. It's late. I mean, it's late." He leaned forward and squinted into the night. "Be careful. You have your cell phone?"

"Yes, Dad."

"All right. Well. All right."

The rotary clock atop the night stand at the side of Leslie's bed read 3:37 when she returned to her parents' house, lay down, yawned and turned out her bedroom light.

Thoughts of reconstructing some of the houses and shops in Harlem with the profits from *Pack It Up* gnawed at Robin's conscience. In the midst of the renovations, she told herself she would fly home to Johnson City. She telephoned Sharon and Trisha and asked if they would meet her at John F. Kennedy International to fly South.

"Sharon?"

"Rob, is that you?"

"Yes."

"Rob!" Sharon sat on the edge of her bed. She wrapped the telephone cord around her fingers and smiled into the receiver. "It's so good to hear your voice!"

Robin swallowed hard and placed her hand against her racing heart. "Yours too! I just got off the phone with Trish. We're flying home to Tennessee together, flying home for Christmas."

"How is Trish? How are you?"

"We're both doing good. It's been so long since we've talked."

"I heard about *Pack It Up*. I heard it's your best work so far. I also heard that Leslie is blowing up the spot."

"You know Les."

Lowering her voice and shaking her head, Sharon said, "Girl, I miss you."

Robin sat up straight. "I miss all of you. I haven't kept in touch like I should have."

"None of us have."

"Really? I thought it was—"

"Only you." Sharon laughed. "You always did think you were standing on the outside of the circle when something didn't go right."

"Not all the time."

"A lot of the time."

"True. I just wish I had kept in touch better. I wish we all had kept in touch better. We were always the best of friends. We did so much together. I wonder if Johnson City has livened up any since we were last home."

"Mom tells me the Smokey Mountains and Pigeon Forge are booming."

"I know. From what Dad tells me, the Smokies and Pigeon Forge are becoming like Manhattan, so commercialized."

"I miss the mountains."

"Especially in the spring and summer."

"We've gotta get back. When are you and Trish heading out? What flight are you catching?"

"We're leaving this Saturday. Catching a 10 am flight." She raised her voice. "Come on, Sharon. Go with us." She shook her head. "It won't be the same without you."

Sharon was quick. "Hang on." Then she stood. "Let me check my schedule. I don't think I have anything to do, but I want to make sure I don't buy a ticket when I'm scheduled to teach a class. Hang on. I gotta go get my calendar."

"I'll be here when you get back."

When Sharon returned she exclaimed, "I'm there! My calendar is clear! I don't have to teach a class! Hold me a seat, Girl!"

They talked for an hour before Robin said, "I better go. I'll see you Saturday morning. Can't wait to see you. It's gonna be good." After she hung up the telephone, she turned her gaze to the ceiling and mouthed the words, "Yes. Yes. Yes." Then she lifted the receiver and dialed Betsy's phone number. Since Betsy wasn't home, she left a message on her answering machine. "Betsy, it's Rob. Just got off the phone with Sharon and Trish. We're flying home this Saturday. Flying home for Christmas. Call me as soon as you get in. Come and go with us. Come and go with us, Betsy!"

Robin stayed on the telephone for two hours after Betsy returned her call. She laughed so hard with Betsy her voice was coarse when she hung up. She raised her hands toward heaven and thanked God her sorority circle of friendship went unbroken.

****

Yellow curtains hung from the kitchen window directly over the sink. Bertha told Aretha she could move in with her, but Aretha, proud of her financial independence, refused.

Months later, Bertha entertained the idea of marrying a man named Jonathan. She met Jonathan, a nightclub owner, at his club. *Adam's* was an up and coming place, big for drawing popular jazz musicians to its glass stage. Jonathan and Bertha dated two weeks when Jonathan proposed. Kathleen told Bertha it was the holiday season and that she would get over the feeling of being in love. Aretha, though agreeing with Kathleen's surmise, was silent.

"You don't love Jonathan. He makes you laugh, and he's an understanding man, but you don't love him. You don't love each other. It's that simple. Bertha, when are you going to realize you can't love someone you don't know." Kathleen was quick. "Besides, Jonathan's got a temper. I can see that. As sharp as you are, Bertha, certainly you see that too. I can understand your wanting to try to make a go with a man, but think about how he grabs you. He squeezes you hard. He pulls on you. He pushes you when he's angry or drunk. He's mean. Jonathan can be mean, Bertha. I know you see that, and that meanness is dangerous. Just a few weeks ago you were asking Aretha to move in with you and now you're talking about getting married. Doesn't make sense. Bertha, you know that. I know you know this doesn't make sense. You're just lonely and looking for a security blanket. Well. Let me tell you, and I'm not saying this because Jonathan is a man, but, Jonathan ain't nobody's security blanket. Jonathan is trouble. Jonathan is mean."

Across town, Aretha struggled with her nemesis. Each time she gave in to her narcotic appetite and snorted cocaine, she told herself if she didn't know where to get the drug, cleansing her appetite for it would be easy. Yet, she was clean nearly all the time. She very rarely used. And she didn't mix drugs; she didn't run from coke to heroin to booze to cigarettes, nor had she packed on unwanted pounds. She had a new strength, and she knew it.

It wasn't until late at night that life got hard for Aretha. Hunger for cocaine shook her at midnight, seemingly closing in the area around her bed until her eyelids shuddered, and, quick flashes of light searing her consciousness, woke her from sleep. She vomited what seemed against her will. Her mind raced to her past and dug up every misdeed she ever performed. Guilt covered her thoughts. Shame took smiles away from her face and laughter out of her chest. She told herself she was a stain. At night when she woke from the fitful bits of sleep sweat drenched her body. Many nights she wept. Climbing to her knees, she even tried prayer. She begged God to forgive her, to accept her inside the ark of grace. Her prayers, seemingly empty of integrity, she screamed into the darkness. She was tired of being alone, but she didn't just want company. She didn't want just anybody around her, filling her head with words. She wanted to be loved.

She wanted somebody to really care about her, just the way she was. Whether on her knees talking with God or coiled on her side in bed, she promised herself and the spirit called God that she would fight until she reached a breakthrough.

Despite her mounting literary success, twice a week Robin drove to Studio 63 and visited with Aretha. They talked about fashion, mothers, heartache, work, the theatre, Manhattan and good friends. After she left Aretha's, Robin drove to New Salem Baptist Church. "Come on. Go with me," she always called out to Aretha when she headed for church. Aretha just shook her head and smiled at her. It took months. "Hold up. Let me get my jacket. I want to go to this church you keep telling me about. Sure must be some nice people there the way you keep talking this church up. I want to go see for myself. Wonder if they have room in their hearts for a woman like me." Then she laughed and went across the floor to get her jacket. "I'm not going to change, Rob. I am who I am. If those church folks can't love me the way you do, I'm never going back. Hear me?"

Robin nodded.

"I'm never going back."

Not every week, but occasionally she joined Robin and accompanied her to church to attend Bible Study. Robin didn't make it her business to tell Aretha what was right and what was wrong. She just handed her a bible, and let her talk with God for herself. "I can't get you to heaven."

Aretha chuckled. "You say that a lot."

"I can't. I can only tell you that God loves you and give you a bible. You have to talk with God for yourself. I can most definitely assure you that God loves you."

She shook her head. "Rob, I don't get you sometimes. Miss never misses a Sunday church service accepts any and everybody at the snap of a finger. You just don't seem like a Christian."

Robin tossed her head back and laughed. "Sometimes I hate that word. I prefer to tell people that I believe in God and the bible and leave it at that. I don't wear my belief like it's a badge. Something I can show off and kinda walk around like I'm the sheriff."

Aretha laughed.

"I'm serious. Accepting a person doesn't mean you agree with everything they do."

"Here it comes again."

"No. Aretha, you know I believe homosexuality is a sin. I also believe lying is a sin and I've done that. We can't say everything is okay."

"Rob."

"You can't say something wrong is right just because you love someone."

"I know that."

"I'm sorry, Are—"

"No. That's okay. I know you're not judging me. And I know you know I wouldn't give a flip if you did. I'm me, and that's that."

"Stop being you and I won't come around you anymore. You know, you and Les are a lot alike. You both take all on-comers head on. You are two not backing down women."

"We're all alike, Rob. The whole crew. We know how to take a good, hard blow and still come up swinging. Ain't no quit in us. That's what it is."

"That and the fact that when we first met, we all were too broke to afford anybody else's time."

"You and Les were broke. Trying to live like big time celebrities. I had me a little piece of money back then. You and Les were just two broke sisters back in the day." They laughed while Robin pulled into the studio parking lot.

****

Michael and Company filled in for five of *Pack It Up's* ailing opening dancers early in December. *Pack It Up's* dancers suffering from the flu, Robin spent December 12-16 showering Michael and Company with flowers, cards, catered meals and gratitude.

Michael almost blushed the times Robin and he shared each other's company. It mattered not that others were in their presence or that they were alone. Heartaches and bitterness dispatched into nothingness the second they beheld one another. Robin thanked God in the quiet of her thoughts when she found Michael doing well. It took awhile, but she noticed his appetite for rigorous dance was fading. Where he once pleaded with presidents of dance companies to include him in more of their numbers, he now complained of being over worked and famished for sleep and rest. Dancing less frequently, he was practicing his skill at a refined level. When he was away from her, Robin teased herself with what could have become of their relationship had they chosen to stay the path. His conditioned body aided her thoughts. December 12-16 was a long week for her. She was glad when it passed, and, Michael, still the only man she mounted the courage to express deep emotion and intimacy for, stepped again, with a warm smile and a farewell greeting, from her presence.

****

A note was taped to the back stage door of the small room just to the right of the main stage that Robin called her office. Theo was glad to hear that she was coming home for Christmas. He also wanted her to stay for New Years Day, and, if time permitted, the first two weeks thereafter.

She pulled the note away from the door and smiled. When she finished reading it, she blinked and swallowed hard.

Michelle agreed to drive her to the airport on December 23, the day before she was scheduled to fly home to Louisville. "Can you believe I haven't been home in three years?" She exclaimed more than questioned Robin the evening of December 20th, the night Robin called and asked her if she would drive her to the airport. "My little sister, Gloria, got married a year ago. Her and her husband, Calvin, have a two month-old baby girl. Rob, I'm so excited to see her." When she worked to picture her niece, she smiled into the receiver. "I know she's adorable, as cute as she wants to be. My sister's attractive, and I heard Calvin's a fine Brother." She smiled again.

"When are you going to get married?" Robin stressed the word 'you'.

Michelle waved her hand. "Oh, stop."

"No. No. Answer me. I'm serious."

"Oh. I don't know."

"Do you ever think about it?"

"Of course."

"I like Benjamin."

Michelle blushed before she said, "I do too. I don't know. I think about marrying him sometimes. I think he'd make a good husband. He's a born again Christian, as you know. That's most important, because we're not to be unequally yoked as the Bible says. Benjamin is so understanding. He is an unusually understanding man. I love talking with Ben. He always listens. He always hears me. And, after trying to love three psychologically abusive men, two who couldn't get enough of sleeping with other women, it's a thrill to be loved by a strong man who doesn't use abuse or control when he's with the woman he loves. Ben is so sexy too." She laughed. Then she asked, "How about you?"

"How about me, what?"

"Oh, now. Come on. Don't. You know what I'm talking about."

Robin chuckled. "I don't know. Well. Yes, I do. I want to marry a moving on Brother one day, and I hope that God doesn't require me to wait years."

"Do I hear a plea?"

"I have to admit, I want to try to make a relationship grow again. I learned a lot from Michael and my relationship. And, you know, I used to be angry with Michael. I blamed him for the failure of our relationship, as if

327

I had nothing to do with it. I was bitter for so long about the end of our relationship. I still love Michael. I realized that when I saw him a week ago. I always will love him, but, thank God, I'm not in love with him anymore, because it's not meant to be. Michael and I aren't meant to be. We're not supposed to be together. Yet, it was with Michael that I learned how to open up more. I learned not to be afraid to fall in love. If I live life afraid of heartache, I'll never enjoy all there is inside a God approved relationship with a positive, loving Brother."

"That said, why aren't you dating?"

She laughed. "I'm scared."

"Rob!"

"I know."

"And after all you just said."

"I know."

****

Pack It Up's success mounted. The night's audience laughed so robustly they shook the rafters. Robin smiled from her small office, a room minus windows or air conditioning. Half an hour into *Pack It Up*, she stood from her brown, swivel chair, and, walking to the door, titled her head and pressed her ear against the laughter hanging in the air. Although regular theatre-goers told her they missed Leslie while she was away on vacation, they also told her how talented Leslie's stand-in was. Memory taking her to the first play she wrote when she was only twelve years old, she longed to dismiss herself from the backstage area and take an inconspicuous seat at the back of the theatre. She only saw *Pack It Up* on its opening night. She missed the performance, the expressions on the audience's faces, the curtain calls and the final bows. She wanted to see it all again.

While Robin enjoyed the changing moods of *Pack It Up*'s audience, over two hundred miles away in Connecticut, Leslie examined the six foot fir Arnold pushed in the corner of the living room. A box of tinsel and glass tree ornaments lay at the side of her feet. Joyce said she would make popcorn later in the day. Leslie told her she would help string the popcorn and wrap it around the tree.

Leslie's gaze raced through the box of Christmas decorations. It wasn't long before she bent and turned ornaments over in the box. The familiar Christmas tree topping escaped her search. She stood and massaged her lower spine. She scowled, and her mind reeled to the past.

When she was a little girl living at home, Arnold took her with him to pick out and cut the Christmas tree. Joyce always remained at home baking holiday cookies. "You want that one, Princess?" He beamed while he followed Leslie's pointing finger. Applying force and a sweaty brow, Arnold would crush the stump of the tree with the ax he put in the trunk of his jeep before leaving home until the tall fir fell with a loud noise to the ground.   Leslie jumped and plugged her fingers in her ears while she watched the tree fall.

Arnold and Leslie sang Christmas carols during their ride home. Once home, Leslie marveled at how Joyce always had the cookies baked and cooled before Arnold and she bound, tree in hand, through the front door.

While she stared into the ornament box, Leslie told herself to be nice, be nice and not confront her father with hard issues.   She knew how much Christmas meant to her mother.   All her life she watched her mother strive to turn December 25 into a perfect day.

She almost shook her head.   "No," she told herself when the desire to ask her father if he'd seen Jack welled up in her.   She wouldn't mention Bob or Jack during this visit home.   "After all," she thought, peering up at her mother, "She deserves to be happy."

Chapter Twenty-Two

Every winter since Robin was a young girl she hoped for a white Christmas. It never happened. The trees were bare; dirt always showed on the ground. Joggers and 10K road racers traipsed through the city dressed in brightly colored, lightweight running suits. Behind it all, sun rays beamed against glass windows of tall buildings and sent long stretches of light from the tops of the buildings to the sidewalk. Robin marveled at how she and other Tennesseans refused to give up hope that it would snow on Christmas. She felt light years away from the sub-zero temperatures blasting New York City. No wind howled. She didn't miss thirty-four inches of snow eight days of continuous precipitation sent to earth. The entire East Coast and large portions of the Midwest was immobilized under a heavy snowfall. She didn't want that; she simply wanted it to snow a few inches on Christmas Day this year while she was in Tennessee.

When Trisha, Sharon, Betsy and she flew through Cincinnati, the pilot gave a warning of, "We may experience turbulence. Once we are out of Cincinnati, all should be clear." At the silence of the pilot's voice, Robin gripped the arms of her seat and stared directly ahead. When Flight 237 flew over Kentucky and the pilot described the weather, "Light snow and sleet," she smiled. She couldn't count the times Michelle told her she wanted it to snow this Christmas. The weather seemed perfect.

Flight 237 bumped the Alcoa International Airport domestic runway. Robin turned and examined Trisha, Betsy and Sharon's faces. "Think it'll snow for Christmas?"

They chorused, "You know it won't."

Robin talked fast while they walked down the ramp leading to the airport's main terminal. "Come on. Let's get our luggage then hurry and rent a car."

"What type of ride do you want?" Sharon asked.

"Do you think one car will do, or should we each rent our own car?" Trisha turned from Sharon to Betsy to Robin.

"I think one car is enough. Dinah has a car. She'll play taxi. She's probably been borrowing her parents' car for the last two days she's been here. Plus, Dad will give me the keys to the Buick any time I ask. He said Mama hardly drives that car anymore, as it is."

"My mama doesn't drive much anymore either. Dad told me the last time I talked with him on the phone." Sharon added.

"I remember a time when if you saw a woman driving and a man riding in the passenger seat, it was a big deal."

Robin faced Trisha. "Down South?"

"Girl, yes." A second later she raised her voice and said, "Here comes our luggage." She bent and pointed. "Sharon that looks like your bag, right there."

They grabbed their bags and hurried toward the terminal doors.

"Girl, I can't wait to see my mama." Trisha struggled to even her breath while she walked, both her hands groping the suitcase handle.

"Daddy's the one I want to see. Mama said Daddy's going bald."

Robin slapped her hand over her mouth. "Ewww."

"That comes from living with your mama for more than twenty years. Don't worry. My dad's going bald too."

"Eww, Trisha."

"Shut up, Rob. You're dad's balding too. Your mama gets on your dad's last nerve, and you know it. She gets on your dad's nerves as much as she gets on your nerves. That's why you don't go home more than you do."

"Now, you shut up."

"Come on, Girls. Let's rent a car. These suitcases aren't getting lighter, and my backs starting to hurt."

"Stop whining, Sharon. We'll get you home soon enough." Robin pressed her back against the glass door and waited for them to pass.

Marcia was standing in the front door when Trish pulled up.

"Come get me tomorrow morning. We'll do breakfast together." Robin called over her shoulder while she climbed out of the car.

"Trish stuck her head out the window. "Hi, Mrs. Carlile!"

Marcia smiled and waved at Trish, Betsy and Sharon. "Hi, Girls."

"Rob," Trish said, "Why don't we say I pull up around nine tomorrow morning?"

"Sounds good."

When Trish honked the horn, Robin hurried up the walkway.

Marcia's arms were crossed. "Your father's not home." Her mouth was straight. Covered in burgundy lipstick, it looked like a painted line.

Robin bowed her head. Then she raised it. "Mom, I came to see you too."

"Sure you did."

Blinking back tears, she said, "It's Christmas time, Mom."

"I haven't enjoyed a decent Christmas since—"

"I know. I know." She swallowed hard. "You haven't enjoyed Christmas since Sonia died. I know, Mom. Sonia was your world."

"Wait until you have children of—"

"No. No. I was wrong. Forgive me. I was wrong. I certainly was wrong. For sure I was wrong. Sonia wasn't your world. Sonia is your world." She pulled up on her suitcase handles and stepped forward.

331

"Coming in here with that attitude?"

"Mom, I haven't been home for more than a couple of days in nearly two years."

"You don't have to come home every year."

She dropped her suitcases to the porch floor. "Did you have but one child?"

"Might as well have. You belong to your father. Always ha—"

"I have not always belonged to Daddy. Once I was your little girl too."

Marcia's brow tightened. She ran her hand through her hair then she glanced at her neighbor's houses. Seeing their curtains drawn, she continued. "You've always sat up under your father. You've always been his little girl, his favorite."

"Do you mean to tell me you feel threatened for your own husband's attention by your own daughter?"

Her hand lowered. "Damn you."

Robin blocked the blow, then she stepped back. "Now you're going to take to hitting me? You want to beat me, Mom. Knock me down? Kick me? Is that it? Can't crush me with your words and your icy stares, so now you're just gonna out and out knock me down?"

Marcia hissed. "You never did respect me. You were never like Sonia. You. You only respect your father. It was always him."

"He was there for me. You couldn't move beyond your grief. Dad stepped in and became my mother and my father. If not, both of your daughters would have died. The good Lord knows for so many, so many years of my life I was dead, all dead and gone on the inside."

"It's not normal for a girl to be so close to her father."

"Ours is not a normal family, Mom. Have you not yet noticed that?"

"You know. I did some researching. Checked with the hospital and all. Went through some records. Did you know Sonia had traces of iodine in her blood?"

"Mom."

She clenched her teeth and glared at Robin, "Did you?"

"No. I didn't. Sure. I spent enough time with her to be her mother while you were always cleaning up around the house, but I didn't see her drink iodine. Not that I was old enough to know what iodine was."

Marcia pointed, "Don't you get—"

Robin sighed and shifted her weight. "We both know what Sonia died from. She had cancer. Are you gonna accuse me of giving that to her next?"

"Stop sassing me!" The neighbor across the street opened her front door. Marcia stepped back and smoothed out the front of her cashmere dress with her palms. She went to her toes. A smile stretched across her entire face. "Hi, Gloria! How're you and Frank getting along?"

"Fine. Just fine. Who's that pretty young lady I see standing on your porch?"

Marcia waved. "Oh. Just somebody. She won't be here long."

"For a minute there I thought it was Rob. She's the prettiest, sweetest thing."

"Well, Gloria. I'm not going to keep you. I know you have things to do. You and Frank always do stay so busy. Such wonderful, helpful people."

"Thank you, Marcia. You and Theo are gems too."

Marcia waved over the top of Robin's head. "Take care."

"Love you!"

"Bye, Girl!"

Robin stood with her head bowed.

"So, now you're gonna act shy. Couldn't even speak to Mrs. Johnson. I know I taught you better manners than that."

"It's not like you told her I was your child."

"You're old enough to speak for yourself."

"And still young enough to want my mother to claim me as her own."

"I'm not going to pamper you, Girl."

"How about just letting me in the house?"

"I told you. He's not home."

"Well. Where did he go, Mom? Straight to the moon?"

"Don't you get fresh wi—"

She blocked Marcia's hand. "Better not. One of the neighbors might be peeking out of those pretty designer drapes of theirs. Wouldn't want anybody to see you being anything except the best mother in the whole wide world." Then she stepped around her.

Marcia turned and faced her moving back. "What has gotten into you lately? You are just down right rude, and I'm not sure I want you in my house."

After she placed her suitcases at the foot of the living room stairs, Robin turned and walked into the dining room. She sat at the table. "This is my house too. Full of love or cold as ice, it's home."

At the edge of the table, Marcia stood akimbo. "I am not going to tolerate one more remark from you, young lady. You are not going to disrespect me in my own home. I will not stand for it."

"Does that mean you can talk to me any way you please?"

"Robin, you can pick up your luggage and head right on back out the door. I'm telling you. I am not going to tolerate this abuse from you."

Robin stood. "I am not abusing you, Mother. I'm simply standing up for myself."

After she spread her palms, Marcia laughed. "From what? Standing up for yourself from what?"

"From you."

She stepped back. "From me. Robin, I have sacrificed half my life for you. As hard as Sonia's death was on me. Do you think I had to keep you? I went through a lot after Sonia died. I almost fell apart. You don't have children so you don't know what that feels like. You cannot possibly understand where I am coming from."

"Sonia was my sister. I lost my sister. You don't think I hurt? Don't think losing Sonia hurt me?"

"It's different! It's different. It's just different." At once, she turned and marched across the floor.

Robin followed her. "Where are you going? You never could take a confrontation. Never could stand for someone to stand up to you. You always were a bully. You bully Dad. You bully me. Truth be told, if Sonia had lived, you would have bullied her too."

A second later, she cried when she stood erect. She rubbed the spot on her face where Marcia slapped her. "Tell Dad I came by."

"Where are you going?"

"I'll get a hotel."

"What will your father think?"

"Don't know. Tell him and see."

She raced to the door and stood in front of it. "I'm not letting you leave."

"Mom, have you lost your natural born mind? First you didn't want me to come in the house. Now you don't want me to leave?"

"You're father will nev—"

"She dropped her suitcases to the floor. "Tell you what, Mom. If you don't look me in the eye right now. Right this second. This very second, Mom and tell me you are sorry for slapping me. Gravely sorry and ask me to stay because you want me to stay, I'm out the door."

She bent and reached for the suitcases, but Robin grabbed them before she could get her hands on them.

Reaching for the suitcases again, she said, "Give me those."

Robin jerked the suitcases back.

"You are not leaving. You are not going to make me suffer your father's wrath."

"Dad wouldn't do anything to you. He's never even raised his voice at you. Not that he ever shouldn't have."

"Okay. Okay." She stood erect and smoothed out the front of her dress. "I'm sorry."

"Sorry for what?"

"For slapping you. That was wrong. Slapping is not a Christian thing to do. I shouldn't have slapped you, and I apologize. Now put your suitcases down and stay. Your father should be home in about half an hour. He just ran to the hardware store."

Pulling up on the suitcases, Robin stepped forward. "I said I was sorry."

"And—"

"And I want you to stay so your father won't get upset with me."

She lowered the suitcases to the floor. "Mom, what did I ever do to you? Please just tell me, because I sincerely do not know."

"Know what you did the day Sonia died?"

Her heart raced. She tightened her grip on the suitcase handles. "No. What?"

"You jumped on your bed and sang a loud chorus of Miss Mary Mack. To this day I cringe when I hear a child sing that song. You clapped your hands and the whole nine yards. Sonia couldn't have been dead a full hour when you jumped on your bed and made a mockery of her death by singing that song, stupid and loud and long."

Bowing her head, she peered at the floor. "Sorry."

Marcia clinched her teeth. "You remember."

"No. No. I don't remember. But if you said that's what I did, I guess that's what I did."

"That's what you did."

She looked up. "Did I know?"

"Know what? Know that your baby sister was dead?"

"Yes. Did I know?"

"No. You didn't know. Your father and I just found out ourselves. I left you at home with my sister while we went to the hospital."

"Then why was I bad for singing the song?"

"Because your baby sister had just died."

She spread her palms. "But, I didn't know."

"It doesn't make any difference." She pushed her way beyond Robin and hurried through the kitchen into the basement.

"Mom?" Robin called from the foot of the stairs. "If you want me to leave, I will. I'll even go all the way back to New York. Dad'll never know I even was here. I'll never tell him. If seeing me brings you that much pain, I'll just leave." She lowered her voice and stared at her hands. "I don't want to hurt you. God knows I don't want to hurt you."

It was quiet for a long time then Robin heard the faint sounds of a cry. "Mom?"

"Go away."

"Do you want me to leave?"

"No. Just leave me alone."

"Mom?"

"What?"

"I love you."

"Oh, Robin." She sniffed hard and wiped her face. "I know you do."

"Okay. I'm gonna go now. I'll be upstairs in my room."

She sniffed hard again. "Okay. After I get myself together, I'll be up to help you unpack. If you want, you can even help me get the decorations out of the attic."

"All right." When Robin turned away from the foot of the stairs, her shoulders heaved. She bit her bottom lip to keep her weeping silent.

An hour later, Theo was home. He went straight upstairs as soon as Marcia told him, "She's here. Rob came home for the holidays."

"Hey!" He wrapped his arms around Robin. "Thought you might not make it. I'm so glad to see you."

She almost wept on his shoulder. "Thanks, Dad. It's good to see you and Mom too."

Releasing her, he stepped back and asked, "So what have your Mom and you being doing while I was away?"

She turned and faced the folded clothes on her bed. "Oh. Nothing really. I was just unpacking. Think Mom was in the basement doing a load of laundry or something."

"That woman is always finding something to clean."

She raised then lowered her shoulders. "Um-umm."

He sat on the edge of the bed and looked into her face. "Are you really glad to be home? Your mom didn't jump on you, did she?"

She shook her head. "No. Un-un. Mom and I are cool. I just came up here to unpack. That's all."

"You don't look like the picture of joy."

She chuckled. "Dad, how often do I look like that?"

"Rob, turn around."

She did.

"Please be straight with me. Is everything okay?"

"Why do you keep asking me that?"

"Because I know your mother. Because I know you're grown.
Because I know your mom and you relationship is strained."

"Dad, after all these years."

"After all these years – what?"

"After all these years of dancing around the subject, now you want
to address it?"

"I wouldn't talk about it with you when you were younger, because
you wouldn't understand."

"I don't understand now. In fact, it hurts worse now."

"I told your mom not to be this way, not this time, not anymore, not
ever again. What did she say to you?"

"Dad, I really don't want to talk about this. I really don't. I'll be
here through New Years Day."

His shoulders lowered. "Are we ever gonna be a family?"

"I've tried."

"So have I."

"We're getting by."

"This ain't getting by, Rob. This is purgatory."

"You're the one who stayed married to her."

"Rob!"

"Don't worry, Dad. I'll put on a show. I'll be good. I won't stir
the pot, not that it's not already brimming over and hasn't been for a mighty
long time."

He faced the bedroom door. "Tell you what."

She raced after him. "No. Dad. Don't."

"No." He sped down the stairs.

She ran after him calling, "Dad! Dad! Dad!"

"Marcia!"

She looked up from where she sat at the dining room table sifting
through a stack of bills. "Honey?"

"Let's have a talk."

"Sure. I'll be up in a minute."

"No." He pulled out two chairs. "Down here."

She looked up. She met Robin's gaze.

"It's time we addressed a few things before this family falls
completely and utterly apart."

She glared at Robin.

"Dad."

"Please sit down, Rob."

Marcia laid the bills on the table. "Yes. Sit down, Robin. You
started all of this."

"I did not."

"Ran crying to your daddy like you always do."

"I did not."

"Always looking for sympathy."

"No, I don't."

"This from the woman who not once asked me how I felt after I lost my daughter."

"Marcia, please."

"No, Theo. It's time you faced the truth."

"Robin is not the cause of Sonia no longer being here with us."

"She has also never tried to understand how I feel being a mother who lost her daughter."

"Robin is our daughter, and I want you to stop talking like she isn't."

Robin stood. "Dad, I'm going back upstairs."

Marcia waved. "Go on back upstairs. Run. You're good at that."

"Mom, I figure avoiding you is the best way to keep my food down."

Theo's eyes ballooned. "Robin."

"She doesn't want me, Dad, and I'm tired of getting my feelings hurt. Ain't no pain like the pain a little girl feels when her mother makes it loud and clear that she doesn't want her."

"That's not it, Honey. Your mother wants you. She loves you. She's proud of you. It's just that she hasn't gotten over Sonia's death. That's all."

"I don't expect her to ever completely get over Sonia's death. I still get sad when I think about Sonia sometimes. Not like I used to because I turned that over to the Lord and the Lord took care of it. But you can't sit there and make me think your wife loves me."

Marcia stood. She smiled a tight-lipped smile. "Never mind all this chit chat. Tell you what. Robin, I told you I would help you unpack, so let's go upstairs so I can help you unpack."

"I'm almost unpacked."

"Well, let me help you finish."

"All I have to do is—"

Theo turned in his chair. "Rob."

Moving toward the living room stairs, she said, "Okay. Come and help me unpack, Mom. I really would like that."

"It really is good to see you."

She was silent while Marcia and she ascended the stairs.

"Doesn't seem like it's been two years since you were last home. Did you notice that I rearranged the living room and the family room? I even moved some things around in your room."

Robin nodded.

"Got most of the furniture from the best stores in Cedar Bluff and Knoxville. Very high quality furniture. I figure while you're here we can go shopping at the malls. It'll be nice driving into Knoxville again. They even have an East Town Mall now. I don't shop there much. I usually shop at the West Town Mall when I go into Knoxville, but things are picking up. They're working on a new stadium at U.T. I heard they are going to have concerts and everything there. For lunch I figure we can grab a bite to eat from Lobster and Crab Fest. Your dad mentioned something about having dinner at Steak Palace. Your father's really proud of you. He talks about you all the time. You ought to hear him talking about you to your grandparents. A stranger would think you were a queen or something. The way your dad talks." She waved her hand. "That man just talks and talks about you."

Robin grabbed a pile of shirts and placed them inside a dresser drawer.

"Sharon, Trisha and Betsy look good. Don't know why they didn't get out of that car. Come and say hi to me."

"I didn't tell them to stay in the car, Mom."

"I didn't say you did. I just said I don't know why they didn't get out and come and say hi to me. That's so unlike them."

"Maybe they were in a hurry. They haven't been home in awhile themselves. All of their mothers called and begged them to come home. I'm sure they wanted to hurry home and see their mothers. You know how much their mothers love them. Just crazy about them!"

She smiled at the back of Robin's head. Then she picked up a sweater. "So, what lucky young, handsome man are you dating now?"

"Mama, can't you--"

"Rob, how do you like the house? Like how I rearranged the furniture?"

She turned and lowered her hands to her sides. Her gaze darted around the room. "All by yourself?"

Marcia chuckled. "Well, your dad moved the furniture, but I designed it all. I sure am good with a house."

Robin turned and faced her. She forced a smile before she said, "You did a great job, Mom. Both you and Dad. The house looks great. I like it."

"Thanks, Robin. After we put your clothes away would you like me to fix you something to eat?"

"I can really unpack by myself."

"I'm trying to be helpful."

"I know, and I appreciate it. I really do. It's very kind of you. I just don't want to trouble you."

"You're not troubling me. If I didn't want to help you put your clothes away, I wouldn't."

She laughed. "That much is true."

"At least I'm not a phony."

"Neither am I. And you don't have to fix me anything to eat. We can go out and grab a bite. My treat." She glanced over her shoulder. "Unless you and Dad have plans."

"Theo and I don't have any plans. But I don't really feel like going out." Running her hand over the top of her hair, she added, "I haven't been to the beauty parlor in nearly a week. I really shouldn't go anywhere looking like this."

"You look fine."

"By whose standards?"

Robin was silent.

Marcia picked up another sweater. She wore a lopsided grin. "You didn't answer the question I asked you moments ago."

Robin's hands slowed. One of her suitcases was unpacked. The other was half empty. Pants and sweaters were folded and pushed inside her old dresser drawers. Dresses, skirts and silk blouses hung from wire hangers in the closet. After she pulled the remaining clothes out of her second suitcase, she walked to the window, and, folded her arms. While she looked out the window, she watched birds peck and flutter their wings in falling snow. She almost smiled.

"So?"

She turned and faced her. "What question?"

Marcia snickered. "Girl, you know what I'm talking about."

Robin shook her head. She searched her mother's face. "No. I don't. Mama, what are you trying to ask me?"

"The question I asked you only minutes earlier."

"And what was that? I honestly forgot."

"I asked you what lucky, handsome, young black man you were dating." A smile widened her face.

"I'm not dating anyone right now. You know that. You ask me that every time we talk."

"Honey, I just wondered."

"I know."

She looked at the piles of clothes on the bed. "Where'd you get that cute blouse?"

Robin stared at the clothes on the bed. "Which one?"

"The pretty, light green one?"

"From a small boutique in Greenwich Village."

"That dive."

"It's building up again."

She pushed two of Robin's jackets down the bed then she sat. "So, who did you say the lucky fella was?"

"No one. I said I'm not dating right now."

The volume in her voice dropped. "Oh. That's right. When do you think you'll start dating again?"

She shrugged. "I don't know."

"You don't have any idea, not the slightest inclination?"

"Mom."

"Mom nothing. I want to know. You are your father and my only chance at a grandchild, and, at the rate you're going just to find a man to call your own, it looks like you're going to deprive us."

"Maybe Dad and you should have had more children, increased your chances for grandchildren."

"Nothing's wrong with you, Girl. You can have children."

"I know nothing's wrong with me. You're the one who doesn't realize that."

"Well, Michael has been the only special man in your life. That's not normal."

"Please."

"Have you met anyone since Michael?"

"No."

"Has Michael met anyone?"

"I don't know."

"I thought you said his dance company filled in when some of your dancers took sick."

"They did. Michael danced too."

"Well?"

"Michael and I are merely friends."

"That's your fault, you know?"

"It takes two to tangle."

"So, it does."

"When I get married, I want it to last and be good. I want it to be real. I want my home to be full of love, love with integrity, real love. I'm in no hurry. I have time. I know that."

"You're thirty-four."

"I know how old I am."

"I see I'm not going to get anywhere with this." She stood and ironed the back of her pants with her palms. "Let me help you put the rest of your clothes away."

"That's okay."

"I don't mind."

"I know you don't, but I want to be alone for awhile. I want to watch the snow fall out of the sky. That's a first for me. Seeing it snow so close to Christmas. I want to relax and enjoy it."

Marcia walked toward the bedroom door. "All right, then."

The two weeks Robin was home passed quickly. Marcia baked her favorite dishes those two weeks: pineapple upside down cake, cherry cobbler, blueberry muffins, oatmeal raisin cookies, butterscotch pudding, zucchini, squash, collard and turnip greens and macaroni and cheese. She never told Robin the dishes were for her. Dinner ready, she simply called out, "Come and eat!" Theo hurried into the kitchen and sat at the table. "Come and eat! Come and eat!" Marcia would have to call again before Robin came slowly out of her bedroom or stopped watching the Bravo! Channel in the living room. Once she sat at the table, Theo prayed grace. She was rarely hungry. She drank so much soda and juice throughout the day, come dinner she rarely had an appetite. Yet, she ate faster than Marcia or Theo. She raced through her food. Marcia glanced across the table at her. Feeling her mother's gaze on her, she ate faster. Despite her thoughts going to Manhattan to the theatre to her upcoming motivational speaking engagement at Lenox and Jayson, a leading international medical firm, somehow Robin never forgot to mouth the words, "Thanks, Mom. Thanks," before she pushed away from the table. Marcia just bowed her head. Not until the last day she was home did Marcia smile at her show of gratitude. When she finished eating then, Marcia looked up, smiled and winked at her.

Robin visited with her grandparents everyday while she was home. Their houses were laced with good memories. They still had the Barbie dolls Robin played with when she was a little girl. Their houses kept photo album after photo album of family pictures. She'd seen them more than a dozen times. Nevertheless, she looked through them each time she flew home from Manhattan. Nostalgic and looking for chunks of the past to take back to Manhattan with her, the pictures served to make her feel that her family was more strong, more healthy, more loving than it was dysfunctional. The faces in the pictures spoke to her. They told her to press on, to keep faith in God, to believe in her God given talents, to strive, to dream, to soar. There were so many faces. Her great-grandparents, her great aunts and great uncles, her cousins, old classmates who visited often, Dinah, Betsy, Sharon and Trisha, old portraits she took with her parents, and Sonia. Sonia laying on a blanket on her parents' bed. Sonia sucking her thumb. Sonia trying to stick her feet in her mouth. Sonia blowing bubbles.

Sonia crawling. Sonia laughing. Sonia with her arms wrapped around Robin's neck. Kissing Robin. Smiling hard.

More than thirty relatives came to the Carlile's for Christmas Eve. Robin and Marcia decorated the Christmas tree without criticizing each other's hanging skills. Robin's maternal grandmother, Dorothy, baked Robin a tin pail of her favorite oatmeal raisin cookies to take to New York City. Loud Country and Rhythm and Blues music played on the stereo. Laughter filled the room. There was more picture taking. Robin chased one of her cousin's infant daughters. She giggled while the little girl raised her fat legs and ran across the room. Marcia was sitting on the chair next to the front door. Her cousin ran behind the chair, covered her eyes and started peeking at Robin and saying, "Boo. Boo. Boo." She laughed each time she peeked at Robin. Dorothy went and grabbed the camera. She pressed down on the button. The flash exploded. Everyone waited. When the picture came out all it showed was Robin leaning close to Marcia's shoulder. It looked like mother and daughter were giving each other a kiss. Both were smiling. It was the last picture Robin took while she was home. Outside it was snowing.

****

The tree was down. Leslie dragged it to the back of her parents' garage, at the edge of the alley and dropped it. Her mother was standing at the back door. "Thanks, Baby," was the first thing she said when Leslie entered the house again.

She reached out for her mother. They held one another tightly.

"Les! Joyce!"

Turning and stepping away from Leslie, Joyce called out, "Yes, Honey?"

"I'm going out."

"Now?" Joyce asked.

"Yes. I won't be long. I have to make a run."

"Today? It's New Years Eve."

"I know, Joyce. Said I won't be gone long. I'll be back. Soon."

Her brow lowering and her voice dropping, she turned to Leslie. "Well. What time did you say you were leaving?"

"I was gonna leave in an hour. Catch a two o'clock flight." She smiled softly. "But I'll stay until tomorrow. I don't have to party on New Years Eve. I can hang out with you and Dad."

She turned her back to Leslie again. "Arnold, let's go somewhere, do something special. Les said she's gonna spend the holiday with us!"

He hurried to the edge of the kitchen. He was wearing his long leather coat. "Thought you said you were leaving today. This afternoon."

Leslie's brow tightened. She felt her hands going into fists. "I changed my mind. I'm gonna stay and help Mom bring in the holiday."

He pulled up on his coat collar. "Good." He nodded. "Good. I wouldn't want your mother to bring in the New Year alone."

"We-Well."

"I had plans, Joyce. I can't just cancel my plans all of a sudden because you took it upon yourself to talk Leslie into canceling her New Years Eve plans. I can't just drop what I was going to do because at the last minute you decide to change everybody's life. No. I can't. I have somewhere I said I would be for the holiday. Months ago. This isn't something new that came up for—"

She raised her hand. "Never mind. Forget it. Les and I will bring in the New Year together. You go ahead and go wherever it is you say you have to be."

He looked at Leslie. Then he looked at Joyce. Then he looked back at Leslie. Joyce. "Don't put this on me. Don't make this my fault. Told you this isn't some new plan I had. I've had plans for New Years Eve for months."

"And they never included Mom?"

He chuckled. "You know your mother never liked to socialize, to mix with other people. She's a homebody. As much as you get out and about, as much as you love people, Les, you know that."

"Dad, where are you really going? You never know, this could be the last year we spend New Years Eve together as a family."

His brow went up. "Why do you say that?"

"I just do. Who knows what tomorrow is going to bring. I don't. I've had my share of surprises in life. Haven't you?"

He chuckled again. "No. I plan well. Thought I taught you how to do that." He shook his head. "You're too much like your mother sometimes."

"You didn't answer Leslie's question."

"What question?"

"She asked you where you were going."

Crossing her arms, Leslie moved close to her mother. Their shoulders touched. "Yeah."

He looked at them. Then he smiled. "I'm going out."

"To see your girlfriend?"

"Joyce!"

"I've known. Arnold, I've known. All these years, I've known."

He waved his hand. "You don't know what you're talking about."

"Oh, no?"

He turned to leave. "I don't have time for this. I have to go."

"Don't keep her waiting."

He turned and pointed his finger sharply. "You young lady are my daughter. I will not have you talking to me like you're my equal."

"I'm helping you, Dad."

He was silent.

"Helping you face yourself. See yourself. See how much you hurt people."

He stuck his hands in his coat pockets and hurried out of the house. He didn't close the door before he hollered, "Leslie, when I get back hopefully you won't be here."

She threw an arm across her mother's shoulder. Her mother wrapped an arm around her waist. It rained outside. Rained on top of eighteen inches of newly fallen snow. Then the rain froze. They sat in the living room watching old movies, listening to old records and sipping ginger ale. They pulled off their shoes and laughed at the same jokes.

Chapter Twenty-Three

Leslie and Darryl, an architect, met and married six years after Bob and Leslie's divorce was final. They had three children, Darryl Jr., five; Chris, four; and Robin, two.

Robin and Carl, a world famous guitarist, were married five years. They had two children, Jerome, three and Greg, nine months old.

They made their home Atlanta, Georgia, Carl's birthplace. After travelling the world twice completing documentary filming and studying, Robin was glad to spend two to three quiet hours in the evening pulling weeds from Carl and her half acre garden and walking barefoot in their front and back yards after the sun sank over the hill.

Leslie, Darryl and their three children made their home Kansas City, Missouri. To Robin's surprise, Leslie moved with Darryl to Kansas City one month after they married. Robin moved out of Apartment 1201 six weeks later. Two weeks later she met Carl. Leslie was throwing a house warming party. Carl was an old friend of one of her former boyfriends. Although she lost all contact with the boyfriend, she spoke to Carl when their careers brought them together at awards banquets. A rock and roll fan, she made it her business to catch Carl and the band, Razor, he played lead guitar with, perform when they were in concert. "Carl's one of the world's greatest guitarist. He writes his own music. He speaks four languages fluently. He's bright. He's been on the cover of more magazines than I have. Although he's quiet, he's a rock and roll star through and through." Leslie walked through the kitchen telling Darryl when he asked her who people on their guest list he hadn't met were.

It took her as a total surprise when Robin entered Carl and her 100 acre farmhouse and seconds after they hugged and kissed, gazed across the living room and immediately caught Carl's eye. The room was full with company. Not long after all the guests arrived Darryl started a game. While most of their guests played along with Darryl in the living room, Carl and two of his friends excused themselves into the basement where they shot pool. After she tossed a salad, Leslie wiped her hands on her apron then descended the stairs. "Carl?" she called from the center of the stairs.

"Yea?" He didn't look up. He narrowed his brow and concentrated on getting his ball in the right, corner pocket.

Leslie watched the ball roll into the hole. "Can I speak with you for a sec?"

"Yea." He stood erect. "Yea." Crossing the floor, he neared her. "What is it?"

She placed her hands on her hips and smirked. "I saw you checking out my best friend."

"Who? Who's your best friend?"

"Oh, Carl. Everybody knows Robin is my best friend."

"Who's Robin?"

She leaned back. "You don't know?" Then she leaned forward. "You really don't know?"

He shook his head. "No. I don't."

"She's the super fine black woman who walked in here about twenty minutes ago. The one I was so happy to see. The Sister with the long, pretty hair. She had on a tight pair of jeans and a soft, pink cashmere sweater."

He started to laugh. "Oh, her." Then he lowered his head sheepishly. "Yea. I saw her."

Leslie pointed a finger. "Let me tell you something, buster. You better not hurt her."

He raised his shoulders and spread his hands. "What? Wha-- I don't even know her."

Leslie turned to leave. Near the top of the stairs she turned, "Carl?"

"Yea?"

"We both know you're going to make it your business to get to know Robin real good. Don't be a rock and roller with her. Be yourself. Just be yourself." Then she walked to the top of the stairs and entered the kitchen.

Carl stayed in the basement shooting pool with his friends for an hour. As soon as he climbed the stairs and rounded the corner, the first person his gaze landed on was Robin. She was sitting on the edge of the sofa talking to Leslie. Everything they said was mixed with laughter until Carl crossed the floor and asked Leslie, "Where's the bathroom?"

Silence.

Carl glanced at Robin then he returned his attention to Leslie. "Where's the bathroom, please?"

Leslie stood. "It's right around that corner."

Robin grinned while he walked away from them.

"He's mixed."

"I didn't as—"

"His mother is black and his father is white. He was born in London. He came to L.A. when he was a teenager. He's this rock and roll guitar star. Big like Jimi Hendrix. Well." She sat back in the chair. "He's bigger than Hendrix. Played with some of everybody. He's so down-key you'd never know he was famous if someone didn't tell you. He's quiet." She chuckled. "I almost dated him once. His name is Carl Sallis."

Sitting back on the sofa, Robin smiled coyly while she crossed her legs. "I'm glad you didn't. I always promised myself that I'd never date a man my best friend did."

Leslie sat forward. "You just be careful. He ain't no choir boy. One thing I can say about Carl though. Remember that talk we were having about male singers with Liz a few years ago?"

"Yea."

"Well, Carl's never been a player. I think he slept about when Razor first found fame. I don't know. Maybe about 6 months. I heard a lot about him from friends. You gotta remember he had my interest for awhile. I never told him. He still doesn't know I was ever interested in him, but I know enough about him to know he won't cheat. A man with as many opportunities to sleep around as Carl has who doesn't won't cheat. I mean. He's single. He's not even seeing anyone right now and he still doesn't sleep around. But," she pointed a finger. "He still ain't no choir boy."

"He drinks?"

"Sometimes."

"Drugs?"

"Nah. Not anymore. He gave those up about the same time I did."

Robin sat back. "You really know this Carl—"

"Excuse me?"

Robin's eyes ballooned. She turned slowly to stare into Carl's brown eyes. She watched his thick, curly hair dip well below his shoulders. She wondered if it was as long as hers was. Then she smiled coyly. "Ah. I was. Just. Tal—Talking with Leslie and your name came up." She turned back to Leslie and gawked at her.

Leslie smiled. "She was asking me how she could ask you out. She was telling me how good she thinks you look in those jeans you're wearing. She also noticed the hair curling off your chest." She almost stood. "You know. Where your shirt is unbuttoned to the – what is that? To the third button from the top?" She sat all the way back down. "Stuff like that."

Robin's mouth was opened.

Carl extended his hand. "Nice to meet you. Ah—"

"Robin. Robin Carlile."

He nodded. "Ni—Nice to meet you Robin. And don't worry. I know Leslie made all that up. You look too shy to say something like that."

"I was also asking her if you drink or do drugs. You know how you rock and rollers have a rep to protect."

He laughed. "Oh. Do we. My. Fifteen years in the business and I didn't know that. I always thought all I had to do was play a mean guitar."

Robin was silent. She tried to stop grinning, but her face wouldn't allow for it.

"I don't do drugs anymore. Stopped years ago. I only drink occasionally, but to tell you the truth, I'm getting tired of that. Same old scene. Just getting tired of it. But I'm not an alcoholic."

"They all say that."

"Who's they?"

She was silent again. Shame coated her face.

Leslie winked. "Told you he was sharp, Rob. Gotta watch him. Can't take your eye off of him. Never know what he's gonna do next."

He sat on the sofa next to Robin. "Oh, Leslie, I'm not that unpredictable and you know it. I can't be. You seem to know me as well as my own mother does and I hardly ever see you. I see my mom all the time."

Reaching across the sofa, Leslie swatted his thigh. "Shut up."

Robin turned on the sofa and faced him. "So, how long have you been playing the guitar?"

"Seventeen years."

"That long?"

"Yea. My grandmother gave me my first guitar."

"You must really be close to her."

"Yea. I was." He stared at his hands. "She passed away four years ago."

"I'm sorry. I'm sorry to hear that."

He looked up. "It's okay. You didn't know."

"How come you rock and rollers come off as being so sweet and sensitive?"

"Well. I'm only one man. I'm not every guy who was ever in a rock band. I can't speak for everybody. Me. I'm sweet, but I'm not that sensitive." He raised his hands. "See these hands?"

Robin nodded. "Yea."

"Touch them."

She looked at Leslie.

Leslie spread her hands and raised her shoulders.

She returned her attention to Carl. "What are you smiling about?"

"You."

"You're cute and you're scared. You keep looking at Leslie like you think I'm gonna jump you or something."

She crossed her arms. "I'm not scared. I'm not scared of you."

"Then raise your hands and put them up against mine."

"Why?"

"I want to show you something."

She raised her hands slowly. They shook until they touched his. Then she felt a warm, tingling sensation start in her palms and work its way down to the center of her spine. She also felt the coarseness on his hands. "You have calluses."

He laughed. "Told you I wasn't sensitive. Playing the guitar won't allow for it."

It was her turn to laugh. "Play the guitar with your heart too?"

He smiled at her. "Well, now. I can't think of an easy way for you to find that out. And if I told you, you wouldn't believe me. Women never believe men when they tell them good things about themselves. So, I won't bother. But I do know of a way I could start to let you find out for yourself."

She glanced over her shoulder. "Les. Les?"

"She went in the kitchen a couple of minutes ago."

"Oh."

"So?"

"So, what?"

"You wanna test my heart?"

She smiled at him. "Why not?"

"Exactly. So go out with me to a real good scary movie tomorrow night."

"You don't even know where I live."

"I will after you tell me."

"I mean. I don't live in Kansas."

"Well. I knew that. You didn't say your name was Dorothy."

She laughed. "Stop it. Stop it right now. How do you know you can get to where I live in time for a Friday night date?"

"Who said anything about a date?'

"Okay, Funny Guy. Where do you live?"

"L.A., of course. I thought you knew that. Every musician in the whole wide world lives in L.A."

She laughed. "I like your sense of humor."

"And I like your sweater. And your jeans. And your smile. And your eyes. And your hands are real soft too. And from all the way over here I can tell you've got a good heart."

"I live in upstate New York, close to one of my sorority sisters."

"Yea?"

"Yea."

"Used to live in Manhattan. Moved when Leslie got married."

"You. You. You were Leslie's roommate?"

"The one and only."

"I saw you at the Grammy's a couple of years ago."

"That was me."

"Was that your boyfriend you were talking to backstage?"

"We were trying to be alone."

"A good looking woman like you is very hard not to notice. Hard to leave alone."

"He was my ex-boyfriend."

"Have any current boyfriends?"

"I never was one to date more than one man at a time."

"Current boyfriend then?"

"No. And," she stared at her fingers. "Why a scary movie? I don't like scary movies."

"See. I knew that. I also happen to know that you only don't like scary movies because you have a vivid imagination. See. I just bet you do. I bet you have a vivid imagination. You'll need someone to sit with you in your apartment for awhile after you see a scary movie. Does that answer your question?"

She chuckled. "You're bad."

He smiled at her. "And you're still here."

The next Saturday, Carl flew into JFK International from Los Angeles. Due to a delay his plane was half an hour late. With a sports bag strapped over his shoulder, he ran to a row of pay telephones and dropped coins inside.

Robin stopped pacing the living room floor of her townhouse. She pulled down on her blouse and caught her breath. "Hello?"

"Robin?"

"Yes. Carl? Carl, is this you?"

He smiled. "It's me. Look. My plane was delayed. I got held up. I'm here. At JFK International." Turning, he looked over his shoulders. "I'm standing near a donut shop." He went to his toes. "Ahhh. Delicious Dozen. Ever heard of it? Ever been down this way? Do you know where I am?"

"I know exactly where you are. I'll be right there. Carl, don't go anywhere. I'm on my way. I'm leaving right now."

Traffic was thick. It took Robin over an hour to drive to the airport. Once there, she looked at Carl like he was a stranger. She started twisting the ends of her hair and turning her feet over. Although she told herself to look up – meet his glances – she stared at her shoes. Shyness cleaved her tongue to the roof of her mouth. Nervousness sent a flurry of emotional butterflies racing up and down her spine. Then Carl neared her side, took her hand inside his and told her to, "Come on." They walked back to her car and spent the day trading dreams and talking about how difficult it was to maintain success in the entertainment industry. That night Robin kept a promise she made to herself early that morning. She asked Carl to let her take him to the movies then out to eat at a corner café. With a smile and a wink, he obliged. It was 2 o'clock in the morning before they returned to Robin's townhouse.

"I can sleep here on the sofa, if you don't mind?"

Robin stopped just outside the main bathroom. "You don't want me to drive you back to your motel?"

He chuckled. "I don't have a motel. I always planned on spending the night here, on staying with you."

"But—"

"I know. I know. We haven't known each other that long. That's why I said I'll sleep on the sofa."

Returning to the living room, she gazed at him. "Carl, I'm not that kind of—"

"I was hoping you weren't. See. I was right. I keep telling my mom I know a decent woman when I see one." He smiled up at her. "She doesn't believe me though."

Robin laughed. "It's okay if you sleep on the sofa. Do you want to take a shower now or in the morning?"

His mouth opened and formed a circle; he was silent.

"I mean. I was just going to get you a wash rag and a towel and put it on the sofa so you'd have it."

"You know what would be easier?" Leaning across the sofa, he reached out for her.

She grinned sheepishly. "What? What would be easier?"

"Why don't you just show me where the linen closet is. I can get a towel and wash rag myself."

"Trying to show me you know how to take care of yourself?"

He arched his shoulders. "Not really. But," he raised a finger. "It is something I've been doing since I was about what? Ahh.. About five years old."

"Oh. I see. Independent?"

"So are you."

"Why are you watching me so hard? You're learning too much about me so fast."

He leaned back on the sofa. "Too much so fast. Never heard anything put like that before. Too much so fast." He nodded. "I like that." He smiled. "Yea. I like that."

"Well?"

"Why am I learning too much about you so fast?"

"Yea. Yes."

He held out his hand. "Because I like you. And—" He sat up. "Because I want to rush into a good thing."

Stepping back, she peered into his eyes. "I'm not sleep—"

"That's not what I was talking about. And besides. If I wanted to, I already know I could seduce you. Again, that's not what I was talking about. Don't prejudge me. Why don't you observe me and listen to me and get to know me that way. If you prejudge me, you stand a very good chance of getting me all wrong especially since you think guitar players are skirt chasing drug addicted winos."

She stood akimbo and laughed. "Well. Aren't they?"

They stayed up for another hour talking and laughing. Robin blushed a lot. Carl slept so soundly, when Robin woke at 5 o'clock to go into her office and start writing she didn't pull on her robe. Not until she went into the kitchen to pour herself a glass of orange juice did it return to her that she was not alone.

Carl's feet hung over the arm of the sofa. She smiled when she looked at him. Warmth entered her stomach and pulsed. Pulling loose strands of hair off her forehead, she made a wish while she walked beyond Carl and into the kitchen. When she came out of the kitchen, he was still sleeping. Before she left the living room and returned to her office, she turned and stared at him. His chest rose and fell in what, to her, seemed perfect rhythm. His long, thick wavy hair was pulled back and kept together in a braid. Inching closer to him, she wondered how his moustache kept from tickling his mouth. It brushed against his lip each time the living room fan circled in his direction. She almost leaned over him while she stared at his mouth. His lips were thick. The longer she thought about his mouth, the more she thought about her own. Running her tongue across her lips, she wondered what her lips would feel like pressed against his. Then he turned on the sofa. She froze. When he resumed his deep, even breathing she leaned over him. A dark haired woman with a single red rose in her hand was tattooed on his left shoulder. Running her fingers through her hair, she told herself if she wore her hair down and teased it and put a red rose in her hand, she would look like the woman on the tattoo.

He turned again and she stepped away from him.

He stayed an entire week with her. Each night he slept on the sofa. The day he returned to Los Angeles Robin went to a nearby furniture store and bought a king sized bed and two matching dressers. She also telephoned Reverend Julian and asked him to give her signs that would tell her if a man was the "right man" for her. They talked for twenty minutes. Reverend Julian told her to pray about it and to make certain the man had a warm heart that was full of integrity. Then she called Leslie. Darryl answered the telephone.

"Hey, Darryl. It's Rob."

"Hey, Rob!"

"What's up?"

"I'm busy designing a cathedral in Phoenix. Did Les tell you the great news?"

"No. What?"

"We just found out yesterday. We're expecting!"

She screamed. "That's wonderful. That's great. That's fantastic. What a blessing. Oh, what a wonderful, wonderful blessing. How many months along are you two?"

"Nine weeks."

"I am so happy for you. Is Les home?"

"She's out back working in the yard."

"My that woman has changed over the years."

"And she keeps getting better."

"Darryl, you and Les belong together. I'm so glad you found each other."

"Me too. Hold on. Let me go get Les."

Robin whispered thanks to God for bringing a rainbow of happiness around Leslie while she waited for Darryl to go tell Leslie that she was on the line.

"Rob!"

"Les! Girl, Darryl told me the excellent news! Hello, Mommy."

Leslie laughed. "Thanks." Then she ran her hand across her stomach. "I'm so excited. I hope it's a girl. Well. I really just want a healthy baby. Darryl and I are really looking forward to becoming parents."

"You should be. You're going to bring your little one a world full of joy and promise."

"Thanks, Rob. So, what's up? Oh, and, how's Carl?"

"He's the reason I called."

Leslie sat in the chair next to the telephone. "Carl is real quiet. Sometimes he doesn't know how to tell a woman how he really feels—"

"No. No. It's not that. Carl is warm and loving. He's very caring and expresses himself very well. It's not that at all. I know it's soon and I know this is not like me at all, but I'm starting to have strong feelings—"

She chuckled. "You're falling in love. I knew you were going to fall in love with Carl. He's in love with you too."

"How do you know?"

"Think he hasn't called me?"

"He has?"

"Just once. He wanted to know why you sometimes pull away from him."

"Pull away from him how?"

"Pull away from him when he tries to kiss you passionately or tries to caress you."

"And what did you tell him?"

"I told him you don't believe in having sex before you are married."

"Les, did you tell hi—"

"No. I didn't tell him that you're a virgin." She laughed. "As if that would make a difference. I think he figured that out the first time he met you."

"It's that obvious?"

"Rob, you are not an everyday woman. You have a lot of rare and standout qualities."

"Thanks." She lowered her voice. "Do you think Carl regrets trying to get to know me?"

"Not at all. I told you he's in love with you."

Her heart raced. "So soon?"

"You're falling in love with him this soon."

"I am. Les, I have never felt this way about a man, not even about Michael. Carl does something to me every time I see him. I get so nervous around him. Sometimes I even get light headed. My hands start to shake, and I just get so nervous. He's so incredibly handsome. His eyes. His nose. And his mouth. He has the sweetest looking mouth."

"Well, why don't you ask him if you can taste it?"

"Lesl—"

"Well. What are you going to do? Are you going to tell him how you feel or are you going to make him toe the line and keep your feelings to yourself so you can one day cry the blues over losing him?"

"Les—"

"I'm serious, Rob."

"I have to know if he's the right one."

"The right one for what?"

"For me."

"Do you actually think there is one right person for everybody walking the face of the earth?"

"Well."

"You could probably have a very rewarding and loving relationship with about thirty to one hundred men, Rob. Tell Carl how you feel. Ask him if he wants to take your relationship to another level and if so, when. Keep reassuring him of your love. Treat him like you want him."

"But I'm sca—"

"Scared."

"Yes. I'm scared. I'm terrified."

355

"You're heart is exposed. You should be scared. It's normal. That exposure can lead to very, very good things, Rob. Of course, it can also lead to heartache, but I know Carl enough to be able to say this exposure will lead to very, very good things."

"What if he's not faithful?"

"Any man can cheat on you. Now or twenty years into a relationship. Gonna let that fear stop you from experiencing true love with Carl?"

"No."

"Then why don't you just hang up the phone and dial Carl's number and tell him everything you have just told me?"

"Les."

"No, Rob. Do it. I want us both to be happy. Don't cheat yourself out of this opportunity for true love and romance."

"Okay. You talked me into it. After I hang up from talking with you, I'm going to call Carl."

That telephone call to Carl lead into places Robin had never been before. She was crying when she returned the receiver to its cradle. Carl kept telling her how much he loved and missed her. She promised to fly to L.A. Saturday morning. She spent two weeks with him. The first week she slept in one of his four guest bedrooms. The second week she climbed into bed with him and curled up against him. She lay her head against his chest and ran her fingers over his chest hairs. They held one another and talked until they drifted off to sleep. At the end of her visit when he drove her to the airport she kissed him with passion and pulling him close to her, she told him, "I want to spend the rest of my life with you, Carl."

Three months later they were married in Darryl and Leslie's back yard on a hazy Saturday afternoon.

Joyce caught Robin's bouquet. Immediately she turned and peered at Arnold. He looked at her sheepishly then he turned and looked at the ground.

"Congratulations! I love you, girl!" Leslie screamed as soon as Carl and Robin reached the edge of the lawn and freed each other's hand. She pulled Robin close to her. "I knew it. The second I saw you two together, I knew it. You make a beautiful couple, inside and out, you do. You're going to make each other so happy. You're going to bring each other so much joy! Oh, Rob! I'm so happy for you! I love you, girl! You're my best friend!"

Warm tears inched down Robin's face and landed against Leslie's shoulder.

Stepping back, Leslie smiled at her and said, "I'm glad your father made it up. I know you're happy to see him."

A cool breeze brushed the side of Robin's face when she turned and glanced over her shoulder. Her gaze landed on her father's taut, square jaw. "I wouldn't have gotten married without my dad being present."

"Rob!"

Leslie turned. "Hi, Mom."

"Hi, Baby." Joyce moved beyond Leslie. "Come here, Rob and give me a big hug. You. The woman who just made that rockin' guitar player one of the most blessed men on the face of the earth. Come here and give me a big, warm, tight hug."

She kissed the side of Joyce's face while they embraced. "I love you, Mama Fletcher."

"I love you too, Sweetheart. You're the sister Leslie always wanted and the second daughter I spent years trying to have."

Choking back tears, Robin stepped away from her and whispered, "I wish you were my mother."

Joyce's face tightened. Leaning forward, she asked, "What, Sweetheart?"

With flutters of her hand, Robin said, "Never mind. Sorry. Never mind. I was wrong. I shouldn't have said what I did."

Joyce leaned forward again. "I didn't hear you, Honey. What did you say?" Her brow went up.

Pulling down on the front of the white lace dress she wore, Robin cleared her throat. "I said Leslie's lucky to have you for a mother." A lump formed in her throat while she gazed at Joyce.

The blue in Joyce's eyes slowly began to fade to pink. She saw the lump in Robin's throat moving up and down. She knew she was working to keep the lump from choking her with emotion. She turned away from her. Then she faced her again. "Thank you, Sweetheart."

Robin bit down on her bottom lip. "She's not here, Mama Fletcher. She's not even here."

Joyce twirled the end of her hair around one finger. "But you said she was sick."

Robin looked at the ground. "I always say that." Then she looked up. "She always says that."

"Oh, Honey. The flu gets more than a few people down. The timing was just off. That's all. But, look," She turned and gazed over her shoulder, "How many of your friends flew in to see you get married. Leslie's tickled to no end that Carl and you were married at her home. She's been talking about Carl and you for I don't know how long. She's very happy for you."

"You know. She always knew what I was feeling for a man and I always knew the same about her. We never could fool each other when it came to men."

"Well." Joyce chuckled. "Carl gives it all away. He always has this sparkle in his eye when he's around you."

"I'm glad you like him. I can't tell you how many people warned me not to get involved with him."

Joyce stepped back. "Why?"

"Because he plays in a rock and roll band. But Carl's nothing like the rock and roll image. He went through that period early in his career. He learned the very hard way that he couldn't feed into that image and stay alive or be truly happy."

"And his lesson was? His lesson came through what profound event in his life?"

"He was in a serious car accident. He almost died. The person who was in the car with him was in a comma for six months."

Joyce's mouth opened. She stared at Robin gape-eyed.

"They are okay now, after years of physical therapy."

"He was drinking?"

She nodded. "Yes. Said he tried to drink himself into a successful suicide three months after the accident. Then, like a light coming on in a dark room, he came to his senses. Just like that. Boom! No long stretched out period of time. Just like that, he decided to stop drinking and he did."

"Giving up booze is no easy trick."

"No. But he gave it up. And thank goodness he got chasing women out of his system too, because I am not about to go through that again."

"Don't you dare."

"It's amazing what some people go through before they find their route in life."

"It is. But it was worth it." Turning, she glanced at Carl again. "He got on track and landed smack dab in the center of your heart."

She lowered her head and chuckled.

Not half an hour passed before it started to rain. Leslie and Darryl hurried everyone into their finished basement. Joyce, Arnold and two of Leslie's neighbor/friends grabbed platters of food and set up refreshment tables against the basement wall. After Robin and Carl cut their wedding cake, they spent the next four hours dancing, laughing and trading stories with friends. Darryl kept jazz blasting on the CD player. Near the end of the evening, Leslie formed a line and led the procession while everyone snaked around the basement doing popular dances from the 70s and 80s. At the end of the dances, Robin sat on the sofa and let out a deep breath. Leslie chuckled when she saw her fanning her face with a napkin. "Tired, girl?"

"Child, I'm worn out."

"We had a blast."

"I can't thank you and Darryl enough for all you did to make Carl and my wedding so memorable." She leaned and kissed the side of Leslie's face. "Thanks, girl."

"You bet. And speaking of Carl, here he comes." She stood and smiled at Carl.

He hugged her. "Thanks, Les." Then he turned and looked at Robin. "Ready to go, Baby?"

She let him take his hand inside hers before she answered, "Yes."

Darryl let Carl borrow a stack of his jazz CDs. Leslie told him how much Robin enjoyed jazz, and, she told Darryl, "I don't think Carl has any mean jazz cuts, so why don't you let him hold on to a few of yours for awhile."

Carl drove to the airport. Robin squeezed his arm when they boarded the plane and headed for Maui, Hawaii. Although he was tired, Carl couldn't sleep on the plane. He spent the flight watching Robin sleep soundly with her head against his shoulder and looking out the window at the tops of clouds. Not one relative or friend thought he'd be sitting where he was. Next to a warm, loving woman whose life was full of promise. Next to a woman who knew the "real" him and chose to love that man rather than stroke the mirage that was his stage presence. Next to a woman who his mother called out, "Hey, girl!" to when they visited, a woman his parents bragged to their friends was "in love with their son".

"Thought I'd marry some dope addict. Some woman who had four or five kids by three to four different men. Some woman who chases rock stars and sleeps with as many guys in the band as she possibly can. That's what they all thought," Carl told himself. He saw the looks on their faces, the glare in their eyes. He knew outside playing a mean guitar, his family thought he wouldn't amount to much. He knew the guys he used to hang with spent years keeping him drunk because they didn't think he'd have anything constructive to do with his life while sober.

He turned, looked at Robin and kissed her forehead.

"They were wrong." Leaning into the headrest, he listened to the sound of faraway voices taunting him. "Zebra. Half breed. Light bright. Red bone. Mulatto. Mutt." He closed his eyes and silenced the voices. From grade school through high school, classmates teased him about his mixed heritage. It was as if the entire world knew his mother was African American and his father was Scottish. Whenever he formed a new group of friends, it wasn't long before they got around to discussing the fact that his mother was black while his father was white. If not for his maternal grandmother's unending love, he felt sure that he would have crumbled beneath the pressure. After his grandmother gave him the guitar her grandfather played at the close of a Saturday evening while the family circled him on the front porch, Carl's life changed. Doors that he never presumed to exist opened and he walked into a world of fantasy. He went from being an un-cool, long haired skateboarder to being a talented guitarist. During the summer months when he stayed with his grandmother in Alabama, he sat in his room and practiced the guitar for as much as eighteen hours a day. Not once did his grandmother tell him to stop strumming the instrument. She believed in him; he knew it.

He raised his arm and stroked Robin's hair. "I love you," he whispered to her. One regret alone trailed his words. He wished his grandmother had lived long enough to meet Robin.

He and the airline staff were the only passengers awoke when the plane landed. As soon as the Unfasten Seat Belts light went on, he reached over and shook Robin's shoulder. It took him awhile to wake her. She sat up and grinned at him.

"You were sleepy."

She wiped her face with her hands. "Oh. My. Gosh. I was exhausted, and I don't know why. Sometimes I just get so tired."

"I'm just glad you're rested."

"Me too."

He grabbed both their overhead bags and followed her off the plane. "Let me carry a bag," she called out.

"No, Baby. I've got it. They're not heavy," he told her while he chuckled and said, "Besides, something tells me you wouldn't look as fine as you do from back here if you were had a traveling bag banging against your hip."

She laughed. "I forgot how late it was," she said when they exited the plane and she looked outside and saw the sky blanketed in the color that is night.

"Let me just go get our luggage so we can head to our suite."

With their luggage in tow, he flagged a cab. Robin sat next to him twirling the ends of her hair. He smiled at her nervousness. Then he leaned into her shoulder and told her, "Promise I won't bite you if you don't bite me."

She clucked her tongue before she poked his side with her elbow. When she sat back, she swallowed hard. After he wrapped her shoulders in his arms and kissed the side of her face, she blushed and whispered, "I'm scared."

It took them half an hour to reach their suite. Straightway he hunted for a CD player. She went into the bathroom. When she came out, he was lighting a scented candle. He turned slowly and looked at her.

She stuttered, "I forgot my negligee."

He reached for her as soon as she turned to re-enter the bathroom. "Don't."

She looked at him with intent.

"I don't want you to put on a negligee. I don't want you to get dressed up to make love with me. I want you just like that. Just the way you are. Right now. You're very beautiful just the way you are."

She gazed at the floor.

"Raise your head, Beautiful. Look at me. I want to look into your pretty, brown eyes."

She glanced up. "You're making me blush."

"I don't mean to. I want to enjoy you in every way possible."

While she fidgeted with her shirt collar, she whispered, "I want to enjoy you too."

He stretched out his hand. "Come here."

She moved toward him slowly. He encouraged her by tugging on the ends of her fingers.

She stood inches in front of him. He kissed her forehead, her nose, her mouth. When he wrapped his arms around her waist, he let his hands rest against her hips. He kissed her mouth again and she wiggled inside his embrace. He kissed her until the heat from her body went into his mouth. Then he closed his eyes and parted her lips with his tongue. She clutched his back and pushed her tongue across his. When he took his hands over her butt and squeezed softly, she moaned and pressed her groan against his. She hung her head back when he took his tongue from her mouth to her neck. She gripped his back again when he started stroking her neck with the tip of his tongue. Her breathing thickened and he pulled her so close to him, he felt the hardness in her nipples pressing against his chest. He whispered, "I love you," in her ear and she wept. Twenty minutes later, she threw her head into the pillow and screamed when the pressure at the center of her stomach exploded into several rounds of ecstasy.

Making love with Carl became the sweetest release Robin knew. They made love in every room of their new home. They spent entire weekends enjoying each other's body. Life seemed different to Robin now that she was married to Carl. They stayed up late at night sitting beneath a blanket on the living room sofa watching old comedies. Robin traveled with Carl the first two summers his band, Razor, toured the world. She visited beaches, museums, researched at international libraries and wrote while Carl went to rehearsals. At night when Razor performed, she was always in the audience.

The third year of their marriage when Carl came home from a band meeting and told her Razor decided not to tour for at least two to three years, Robin hurried inside his arms and told him, "That's great. That's great because I'm pregnant. Honey, we're going to have a baby."

Razor toured two more times during the next six years. By the end of the last tour, Carl and Robin's youngest son was walking. Their oldest was in the kindergarten. Then Razor went into the studio to lay the tracks for their tenth album.

****

"Les. Hey, girl. I thought I was going to have to leave a message on your machine. I'm surprised you're home."

"Rob. What an unexpected treat, hearing from you. I'm so glad you called. I wasn't supposed to be home yet, but shooting wrapped up early yesterday. I flew in this morning." She fanned her face. "Flew into all this heat. Whew! It's hot for real."

"Who are you telling? Girl, I left a sweet potato pie I brought home from church at a dinner for the homeless in the back seat. When I went back out to get it, the bottom of the aluminum pan burned my hand. I only left it in the car for about twenty minutes. It was as if it came out of a hot oven." She chuckled. "Yea. It's been hot. How are the kids holding up in this weather?"

"They're doing good. Keeping busy. Robin's trying to sing. You ought to see her."

"Oh, my goodness. When did that child start singing?" Before she answered, Robin turned and looked down the hall. When she heard the bars of Drew's crib knock and bang a second time, she knew Drew was waking from his nap.

"Oh. She's just fooling around, but she has a good set of pipes on her. Who knows? Maybe when she gets older Carl can hook her up with a good record deal." She laughed.

"I see you all over the place."

"The studio has me hyping the movie right now."

"I know how much you love that."

Drew lifted his head then lowered it again and started rubbing his eyes.

"Oh, yeah. I just love traveling the world pushing a movie."

They both laughed.

"I heard Razor's back in the studio."

"I'm glad they are. Carl loves to create. He's written so much new music. This next album by the band is going to be tops."

"Razor rules. I keep telling people that the bands that will endure are the bands that are clean. No one is sharp when they are drunk or stoned."

"You're telling me. I have seen some of everything since Carl and I got married. Some of the guys in some of the bands Razor toured with are way out there. I'm glad Carl can spend more time with the kids. They love their daddy. When he walks through the front door, they get so excited. Carl being in the studio means he's home every night, which gives me a chance to rest. I've been so tired lately, especially last week. Feel like I have the flu or something. And my appetite has literally been non-existent. I haven't felt like eating anything, not even fruit, and you know how much I like a good bowl of cold fruit."

"Tell me you're not out running in all this heat."

Drew raised his head again and looked out across his room. He followed the sound of Robin's voice. A second later his head bobbed. He turned and looked out his bedroom window. He smiled at the bald man waving at him on the other side of the window.

Robin leaned forward and moved the receiver closer to her mouth. "I'm not. Well. I was, but I had to stop."

"Why? Did your doctor tell you to stay out of the heat?"

"No." She covered her mouth with her hand and lowered her head. "I passed out a week ago.

"Rob."

"Don't worry. I was close to home. A neighbor saw me laying on the sidewalk and rushed to my aid."

"When are you going to learn?"

"I know."

"You're not a spring chicken anymore. You're going to get heat stroke. You better stay indoors and out of this heat."

"I know. It's just that I have to exercise and keep my health up. I get so tired so easily."

"Running in heat won't fix anything."

"I know that, Leslie. I just want to stay in shape."

"What did your doctor say was causing the fatigue?"

"She doesn't know."

"Rob."

"Les, I know what I have to do. I'm cutting back on the amount of fatty foods I eat, and I'm drinking a lot of water."

"Rob, you've always ate healthy foods, drank lots of water and exercised. Ever since I've known you, you have. Go see your doctor. Tell her that you've been extremely tired lately and that you are not working harder than normal. Don't take your health for granted."

"There's nothing wrong with me, Leslie. I'm just tired, that's all."

"Then why did you take the time to tell me how you've been feeling? If it's nothing. If nothing is wrong with you, why did you even bother to tell me that you've been real tired this last week? If it really was nothing, we both know you would have given it no time. You wouldn't have thought about it. But apparently you have been thinking about it. It's one on the first topics you brought up after I picked up the telephone."

"I'm just tired. That's all. I'm as fit as a race horse. I keep telling you we're going to live to be old, wrinkled women." She laughed.

Drew pulled himself to his knees. He stared at the window for a long time before he started to whimper.

"Rob, I'm not going to get on a merry-go-round with you. Go to the doctor. It's that simple."

"Bu—"

"Besides."

"Wait."

"What? What is it?"

"Thought I heard something." She shook her head. Nothing. It's nothing. Go ahead. Go on."

"Want to go get the kids? You probably heard the kids."

"No. Sounded like I heard something move in the front room."

"Where are you at?"

"In the kitchen."

They laughed while they talked in unison. "Cell phone."

"Thought you told me you had a check-up three months ago. How did that go? Were you feeling tired then?"

Drew whimpered. His eyes ballooned when he saw the man again.

"I wasn—"

"And you know, it's a waste of time to visit the doctor if you have something ailing you, but you never voice it to your physician. What do you do? Go to the doctor and tell yourself, if she doesn't discover anything wrong with me through her routine exams, then there must be nothing wrong with me?"

"Les—"

"You have to work with your physician, not play hide and seek with her with your health."

"I know tha—"

"You've always reviled in being strong. I like your inner strength. It's very attractive, but you aren't a stone, Rob. If something happened to you, I don't know what I would do. You're my sister. You know that."

"Let's change the subject."

"Just as long as you heard me."

She chuckled. When she turned and looked at the kitchen wall, her gaze fell across a picture Jerome sketched and colored last week. She swallowed when the colors ran together. Then she clenched and unclenched her left hand and massaged a sore spot in her left shoulder. "I did."

"So, how are my boys?"

"Busy as ever. Keeping me on my toes." She took in a deep breath. A second later she closed her eyes against the pain shooting through her chest.

"It's an amazing thing, isn't it? Being a mother?"

Drew grabbed two of the bars on his crib and pulled himself to the edge of the mattress.

After she took in another deep breath, she leaned back in the chair. "It is. Watching tiny babies grow up. It's something. Children have so much of both of their parents in them, and yet, they have their own personalities. Jerome likes playing with a guitar already. Plus, he draws. I think he's going to be an artist. Right now he's in la-la land. We took the kids to the drive-in last night. Jerome got to stay up as late as he wanted. Do you know that boy didn't go to bed until after three. Tell me he's not tired. He had the nerve to get up at 8 this morning. He's been sleeping for half an hour. Literally passed out." She chuckled. "I don't think he'll be waking up any time soon. Drew. What do I think he's gonna do when he grows up? It's too young to tell about him. The biggest thing for him right now is walking across the front room without falling on his butt."

"He's so cute. That boy is one cutie pie. They both are. Drew's got your nose. Jerome has Carl's eyes."

"Everybody says that. I'm glad they're close and that they don't fight. I have heard horror stories about brothers fighting from very early ages."

"You already told me Jerome's knocked out. Where is my baby Drew?"

"In bed. I can hear him starting to wake up. He's starting to whimper. Pretty soon he'll be standing up in his crib and making it real clear that he wants me to come lift him out of his crib. That boy does not like staying in his crib a second after he wakes up."

Leslie chuckled. "Kids are smarter than adults give them credit for being. Just a few weeks ago, Robin asked me to watch her go down the sliding board at the park. I was studying my lines—"

"Wait." Robin stood and looked over her shoulder.

"What's bugging you?"

"Thought I saw a shadow, but think it was just the clouds. It needs to rain here. It's been dry here for so long." She returned to her seat. "Back to what I was saying. So you're studying for that new television pilot I heard about?"

"Yes."

Closing her eyes, she lowered her head and waved a show of gratitude to God for allowing her to catch her breath. "Thanks for telling me about it."

"Girl, I didn't know that show was definite until three days ago."

"Are you serious?"

"I certainly am. Don't tell anybody, but I don't think I'm up for this part. It's going to be a serious stretch. Playing the role of a successful playwright. You've gotta be kidding. You don't know how much of a stretch this show is gonna be for me."

Drew rubbed his nose and whined.

Robin looked up. Her heart stopped, then it pounded in her chest.

Jack knocked the telephone out of her hand and kicked her in the skull. She fell to the floor and clutched her heart.

"Keep talking," Jack whispered, his breath hot and funky, his face brushing Robin's skin.

Robin moaned.

Jack removed the needle from her shoulder. Then he kneeled back and nodded. "Keep talking, I said." He jammed the gun barrel against her temple. "Keep talking to her."

The television screen blurred.

"Robin?" Leslie said.

"Stop." She jerked her shoulders until Jack's hands fell off her shoulders and down her back.

Leslie raised her voice. "Rob?"

Robin's head bobbed. A wave of nausea rushed over her.

"Rob?"

"Talk to her or this'll be the end of you. Then I'll go get that pretty little boy in the other room."

"No."

Leslie squinted. "What?"

"No. You—"

"Rob, are you okay? You sound like you're drunk."

The gun scratched the side of her head. When she heard Drew whimper, she said, "It's nothing. I'm okay. You're up for this role and you know it."

Leslie sighed. "It's just the weekly commitment. It's been awhile since I've worked on a series."

Jack grinned when Robin closed her eyes. "The solution's taking affect," he mused to himself. Teach you to mess around with me, Leslie. Making all that money and not giving me none. All I did for your daddy, getting him out of that bind. Why. I'm like kin to you. You're gonna see how serious I am now. Ain't nothing like losing your best friend. You'll come through the next time I tell you what to do."

Robin swallowed hard and coughed. "My babies. Oh, goodness. My babies." She took in a deep breath.

"Rob, what are you talking about? What's going on?"

Robin strained to open her eyes, but her eyelids were too heavy. She took in another deep breath.

"Rob, are you getting sick on me?"

Robin grimaced and clutched her chest. She coughed hard twice and gulped air.

"Your health is very important. You know that."

Her hand landed against Jack's foot.

"You know how important it is to get plenty of rest. I don't have to tell you that."

Saliva spewed out of her mouth.

"Oh. I forgot to tell you. A friend of mine saw your latest play on Broadway. She and her family were on vacation in New York when they stopped and saw your play. She didn't know you wrote the play until I told her. Said she loved it! But that comes as a surprise to neither of us. You are good. As you always say, God gave the two of us wonderful talents."

Drew squirmed in his crib. Jerome rolled to his side in his bed and wiped a layer of slobber off his chin. Then he closed his eyes and went back to sleep.

"Do you still go and watch your plays the way you used to when we lived in Manhattan?"

Drew raised his head and whimpered. Pulling up on the bars of his crib, he called out, "Mah-mee."

"Stop being modest. Well. You probably don't go see your plays the way you used to. Every other year seems like you have a hit play out. This one's gonna win an Emmy. Watch and see. Mark my word. This one is a sure-fire winner. Well. Every play you write is a sure-fire winner, but this one has something extra. Not sure what it is, but it's there. You're getting better. There was a time when I wondered if you could improve, but you're getting better."

"Mah-mee."

"Is that my baby Drew I hear in the background?   What's he doing?"

"Mah-mee."

"Go ahead and get him. I can wait."

"Mah-mee."

"Rob, you won't be spoiling him if you pick him up."

Drew stood up in his crib and huh-huh-huh'd his way into a loud wail.

Leslie pulled the receiver closer to her ear. "Rob?"

Drew screamed until he choked and coughed on his own drool.

Leslie stood. "Rob? Rob? Rob!"

Drew caught his breath then pushed his head back and wailed again.

Leslie screamed, "Rob? Rob? Rob? Rob?" into the receiver.

Drew pulled on the crib bars while he wailed.

Leslie drew her hand into a fist. "Rob, are you there? Rob, do you hear me?"

Drew screamed until his cries pierced the air.   Snot dribbled down his mouth and chin.

Leslie's eyes bulged. "Rob? Rob! Rob!" A second later she hung up the telephone and dialed 911 and paged Carl.

Carl reached the ranch before the ambulance. He raced through the front door. Drew's whimpers shook him. His gaze darted. He hurried around the corner. After he took Drew out of his crib and soothed his fears by sshing him while he kissed his forehead, he looked in Jerome's bedroom. He swallowed when he saw Jerome sleeping soundly on his stomach. Turning, he walked through different rooms of the house calling out, "Rob? Honey? Baby?"

Drew rested his head against Carl's shoulder. When they neared the kitchen, he raised his head and whimpered. Following Drew's gaze, Carl looked at the floor just in front of the table. His hands shook and his mouth went open. The last thing he heard was Drew saying, "Mah-mee."

Chapter Twenty-Four

"Precious Lord, precious Lord, precious Lord. Keep me in the shadow of your wings, the hallow of your hand. Catch me when I stumble. Provide escape for me least I fall. Precious Lord, precious Lord, precious Lord." Thelma lifted her head and raised her voice. While the choir sang chorus, Theo sat on the front pew biting back tears. Next to him, Marcia sat with her shoulders taut.

At the song's end, Reverend Julian stood in the pulpit. "When you are loved, folks show up in large numbers to say farewell. I can't count the cards and letters that came pouring in to the church office. It would take more than a day to stand here and read them all." He lowered and shook his head. "She was loved. A true believer. She touched so many in so many loving ways." He raised his head and looked into the waiting congregation. "We will now have about a dozen of the thousands and thousands of cards and letters read by our church secretary, Sister Janice Adu."

Janice sniffed several times before she opened the first card. "To the Sallis Family. 'We do not always know why things happen the way they do. But God is faithful. He will carry you through. Open your heart to God's love. Trust God at this trying time and know that earth has no sorrow that heaven cannot heal. With deepest sympathy,' Reverend Keith Julian and Family and the entire New Salem Baptist Church."

Aretha shifted in her seat and wiped away a tear. Beside her Kathleen and Bertha strangled pieces of kleenex. Bertha leaned forward and peered at Aretha. When she sat against the back of the pew again, she pulled her bottom lip inside her mouth and wept softly.

Janice cleared her throat. "To the Carlile Family. 'May God's peace be yours at this time of great loss. May you treasure the many memories you have of your departed loved one. May you lean on God who cares for you as you seek comfort in God's word, in God's many promises.' You have our prayers and our support. We love you. Darryl, Leslie and Family."

The last card she read was sent from the president of Sigma Gamma Rho Sorority, Incorporated. The church was filled from front to back. Cars crowded the parking lot and double-parked along the street. Television camera crews stood outside the church doors. A few cameramen sat amongst the mourners taking photographs. Several Arts cable channels covered the life and works of Robin during the funeral. Every major television station in the country and many around the globe mentioned Robin's passing throughout their news broadcasts. Memorials dotted roadways in Tennessee, New York and Atlanta, Georgia. Cards and flowers overflowed at Georgia Medical Center, the hospital Robin was rushed to in an ambulance before she was declared dead on arrival.

Theo sat in his seat thinking about the autopsy report. Heart disease. His daughter died of heart disease. He rubbed his brow. He refused to look at Marcia. He asked himself how Robin could have heart disease when she was a picture of health. She wasn't a pound overweight. She exercised religiously. She ate no fried foods and ate more fruit and vegetables than any vegetarian he knew. He lowered his head. Marcia. Her name rang in his ears.

"Son?"

It was his mother. He looked up at her.

She mouthed the words, "Are you all right?"

He nodded and bit his bottom lip.

Reverend Julian's eyes turned pink as he finished the eulogy. "At many funerals a preacher has to struggle to speak well for five to ten minutes of a person without lying before a righteous God." He shook his head. "But not so with Robin Sallis. No. Not so with her. Robin was a woman who cared about people. She saw people. She saw people. She actually saw everyone who came into her life. She saw you for who you were, and regardless of who you were, she saw something good in you. She feasted well at a table God set before her enemies. Those who wished to see her fail, watched her triumph. Those who envied her talent, watched her soar. Those who hoped for her ruin, watched her break down barriers. Those who wished failure upon her artistic efforts, watch her raise the standard for good writing. She was a woman who dared to dream. More than that, she was a woman who always gathered the courage to work with God to turn her dreams into reality. She left her family, friends and loved ones an awesome legacy. She served her community well. She was an excellent mother and a loving wife. She loved her husband and her children with a deep-down love. Her husband and her children returned her this enormous love, and, as she told me, this and the love of her good friends is what made her so truly and utterly happy. She was a fair woman who judged people by the content of their character. She was not ashamed to declare her love and belief in Jesus, the Christ." He shook his head. "How many times did she tell me John 3:16 was the greatest gift anyone, any spirit, God could ever give her. How many times? This declaration she made before the entire world. Hers has been quite a journey. She has traveled from God's highest thoughts to her mother's womb, around the world, back into the arms of a loving God. She was an excellent example of a true believer. She knew her station in life. She was an encourager, a great encourager and a woman who shall be sorely missed. A great woman has gone away from us to a place we too shall one day be if we live like she did. If we believe in God and accept Jesus' sacrifice the way she did. If we give ourselves, all of ourselves, fully up to God through faith the way she did. She was a mighty warrior. Today, amongst us, a giant sleeps."

At Theo's request, Leslie stood and took her place at the edge of the choir loft. She scanned the pews. It both comforted and crushed her to see tears in so many eyes. Michael. Sharon. Trish. Betsy. Bertha. Aretha. Kathleen. Her own mother. Theo. When her gaze fell across Marcia's brow, she lifted the microphone and started to sing, "Like a dove with an eagle's wings, fly away my friend to the place where you have always belonged. Be received at the edge of paradise and let hallelujah be part of your daily song. Fly away. Fly away. Like the dew on a morning's dawn. Take my heart and seal it with your dreams so that I can remember you and be strong. Fly away. Fly away. Like the dew on a morning's dawn." Tears streamed down her face. Her voice quaked. Her hands shook and her knees buckled. In the pews hushed up tears turned into loud moans. Theo looked up at her and smiled through a pool of tears. She smiled back at him, tossed her head back and sang until the moans silenced and the bereaved stood and applauded. Before she returned the microphone to the podium, she said, "She was my best friend." Then she exited the choir loft and walked inside Darryl's arms.

That evening, Robin was cremated. Her ashes were flown to Tennessee and sprayed across the Tennessee River.

Chapter Twenty-Five

Leslie sat on the edge Darryl and her bed. Hot tears streamed down her face. Her tears fell against the letters. A dozen. She wept while she read them.

"By golly, your friend sure sleeps hard. I should have stayed longer hunting for that money. I know your father sends you money. He sent you a big ol' check a few days ago. Guilt money. His pay to you for his not being a father. Not really much of a father, you know? All them whores he's had. My. My. My. I do remember one. Pretty little red head she was. You people owe me. The whole lot of you do. I'm gonna get my payback, Leslie, little miss super star."

She ripped the letter into small pieces then she picked up the second letter.

"Your roommate sure knows how to have a good time. Had me a blast in Jamaica! I've always loved Jamaica. For as long as I can recall. Even hit it off with Mark. Spent two nights at his house. Right there by the ocean. Should have seen us laughing and trading stories together. Even loaned him my ID so he could get in the boat house I bought with the money your father paid me all those years ago. Oh, Leslie. I sure had a ball."

Her hands shook while she unfolded the third letter.

"Next time I tell you to meet me somewhere, you do it. You hear? You owe me, young lady. You and your whole family do. Owe me. All of you! I ain't going to hurt you if you give me what I want. I'm giving you one more chance. Don't blow it."

She pulled at the letter until it fell apart.

"Listen, little miss super star, You best meet me downtown next Monday at 7. You know your way around town. I've seen you around them drug lines. Mess with me this time and I'll make sure your friend Aretha gets a bad fix. I want my money, little miss super star. If it wasn't for me your daddy would have went to jail. I could still put him away. All the stuff he's messed up in. But that would put too much of a spotlight on me and I ain't exactly been the choir boy. Meet me Monday right outside Mavis', and you better have ten million dollars with you. Don't try me. Don't you ever try me again."

"Oh, Robin. Robin. Robin. Robin. Please understand. I was so scared. I wanted it to just go away. I was too scared to tell you. Please. I didn't know it would end this way. I didn't." She shook her head. "I didn't."

So you decide to blow me off. We'll see. We'll see. Oh. Make sure you look real pretty next weekend cause little girl, I'll be making your wedding."

Snot dribbled out of her nose. She sniffed hard.

"You sure got a good friend in that Robin. Smart thing you did putting that ad in the paper. Guess I spooked you with all them phone calls. Didn't want to live alone no more, did ya? Did I scare you when I called, little miss super star? Called and hung up on you. You picked a good one. Wish I had me a roommate like Robin. Picking you up off the floor when you're drunk and all. My. You sure got yourself a good friend, little miss super star. Too bad you're gonna make me kill her."

Leslie gazed at the ceiling. "Rob, this doesn't have anything to do with you. Really it doesn't. It goes way back to my father. Told you I didn't like him. Told you I hated my father, but you always told me I shouldn't. 'You shouldn't hate your father, Les.' That's what you told me. Now you see why. My father ruined my life. He ruined my life even before I was born. Always a hustler. Always working below level. Mr. Underground. My father. Oh, God. Oh, God," she cried out while she rolled to her side on the bed. "Why couldn't it have been me? Why couldn't he just have killed me? Robin never hurt anyone."

They called it a heart attack. Should have told Robin to take better care of herself. She had all the signs of a woman with hidden heart disease. How many times did she pass out while running? Leslie, you knew this. Why didn't you help her? You know. You're so much like your father. Always thinking about yourself. Even now I bet you're crying, crying for what you've lost."

She sat up and stacked the rest of the letters together. She pulled at them until they broke into shreds. "Rob, I couldn't tell you. I couldn't. I just couldn't. I needed you. You would have run. If I told you. You would have left me and you were the only friend I ever had. I couldn't let you go. I couldn't." Pushing off the bed with a long sigh, she walked to the window. She gazed up at the blue sky and cried for a long time.

To order more copies of <u>Love Has Many Faces</u>
Call TOLL FREE: 1-800-929-7889 or
Mail $20.00 (shipping and handling is FREE) to:

Chistell Publishing
2500 Knights Road, Suite 19-01
Bensalem, PA 19020

<u>Visit us online at:</u>
<u>http://www.chistell.com</u>

THANK YOU!